The Au Pair Affair

a novel

TESSA BAILEY

AVON

An Imprint of HarperCollins*Publishers*

THE AU PAIR AFFAIR. Copyright © 2024 by Tessa Bailey. All rights reserved. Printed in the United States of America. No part of this book may be used or reproduced in any manner whatsoever without written permission except in the case of brief quotations embodied in critical articles and reviews. For information, address HarperCollins Publishers, 195 Broadway, New York, NY 10007.

HarperCollins books may be purchased for educational, business, or sales promotional use. For information, please email the Special Markets Department at SPsales@harpercollins.com.

FIRST EDITION

Interior text design by Diahann Sturge-Campbell

Hockey illustration © OSIPOVEV/Shutterstock

Library of Congress Cataloging-in-Publication Data has been applied for.

ISBN 978-0-06-330843-5 (paperback)
ISBN 978-0-06-330842-8 (library hardcover)

24 25 26 27 28 LBC 5 4 3 2 1

ACKNOWLEDGMENTS

Basically, I just have a lot of gratitude to express here! It's rare to have a publisher who trusts an author so completely that they can swing wildly from golf to hockey, based on what they are feeling passionate about writing next, no questions asked. I'm lucky to have found that with Avon Books. My long-time editor, Nicole, left me in great hands with my new editor, May Chen, and I'm so glad we're working on sports books together, even though I suspect both of our favorite sports are lunch and wine! Thank you for letting me have fun with *The Au Pair Affair* and email you out of the blue with questions about secondary characters like, "Would you guys actually let me publish this??" (You'll know what/who/which characters I'm talking about when this book is over.) So, thank you to my publisher. Thank you to DJ and Danielle and Shannon, too, for all of your hard work. I appreciate you. And thank you, READERS. I owe you the happiness I get to experience every day in making this my job, and I'll never take you for granted.

The Au Pair Affair

CHAPTER ONE

Tallulah Aydin had never seen blood droplets sail through the air quite so gracefully.

She turned the phone sideways and enlarged the hockey highlight to full-screen mode, tapping the volume button in order to hear the commentator's voice.

Abraham with the vicious elbow to O'Hanlon's nose. Oh mama. Somebody call the trainer. O'Hanlon just learned the hard way what we've known for years. Players risk bones and cartilage when they enter Sir Savage's house as he's just proven once again tonight . . .

Tallulah exited the video and set her phone down, queasiness rolling in her stomach.

This afternoon, she was scheduled to begin shacking up with the homicidal hockey player from that very SportsCenter highlight. Sir Savage. If the algorithm gods hadn't creepily recognized her location as Boston and placed that nose-crunching clip from last night's preseason game in her path, she would already have left the smoothie shop and entered the landmark doorman building across the street to begin her employment as an au pair for his tween daughter.

She'd agreed to the arrangement *months* ago. Back when the whole idea hadn't seemed so unnerving. Now, however, the white plastic seat in which she'd been parked for over an hour was rapidly making lattice patterns on the backs of her legs. Blenders whirred in her ears. She'd been rendered unable to stand up and cross the road. Which was galling, considering she'd just spent a year in Antarctica studying the migration habits of the Adélie penguin.

A nanny job should be a cakewalk, right?

Thanks to a twist of fate, she'd landed a swanky place to live in Beacon Hill while she earned her master's in marine biology at Boston University. In return, all she had to do was nanny for an already self-sufficient twelve-year-old girl while her daddy apparently went out and flattened perfectly good noses on the ice.

It was the latter that kept her glued to the uncomfortable chair.

Tallulah reached for the paper cup holding her peanut butter–espresso blast and noticed her hand was trembling oh-so-slightly. She gave herself an impatient eye roll and snatched up the cup, swigging what remained of her smoothie. The guy behind the counter obviously heard the empty vacuum sound coming from her paper straw and gave her the Boston eyebrow. Head cocked, impatient, one brow raised. Like, *are you done here or would you like to lick the napkin dispenser, too?*

She'd clearly overstayed her welcome at the Joyful Juicer.

Message received, Tallulah stood up, crossed to the trash can, and tossed her cup before returning to the table and gripping the handle of her suitcase. Staring through the picture window of the shop at the ten-story brick building on the other side of the road, her stomach sagged somewhere in the vicinity of her knees. On paper, she didn't have any reason for the alarm weaving through her ribs.

After all, her best friends, Wells and Josephine, had vouched for the Boston Bearcats team captain, Burgess Abraham, also known as Sir Savage. He didn't have any criminal history that she could find on the internet. In fact, he was known for being a terror on the ice, but stoic and reasonable once he entered the locker room. As evidenced by the time Tallulah had spent watching postgame interviews with his sweaty black hair plastered to his forehead, his denim-blue eyes intense as he considered every question like the answer was deeply important.

And no, she hadn't purposefully searched for shirtless interviews, thank you very much.

They'd come up as a *suggested* Google search. She couldn't simply ignore that kind of search engine divine providence. It would be irresponsible. Nor could she ignore shoulders thick enough with muscle to seat a couple of baby walruses—and those suckers had *heft*.

But right now, when she was an hour late to arrive at Burgess's penthouse to view her new living space and go over the particulars of their arrangement, all she could see was that brutal elbow slicing through the air, the accompanying expression of malice.

Like a peek inside some hidden part of the man?

Accepting this job had seemed like a great idea when she'd met Burgess at that golf tournament in California last summer. But she shouldn't have been so impulsive when it came to something so huge, like living with a man who she barely knew. One who could have all manner of lurking issues. In her experience, men could be mild mannered, charming even, on the surface. Easygoing, friendly.

They could also be dormant volcanos waiting for the right moment to erupt.

Ignoring the sigh from the dude behind the counter, Tallulah sat back down.

Moving in with this near stranger was a bad idea. An error in judgment.

Thankfully, she hadn't moved in *yet*. If she was going to change her mind, it had to be now. Before she wasted valuable time Burgess could be using to find a new au pair. She could check into a hotel tonight and use tomorrow to view apartment share opportunities. With other women. The apartments probably—no, *definitely*—wouldn't be in neighborhoods as nice as this, nor would they be penthouses, but at least she'd be able to sleep at night.

Decision made, Tallulah slipped the phone out of the front pocket of her windbreaker and prepared to call the Bearcats defenseman. Being so unprofessional about this rankled. She should break their deal in person. But what if he reacted badly? Got upset?

A phone call was better. Safer.

Before Tallulah could dial, a bell tinkled above the door.

And Burgess Abraham himself entered the smoothie shop.

Holy shit, she'd forgotten how . . . hulking he was. Six-three, give or take an inch. Broad as a barn. And grizzled. Sir Savage had entered the second half of his thirties and he already had a hint of salt and pepper buffering in his black beard, his temples. He walked with leashed confidence. It wasn't the stride of a man who needed to be noticed. Or feared. It was a one hand in his pocket, the other loose at his side, eyes forward, unhurried but goal-oriented gait. He didn't bother stopping at the register to order, just signaled the employee with a salute.

"Your usual, Savage?" The smoothie guy got working, tossing frozen fruit into the clear blender, adding juice and three heaping scoops of protein powder. "I live in hope that someday you'll come in and try something new."

"I like what I like," Burgess muttered, frowning at the screen of his phone.

Was he checking to see if she'd called?

Probably. She was now sixty-seven minutes late.

With an inward wince, Tallulah tapped call and held the phone to her ear. When the device started to buzz in Burgess's hand, a ripple went through his back. He dropped the phone to his side and looked straight ahead for a moment, then back at the phone, coughing. Rolling a shoulder. She could only see his profile, but his lips moved slightly like he was practicing his greeting—and that's when Tallulah remembered *why* she'd agreed to take the live-in au pair job with someone she barely knew.

Time had obviously blurred the memory of Burgess.

There was something about his energy that read . . . safe.

Very safe.

Protective.

Along with her friends' faith in Burgess, she'd trusted her gut.

It was going to be a shame to break the agreement. It was for the best, though. There was no guarantee he'd be civil off the ice one hundred percent of the time. Wells and Josephine might wholeheartedly believe in Burgess's good character, but Tallulah had done the same with people throughout her life and gotten burned when their true selves were revealed.

You just never knew.

Tallulah watched as Burgess tapped the screen and held the phone to his ear, plugging the opposite one with his finger to drown out the screaming blender.

"Hello," he said, staring intently at the floor. "Tallulah."

Best to ignore that hot shiver that trekked up her inner thighs at the basement baritone version of her name. Blame it on her recent lack of anything resembling a sex life.

Watching penguins mate didn't count.

"Hi, Burgess," she responded, waiting for him to register the blender sounds in the background of her call, too. When he did, his gaze zipped to where Tallulah sat, a grunt brushing up against her eardrum.

They both ended the call, looking at each other across the smoothie shop.

It was very hard to tell what Burgess was thinking. But he *was* thinking. A lot. Intuitive blue eyes traveled between her and the suitcase, a slight wrinkle taking up residence between his brows, though the rest of his expression remained carved in stone.

Without taking his attention off Tallulah, Burgess reached out and accepted his smoothie over the counter, and that casual competence was . . . dangerously attractive. It was all coming back to her now. The hot spark of attraction she'd felt for this man all those months ago. She'd flown into California as a surprise for her best friend Josephine's birthday. Burgess had been in attendance as a spectator at the same golf tournament where his friend, Wells Whitaker, had been competing with Josephine as his caddie. Brought his daughter, Lissa, along, too.

The five of them had unexpectedly had lunch—and when Burgess sat down beside her at the table, she'd been caught off guard by the ribbons of electricity that had only fluttered with more persistence every time his voice did that deep, boomy thing. There'd been no reason to question his outward calm while at lunch with other people, but she couldn't discount her current apprehension at the prospect of being alone with him. In an apartment. Day in and day out. Knowing he was capable of breaking someone's nose with all the fanfare of a sneeze.

As Burgess approached the table, the sound of his bootsteps was muffled, her palms growing soggy, but she also couldn't help but notice the way his God of Thunder thighs were almost too robust for his jeans. He wore a loose navy sweater, like a man in the middle of a relaxing Sunday, and she wondered if he'd stretched out the neckline to show off the sharp cuts of his throat and collarbone.

Instinct told her no. That he'd just thrown it on.

But instincts weren't always enough when it came to men, right?

When Burgess was five yards from the table, Tallulah shot to her feet with the brightest smile she could muster and held out her hand for a shake. "Burgess. It's so nice to see you again." She pressed her toes into the soles of her ankle boots when their hands connected, coarse into smooth, twisting the ball of her foot into the soft leather, because the clash of awareness and misgivings was so peculiar. And noisy. She could hear herself *swallow.*

Dang, he was tall. Mean appearance, collected demeanor. So confusing.

"I'm so sorry, but unfortunately I won't be able to take the au pair position, after all."

CHAPTER TWO

"I'm so sorry, but unfortunately I won't be able to take the au pair position, after all."

Burgess was so busy trying to put a lid on his physical reaction to this woman those words almost didn't reach his brain. That sentence had a lot of hurdles over which to leap, starting with the way her scent smacked him in the senses like a puck to the chin. A few years back, he'd been forced to attend the wedding of one of his teammates and they'd had a signature cocktail. He'd felt like an ogre holding the ridiculous crystal glass between his thumb and index finger for the toast, sort of how he'd used to feel having tea parties with Lissa, but the taste of the drink had been unusual enough to stick with him.

Blood orange and basil.

That's what Tallulah smelled like. Fresh and sensual.

As they shook hands—and she apparently gave her notice to quit before she even started—he could taste the orange in the back of his throat. And speaking of throats, he couldn't seem to take his eyes off hers, because she seemed to be having a very difficult time swallowing, if the visible knot below her chin was any indication. Her palm was a little damp, too, which didn't bother Burgess, a man who spent hours every week surrounded by sweaty athletes and their, oftentimes, putrid stenches. Hell, their goalie had a good luck jockstrap that he didn't wash during winning streaks. Sweaty palms were a pleasure.

But why did *she* have them?

Their meeting in California had gone in three stages.

One: he'd been caught off guard by her beauty. The almond shape of her bottomless brown eyes, framed by sweeping black brows and brimming with intelligence, inquisitiveness, kindness. The tan glow of her complexion, the way she wrinkled her nose to acknowledge someone's point. All of her. Later, he'd found out about her Turkish heritage and that she was born in Istanbul, where her family still resided . . . and he'd Googled whether or not they played hockey in Turkey, immediately feeling like a jackass.

Two: he'd been further blown away by her sense of humor and ability to connect so easily with his daughter, which was no easy feat. He was considering hiring a parenting coach at this point. These days, the kid was either outright ignoring him or crying hysterically.

Three: he'd realized Tallulah was eleven years his junior, a future grad student who had plans to get plugged into the Boston social scene—thus, his polar opposite—and promptly categorized her as someone who would be inappropriate for him to pursue romantically.

Labeling her off-limits, however, hadn't stopped him from offering her a room and a job in his apartment, but yeah. His uncharacteristic impulsiveness that afternoon was a discussion for a different day. The topic on the table was the fact that she'd already decided to quit—and after spending a week debating whether an aspiring marine biologist would prefer her pillows firm or floppy, he wanted to know why.

Burgess set down his Protein Avalanche smoothie and took a seat at Tallulah's table, waiting for her to sit down across from him, which she did after a moment. He considered the stiff set to her shoulders, the way she continued to grip the handle of her suitcase, and decided he didn't like any of it.

With a quick clear of his throat, he leaned forward, folding his hands on the table. "You packed and got all the way to my smoothie shop before deciding to quit. What happened?"

She slowly sat down, wet her lips, her eyes dropping briefly to her phone. "I'd prefer not to say."

"Is it the neighborhood? You don't like it?"

"The neighborhood is gorgeous," she scoffed, looking out the window toward The Beacon, where he resided on the top floor. "The building is lovely, too. I'm starting to regret choosing marine biology over professional hockey."

His grunt passed for a laugh. This was the person he remembered from lunch. Direct and clever. A little self-deprecating. Wildly unique. *I should let her quit. It would be easier on my sanity to not have this beautiful girl sleeping under my roof.*

Or would it be the opposite?

"Then what's the problem?" Burgess asked. "You don't want to be Lissa's nanny?"

"Oh no, that's not it at all. Lissa is a sweetheart and she'd barely need me, she's such a little grown-up." She waved a hand and his eyes caught on the simple silver bands that were such a contrast to the natural tan of her fingers. "You made me such a generous offer. And Wells and Josephine speak so highly of you. Really."

Burgess took the lid off his smoothie, sipped and waited.

"I'd be happy to help you find someone else. I'm sure people would be trampling me to get this position. It's kind of a dream come true," she said, giving him a bright smile, a dimple appearing in the apple of her cheek. Damn, she was . . . a very disquieting combination of hot and cute. She had these long waves of black hair that almost reached her elbows where she propped them on the table, hugging them almost . . . nervously?

That hair acted as a shield for her body, which happened to be the hot part of the equation. So it was probably a good thing he couldn't see a lot of it from across the table, because he was having a hard enough time concentrating with blood oranges juicing themselves on his brain and every downward sweep of her eyelashes making his thoughts fuzzy. This is how it had been in California. One measly lunch had led to months of staring off into space trying to remember the exact shade of her eyes.

Stay on track. "If a position as my nanny is such a coveted one, why don't you want it?"

She took a breath, pulled her elbows in tighter. Watched him closely, as if weighing his reaction. "I'm nervous about living with a man I don't know very well."

While her answer caused an unpleasant shift in his stomach, he'd sensed a difficult explanation coming from the time he'd glimpsed her across the smoothie shop. Something in the way she'd braced as he approached had tipped him off. Was he insulted? No. Actually, he felt like kind of a moron for not considering before that she might be hesitant to live with a near stranger. Neither had Tallulah, apparently.

Until the very day her employment was set to begin.

Burgess started to ask Tallulah whether the sudden change of heart stemmed from a healthy fear of strangers or something else, but her phone buzzed with an incoming text. Murmuring an excuse me, she slid a finger across the screen.

Tapped an icon.

A video popped up that he recognized all too well.

Because his agent had sent it to him this morning.

Apparently his shot to O'Hanlon's nose had gone viral.

Was . . . *this* the reason Tallulah had stalled out in the smoothie shop? Yes. The answer was obvious. She'd been watching it before he arrived. Did that mean . . . was she *scared* of him?

"Sorry," she blurted, fumbling with the phone to get her text messages open instead. "Wrong app."

"Tallulah, I saw it. The video." He braced himself for the conversation ahead. She could be scared of him. That possibility settled on his chest like a thousand-pound weight. "Is that what's going on here? You saw a clip from a preseason game and it . . . made you nervous? About me?"

It took her a moment to respond. "My instincts are telling me it will be safe to live with you, but I have a hard time relying on my instincts when it comes to men. In other words, I don't. My gut feeling is not always accurate. And I thought it would be enough that Wells and Josephine trust you, which is how I made it all the way to this smoothie shop with the terrible chairs. But the video . . . I guess it reminded me that people aren't always what they seem."

"I see." Her explanation filled him with a sense of dread, but he kept his hands loose on the table, despite the urge to curl them into fists. Had Tallulah had a bad experience with a man? It seemed so. And right then and there, looking into her honest eyes, Burgess knew if he ever found out who it was, a broken nose would be a pleasure compared to what he'd do to them. "The way I play hockey is not an indication of who I am in real life. I think the same could be said about any player. It's the sport. Sometimes it's brutal."

"I realize that. I do," she said quickly, wetting her lips. "The video isn't the reason I'm declining the job. It was more of . . . of a prompt. For me to take a step back and examine my choices. Sometimes I make really impulsive decisions and regret them later. Like now."

"What kinds of impulsive decisions do you make?"

"Ordering a peanut butter and espresso smoothie on an empty stomach, for instance."

Burgess couldn't hide his incredulity. "Jesus Christ, you ordered that? I thought it was on the menu as a joke."

"It should be," she breathed, feeling her forehead with the back of her wrist. "I feel like I'm leaning up against an electrified fence."

He hummed. "Caffeine jitters."

She looked around. "Is everything supposed to be glowing?"

A low laugh made its way free of his throat, a bit like an engine chug. The rusted sound caused her to look up, making eye contact. And they stayed that way for several seconds, hers curious, his rueful. Just this once, why couldn't he have kept his fucking elbow to himself? "I wouldn't have pegged someone who studied penguins in Antarctica for a year as impulsive," Burgess said, knowing it was pathetic to try and prolong his time with her, but he couldn't help it. "I'd call it adventurous."

"You'd be surprised," she responded.

"Would I? Try me."

She tapped a finger to her lips, as if deciding whether or not she should cut their talk short and leave. Or stay and brighten his afternoon a little bit longer. "I do love an adventure. In theory, anyway. I used to love trying new things," she started slowly. "But in the case of Antarctica, I was playing it safe. Living in an isolated research center in the cold, where I feel most at home. Seeing the same five faces every day. The familiar repetition of research. Documenting." She paused, looking down at the table. "Before that, I lived on a boat for six months, interning on a coral reef conservation initiative in Mexico. Seychelles prior to that. If anything, I've been hiding."

Knowing his voice would sound unnatural if he spoke right away, he swallowed hard twice before asking, "From what?"

"I think I should go."

Burgess forced himself to accept her choice with a stiff nod. "Is there anything I can do to change your mind about taking the job, Tallulah?"

"No." She pressed her mouth into a straight line. "Again, I'm sorry to do this on short notice. But like I said, I'll help you find a replacement."

Burgess chose to ignore that offer for now. He'd handle one problem at a time. "What is your plan from here?"

"Get a hotel room for the night. Go visit some apartment share listings tomorrow."

Instantly, he was not a fan of the plan. Too much shit left to chance.

Burgess didn't have any say in what Tallulah did. None whatsoever. She was a grown-up who obviously had no problem safeguarding herself. Unfortunately, there was a protective hum in his chest that grew louder the longer he looked at her. Tallulah was the best friend of his best friend's future wife, right? An argument could be made that he was looking out for her safety.

As a favor.

Sure.

He'd lived in Boston for fifteen years and knew it better than anyone. And the idea of her settling for a place to live that was even one iota less safe than The Beacon wasn't sitting well with him. At all. But he thought of his daughter. How he would want Lissa to be treated when she grew up and struck out on her own, vulnerable to the world. He definitely wouldn't want some burned-out hockey player elbowing his way into her life as some kind of protector. Not unless she asked for it first.

Imagine this beautiful woman asking you to be her protector.

Burgess swallowed hard. "What is your ideal living situation?"

She seemed surprised by his question. "Um . . . well. In a perfect world, I'd be living with Josephine, but your grumpy golfer friend went and stole her out from under me." His lips twitched at that. "Considering that's not an option, I'll look for another female student who is renting a room in a neighborhood that has good transit options. Being that it's already late September, I might have some trouble locking down a decent place, but I usually have good luck with these sorts of things."

"Do you have a budget?"

"It's not exactly fat, because I've been interning for minimal cash. But I can float seven hundred a month for a room. For a while. Then I'll need to find some lab assistant work in the near future to replenish my funds."

When he wanted to wince, he nodded, instead.

Seven hundred dollars wouldn't put her somewhere safe in Boston.

Even if she managed to find a room, it would likely be the size of a broom closet.

"What?" she prompted.

Burgess couldn't quite stop himself from interfering, despite the fact that she clearly wanted to get the hell away from him. He shouldn't question that. He should let her. But he couldn't release her to the wilds of Boston real estate. Nor could he imagine a world where this was the last time he saw Tallulah. If there was a way to keep an eye on her without being in her face, shouldn't he try? For her safety as well as his own peace of mind?

"I know someone who has a room for rent," Burgess said before he could shame himself into letting her fly free. "In a building like mine, but in the North End. My teammate rents this place for his future stepsister."

Tallulah sat up straighter. "Oh. How much is the rent?"

"It's in your range."

She squinted a skeptical eye. "Are you sure?"

"Yes," he lied, fully prepared to pay the difference between seven hundred dollars and whatever astronomical amount the rent happened to be, out of his own pocket. "I'll speak to my teammate and send you the information, but Tallulah . . ." Okay, this part wasn't planned. The words just flowed out, urged by some intuition that he'd never have this chance again. "If you change your mind and want to come live with me, I'd do whatever it took for you to feel safe with me. All right? I'll install locks on your bedroom door and give you the only key. Just . . . don't compromise your safety. I don't think I could sleep at night knowing you compromised it because of me." Knowing he'd pushed enough, Burgess stood, reluctantly picking up his smoothie and trying not to be obvious about memorizing her face, just in case. "Good luck."

She stared up at him looking kind of astonished. "Thank you."

Burgess grunted and left, hoping like hell he'd said the right thing to a woman for once . . . and praying like a son of a bitch that it wasn't the last time they crossed paths. As soon as he made it to the other side of the street, he tugged his phone out of his pocket and dialed Sig Gauthier, center for the Bearcats and one of the only teammates he could tolerate off the ice. Most of the time, anyway.

"Hey, man," Sig said, yawning into the phone. "What."

"Didn't you rent Chloe a place in the North End?" Burgess asked, referring to Sig's future stepsister.

The creak of bedsprings as Sig presumably sat up. "Yup. She's used to the finer things, so I found a place she'd be comfortable." He laughed under his breath, sounding almost fond. "Didn't realize how much comfort costs when it comes to Chloe."

"Meaning what?"

"We made a deal—she pays half the rent. And she did. *Once.* Meanwhile, I go over there and she's got eighteen billion Sephora bags stuffed into the garbage can. Did you know girls put *primer* on their fucking faces? Foundation isn't the foundation anymore. It's out of control."

"Jesus. Lissa has been asking to go to Sephora lately."

Sig's laugh almost burst his eardrum. "Welcome to the beginning of the end, man."

Burgess grunted into a hard gulp of his smoothie. "Does Chloe have parties? What are her friends like?"

A long pause ensued. "Why are you asking?"

"Just answer."

Sig let out a breath. "She's not a partier. Guess you can't afford happy hour when all of your money is being funneled into the beauty industry."

"No sketchy boyfriends? No drugs?"

"You think I'd let some lowlife hang around with *Chloe*?" the center shouted. "No. None of that. And no drugs. She's in her final year of conservatory. You should hear her play the harp, man, she's . . ." Without seeing Sig in real life, he knew the guy was gesticulating wildly, same way he did while disputing calls with the referee. Creep up on Sig while he's telling a story and risk getting knocked the fuck out. "Never mind. What is this about?"

One of the perks of being team captain was that Burgess didn't have to answer anyone's questions. It was, perhaps, the best part of having the title. "Maybe Chloe would be able to afford half of her rent if she got a roommate."

"So, I've told her."

"What is the rent on the place?"

"Five K. You'd think it came with a goddamn butler."

This was exactly what Burgess had been afraid of. Nothing that couldn't be handled, though. Honestly, he would have paid ten times that amount to know Tallulah had a secure place to live. "So her roommate would be expected to pay twenty-five hundred?"

"Yup. It's a nice room. Sunlight. Closet space."

"Great." Burgess tamped down on the urge to turn around

and look back at the smoothie shop. Was this his last chance to see her? "I've got someone. But she's only paying seven hundred."

"I'm hanging up now."

"Relax. I'm good for the rest. Send me the info." He rubbed at the sharp object in his throat. "It's my fault she has to find a rental in the first place. It's the least I can do."

CHAPTER THREE

Tallulah skidded to a stop in front of the building and her jaw unhinged, drooping to the vicinity of her ankles. This was the place Burgess expected her to rent a room? Did he somehow misinterpret her budget to be seven thousand a month, instead of seven hundred?

Modern lines, gray stone exterior, mums peeking out of window flower boxes, gas lanterns hanging on either side of the glass door. The place was a Boston postcard.

"The apartment is probably a front for a commune of clowns," she muttered, walking inside and searching the vertical row of buzzers for 3F. "Or Chloe is the code name for a ring of rich financiers who need a place to convene for nightly pagan rituals. I'm obviously tonight's sacrifice." She stabbed the buzzer. "Weird that I still want to rent the room?"

"Nope. It's a great room!" enthused a voice on the other end. "I'm Chloe. Come on up!"

Tallulah winced. "On my way!"

Chloe was obviously bait.

How many people had been lured to their deaths here by the promise of an affordable cost of living? At such a cheap rent, how had this place not already been rented?

Not for the first time that morning, she wondered if she'd made a huge mistake turning down the free room offered by Burgess.

Burgess.

Was she continuing to think about him out of guilt? Because she felt bad for breaking their deal? Or was it the fact that his thoughtful composure just . . . appealed to her? Tallulah was really good at making small talk. When one worked in research labs in Antarctica and elsewhere with a bunch of introverted biologists, one learned to fill the silence. And her gift of the gab had been honed on many a night out during undergrad.

Yesterday with Burgess, she'd skipped the small talk.

They'd bypassed it completely—and nothing about it felt too soon. Or uncomfortable.

There was no explanation, except that something about his intentional gaze made Tallulah feel like they were past pleasantries. Sure, they'd met once, months ago, but that shouldn't have been enough to compel her to open up so quickly.

What *was* it about him?

Shaking off her useless musings, Tallulah walked up the stairs, slowly, on the balls of her feet, finger on the trigger of the pepper spray she'd uncapped in her pocket. Overhead, she heard the gentle creak of a door swinging open. So far, she didn't hear any chanting, but the evil oligarch financiers might just be at work. *Someone* had to pay the rent on this place. Obviously, it wouldn't be Tallulah—she would be dead. Sacrificed to the god of prosperity or something.

She rounded the railing at the top of the final staircase—

And found an ethereal blonde staring back at her from an open doorway at the opposite end of the hall, gel patches shaped like half-moons stuck beneath her eyes. "Are you Chloe?"

"Yes," whispered the blonde. "Hurry, before the landlord sees me. He knocked on my door for the rent earlier—and I have it. *Most* of it. Sig gave me a check for September and I deposited it, like I was supposed to. But I might have withdrawn a little chunk for essentials."

Tallulah moved down the hallway. "Such as?"

"Oh, this and that." Chloe stepped aside to allow Tallulah into the apartment, her bright smile dissolving into dread. "One of the building amenities is Wi-Fi. Do you think the landlord can see what I'm buying online?"

"I don't know," Tallulah said honestly.

"I bet he can. Oh boy." Chloe ripped off the gel patches from beneath her eyes, tapping and pressing the dewy, uncovered skin, as if to see if the patches had made a difference. "Let me show you the room."

For the first time, Tallulah turned to look at the apartment—and only grew more suspicious. It was a palace of high ceilings, awash in sunshine. An incredibly spacious open floor plan with a chef's kitchen on one side, a sunken living room on the other. Greenery galore. Tastefully decorated down to the woven basket full of throw blankets. Well, apart from the framed Gauthier jersey and Boston Bearcats pennants over the couch, anyway.

Chloe bounced ahead of her to the far end of the apartment where a short hallway was located. She toed open a door and executed a sweeping bow. "Thy chambers, milady."

"How many oligarchs are hiding in there?"

Chloe gasped. "What's that?"

"Never mind." Tallulah didn't even have to cross the threshold to know the room was a dream come true, probably even had an ensuite bathroom. "Chloe, there is no way you're renting out a room in this apartment for only seven hundred dollars a month."

Her smile never wavered. "Yes, that's what Sig told me to do." She flinched, slapping a hand over her mouth. "I mean . . . yup! That's the price."

Suspicion prodded Tallulah. "Are you sure? Sight unseen, I'm thinking you could get quadruple." She sensed that Chloe was trying to do mental math and perhaps not having the easiest time. "That's closer to twenty-eight hundred, babe."

"Right." Chloe nodded like they were both in on a big secret. "I don't know. I just live here and hope it all works out."

Okay. No.

Someone could easily take advantage of this girl—and it wasn't going to be her. "Chloe, I think you should rent the room for a better price, okay? I can't imagine what the cost of this apartment must be on a monthly basis, but you could one hundred percent find someone willing to pay more. Wouldn't that make things easier for you?"

"I don't know," she responded slowly. "Everything is pretty easy, as it is."

Tallulah's lips twitched. "I'm happy for you." She hesitated, but decided she wouldn't be able to live with herself without offering some assistance. "Look, I'm going to give you my phone number. When you relist the room, call me if you need help weeding through applicants."

Chloe's shoulders slumped. "So you're not going to take it?"

"No."

"Oh boy," the blonde said, pacing into the room, turning gracefully and coming back out. "But I did exactly what Sig told me to do."

An alarm bell started to tinkle in Tallulah's head. "Which is . . . ?"

"Charge you seven hundred and he would get the rest of your share from Burgess." After a prolonged moment of staring at the ceiling, Chloe sighed. "I can't remember if I was supposed to tell you that. Sig knows not to call me during my nighttime routine. It's like he *wants* me to have clogged pores."

While Tallulah stood in place, reeling from that information bomb, Chloe moped her way into the living room, plopping down on her gray upholstered couch and hugging her knees to her chest. "I know you're friends with Burgess, but Sig is the best one on the team, even though he's not the captain. He *should* be. I don't care if you tell Burgess I said that." She winced. "Actually don't. He's even scarier than my landlord."

"Whoa whoa." Tallulah waved her hands, desperate to regain control of the situation. "Let's start from the beginning. Burgess was going to pay my rent?"

"Most of it, yes." Chloe pursed her lips. "Aren't you supposed to be happy about that?"

"*What?* No!"

"Why?" breathed the blonde.

"Because I want to pay my own rent," Tallulah sputtered. "I don't want to owe him anything."

"But you were never supposed to know." She dropped her voice to a whisper. "Just pretend you never found out."

"*Chloe.*"

"*Well.*" Her might-have-been roommate was thoughtful for a moment. "Sig said Burgess thought it was his fault that you had nowhere to go. He said footing some of the rent was the least he could do."

Tallulah's heart started to rap faster, the moisture fleeing from her mouth. "I . . . can't believe he did that."

"Are you mad about it?"

"I freaking should be!" she managed, forcing herself to take a deep breath.

"Still not clear on why," Chloe drew out. "It's like a present. A monthly one. And everyone loves presents."

Tallulah wasn't very clear on why she was mad, either. Or if she was mad at all. She kept waiting for the indignation to take hold, but all she felt was kind of . . . touched. Wasn't that ridiculous? Yes! It was! But she couldn't help but remember that yesterday, when she'd explained her reservations to Burgess in the smoothie shop, he'd acknowledged them without making her feel silly or like she was overreacting. He hadn't tried to badger her into changing her mind. He'd just quietly gone and done something to help without getting any credit.

"I'm mad because he . . . maneuvered me," she explained, though her heart wasn't in it. "I don't need his help. I could have found a totally suitable place on my own."

"And yet . . ."

"And yet he wasn't even going to tell me."

"Sig must have failed to mention to Burgess that I'm a big mouth."

"You're not a big mouth. You're just . . . guileless."

Chloe laid a hand on her chest. "Thank you."

"You're welcome. Listen, Chloe. If you do try again to rent the room, call me, so I can help. But I'm not taking advantage of you like this. Or Burgess, for that matter. I can't." She crossed the room and put out her hand for a shake, remembering her vow to make bigger efforts to be social. "Matter of fact, call me even if you don't need help renting the room. We should get a drink, right?"

"Really?" Chloe jumped to her feet and wrapped her arms around Tallulah's neck, knocking her back a step. "Yes! I would love that."

"Me too." Amused, Tallulah patted her back. "I'm glad you're not an oligarch."

Chloe stepped back, beaming. "I still don't know what that is."

"They're even more overbearing than hockey players." Tallulah backed toward the door, waving on her way. "But only slightly."

Tallulah didn't remember walking down the stairs, she was so deep in thought. This near stranger had attempted to orchestrate her living situation. Had been willing to shell out just under two grand a month on her behalf. Because he felt responsible for her situation?

Unreal.

She was pissed. Or trying to be, anyway. Mainly, however, she was confused.

And also . . . what? *Intrigued?*

He'd gone out of his way to help her at a cost to himself. After all, if she hadn't been able to find an affordable room to rent, there was a possibility she would have had no choice but to crawl back to Burgess and take his offer of a locked bedroom door, thus landing him an au pair *and* freeing him from the tedious job of interviewing new ones.

But could his motive really be her safety? Coupled with his own guilt?

If so, were his actions controlling or . . . a misguided attempt to be helpful?

Tallulah didn't know, but she was going to find out.

Meaning, she'd be seeing the Goliath single father again.

And her stomach wasn't elevating with excitement over that fact.

Definitely not.

CHAPTER FOUR

Burgess watched the French braid tutorial on the screen in front of him, wondering how in the hell it could grow more confusing each time he restarted the video. Simply put, his fingers didn't move like that. Thumb cradling the bulk of the hair; pinkie hooking here, there, everywhere; middle and index weaving in and out as if they were totally independent from the disembodied hand. What the *fuck*.

"Dad," Lissa wailed from her position face down on the couch. "If we don't start soon, I'm going to miss my bus."

"I need to watch it one more time." He dragged the dot back to the beginning. "The method has to click eventually."

"It won't!" She sat up and glared at him, the shoulders of her school uniform wet from the dripping ends of her dark hair. "The look on your face is the same one you had when I tried to explain bra sizes."

"Someone needs to burn that system and start over."

"It makes sense to us!"

"Oh yeah? Then why are eighty percent of women wearing the wrong bra size?" He stabbed the pause button. "Read that interesting tidbit in the pamphlet they sent with your bra order. Eighty percent. *No one* gets it."

She slapped a pillow over her face and screamed into it.

Burgess wished he could do the same. He was exhausted from a late practice, after which he'd driven to Westford to pick up

Lissa from her mother's house. By the time he got home with his daughter in tow, he'd been too tired to talk to her about anything important. To try and connect, like he always promised himself he would try to do. Mental and physical exhaustion always seemed to get in the way now. He didn't recover from practice the way he used to in his twenties. Recovery now required ice and ibuprofen, neither of which he'd had time for last night. The throb in his lower back was a constant reminder that he'd lost a step.

That he'd probably lose another one every season until he retired.

Sighing over the unwanted thoughts, he hit play again on the tutorial, though he wasn't really seeing it now. He was thinking about Tallulah—again—wondering if she'd connected with Chloe and started the move-in process. He'd searched crime statistics in the neighborhood and done a Google street view of the building, satisfying himself that it was safe.

Did *she* like it, though?

"Dad, can you just *try*?"

He dragged two hands down his face. "Why the sudden need for this complicated hairstyle?"

"It's *not* complicated. We have a volleyball scrimmage today and everyone on the team is going to have their hair French braided. I was the only one who didn't have their hair braided last time." She plucked at the black hairband around her wrist. "I don't want to be left out again."

Sympathy nudged him in the chest. "Did they plan it without you?"

Her face turned red, eyes suddenly full of tears. "Why would you ask me that?"

"I don't know. Sorry." Christ, he didn't understand his own daughter. Every time he opened his mouth that became more and more obvious. He'd had no sisters. No siblings at all growing up. His youth was nothing but hockey, as was the entire life that followed. French braids and training bras and the politics of elementary school girls were an alien language to him that became more indecipherable by the day. Whenever it was Burgess's turn to have Lissa, she grew more unreachable. Or he grew denser. It was hard to say which.

"All right, let's do it." He stood up and circled the couch, accepting the comb she handed him. "Trial and error is obviously how I'm going to learn, because Braiding Besties on YouTube isn't cutting it."

Lissa turned so her back was propped up against the arm of the sofa, muttering, "It doesn't have to be perfect."

Guess what? She was lying.

Yes, it fucking *did* have to be perfect.

Burgess watched his blunt, crooked fingers move in an unnatural pattern, attempting to weave hair into something resembling a braid, but one section went misplaced every time. The three pieces were uneven, leaving him without enough hair to complete the braid. Or bumps. Bumps appearing out of virtually nowhere. And bulges. Plus, she kept pulling out these little strands around her temples *on purpose.*

"Why are you doing that?"

"It looks cuter that way."

"They didn't do that in the video."

"Oh my gosh! So *what*?"

Burgess shut his mouth and reached for the rubber band, securing the uneven bottoms of the three sections, praying to the God of Single Dads that it was good enough. When he heard tears coming from the bathroom a minute later, he knew the braid hadn't passed muster and he hung his head, massaging both eyes with his thumb and forefinger.

"I'm not going to school."

"You *are* going to school," he said patiently. "I have a meeting with the Bearcats manager this morning and practice in the afternoon. I won't be home to watch you today."

"Can I go with you?"

The desperation in her voice raised his antennae. Was something going on at school with her classmates? Was her whiplash mood about more than a braid? And if so, was he even qualified to handle the problem? "Lissa—"

The apartment buzzer rang, cutting him off. Both of their gazes zipped to the door. It wasn't unusual for Burgess to get deliveries. There was always stuff coming in. Equipment samples, shit he needed to autograph, game footage sent from the coaching staff. However, the doorman usually accepted the delivery for Burgess to collect later. No reason the buzzer should be going off.

"Hold on a second," he said, crossing the floor of the living room to the electronic panel on the wall, tapping the button that would bring up the security feed from the lobby.

Tallulah stood there with her arms crossed.

Just like every other time he saw this particular woman, the muscles in his stomach flexed involuntarily, his pulse doing something ridiculous in his neck. He got sweaty without actually being sweaty, which made no sense. This morning's reaction was no exception. Although this time, a touch of dread crept into the pleasure he got simply from looking at her.

Because that was one ticked-off lady.

His love life might be nonexistent now, but he'd gone through a divorce.

Therefore, he knew.

Although, she seemed sort of conflicted, too, and he had no experience with that combination. The doorman who stood behind Tallulah signaling him with a finger slashing across the throat must have been equally alarmed by a woman who looked unsure about how much anger she would be unleashing, as well. At least he wasn't alone.

Still . . . "Shit."

"Dad."

"Sorry."

"Who is it?"

"Tallulah."

Lissa gasped. "Really? She's *here*?" She was already clawing down his attempted hairstyle, his pitiful handiwork gone in seconds. "Do you think *she* can braid my hair?"

"Something tells me she isn't in the mood." With a long exhale, Burgess pressed the buzzer that allowed her into the lobby, not even remotely surprised that his pulse started to beat faster. Because pissed or not, he *wanted* to see her. Was looking forward to it, even. When she left yesterday, he wasn't sure he'd have the privilege again.

Burgess leaned a shoulder against the doorjamb, crossed his arms, and waited for the elevator doors to open. As soon as they did and he got eyes on Tallulah, his fucking heart started to hammer. Yeah, it had a lot to do with her tight jeans. But hell if the flush on her cheekbones, the delicate notch of her throat, even the purposeful way she swung her arms didn't fascinate the shit out of him. Uncharted waters—that's what this was. His ex-wife had never done this to him, even when they first started dating.

No one had.

Ever.

Roll your tongue back into your mouth before you humiliate yourself.

He was verging on retirement and this woman's life was only beginning.

Burgess stood very still as Tallulah marched right up to him, indignation crackling in those gorgeous brown eyes. And oh yeah, she definitely knew what he'd done. Any second now, she was going to open her perfect mouth and tell him to go straight to hell. That she could take care of herself. That he'd had no right to interfere. She would be right, too.

"Tallulah?" called Lissa behind him. "Hey! Do you know how to French braid?"

Tallulah flicked a softening glance over his shoulder, then returned her attention to him. "We'll talk about Chloe's apartment later."

"I believe you."

She hummed in her throat. "Fishtail? Pigtail? Or regular, Lissa?"

A cry of relief came from the apartment.

Lissa pushed past him into the hallway and hesitated awkwardly in front of Tallulah. But when Tallulah opened her arms, his daughter walked right into them, resting her chin on Tallulah's collarbone. Burgess spent the next few seconds pretending the sight didn't affect him. It did, though. He hadn't imagined the seemingly immediate bond between his daughter and Tallulah. And he was as envious of it as he was grateful.

"Hey, girl," Tallulah said. "You still have those fire dance moves?"

Lissa giggled. "Maybe. I haven't danced since the last time."

"Not even in the shower?" exclaimed Tallulah.

"People don't dance in the shower," scoffed his kid. But she was smiling.

Tallulah gave an exaggerated toss of her hair. "I do."

Burgess would be mulling over that piece of information for the rest of the day.

Month.

Year.

Decade.

Dangerously close to thinking about slippery flesh at the absolute worst time, Burgess cleared his throat hard and pushed himself off the doorframe. "Do you want to come in?"

"You *have* to come in," Lissa said, taking Tallulah by the wrist. "I need to leave for school in five minutes and he just keeps watching tutorials like a zombie."

He made eye contact with Tallulah as she was dragged past, her blood oranges and basil scent like a grind of a fist to his belly. And there she was. In his apartment. Setting down her purse, shrugging off her bomber jacket, and getting down to business. He stood there in astonishment as she twirled the comb in her hand in fast motion, dividing Lissa's mass of hair into three equal parts. As in, he could actually see the white lines of his daughter's scalp.

Wow. They did exist.

"For the record, I did try," he said, berating himself for the creepy tendency to fall quiet in Tallulah's presence. "A seven-game playoff series is easier."

"Do you have to relate everything to hockey?" complained his daughter.

"Yes."

"It's a learning process. Everyone has to start somewhere," Tallulah murmured. "Who normally braids your hair? Mom?"

"Nobody, really. I usually wear a ponytail or just leave it down, but all the volleyball girls do it like this on game days and I'm the only one who doesn't."

Tallulah's fingertips took a very tiny pause. "Oh yeah? You play volleyball?"

"Yes. When the coach puts me in, anyway." A beat passed. "I'm on the team, but I'm not on the *team*, you know?"

"If you're on it, you're on it."

Lissa exhaled into a smile, nodding. "Yeah."

Burgess assumed that would be it. His kid tended to clam up after giving only the barest amount of information. To his surprise, though, she kept going after an extended silence. "I suck at volleyball. They rolled their eyes when they found out I got put on the team."

"I'm sorry." Frowning in concentrating over the movement

of her fingertips, Tallulah continued. "I think I'd rather suck at volleyball than suck at being nice. What about you?"

His daughter let out a watery laugh and swiped at her eyes. "Yeah. Me too."

Tallulah wrapped the rubber band around the end of the most perfect braid Burgess had ever seen in his life and he didn't know what to marvel over first. How quickly she'd created that masterpiece or how easily she'd turned Lissa's problem into a positive thing. "You're good to go, kid. You might not have the best serve today, but that braid is unmatched."

"Thanks, Tallulah."

"You're welcome."

The buzzer went off again, followed by the doorman's voice crackling through the electronic speaker. "Bus is downstairs, Sir Savage."

Lissa gasped and jumped to her feet, swinging her eight-million-pound backpack off the floor and running out the door of the apartment, shouting, "Bye, Tallulah! Bye, Dad," over her shoulder.

"Bye," Burgess called after her, feeling like he'd just witnessed a divine miracle. "Thanks for doing that." He winced at the wall-rattling slam of the door, before turning to Tallulah who had gone back to her unique combination of confused irritation. There was something else in her expression now that hadn't been there before, however, and it was apprehension.

To be alone with him in the apartment?

A stick prodded at his jugular.

Yeah, he kind of thought that might be the reason.

Make her comfortable. Now.

"I usually head down for a smoothie this time of day. Want one?"

The clock ticked while she gathered herself. Or maybe it was his pulse.

"Sounds like you want witnesses for the lecture I'm going to give you about personal boundaries," she said, faintly. Visibly holding her breath.

Brave, but not confident with it.

What the hell had this girl been through, and who was he going to kill?

"You're not wrong," Burgess said, tipping his head at the door.

Tallulah nodded, keeping an eye on him while she collected her purse and jacket, folding it over her arm and leading their party of two into the hallway. They were quiet as he locked the door, quieter still while taking the short elevator ride down to the lobby, but her shoulders visibly lost their tension as soon as they were outside.

"Whatever you do," she said, walking past him when he held the door of the smoothie shop open for her. "Please don't let me order the peanut butter and espresso smoothie again."

"I still think that's on the menu as a joke."

"If it is, I fell for it. And so did my taste buds." They stopped at the counter, side by side, looking up at the menu fastened to the far wall. "I'll take one peanut butter and espresso smoothie, please."

He dropped his chin. "I'm afraid I can't let you do that."

"I can't *not* order it."

"Be strong."

"Be strong," she mimicked, adorably. "You can't do a French braid, but you can concoct a whole scheme to funnel me into an apartment of your choosing?"

"You're not even going to wait until we order our smoothies to address this?"

"The fact that you're making *light* of it—"

"I'm not making light of it," he rushed to say. "That being said, I came up with the idea knowing full well that if you found out, you would hate me, but at least you were going to be somewhere safe. It was a conscious trade-off."

"That's . . . why I'm having trouble being as mad as I would like to be." She gave a sharp cluck of her tongue. "It's very annoying."

"I'll take annoyed over you hating me."

"I don't hate you. And it's *not* your fault that I'm apartment hunting."

"Yes it is." His voice scraped like gravel. "You're scared of me."

"I'm scared of a lot more—" She snapped her mouth shut. "It's not *only* you."

Burgess had the most inappropriate urge to pick her up and hold her. He couldn't think of a better use for his strength than wrapping it around her after an admission like that. It wouldn't be welcome, though, so thankfully the smoothie shop employee chose that moment to pop up from behind the counter.

"Can I help you?" he asked.

"The usual for me," Burgess said after a moment. "Don't give her that peanut butter and espresso smoothie."

"Give it to me." She shielded her mouth with her hand, whispering to the smoothie shop employee. "Extra espresso, please."

Smirking, Burgess tossed a twenty on the counter. "Can we sit down?"

"Maybe." She sucked her teeth at him on the way to a table. "Is this one good or do you want to choose a different table behind my back?"

He squinted an eye. "I'm picking up on some sarcasm."

"Good."

She sat down, crossing her legs . . . and he heard the slightest creak of her too-tight jeans. Felt that sound deep in his Adam's apple. It would take some work to get that denim peeled down her legs. He'd have to rough them down her hips, probably taking her panties along with them. Now *that* was a task his hands could perform without watching a tutorial. Because he'd been undressing Tallulah in his dreams since meeting her last summer.

Burgess took the seat across from Tallulah, ordering himself to act natural, despite the semi he was sprouting in his briefs. "I assume you took the room with Chloe, regardless of my meddling."

"No, I did not," Tallulah answered, very succinctly. "That room is worth four times the rate advertised. Renting that room for seven hundred dollars a month would be a crime. I'd be taking advantage of you both."

"A small price to pay for . . ."

Jesus, he was revealing way too much. She'd come here to hand him his balls and here he was, making his admiration of her painfully obvious. He might as well be wearing a sign around his neck that said OUT OF PRACTICE.

"A small price to pay for me being safe?" she supplied, quietly.

Burgess grunted at the table, no idea how to respond without sounding ridiculous.

Tallulah remained silent for several seconds. "Maybe I just don't have a lot of experience with athletes, especially hockey players, but you come across as such a contradiction, you know? Is it possible to have so much aggression inside of you and still be so . . . worried about someone you've only met twice?"

More than possible. It was reality. "Yes."

"I wish I could know that for sure," she whispered, seeming to surprise herself by letting that slip. "Um. Could you satisfy my curiosity about something?"

"Shoot."

She squinted one eye. "Do you feel bad about breaking that guy's nose?"

The question caught him off guard. "Do I feel *bad*?"

"Yes."

Burgess let his breath hiss out slowly, knowing he couldn't be anything less than baldly honest with this woman, at all times, even if that honesty probably wouldn't earn him any points. "He'd been high sticking all night. I've been playing against that jackass for six years—he should have known me well enough to know a warning was coming and protected himself better." He really wasn't doing himself any favors here. *At all.* But he didn't know how to do anything but impart the ugly truth. "I guess I didn't mean to *break* the damn thing. If it makes you feel better, I sent a six pack to his hotel room after the game."

That made her sit up straighter. "Did you really? What kind?"

"Sam Adams. Obviously."

She snorted. "A beer originally brewed in Boston. So really, it was just another dig."

"How can I explain this . . ." He drummed his fingers on the table. "If I'd sent him an apology, it only would have made the broken nose sting harder. Sam Adams was a way of saying I'm sorry, man, but also fuck you. He keeps his pride that way. Much better. See?"

She blinked. "Hockey players are built different, aren't they?"

"You have no idea."

Tallulah picked up her smoothie and sipped from the straw. He did the same. They considered each other across the table like debaters preparing for the next question.

"I'm just going to come right out and say something, Tallulah, because it feels like it needs to be said." This could be a huge risk, but the verbal reassurance wouldn't stay locked inside. He'd always been blunt and direct, often to his own detriment, but Tallulah was too smart to buy any bullshit and he didn't want to sell her any, either. "I've never laid a hand on a woman in my fucking life and I never will."

Her chest sank all the way down and fired back up, her fingers twitching around her smoothie cup. She started to say something, but no words came out. That telling reaction caused Burgess to dig his fingertips into his thigh hard enough to cause pain, his pulse pumping loudly in his ears. *Name the dead man who hurt you.*

His throat burned with the effort of keeping that inquiry to himself, because it would be too far. Too fast. He might have spent the last few months replaying the afternoon they'd spent together, but there was no reason to think she'd done the same. He was just a potential employer to her. Not a friend. Not someone to whom she'd be interested in spilling her guts.

Definitely not a romantic prospect.

"Maybe I could come to dinner," she said slowly, as if measuring her words.

Burgess held his breath, a weird sensation—was it hope?—giving him pins and needles at the top of his scalp. Whoa. What was happening here? "Yeah?"

"Yes, I mean, I'll stay in the hotel for now, of course, but I didn't get a long enough visit with Lissa this morning and . . ." She cocked her head. "Are you picking up on the mean girl vibes?"

"I . . . what? What the hell is that?"

"Like maybe the girls at school aren't being very kind to her."

"Yeah." Relief almost had his giant ass sliding off the chair. "You think so, too?"

She gave a reluctant nod.

He prodded at the discomfort in the chest. "Oh God, I don't like knowing that. At all."

Tallulah followed the motions of his hand, looking almost curious. "I don't want to overstep—it's probably a job for Mom. But as a former brownnosing science freak, I *do* have some experience with mean girls."

Yesterday, he'd been prepared to let Tallulah pass on the au pair job, because the last thing he wanted was to force her into a situation that made her uncomfortable. However, now that there was a chance she could change her mind, he was determined to show her that his home was the safest place for her in Boston, possibly the world.

Starting with dinner.

There was just one problem.

"Tallulah, I can't cook for shit. I'm on a high-protein, low-carb diet, so I basically eat meat and steamed vegetables. Fish twice a week. I was planning on ordering takeout for Lissa tonight."

She pouted. "Oh, Burgess, you need help, don't you?"

"Help me," he said, hoarsely. "I can't do what you did this morning. You made straight, white lines in her hair. *While* talking. I can't do either one of those things with her. Not even one at a time."

"I'm . . . thinking about it." They continued to stare at one another so long, his body started to respond to her prolonged interest and he had to shift in his seat. Focus hard on keeping his breathing even. God, this woman ruled his dick and she had absolutely no idea. Maybe allowing her to move in was unethical. The need to be around her won, though. It drowned out everything else, including his conscience, apparently. "In the meantime, I have a meeting with my counselor about my course schedule. I guess I'll see you tonight?"

"Tonight sounds amazing," he said, adding, "We'll take it slow. See how it feels. Okay?"

She exhaled, relaxing another degree. "Okay."

Tallulah pushed back from the table and stood. Burgess did the same. He had no idea what to do with his hands, so he put the right one out for a handshake. Tallulah rolled her lips inward, seemingly to hide a smile, and slipped her fingers into his grip, the contact sending a slow sizzle down to the soles of his feet. *Soft. Strong. Perfect.*

He watched as she shouldered her purse and picked up her smoothie, obviously preparing to bring it with her. Before she could breeze past him to the exit, she stopped, hesitated, then lifted the straw of her drink to his mouth. "I dare you to try this and tell me it isn't amazing."

Burgess grimaced. "I don't drink caffeine."

Briefly, she pretended to choke. "One sip isn't going to kill you, protein pants."

"Jesus. Fine." He closed a hand around her wrist and guided the drink higher, closing his teeth around the straw and tugging it upward, so he wouldn't have to crane his neck. And hell if he didn't feel the pulse leap in the small of her wrist. Her eyelashes fluttered ever so slightly, her gaze trained on his mouth as he sucked down a healthy gulp and let go of the straw, licking his lips. If she wasn't a stupefyingly gorgeous, intelligent, and *young* grad student who could have her pick of any man *her own age* in Boston, he might have wondered if she was attracted to him, too. But there wasn't a shot in hell.

"Well? What's your verdict?"

Only the truth for this woman. "That's vile, Tallulah."

Her mouth fell open. "You don't even like it a little bit?"

"I like knowing what you like." It took him a moment to register what he'd said—and more importantly, that he'd said it out loud. She was blinking up at him, obviously thrown off by the statement, as well, so he backpedaled as fast as he could. If he wanted her to reconsider the au pair position, the last thing he needed was Tallulah being aware of his totally pointless mega crush on her. "I mean, knowing you happily drink liquefied dog food will make me feel less self-conscious about my terrible cooking."

A smile lifted one side of her mouth. "See you later, Burgess."

"Bye, Tallulah."

He inhaled her basil and orange scent as she skirted past him to the door, then turned and watched her ass move right to left in a hypnotic sway until she was out of sight. A chuckle from behind the counter snapped Burgess out of his trance—and there stood the smoothie guy behind the register, smirking and drying his hands on a white towel. "Would you look at that? Sir Savage has got it bad."

Burgess gave him the middle finger on his way out, but the guy only laughed harder.

Not until he was inside the elevator did Burgess allow himself to smile.

Tallulah was coming to dinner.

CHAPTER FIVE

Tallulah selected a Styrofoam tray of chicken breasts from the refrigerated trough, making a face as she tossed it into the red handbasket. As a vegan, she didn't make a habit of handling raw meat, but she could tough it out for one single meal—and once she reached the produce section, she planned to gather eggplant, zucchini, peppers, and onions for a vegetable dish for herself. Her mother's Saksuka to be exact.

What a difference a day makes. Suddenly, she was shopping with a man's dietary restrictions in mind. High-protein, low-carb. *Blech.* Why was she in the store buying supplies to cook dinner for this man and his daughter, anyway? She didn't have an answer to that. Except her mind continued to replay his rasping plea of *help me* across the table in the smoothie shop . . . and she'd kind of just ended up at the closest market to The Beacon.

One time.

She'd cook *once.*

Even if a miracle happened and she changed her mind about living with Burgess, her duties would *not* include cooking. This was a favor. A whim. Nothing more, nothing less.

She hung a right out of the refrigerated section and came face-to-face with an endcap full of peanut butter jars. As if she needed a reminder of Burgess taking a sip from her smoothie that morning. She'd only been thinking about it *since it happened.* During her meeting with her counselor, the woman's mouth had been moving, but no sounds were registering, because every last one of Tallulah's thoughts were on those strong white teeth. How they'd yanked on the paper straw, somehow contracting muscles in her tummy that hadn't been exercised in far too long. That imagery was plenty distracting on its own, but throw in the flex of his throat as he swallowed, his eye contact intentional, curious, and the memories had caused her to leave the air-conditioned administration building flushed head to toe.

Now she had *two* reasons not to take the au pair position.

One: she didn't want to live in a constant state of worry that Burgess's temper might extend beyond the ice, an invisible boil just below the surface.

Two: she suddenly wanted to know if he'd use those same teeth to take her panties off.

The combination was alarming, to say the least. To be attracted to a man without knowing exactly what lay under his hood. Although, did anyone ever truly know what was lurking inside of someone? No, right? She'd been tricked before.

The monster had hidden himself so well. *So* well.

Tallulah tore her unseeing eyes off the peanut butter and headed for produce. She'd already picked up the chicken. Now she threw a green pepper, an onion, a lemon, and a garlic bulb into her basket. A potato, too, which was *not* part of her mother's Saksuka recipe and would probably get her disowned, but the call of carbs drowned out the shame. Hopefully Burgess had a few basics in his kitchen, like cooking oil, sugar, and vinegar, or she'd have to send him knocking on his neighbors' doors.

At the cash register, she paid for the ingredients, wrapping her arms around the big brown paper bag and stepping out into the Boston evening. And she had to admit, she liked Burgess's neighborhood. A lot. People-watching in parks was kind of her thing, as it was free, relaxing entertainment, and there were plenty of green spaces in Beacon Hill. Burgess lived right down the road from a giant public park, not to mention one of the original sell-ing points of the job had been the rooftop garden on his building.

Streetlights were beginning to flicker on, along with gas lamp posts, lanterns adorning stoops of three- and four-story brick buildings. Green ivy clung to the sides of every other structure, mums peeking out of immaculately painted flower boxes, bright-ening every residence. A lot of people living on the first floor didn't even bother with blinds, so she could see them through their windows as she passed, kids doing their homework at the kitchen table. Lissa would probably be doing the same right now. Would Burgess be helping her?

A postbox on the corner jogged Tallulah's memory and she stopped in her tracks, setting down the sack of ingredients on the sidewalk. She reached into the pocket of her coat and took out the postcard she'd snagged earlier that day in the more tour-isty section of town. On it was a picture of Quincy Market and scripted words that read GREETINGS FROM BOSTON. She read over the short message she'd penned to her sister, Lara, along with the Istanbul address she knew by heart. A lump began welling in her throat, but she dropped the card into the slot before tears could form in her eyes and continued on.

She didn't stop again until she reached the corner across the street from Burgess's building, her gaze traveling up to the top floor. She didn't actually expect to see anyone, so she almost dropped the bag of groceries when she caught Burgess's outline in the window, a Goliath-sized figure pacing back and forth, a phone pressed to his ear. And oh lord, she couldn't pretend away the pressing fist of attraction beneath her belly button.

Since the incident that took place during her final year of undergrad, Tallulah had found it very difficult to abandon herself to chemical attraction. Or even experience the feeling. Appreci-ating men for what they could offer her physically had never been an issue in the past. Not at all. She'd *loved* men, prior to her string of internships around the globe. Flirting, too. The excitement and pleasure of a biological reaction to a stranger. That buildup of tension, the snap of release. Now when she ventured out to socialize, her nervous system went on high alert around men. She couldn't function, worrying she wasn't seeing the whole picture. Wondering what they were *really* like. And most importantly, what they were capable of.

She wanted freedom from the fear. Badly. Over time, she'd hoped that either she would overcome it or someone would simply strike her as different. Trustworthy. *Not* a monster.

Why did her libido have to make its illustrious return with her potential boss?

Like, come *on*.

A whole lot of complications could arise while living with a man she wanted to saddle up and ride. For one, he had a kid. Their age gap was notable. Tallulah wanted to get back to living, to making the most out of her twenties. Not settle down. No, thanks. She'd spent years hiding on research missions, but it was time to start fulfilling the promise she'd made to her sister, Lara, who'd been there to witness the incident and see Tallulah in pieces of emotional wreckage. Pieces that had taken a long time gluing themselves back together to form a whole.

Now was the time to get out and *do*.

Until she started keeping her word, she'd continue communicating to Lara through postcards. They made it so much easier to delay the disappointment—or worse, the pity—she knew she'd hear in Lara's voice if she ever got the courage to call.

One hurdle at a time, though—and tonight was a big one. Six-foot-three, to be exact.

"It's just dinner," Tallulah said on an exhale, glancing left down the one-way street before crossing. The doorman gestured her through the entrance with a broad smile, like he'd been expecting her, and she rode the elevator up to the top, stepping out—and halting in her tracks at the sound of the argument coming from Burgess's apartment.

"Hang up, Dad! It's not going to help."

"I can't just do nothing, Lissa."

"Yes, you can! Oh my God, you're making it so much worse."

Tallulah took one hesitant step. Then another. And stopped. Did she really want to get involved here? Because she wasn't a fly-by-night kind of person. Once she got involved, she stayed there. This was only supposed to be dinner. A chance to pass on some words of encouragement to Lissa and maybe—and that was a teeny-tiny maybe—reconsider the job offer. But Tallulah's instincts were telling her there wasn't going to be anything casual about inserting herself here. Did she want to do that, considering her misgivings?

A gulping tween sob from inside the apartment propelled Tallulah forward, her sympathy making the decision for her. Propping the groceries on one hip, she rapped hard on the door three times. Silence greeted her from the other side.

Footsteps.

A scowling Burgess opened the door holding a phone to his ear, feet bare, hair wet, dressed in black sweatpants and a white T-shirt with the Bearcats logo emblazoned across the front. "I wasn't going to be wearing this when you got here. But shit happened."

"I can hear the shit from the hallway."

He closed his eyes briefly, before settling them on the brown paper bag she held. "What's in there?"

"Ingredients for Saksuka and some lemon chicken."

The intensity of his scowl lessened dramatically. "You're going to make that? For us?"

"Yes."

"Please, for the love of God, come in."

He stepped aside and Tallulah entered, trying very hard not

to notice what the freshly showered professional athlete smelled like. But she failed. The answer was . . . delicious. Like he'd still been sweating when he got into the shower and hadn't quite stopped by the end of it. The result was a drugging combination of menthol and musk that brought about a flip in her belly.

Thankfully—or not—Tallulah was instantly distracted by the girl sitting on the couch with the tear-streaked face. "Hey." Tallulah crossed the room and set down the groceries on the coffee table. "Rough day?"

Lissa crossed her arms over her stomach and nodded miserably.

Tallulah nodded. "I can't help but notice you took out the French braid."

"None of them had braids today. I looked pathetic."

Sympathy crowded in her throat. "I disagree that you looked pathetic. That's impossible. But why don't we worry about what's happening right now. What's the problem?"

Lissa erupted. "Dad is calling the school to tell them I'm being bullied, but I'm not. Not really. It's . . . I don't know. It's more complicated than that."

"They're bullying you without bullying you."

"Yes!" She flung an arm out at her father, who was now pacing back and forth in the open kitchen fifteen yards away. "He's going to get them in trouble for nothing and it's going to be way worse tomorrow."

Tallulah shared a private wince with Lissa. "Let's see if I can distract him."

The girl swiped at her wet cheeks, looking hopeful. With a deep breath, Tallulah picked up the bag of ingredients again and made her way to the kitchen, setting it down on the counter. "Hey." She took out the onion, pepper, garlic, and potato, setting them on the cutting board adjacent to the sink. "Can you chop these up for me, starting with the onion?"

"Me?" Burgess asked, stabbing a giant finger between his pecs.

"Yes."

"I only have one hand right now."

"Then maybe you should hang up?" She dropped her voice to a whisper. "Translation: you should definitely hang up."

His brows slashed together like twin swooping black kites and her heart started to pump. She'd just come into this man's kitchen and told him what to do. How would he react?

A bony object got stuck in her throat while she waited, her fingernails digging into the palm of her right hand. His attention fell to her fist and that frown only deepened.

Finally, his gaze climbed back up to meets hers. "She came home crying," he said, his voice calm. Even. "I'm supposed to just let that go?"

Tallulah could feel the girl's hopes resting on her shoulders, all the way from the living room, so she held her ground, despite the trepidation. "I think you should, for now, yes." She lowered her voice and turned her back to the rest of the apartment. "I understand the knee-jerk reaction to solve things for your child. I think that's normal and healthy. If there was outright bullying involved or she was being threatened, adults would need to step in. But this sounds like typical girl politics to me. She's twelve and she has to solve this problem for herself."

"I don't like it when she cries," he said, enunciating every word.

"That's normal and healthy, too."

He grunted. "So you want me to hang up and chop an onion."

"Yup. Your turn to cry, Sir Savage."

Burgess ended the call with a surly grimace and shoved the device into the pocket of his sweatpants. Frankly, he looked disgusted. Yet he took the knife out of the block, examined the onion a moment, and started chopping, a sharp muscle popping in his cheek. And Tallulah slowly let out the reserve of breath she'd been holding, shaking out the hand that now displayed a quartet of half-moon indentations from her nails. When she felt eyes on her, she noticed Burgess watching her over his shoulder and forced herself into motion.

While removing the package of chicken from the bag, she winked at Lissa over the breakfast bar and the girl slumped backward onto the couch like a puppet who'd had its strings cut. Tallulah found a sauté pan in one of the lower cabinets, olive oil in another, and got to work cutting the chicken into pieces. She had been working in silence for a few minutes when Lissa appeared at the entrance of the kitchen.

"Can I help, too?"

"Of course. You can brown this chicken for me."

"I can?" She approached from Tallulah's right looking bewildered. "How?"

"Sprinkle some of that olive oil into the pan and heat it up."

Silence stretched. "I don't know how."

Tallulah set down the knife and washed her hands, then gestured for Lissa to join her at the stove. She could feel Burgess's eyes on her back as she walked Lissa through the motions of turning on the burner to the correct setting. They salted and peppered all of the chicken chunks together and added them to the pan, along with a dollop of butter and a hearty squeeze of lemon, Lissa jumping back when the sizzling oil popped. "You don't help your mom cook?"

"No, she just does it by herself."

Tallulah hummed. "She's going to be excited to have a helper now."

"Yeah."

"Just don't use the stove without an adult around. Your parents will probably get touchy if you burn the house down." Tallulah searched the drawer for a set of tongs, surprised when Burgess handed her one over her shoulder. She turned and made eye contact with the hockey player where he stood in front of a crudely chopped pile of onions, watching her with a mixture of curiosity and gratitude. "Growing up in my house, we had a rule. You have to clear the air before a meal. If you still have anger in your throat when the meal starts, you could choke."

Father and daughter looked at her with owl eyes.

"I didn't do anything wrong," Lissa pointed out.

"Neither did I."

"It's a good thing I know the Heimlich maneuver." Tallulah sighed. "Chicken is definitely getting stuck in somebody's windpipe."

"I just wanted to tell you what happened, but you freaked out," Lissa said to her father.

Burgess massaged the bridge of his nose. "I wanted to handle the situation. That's what I do. I'm your dad and I love you."

Lissa's lower lip started to tremble, but she quickly stilled it. "Okay. Me too."

Tallulah found it hard to take a deep breath. "Maybe next time, we'll listen first and handle the situation later, if necessary." She gave Lissa another side hug. "Does that sound good to everyone?"

"Yes," Lissa said emphatically.

After a moment of consideration, Burgess nodded. "Yeah."

Tallulah split a smile between them. "Congratulations, no one is choking to death tonight."

BURGESS NEEDED HELP. Badly.

Throughout dinner, that fact was painfully obvious.

When he looked at his daughter, the affection in his eyes was clear. He simply had no idea how to relate to her. She talked about her favorite band and he grumbled about the lyrics being too mature. She giggled about her crush on the lead singer and Burgess looked like he needed to be sedated. Her desire to get a purple streak added to her hair had him draining his entire glass of water. It went like that.

By the end of the meal, Tallulah had drawn the conclusion that Lissa had gotten older, but Burgess was still mentally parenting a five-year-old.

"That was really good," Lissa commented as the three of them cleared the table, rinsed the plates, and loaded the dishwasher. "What are we making tomorrow?"

Tallulah's chest lurched. "Well, um . . ."

She met Burgess's searching gaze from the other side of the kitchen. "Hey, kid," he said gruffly. "Can I talk to Tallulah in private for a sec?"

Lissa looked at both of them, sharp as a tack. "You're coming back, right?"

"You know how us adults operate," Tallulah hedged. "We have to go over all the boring details before we settle on anything." She looked the young girl in the eye. "But we're friends, Lissa. One way or another, I'll see you soon."

"Promise?"

"Promise."

Lissa scrutinized Tallulah a little too closely for comfort. "Take her to the rooftop garden for your talk, Dad. She has to see it, okay?"

"Uh-huh." Burgess coughed into his fist. To disguise a laugh? "Good idea."

Tallulah narrowed her eyes at Burgess as Lissa danced out of the kitchen. "I'm being played. She remembers that I'm a sucker for gardens."

He shrugged. "You won't like this one. There are too many water fixtures."

"Water fixtures?" she echoed wistfully.

"Yeah, the waterfall gets noisy sometimes." He shuddered. "And it's too bright up there with all of the string lights."

She made a sound. "The ones with the big vintage bulbs?"

"You know them?" He cringed. "Awful. Just awful. You're

there to look at the stars, not a bunch of lights, right? I mean, the stars are *right there*."

A giggle carried down the hallway in the direction of Lissa's room.

Burgess gave her a quick grin. Just a flash of those teeth and her heartbeat doubled. Since when did she have a thing for *teeth*? And if she did have a sudden fetish for chompers, why was it manifesting itself with a hockey player who could easily lose them with one rogue puck to the face? Everything about . . . *noticing* Burgess was inconvenient. She shouldn't be following him to a romantic rooftop garden for a private chat beneath the stars.

But dammit, she really wanted to see that garden. Enough to go somewhere alone with a man, which she hadn't felt safe doing in quite some time.

Did she feel safe *now*?

"There are usually other residents up there," Burgess said quietly while drying his hands on a kitchen towel. "Not a lot, but my neighbor's dog gets the zoomies around this time of night and he brings her up there to run in circles." He set aside the dishrag and slid both hands into the pockets of his sweatpants. "He should be there."

Tallulah studied Burgess, his earlier words from the smoothie shop replaying themselves. *I'm just going to come right out and say something, Tallulah, because it feels like it needs to be said. I've never laid a hand on a woman in my fucking life and I never will.*

Thing was, she was kind of starting to believe him, even if it felt too soon. Too soon to really know someone, especially someone who had a temper and a lot of physical strength. His daughter was not afraid of him, however; that was very obvious. And there was something else. Burgess already had a decent idea of Tallulah's issue, but he hadn't pushed for the details. He was exhibiting patience and understanding, addressing her worries without her having to ask—and he wasn't doing it in a patronizing way. That . . . counted for something.

"Then I guess you should show me this awful garden."

Relief rippled across his features. "Brace yourself," he said, jerking his chin in an indication that Tallulah should precede him out of the kitchen.

"I'm shaking in my boots."

The rooftop garden wasn't awful.

It was *breathtaking*.

Pushing through the metal door at the top of a narrow staircase and stepping out onto soft grass, she had to blink several times before she believed what was in front of her. There were, indeed, string lights hanging in a zigzag pattern from one corner of the roof to the other. Colorful Adirondack chairs were arranged in conversation circles on one side. On the other, a bench sat against a brick perimeter wall that was covered in moss. And the *view*. She could see the uneven chimneys that poked out of nearly every building's rooftop in Beacon Hill. The tree-lined, cobblestone grid of the neighborhood. Beyond that, she could see the concentrated lights of downtown Boston. Cool September wind rustled leaves of potted trees that were already verging on yellow, soon to be orange.

There was no word for this place other than spectacular.

"Oh, this is playing dirty," she murmured.

"No." He drew out the word. "Making us that lemon chicken and . . . Saksuka?"

She nodded, impressed he remembered.

"Making us a home-cooked meal was playing dirty," he continued, seeming relieved to have pronounced the dish correctly. "There's nowhere to go from here but down."

She gave him a pointed look. "Even if I were to stay, cooking isn't part of the deal."

"Of course not."

It was very difficult not to notice the way the breeze was plastering the thin white T-shirt against his pecs. "I mean it."

"I know." His stance was casual, relaxed, but from the corner of her eye, she could see him press his fingers to the base of his spine, massaging in a tight pattern, a slight wince pulling his mouth taut. Before she could ask if he'd received some kind of injury, a little brown Yorkie zipped in front of her. A split second later, it shot by in the other direction.

"Sorry folks," chuckled a man approaching from the far end of the roof. "She's about finished, just needs a few more laps. Don't let her trip you up."

"We won't." Burgess put his hand out for a shake and got a firm one in return. "How are you keeping, Hank?"

"Good. Good."

Burgess tipped his head at her. "This is Tallulah. She's a friend."

"Sir Savage has friends?" Hank hooted at his own joke. "I guess I've seen it all. Nice to meet you, Tallulah."

"Nice to meet you." They shook hands. "Cute pup."

"Thank you. She's a handful, that's for sure." As though he knew the exact moment his dog would run out of steam, Hank hunkered down and scooped up the canine with one arm, where it panted happily, its pink tongue lolling out of the side of its mouth. "How is the team looking this season, Burgess? That pair of rookies you picked up have me excited."

"Honestly, they're annoying as hell, but they can play, so I put up with them."

Hank let out another hoot, delivering a slap to Burgess's shoulder. "And I know you've got some gas left in the tank, too, old man. They couldn't have a better veteran to teach them the ropes. I hope they know it!"

"I'm sure you'll yell it at them from the stands on opening night," Burgess said dryly.

"You're damn right I will." He stroked his dog's head. "Well, I'll leave you to it. She likes to watch *Wheel* after her zoomies run out."

Burgess nodded, but he was looking at Tallulah. "Good night, Hank."

"Night."

As soon as the roof door closed behind the tenant, Burgess cleared his throat. "Are you still good to stay up here?"

Tallulah registered her steady pulse, the lack of cloying fear that usually showed up when there was a possibility of being alone with a man she didn't know and trust. There was a baseline hum of wariness, just not enough worry to return downstairs. Besides, she *did* need to speak to him. She hadn't decided yet whether to move in, but no matter what decision she made, she was hoping Burgess wouldn't mind if she took Lissa out for ice cream once in a while. And again, the fact that Burgess was taking her comfort into consideration went a long way. Was she really starting to feel secure around him? Already?

"Yes," she responded slowly. "I'm good."

Tallulah walked to the far end of the roof and propped her forearms on the perimeter wall, briefly closing her eyes to enjoy the sensation of the wind picking up her hair and blowing it out behind her. When she opened them again, Burgess stood to her left, watching her face with an unreadable expression that he quickly disguised with his usual stoicism.

"So why are the rookies on your team so annoying?" she asked, kind of hoping to stall having to make a choice—move in or move on.

Burgess rolled a shoulder that could have belonged to an ox. "They're just young and cocky. They haven't been humbled yet and it shows."

"Interesting. What does it take to humble a hockey player?"

He leaned forward onto his elbows, seemingly mulling over her question. "Time."

That wasn't the answer she'd expected and she waited, hoping he'd elaborate.

"They have to experience a few hard losses to appreciate winning. The greatest players are great because they can cope with losing. They've been there, been humbled by getting crowned second or third best." He shrugged. "You can take home the first-place trophy, but it won't be as sweet if you've never experienced second. That hasn't happened to them yet."

"Have you told them any of this?"

Burgess made a sound that called to mind a garbage disposal. "I'm not sure why everyone thinks guiding these kids is my job."

"Because you're . . ."

"The veteran." He laughed without humor. "Believe me, I know."

Tallulah studied his face, the downturned corners of his mouth. "You don't like being called a veteran." He grunted in affirmation. "Why? Just . . . vanity?"

"*Vanity?*" he repeated, looking like he'd swallowed a fly.

"Geez. Never mind."

They went back to staring out over the rooftops. Burgess spoke again after a moment, "I don't like the reminder that I'll be retiring someday soon." He paused. "I don't like wondering if maybe I should have retired already. I think that's what happened in that preseason game last week. I got asked before the game started if I still felt capable of playing with the young guns . . . and I don't know. I think I just overcompensated trying to prove I could. I know how ridiculous that sounds."

"I don't think it sounds ridiculous. I don't have the mindset of an athlete, but I can put myself in your . . . skates." They smirked at each other and a little more of her wariness melted away. "Having a long career like yours is an accomplishment in itself. But you're also at a disadvantage, right? Everyone has watched you play for over a decade and they can draw comparisons. Then they have all these *stats* to refer to—"

"This is really helping, Tallulah."

"Sorry." She laughed. "But I do get where you're coming from."

Still leaning on his left forearm, he reached back again and massaged that spot at the bottom of his spine. His low groan was also swallowed up by the wind, but she heard it.

"Back hurt?"

"It's fine," he grumbled.

She raised an eyebrow.

"It *is*." He straightened to his full height and braced his legs apart. Crossing his powerful arms over his chest, causing those sharp-cut triceps to wink at her like they were sharing a secret. "We might as well talk about this nanny gig."

Tallulah pushed off the wall and faced him, squaring her shoulders. "Okay. Let's talk."

"I'll do anything I can to make it work." He looked away from her as he said it, almost like he was slightly embarrassed. "You just waltzed in this morning and . . . Christ. I couldn't even see your fingers while you were braiding her hair, they moved so fast. Then tonight?" He shook his head. "I know it's not your job to be our family counselor, but you've got this way of calming everything down. I really don't like people telling me to pull my head out of my ass—ask my coaches. But for some reason, I really, really don't mind when you do it."

As he spoke, pressure started to build in her chest, like a balloon filling with water, expanding, expanding. She'd already known he needed some help connecting with his daughter—and no, it wasn't her job. But she wasn't a half-in, half-out kind of person. She'd inherited the all-or-nothing trait from her parents, who'd grown up in a closely knit neighborhood of Istanbul, raised to step in and help one's neighbors at a moment's notice without expecting anything in return. It might have been eight years since she'd lived with her parents, but she'd never stop valuing the act of lending a hand, especially her own.

However. This whole situation screamed *messy.*

If only she could stop thinking about him openly saying he loved Lissa in the kitchen and the way her lip had quivered in response. Who *wouldn't* want more of that progress for a father and daughter? And was she forgetting the not so little fact that a room in Burgess's dope as hell apartment came *free?* With a salary on top of it?

At this point, her bank account's stomach was growling.

"Are you ready to tell me what's holding you back from taking the job, Tallulah?" He took a very deliberate breath, in and out. "It's getting harder and harder not to ask what I want to know."

A cold iron pressed to the center of her sternum. "Burgess . . ."

"Did someone hurt you?" he asked, with a steep rise of his chest. "I'm sure you're going to tell me it's none of my business. And you'll be right." She watched his hands turn to fists in his pockets. "But understand me, I will make it my business if you ask me to."

Over the course of their last two meetings, he'd obviously gotten the impression that her wariness of men stemmed from somewhere bad—and he was right. After all, it couldn't come from somewhere *good*, could it? This was her private heartache, though. Did she want to share that with him? She wasn't required to, by any means. Still, she found herself . . . wanting him to know. Wanting him to understand her wariness. Moreover, she didn't want him harboring wrong impressions about what happened. "Nobody hurt me . . . physically. Not in a technical sense."

He started, stilled, followed by his breath escaping in a gust. "No?"

"At least not in the way you're thinking. Maybe what actually happened is better. Or maybe it's worse. I might never know or understand." Images she wanted to forget went screaming through her head like a movie in fast forward. The faint outline of hangers, the sliver of light beneath a door, the hysterical sounds on the other side. "But he would have hurt me, given the chance. And in some ways, I do feel . . . like I'm carrying scars."

His eyes closed momentarily, fingers stretching and releasing at his sides. "I already hate everything about this. Please tell me, anyway."

Perhaps because his concern was so tangible, she found herself continuing in a quiet voice. Working her way up to telling him things that only her family and Josephine knew about. "We moved to Florida from Istanbul when I was fourteen. My father was a developer and his firm had investment properties they wanted him to oversee. My mother had a really hard time adjusting. She missed the old neighborhood. But my sister, Lara, and I . . . we loved it in Florida. Made friends easily. They were *always* at our house." A metallic taste coated her tongue at the simple act of picturing his face. "My sister was more selective when it came to dating, but I was an equal opportunity flirt. One of my sometimes boyfriends, as my sister called them, was Brett—and he *seemed* to understand that our relationship was only casual. We were mostly friends. And everyone adored him, including me. I mean, he was part of our family. He taught me how to drive a stick shift. He gushed over my mother's kofta." In her mind's eye, she could see Brett approaching her on campus, holding a freshly printed class schedule and appearing equally surprised to see her. "Around the time my family moved back to Istanbul, I went to college, roomed with Josephine. Eventually we got an off-campus apartment. I dated. A lot. Brett and I stayed in touch online, but our interactions became farther and farther apart. He seemed to be back home, working for his dad's car dealership. And then one day, my final year of undergrad, he was just . . . there. He'd transferred to FSU and rented the apartment right beside mine and Josephine's."

Burgess dragged a hand down his face, keeping his hand over

his mouth. The words "Jesus Christ" were muffled, but still full of the same dread she could feel building in her chest.

"Even knowing what I know now about him, I'm still not sure I would have noticed the signs that he was a monster." Deep breath. "But he'd been internet stalking me since . . . since I was living at home. It escalated when I left, went to college. And the pictures I would post, having fun at parties or entering short-term relationships . . . it incited him. Later, I found out from the police there were folders on his computer filled with saved pictures. Short stories that amounted to fantasies about what he would do to me one day as payback for not taking him seriously."

Burgess remained quiet. Listening. Watching her intently. His chest moving up and down, faster as she moved toward the worst parts of the recounting.

"He waited until Josephine went home for Thanksgiving to visit her parents in Palm Beach. My family doesn't really celebrate the holiday, so I stayed behind and . . ." She wet her parched lips. "I was in the hallway getting my mail and I felt someone come up behind me and put something over my mouth. A terrible smell and then . . . black. I blacked out. Waking up in the dark is the next thing I remember. I didn't realize until later that I was locked in his closet. He was pacing on the other side. I could hear him muttering, saying these disgusting things about me. This guy from the neighborhood. My supposed friend. I think . . . honestly, based on some of the things he said, I think the plan was to kill me before I ever woke up, but he lost his nerve."

Burgess cursed. Put his hands on his hips and turned in a circle, like he suddenly found himself confined, just like she'd been. "Oh my God, Tallulah."

"He didn't let me out for almost two days." Eight words to gloss over forty hours of sustained terror and uncertainty, fear and discomfort and helplessness. Somehow, however, Burgess seemed to pick up on that. He stopped moving, holding eye contact with her, like he wanted to absorb the worst of her memories. "It was like the entire building was empty except for us, because of the holiday. It didn't matter how much I screamed. Eventually I couldn't anymore. My voice gave out. Someone came to the door—a friend of his—and Brett left with him, probably afraid he'd hear me. I spent an hour prying up a loose floorboard and when he finally opened the closet door, I swung as hard as I could. I knocked him out. And I just started running. I ran until I found someone coming out of a restaurant who could call the police for me. I still couldn't speak, but I wrote down what happened and . . ." She stopped to gather herself, kind of surprised she'd made it to the end of the story. "He went to prison on a five-year sentence, but he didn't make it that long. As I understand it, another prisoner attacked him while in line for the shower." Her gaze turned another shade of serious. "I don't celebrate his death. I also have no idea how I would have lived when he was released, you know?"

"No. I can't imagine. Going through that. Then waiting around for the day he walked free. I just . . ." He huffed an unsteady breath. "I'm not as big a person as you, apparently, because right now I'd like to shake the hand of his killer."

Tallulah nodded in understanding, because she'd been there herself at one time. And in a way, his outrage and shock over what she'd been through was comforting. She'd made the choice to keep her trauma to herself, but sometimes it hurt to watch the world continue on as usual, as if it never happened. He was acknowledging that it happened and it was horrific. Something about that was . . . a relief. An overdue one. "I won't let him put an ounce of hate in my body. He's already put enough fear. But . . ." She gave a jerky shrug. "It's nice to have someone angry for me. I don't feel like talking you out of it."

"I don't think you could."

But she wasn't quite at the end of her story, was she? There was more. And it caused shame to trickle into her bloodstream. "I promised my sister, Lara, that I wouldn't let what happened make me live in fear . . . but I did. I took internships, found comfort in labs. I hid. I haven't . . . God, I haven't seen my family in almost four years. I can't face Lara knowing I didn't keep my promise." Saying it out loud made her neglect of the vow more egregious. "I used to be fearless. I'd try anything once, travel, party with the best of them . . . but I've stopped living. Experiencing. I'm suspicious of men and their intentions. I'm afraid of letting go and enjoying myself, only to be blindsided. I was supposed to *try* and I haven't. At all."

Burgess started to take a step toward Tallulah—to hug her? She never found out, because he changed his mind and remained in place, sweeping the rooftops with helpless eyes. "I'm sorry for what you've gone through. The fact that you walked into my apartment at all with that hanging over your head is a testament to how strong you are." He waited for her to look at him, his voice heavy with sincerity. "For what it's worth, Tallulah, you won. You waited for your moment, you kicked his ass and got as far away as you could. And you didn't let him make you bitter. That's better than I could have done."

She couldn't locate her voice for a moment, because that gruffly delivered assurance had lodged itself between her lungs. How did Burgess know it was the exact thing she'd needed to hear? Even she hadn't known until now.

"And I'm also so glad you're here now," Burgess said, taking a long, measured breath, as if picturing how the outcome could have been even worse. "Give me a chance to show you that you're safe with me."

Earlier in the hallway, when she'd gotten off the elevator and heard Burgess and Lissa arguing, she'd sensed herself standing at a crossroads. She'd knowingly taken the route with a lot of complications, and in truth, she'd already traveled at least a quarter mile, hadn't she? She'd already involved herself. Did she think bailing now would be so easy? It wouldn't. Especially now, after she'd shared so much with him. Shared *everything*.

"Do you have practice tomorrow?"

He seemed to hold his breath. "Yeah. From two to five."

"And Lissa gets off the bus at . . ."

"Three thirty."

"Okay." Despite nerves that were still raw from the traumatic story she'd told, Tallulah held out her hand. "I'll see you around dinnertime, during which I will *not* be cooking. I just feel the need to reiterate that."

He stared at her hand in disbelief. "Are you accepting the job?"

"Can you have the lock installed on my bedroom door by tomorrow?"

"I can," he said, without hesitating, letting the barest hint of sympathy leak into his expression, before putting it in check. As if he could read her and knew it wouldn't be welcome.

"Then yes. I'm accepting the position." She tried to keep her tone brisk and businesslike, but the utter relief blanketing his features turned her words sort of halting. "I'll bring my, um, course schedule over tomorrow and we can make sure there are no conflicts with Lissa's."

Beneath the canopy of lights, with the wind gently blowing their clothes and hair, Burgess's mouth spread into one of those rare and devastating grins. "Was it the garden?"

Why did those four words make her heart elevate toward her throat?

No, it wasn't the garden. Surprisingly, it was . . . *him*? Despite being a giant, growly hothead, he'd somehow reassured her. Which didn't make a lot of sense, but Tallulah's gut told her to trust him. "What can I say? I'm a sucker for a water fixture."

His answering laugh was deep, quick, and just as quickly, he sobered. "Thank you."

Was she fidgeting? She *never* fidgeted. Her hands and actions always had purpose, but right now, they didn't know whether to rest on the perimeter wall or smooth her flyaways. Maybe it had something to do with the very, very brief way his gaze touched on her lips. And the restrained hunger that resulted on his face, echoing in her own belly.

A vibration traveled downward from there, leaving an ache somewhere she had no business hurting for this man. This was her employer now. A kid was in the mix. And he was thirty-seven to her twenty-six. Not always a deal-breaker, but one to think about, because she wasn't ready to settle down. No, her goal was to start taking flight again.

Therefore, no more romantic rooftop strolls with her boss.

"I'll just grab my purse from the apartment and head out," Tallulah said. "See you tomorrow."

"Yeah." He seemed to realize he'd been caught staring and coughed into a fist, crossed his arms. "See you tomorrow."

She pretended not to feel his eyes on her the entire walk to the stairwell.

And she doubly pretended not to like it.

CHAPTER SIX

Burgess skated full speed after the puck, biting down hard on his mouthpiece in frustration when Gauthier got there first. By a hair, but still. They crashed into the boards together, battling it out for the control, a maze of elbows, shoulders, and sticks as more Bearcats entered the mix, resulting in more rattling of the plexiglass and a whistle being blown. "This is *practice*, assholes." Coach McCarren's voice ripped across the ice like metal being sawed in half. "Try not to get injured three weeks before the season starts, would you, please?"

Everyone shoved at each other at once, breaking up the suspended scuffle.

Once the pressure of bodies released from all sides, Burgess's burst of adrenaline capsized, and he became all too aware of the obnoxious throb in his lower back. Coupled with the fact that Gauthier had outskated him, irritation welled in Burgess like black oil out of the ground, his gloved fist bashing into the glass before he could stop himself.

As soon as Burgess performed the action, he regretted it. Losing his temper was endlessly amusing to the rookies, Corrigan and Mailer, and he'd been providing them with way too much entertainment lately.

"Oh shit," Corrigan shouted. "Dad is touchy today."

Mailer chewed on the end of his mouthpiece. "He's going to turn this car back right around if we're not careful. No Disneyland for us."

"If I was your dad," Burgess drawled. "I'd have abandoned you in the parking lot a long time ago."

They laughed in unison and clinked their sticks together, thrilled to have gotten a response out of him beyond his usual death glare. As far as Burgess knew, Corrigan and Mailer had met post-draft, but somehow, they'd morphed into virtual twins already. That afternoon, they'd walked into the locker room with matching Orgasm Donor sweatshirts talking about their romantic escapades the night before when nobody asked.

Burgess might be old for hockey, but he wasn't *old*. Still, he couldn't remember being as young and ridiculous as these two.

"You want to get back to practice, clowns?" Burgess asked, tightening his right glove. "Or is it getting in the way of outfit planning?"

Corrigan belted a laugh. "Don't feel left out, Dad. We can get you a sweatshirt, too."

"But only if you've donated at least one orgasm in the last month," Mailer was quick to interject, bashing his shoulder into Corrigan and getting one in return. "Do you qualify?"

Had he donated any orgasms recently?

Only to himself.

"Since I'm your dad, Corrigan, why don't you just ask your mom if I qualify?"

Mailer doubled over laughing while Corrigan's smile slowly melted off his face. Gauthier skated behind Burgess and they traded a fist bump without looking at each other. Really, that jab had been way too easy—and he liked to think he was above mom jokes at this point—but shit talking was a vital part of the hockey lifestyle that wasn't going away anytime soon. And when it came to insults, offense was the best defense. Honestly, didn't the kid deserve it for buying such a ridiculous sweatshirt?

Coach McCarren blew the whistle again and they resumed

the scrimmage, but Burgess struggled to keep his mind on the game. Which royally pissed him off. Because now he was thinking about the fact that he *hadn't* donated an orgasm in over a year. Had it been a one-night stand on the road in Anaheim, maybe? The memory had been archived almost as soon as it happened, so trying to recall the woman's face only produced a blurry profile. Might as well admit it, his love life sucked. He loved sex. Who didn't love sex? Hookups were great while they were happening, but as soon as they were over and he had a while to reflect, they just seemed to serve as a reminder that his marriage had failed. He'd failed.

There was no reason he couldn't enter into a new relationship. Hell, his ex was already engaged to a new dude—congrats to them. He even sort of *liked* the dentist she called her fiancé now, which was saying something, because he didn't like many people. But a relationship with a new woman meant eventually introducing her to Lissa. That's what held him back. He wasn't even solid with his daughter. What made him think bringing a new face into the mix was a good idea? Nah, Burgess stayed in on his nights off. Didn't date. Refused offers from the players' wives to fix him up with friends and sisters and cousins. Too much work.

He'd rather lust after his beautiful new au pair, who already found his aggression on the ice alarming and had serious and well-founded trust issues with men. Jesus, after her revelation on the roof after dinner, he'd stayed awake all night replaying her ordeal in his head, unable to control his rapid-fire pulse, his only solace being that Brett could never hurt Tallulah again. If her tormentor was still alive, he didn't think he'd be able to function. This woman was so much braver than he gave her credit for. Not only was he outrageously attracted to her, he admired her like hell, this vivacious grad student who would now live with him.

So much easier than casual dating, right?

Wrong. The complications were mounting—yet he only seemed to welcome them.

Great. Let's get complicated.

Corrigan received a pass from Gauthier and blew toward him on the ice, not a hint of restraint or caution in his stance. Not protecting the puck. Was he just that cocky, or did he have so little fear of Burgess handing him his ass?

He could either learn a lesson today or in a future game when it could cost them a win.

Burgess sighed, knowing it had to be now.

Digging his teeth hard into the molded rubber in his mouth, Burgess shoved off the ice and put his shoulder down, colliding with the rookie, slapping the puck out of Corrigan's possession at the same time, Corrigan going down in a screech of metal on ice in the process. The fall was far from enough to hurt him, just to rattle him into keeping his guard up and respecting the defense next time.

Briefly, when the action continued toward the opposite end of the ice, Burgess thought of verbalizing the lesson out loud, but decided against it. If the rookie couldn't figure it out on his own, he didn't belong in the league.

A while later, when practice had ended, Burgess sat on a bench in the locker room with a white bath sheet wrapped around his waist, hair wet from the shower and dripping onto his bare shoulders. He grimaced at the painkillers in his hand, lamenting the fact that he'd been forced to add another one, bringing the total to four. How many more would he add to his repertoire before he told the Bearcats trainer he had a problem?

Thing was, it wouldn't end there. The trainer would tell the coach, the coach would speak to the franchise owner, and he'd be traded or benched or forced into retirement, despite leading the team to three Stanley Cup titles. Already, he was beginning to lose speed. Throw in an injury and he was royally fucked. What the hell else was he supposed to do at thirty-seven? What else *was* there besides hockey?

Nothing. Not anymore.

As a younger man, he'd made his fair share of trouble. He'd been born with a constant flow of adrenaline. Drive. A thirst for sport that never seemed to wane. What he couldn't get out of his system on the ice, he put into women and drag racing on abandoned roads. Swimming contests against his teammates in ice-cold lakes that were half frozen over. He was the biggest dude, so he kicked in the door of the school gymnasium after dark and gave his fellow small-towners a place to party. It was a good—or hell, maybe a bad thing his hockey abilities caused his coaches and teachers to look the other way when he got out of line or he could have ended up down the wrong path.

He didn't, though. Once he got to college and realized he couldn't get by on natural ability alone, he straightened himself out, focused on school and being an enforcer on the ice. He'd worked harder than anyone. Graduated. Got drafted. Looked for stability and learned to ignore the burn of extra adrenaline in his veins.

After the divorce, he'd invested even more of himself into the sport, mentally and physically. Without it? Now? He didn't know what life would look like. Didn't know how he'd be *useful*, especially knowing he sucked at being a family man. Hockey—he was good at it. The only thing he was good at. And he just wanted to be himself as long as possible.

Gauthier dropped onto the bench beside him, staying quiet while he rooted through his Bearcats duffel for a T-shirt, pulling it on over his head. "Advil isn't going to cut it for long."

"It's not cutting it now."

"At least go see a private doctor, man," Sig said. "You could be making it worse."

Burgess was already issuing a grunt of denial. "Leave it."

"The way you left Corrigan on his ass?"

"Yup. Just like that."

"Those fucking sweatshirts."

"I say we burn them."

Sig raised an eyebrow at Burgess, as if to gauge whether he was serious. When Burgess remained totally straight-faced, Sig got to his feet and padded to the end of the row of lockers, presumably to double-check if the rookies were still in the showers, which, of course, they were, since they probably didn't have any responsibilities to get back to at home. The sound of a towel snapping, followed by a pained yelp, echoed through the locker room, strengthening Burgess's theory. *Christ, these shitheads.*

Satisfied that they weren't going to get caught, Sig found Corrigan's and Mailer's bags on the floor of the next aisle down and returned with the sweatshirts wrapped in a towel. "Here, you take one, I'll take the other."

Burgess accepted the Orgasm Donor sweatshirt and shoved it into his bag, covering it with his sweaty socks. "I'm too old for this," he muttered.

"Fuck you, mom jokes. You're never too old for this."

"Touché."

Not two seconds later, Corrigan and Mailer went strolling into their row, midconversation about—what else?—women. "What can I say, I'm partial to blondes," Mailer drawled, earning him a snort and a shove in the back from Corrigan. "Hold up. Speaking of blondes," Mailer called in Sig's direction. "Gauthier, is your stepsister coming to the season opener? I saw her on your Instagram and she is fine as hell." He jerked his chin. "You going to introduce me?"

"Bring her up again and I'll introduce you to the fucking

floor," Sig said, training a deadly look on the younger man. "And she's not my stepsister."

"Yet," Burgess reminded him while pulling a pair of briefs up beneath the towel, then dropping it completely.

"Yet," Sig repeated with forced calm. "Teammates' families are off-limits, rookie, unless express permission is given. You don't have it now and you won't have it ever."

"You just said she *isn't* family yet," Mailer pointed out.

"I know what the fuck I said," Sig snapped.

Mailer raised an eyebrow. "*Do* you?"

Sig turned an incredulous look on Burgess. "I'm going to kill these fucking kids."

Burgess bit back a smile. "You were exactly like them your first year in the league."

"Nope. Uh-uh."

"Yup. Worse, even." Burgess finished fastening the button of his jeans and tipped his head toward the exit, dropping his voice to a low rumble. "We should get out of here before they realize their dumbass sweatshirts are missing."

"I'm right behind you."

Simultaneously, they snapped their lockers shut, throwing their duffels over one shoulder and sailing toward the side entrance of the room, which emptied into the team parking lot. "Say hi to your mom for me, Corrigan," Burgess called over his shoulder, smirking over the resulting wave of laughter throughout the locker room.

"Too old, my ass," Sig muttered, following him outside into the September dusk. They happened to be parked beside each other and they wordlessly got to loading their gear into the rear cab of their SUVs. "Listen, uh . . . speaking of Chloe," Sig said after tossing his bag into the interior and shutting the door. "I hear she didn't quite pull off the whole cheap room ruse. Apparently, Tallulah saw through it pretty fast."

Burgess experienced a twinge of pride that he really had no right to feel. "I should have known she would. She's smart as hell."

Sig shook his head. "She must have chewed your ass out."

"Started that way, but she's moving in tonight."

"No shit?"

Burgess confirmed with a monosyllable, still in shock that it was happening after the rocky start they'd had.

"Chloe says she's a jaw-dropper, B. You interested in this girl as more than a nanny?"

"I'm not answering that."

"Why not?"

Burgess gave him an exasperated look. "Are we really going to stand here and talk about girls like a couple of rookies?"

"As long as we don't use the phrase 'smash that,' we get to live."

"Still no."

"I'll get it out of you eventually."

Burgess stomped to the driver's side of his SUV and hauled open the door. "You won't."

A grin spread across Sig's mouth. "Do I spy a twinkle in your eye, Cap?"

He snatched his shades off the dashboard where he'd left them, put them on, and slammed the door on Sig's knowing face—just in time for the side door of the locker room to fly open, two rookies in towels bursting onto the pavement in nothing but bare feet and towels.

"Dude, give them back," Mailer shouted, jabbing a finger at Sig, who dove into his ancient truck at the speed of light, laughing as he went. And two very mature grown-up men drove out of the parking lot blaring their horns and waving Orgasm Donor sweatshirts out their windows. In other words, just a typical day of hockey practice.

"LATE TO MY first day of class," Tallulah muttered, while hustling down the empty hallway. "Awesome."

She rounded the corner into the lab, giving a tight smile when every pair of bored, jaded grad student eyes landed on her. There was one seat left open beside a guy about her age that she recognized from orientation. Glasses. Commiserating smile. Slouched and grouched, like any self-respecting career student.

Thankfully, the seat was also in the back and she slid into it without the professor commenting, quietly taking a notebook and pen out of her backpack while waving at some of the other friendly faces she'd met a couple days prior.

That morning, she'd been forced to drop her belongings off at Burgess's apartment, because check-out time at her hotel had been 11:00. She wasn't about to rack up charges for another day, even if the detour had ultimately made her late. While at the penthouse she now called home, they'd compared Tallulah's schedule and Lissa's, finding there was blessed little conflict. The custody agreement Burgess had with his wife was pretty amicable and straightforward. Lissa spent the weekdays at his place, weekends with Mom and the fiancé, allowing for adjustments due to special occasions, vacations, or illness.

For instance, today was Friday, but Lissa's mother had a late business meeting, so she'd pick up Lissa in the morning, instead of tonight. Burgess had explained they didn't want Lissa to feel like a business arrangement, and Tallulah couldn't agree more. They were doing it right.

What is his ex like? Tallulah wondered, fully ignoring the professor as he flipped through the syllabus, reading it word for word. More interestingly, what had Burgess and his ex been like together? Really, it was none of her business *at all*. And she totally hadn't Googled *Burgess Abraham Wife* on the bus ride to campus. A few pictures had come up of them at the ESPY Awards a handful of years ago, Burgess rocking a tux, his ex-wife looking happy enough to be there.

Not a lot of chemistry. At least in the pictures. There, she said it.

Was that a salty thing to acknowledge?

No! It was just an impartial observation.

Which had perked her up more than her triple-shot latte.

Ughhh.

"As you'll read on page three of the syllabus, there will be three individual assignments during the semester and one project where you'll be working in pairs. I expect equal effort, people." He stopped and made eye contact with all of them, letting the directive sink in.

"He knows we're not in our first year of undergrad, right?" mumbled her table partner.

"Seriously."

"To make things easy," continued the professor, "your assigned partner is whoever you're sharing a table with today. No doubt you'll need to meet outside of class at least once to complete the assignment, so it behooves you to spend some time getting acquainted."

Tallulah kept her breathing steady, even sending her seat partner a quiet nod, but on the inside, her thoughts were tripping over each other. They'd have to meet outside of class. She'd have to meet with a stranger.

It's going to be fine.

You have to start believing in good people again sometime.

She wouldn't spiral over this. During her remaining weeks in Antarctica, she'd sworn to herself the fear wouldn't hold her back anymore. That phase was over. She just hadn't expected to be tested so soon, so often. But maybe this was normal life and she'd just been hiding from it so long, she'd forgotten.

The rest of class went by in a blur, Tallulah only registering half of the professor's presentation. When he dismissed them, Tallulah gathered her notebook, pen, and copy of the syllabus, looking up with a forced smile when three classmates stopped at the edge of her table. "Hey again, Tallulah. Happy Friday," said Tisha, if Tallulah was recalling her name correctly. They'd spoken briefly at orientation, enough to know Tisha had grown up in India, started her education in medicine, but switched to biology upon realizing her passion lay in lab work and research. "We figured we'd start the semester off right and meet up for drinks tonight. Around nine. You know, in order to establish an official whining circle."

Tallulah nodded. "Negativity. The only way to cope."

"You're welcome to join," laughed the guy beside her. Evan, maybe? "You, too, Finn."

"Sure," responded her table partner.

That's right. Finn.

Tallulah started to decline. They all seemed genuinely nice and there was nothing out of the ordinary about tossing back a few drinks with other students, especially ones who shared the same field of study. But did she know them well enough?

Stop saying no to opportunities. It's time to say yes again.

"Okay," she said quickly, before she could talk herself out of it. "Take my phone number and let me know where you'll be." An idea occurred to her. "Would you mind if I invited my friend Chloe?"

"Not at all," answered Tisha, holding out her phone to Tallulah. "Go ahead."

"Cool."

On his way out of the room, Finn's elbow brushed Tallulah's and she faltered in the act of entering her contact information into Tisha's phone. "See you tonight, Tallulah," he said, adjusting his glasses, before touching her elbow as if to apologize for inadvertently grazing it, which made no sense and only made her creep antennae bleep faster. "Might as well get to know each other now, since we'll be partners, right?"

She laughed, but it came out flat. "Yeah." She handed the phone back to Tisha and dried her clammy palms on the legs of her jeans. "See you guys tonight."

CHAPTER SEVEN

Burgess could confidently say he'd never been happier to walk into his apartment.

Perhaps a little too happy. And he blamed Tallulah's skirt.

When he got off the elevator on the floor of his building, he was met by the sound of music. If he wasn't mistaken, it was the unbearable wailing of his daughter's favorite band, Raskulls. There had never been any love lost between him and the British pop group who wore giant phony heads on stage with freakishly happy faces painted on front. The first time Lissa played them in the car, he'd contemplated crashing into a wall just to end the torture. He was dreading the day she asked him to bring her to an actual concert.

They didn't make strong enough earplugs.

Apparently, Tallulah could put up with the lead singer's high-pitched warble, but he was only going to last approximately three minutes once he got inside.

Burgess pushed his key into the lock and twisted, opening the door and wincing slightly as the worst music ever recorded got even louder. He opened his mouth to complain, but only silence came out. Because there was Tallulah, bent over his kitchen table in a black leather mini skirt and sheer stockings that ended a few inches beneath her ass. She was holding a dirty dinner plate in one hand, as she'd obviously been on the way to the kitchen to put it into the sink when she must have been derailed by Lissa asking for homework help. She appeared to be leaning across the table in order to see a problem in Lissa's math workbook and the timing of him walking into the apartment couldn't have been worse. Or better.

Both.

He was frozen in place, yet burning up with a fever.

She . . . he . . . could see the undercurve of her ass cheeks. The black lace of her panties. The incredibly smooth section of her rear upper thighs. She was the hottest thing he'd ever seen in his life, no question about it. Especially when she laughed and it caused her to fall forward onto the table, barely catching herself on a forearm and the tight curve of that backside got even more dramatic and . . . dangerous. Very fucking dangerous. Because he was imagining the chafe of those stockings against his palms, the supple weight of her ass cheeks in his hands, how she'd shiver and look back at him over her shoulder when he pulled those panties down to her knees.

These were not the types of thoughts he should be having when they were not the only two people in the apartment. Hell, he shouldn't be thinking about taking off her underwear at *any* time, right? She'd given him no obvious indication that she was interested in that. He'd simply walked in at the wrong time, and now he'd be haunted for the rest of his life by fantasies of those stockinged legs wrapped around his neck.

Where was she going in that outfit?

Out?

One thing was for sure, Tallulah couldn't know he'd seen her like this. Their relationship as boss and employee was fragile to begin with, as was her ability to trust men, in general. Getting caught ogling her absurdly hot ass would not help matters. *Don't think about how it would look slapping off your stomach.*

Too late.

Burgess backed out of the apartment as quietly as possible,

making an unnecessary amount of noise when he entered the second time, coughing and ramming his knee into the door, jangling his keys as he locked and unlocked it again. This time, when he walked inside, Tallulah and Lissa were well aware of his presence. Tallulah gave him a light smile on her way into the kitchen and Lissa waved to him from the kitchen table.

"Dad!" Lissa shouted over the music. "She made the chicken again!"

Burgess raised an eyebrow at Tallulah, who gave him a prim sniff—or at least he thought she sniffed, the band from hell was doing everything in its power to drown her out. "We had all the ingredients left over from last night. I didn't want them to go to waste." She turned on the water in the kitchen sink to rinse her dish, casting him another quick glance over her shoulder. "Left you a plate, if you want it."

If he wanted it. Was she serious? The only thing Burgess wanted to eat more than her lemon chicken with a side of Saksuka was . . . her.

And wow, you are disgusting. Obviously, the rookies were rubbing off on him.

Burgess dropped his duffel bag just inside the door, took off his jacket and draped it over the hook. "How was school today?"

"Good. No volleyball practice." Lissa's concentration was back on her homework. "Tallulah moved in, but she's already going out."

"Out?" Burgess asked, casually as possible, while leaning down to untie his boots—and his back spasmed. It was like someone had stuck a plucked tuning fork in his kidney, a painful vibration zooming through the right side of his lower back. His breath lurched out of his lungs and he had to slap a hand against the wall for balance, a guttural sound escaping him before he could lock it inside. *Dammit.*

"Dad?" Lissa called from the table, obviously alarmed.

His daughter's panicked tone was the reason he immediately tried to straighten up, even though his contracting muscles weren't ready for it. Too bad. He pushed through the strain and sent his kid a tight smile. "I'm fine. Just sore."

Burgess looked toward the kitchen to find Tallulah watching him closely.

Too closely.

In her mini skirt and makeup, all dressed up to go meet someone who could bend over and untie their boots without needing painkillers. Lissa still looked worried, so he fought through the pain of leaning down and picking up his duffel bag again, tossing it over his shoulder. "I'm just going to throw these sweaty clothes in the laundry. Keep working on your homework and I'll be back."

His daughter relaxed somewhat. "Okay."

Burgess passed through the living room to the other side of the apartment, down the short hallway where the bedrooms were located, along with one of two bathrooms in the residence. The other was his ensuite. Despite the lock he'd installed this morning, the guest room door had been left slightly ajar, so after checking to make sure no one was watching, he craned his neck to look through the opening and saw Tallulah's suitcase open on the queen-sized bed, her sneakers untied on the floor, jacket hanging on the knob of the closet door.

Had she tried the pillows he'd bought? Were they too firm? Too soft?

They were . . . on the floor, actually.

In place of them, there was a balled-up sweatshirt.

Is that what she preferred to lay her head on at night?

The slightest hint of her orange and basil scent drifted out, diverting his thoughts and making him swallow hard.

Inhaling quietly, Burgess continued a few steps to his bedroom door and nudged his way inside, flipping on the light with his elbow. Now that he was alone, he allowed himself to grind a curse through his teeth, dropping his duffel onto the bed and unzipping it quickly, in search of the white bottle of Advil. The damn music was still on full blast out in the living room . . . which was why he didn't hear Tallulah enter the bedroom behind him. Not until her shadow cast itself over the bed and he turned to find her quietly closing the door, but very deliberately leaving it open a crack.

The pulse at the base of her neck was fluttering slightly, her fingers linking and unlinking in front of her. Being alone with him still made her a touch uneasy, and he wasn't sure he'd ever stop being rageful at the man who'd turned her world into a scary place, but he was going to do everything in his power to make sure it wouldn't be that way for long. Still, no amount of pain in his back could distract Burgess from the fact that he was alone with Tallulah in his bedroom and she looked like a fucking smoke show.

His hookups had been few and far between since the divorce, mainly because they made him feel lonely. The aging bachelorhood of it all was pathetic. But Jesus, if he encountered *this* woman on the road, or anywhere for that matter, he would beg, cheat, and steal to bring her home and sleep with her. The irony of her *already* being in his home—and off-limits—was not lost on him whatsoever.

"Hey." Her gaze flickered down to the white bottle in his hands. "Everything okay?"

"Yeah, just run-of-the-mill stuff," he said smoothly. "I get body slammed for a living."

Her lips jumped. "So you do."

"Lissa seemed happier today."

"Yes." Her smile made his stomach flip over. "She did."

"Thanks for helping her with her homework."

"You don't have to thank me. That's my job."

"And cooking."

"Now, that isn't my job. Tonight was *definitely* the last time."

"Understood." He tried really goddamn hard not to look below her neck, but the strain of making it thirty seconds was taking a toll on his self-control. Burgess made himself a deal. Just her hips. He'd just memorize the line of her hips in that skirt and he'd go back to making eye contact. One, two, three . . .

God.

That leather had been licked onto her by the devil. Cursed with the knowledge that she wore stockings underneath made his balls feel heavy, his hands itchy to touch.

Eyes up.

"Are you going out?" he rasped.

"Yes. That's what I was going to speak to you about."

"You're going to tell me your plans?" She was volunteering them without him having to ask? Awesome. Saved him from looking too interested. Which he was. *Way* too interested in where she was going in black lace panties.

"I mean, no? I wasn't going to inform you of my plans. Should I?" Humor crackled in her eyes. "I was actually wondering if you had keys for me, so I don't have to sleep in the hallway."

"Keys. Right." This wasn't going to be as easy as he thought. "They're hanging by the door—the ones with the pepper spray attached."

Her smile dimmed, her expression growing more curious than anything. "You bought me pepper spray?"

"Did I overstep again?"

"I think so?" She shook her head slowly. "There are a lot of gray areas with you, boss. And I already have some spray attached to my keychain."

"Good." She'd definitely put a little extra emphasis on the word *boss*. "I would want my daughter to carry pepper spray."

Why did he say that? It made him sound old enough to be her father, which thank fuck, he wasn't. Still. Could he call any *more* attention to their eleven-year age difference?

"Since we're already operating in the gray areas, maybe you should let me know where you're going. Just in case."

She studied him, half amused, half searching. "I'm meeting some grad students at a club near the harbor. I met them at orientation, and we share a class." She brightened. "Actually, Chloe is coming, too."

That caught him off guard. "Chloe. As in Sig's future stepsister?"

"Yes."

"How did that come about?"

"Well . . ." Her amusement deepened. Why? He couldn't recall ever *amusing* anyone before Tallulah. "When I made plans to meet for drinks today, I figured the more the merrier, so I texted Chloe to join us." Burgess couldn't help it, he was completely fascinated by that mentality. Making plans with people she'd just met? Mixing friend groups? Where did the chaos end? "If I let too much time pass after meeting Chloe, we'll never hang out. Making friends in a new place means taking initiative."

"How do you know that?"

She tilted her head, causing dark hair to skim against her bare arm . . . and his mouth to go dry. "Are you asking me a lot of questions to stall me from going out, Burgess?"

Was he?

Maybe.

"Why would I do that?"

"I don't know." Her voice was softer than before, almost flirtatious. "You tell me." A fraction of a second after that flirty opening left her mouth, she started, seeming almost surprised at herself and rushed to fill the ensuing charged silence. "I'm trying to relearn how to create . . . social networks, I guess. I need them, you know?" A shadow danced in the brown of her eyes. "I can't stay inside and avoid the world forever."

"Pretty rude of you to call me out like that. First day on the job, too. Is this the kind of abuse I should expect from you?"

A dimple popped in her cheek. "Do *you* stay inside and avoid the world, Burgess?"

"Happily," he replied, no idea if he meant it or not. In the not so recent past, he would have been more positive of his answer. Yes, avoiding people and annoying situations made him abundantly happy. Or at least comfortable. But he wasn't sure if *happy* was the word to describe him anymore. Existing was more like it. Coping.

"Hmmm." She definitely wanted to say more, but her gaze traveled past Burgess and landed on something behind him. "Does that sweatshirt say 'Orgasm Donor'?"

It took him a moment to comprehend the question, because he was so distracted by her incredible lips moving in such a way that they released the word "orgasm." In his bedroom. With that sexy leather skirt on. Had he really set himself up for this kind of continuous torture?

Oh. Shit. The sweatshirt.

"Fuck," he muttered, dragging a hand down his face. "I can explain."

"No need." She dropped her voice to a whisper. "I already know how orgasms are donated."

Could his eyes really be blamed for homing in on her incredible thighs? His sex drive was beyond healthy and he'd been celibate for over a year. Now he was facing the overstimulation of this knockout flirting with him one second, drawing back the next. His cock had no idea what to do, so it just got hard by default. "You don't know how *I* donate them."

"I don't think I'll be finding out," she blurted, sounding suspiciously breathy. "Will I?"

Mother of God, he wanted to chance a step forward, and he came right to the edge of his willpower before reminding himself why she needed boundaries. And how badly he wanted her to feel safe around him. But he would have gladly given his MVP trophy to look down into her upturned face when he said, "Your call, Tallulah."

Because son of a bitch, it turned her on.

No mistaking that.

It wouldn't matter if he went six months or six years without sex, he knew what it meant when a woman looked at him the way Tallulah did just then. As if mentally trying him on for size, perhaps against her better judgment. Her gaze meandered down to his stomach, teasing the button at the top of his fly, flitting across the breadth of his shoulders, dragging up his neck. All within two seconds. But it was enough to make him wonder *what if*. What if they were closer in age and he wasn't a divorced, burned-out has-been hiding an injury? Would it be understood that she was safe with him at all times?

Would he be the one peeling off that tight little skirt at the end of the night?

Yeah, all right. He really needed to quit this line of thought before the situation downstairs got any worse. His back wasn't the only part of him throbbing.

"That's not my sweatshirt, by the way. We stole them off the rookies today."

"Who is we?"

"Me and Sig. Chloe's soon-to-be stepbrother."

A smile danced around the edges of her mouth. "Why did you do that?"

He snorted. "They showed up in *matching sweatshirts*, Tallulah."

"Technically, you all match when you wear your uniform."

"Our uniforms don't say 'Orgasm Donor.'"

"Maybe they should. Think of the crowds."

Softly, she mimicked the sound of an explosion, and he found himself wanting to laugh. Also to ask her to stay home and talk to him just like this. All night. The apartment already felt better with her there and she'd only moved in a few hours ago.

"Um . . ." She looked kind of surprised to still be standing there. "Lissa is almost done with her math homework. She did her English on the bus. There's a science packet due next week, so she should work on that a little bit tonight—kind of bummed I'm missing it. Science is my thing." She drummed her fingers against the side of her thigh. "Break any noses tonight?"

"I considered it." He thought for a second. "The season opener is three weeks from today. If it doesn't interfere with your schedule in any way, maybe you could bring her?"

No doubt about it, the invitation to his game had caught her off guard. "Oh."

It caught him off guard, too. "You don't have to answer now."

"Okay. I'll think about it." After a small hesitation, she backed toward the door. "See you tomorrow."

"Good night, Tallulah." Watching her disappear into the hallway, he struggled against the protectiveness that started to whip its tail around inside of him. And even though he told himself she was a capable adult that didn't need babysitting, he lost. "Be careful."

"I will."

Leave it there. "If you get stuck or something happens, you can call me. Two A.M. Whatever."

Halfway out the door, she paused, studying his face intently. "Good night, Burgess."

CHAPTER EIGHT

Tallulah raised her arms up over her head and absorbed the music, frothiness tickling the lining of her stomach, hips swiveling in an infinity pattern. God, she hadn't been out in so long. Not like this. The kind of out where she lost track of time, every song was the *best song* and she felt free. Alive. Nothing holding her back. No rules to follow but her own.

A huge part of the reason she was comfortable in the moment was Chloe, who danced a handful of feet away in a sequined rose gold skirt and a white one-shoulder tank top, her blond hair in a riot of waves. They merged on the dance floor just as the next song came on, getting into an excited slap fight when it turned out to be yet another banger. The lighting pulsed blue around them, reminding Tallulah of the exact color the sun made when it rose in Antarctica and struck the ice for the first time in the morning. Just the purest electric blue that seemed almost out of place in nature.

"I miss that," she murmured to herself, words instantly swallowed up by the pulsing music. Was it odd to be dancing in the middle of a crowd, reminiscing about her time in Antarctica? Thinking about her favorite penguin, Kirk, and missing the monstrous bite of cold that could rush suddenly at sixty miles per hour and eat straight through five layers of clothing? Yeah, it was slightly odd, but didn't everyone on the dance floor miss something or someone?

That was life, wasn't it? Making connections, bonding with people and places, then moving forward without them. Missing them. Carrying those influence around, sort of like layers of clothing. Her birthplace was one layer, her family another. Her best friend, Josephine. Antarctica. Now Boston. Sometimes it hurt to collect another layer, to make new friends and have new experiences when she still ached for the layers closest to her skin, but she would keep pursuing nights like this, because she'd made a promise to her sister.

She'd sworn she wouldn't let the fear of tragedy keep her locked inside. Otherwise, she might as well still be trapped in that closet, watching Brett's shadow move on the other side. She might have freed herself physically, but mentally? It had taken Tallulah four years to keep the promise she'd made to Lara. But here she was. At least she hadn't broken it, right?

Tallulah danced, half enjoying herself, half melancholy to be in this unfamiliar place, entering a new phase in such a visceral way, her new grad school friends waving to her from the bar, Chloe taking her hands so they could spin in a laughing circle at the crescendo of the song, finally stumbling to a stop at the edge of the dance floor. The song that came on next was a slow one, an indication the club was probably getting ready for last call, filling Tallulah with a combination of disappointment and relief. She was having a great time with her new friends, but maybe when that inevitable melancholy started to eclipse her enjoyment, it was time to go home.

Home.

Where Burgess lived.

Her hot, single dad boss.

Orgasm Donor.

"You want one more?" Chloe yelled over the noise, pointing to the nearly empty amaretto sour in Tallulah's hand. "It's my round."

"Sure. Last one."

Chloe did a little shoulder shake and danced her way back through the crowd. Though everyone in the place was swarming the bar to get their last drink of the night, the bartender zeroed in on beaming-ball-of-light Chloe right away, drawn like a moth to a flame, making Tallulah laugh under her breath.

Tallulah approached the high top where the group had stationed themselves for the night, greeted by smiles from Finn, Tisha, and Evan, the final three remaining out of the six grad students who'd met at Down earlier in the night. Tallulah gave an exaggerated wince at the array of empty glasses and beer bottles on the table, making Finn laugh . . . and it was impossible not to notice the once-over he gave her as she added her empty glass to the collection. He straightened from his lean against the table and angled his body toward Tallulah.

And her stomach immediately drew in on itself.

Finn was good-looking. In his twenties. The clear overachiever type she encountered on a regular basis in the biology program. Medium height, wiry build, round gold-rimmed glasses, and shaggy brown hair. Hot science guy. Who wouldn't be into him?

Orgasm Donor.

Tallulah inwardly winced. Such an appalling sweatshirt—and she believed Burgess when he said it didn't belong to him. But something about the juxtaposition of this big, strong hockey player and the word "orgasm" wouldn't stop punching her in the brain. Even while looking straight into the very earnest, very interested eyes of Finn.

I know how orgasms are donated.

You don't know how I donate them.

I don't think I'll be finding out. Will I?

Your call, Tallulah.

A warm shiver snaked down her spine. What exactly had

Burgess meant by that? Like he'd show her if she simply . . . asked? Her boss would donate her an orgasm?

Finn inched closer to Tallulah, distracting her from thoughts of the towering hockey player, and the fine layer of perspiration on her back hardened to ice, the loud music becoming muffled and distorted in her ears. This tended to happen when a man showed interest in her, and apparently tonight was going to be no exception. Although, she didn't freeze up when Burgess got close, did she? No, just the opposite. She heated like a tea kettle. He had a way of approaching her at just the right pace, giving her room to stop . . . which only made her want *more* of her space invaded by him. *This* guy, however . . .

"I hope you're as good a research partner as you are a dancer," Finn said, close enough to her ear that his breath hit her neck.

Tallulah fought off a cringe. "Oh. Thanks." She wanted to leave it at that, express her lack of interest right away and shut it down, but *why*? When her internship in Antarctica had drawn to a close, one of the biologists had asked her to dinner and she'd said no without thinking. Even though he'd been perfectly nice, like Finn. Probably not a monster.

But was probably ever going to be good enough?

Tallulah *wanted* to meet someone. Or be *open* to meeting someone, at the very least. It had been a really long time since she'd experienced physical satisfaction with another person— undergrad? *Really?*—and she missed the anticipation, the excite- ment, the selfish, human act of going home with someone on a quest for pleasure. Not overthinking, just *feeling*.

Would she ever be capable of that again?

"You don't dance?" she forced herself to ask Finn, while casu- ally glancing over her shoulder to see if Chloe was on the way with their drinks.

Finn shrugged. "Maybe if the right girl asked me, I would . . ." He raised an eyebrow, as if hoping for an invitation.

"Oh, um. I'm probably going to head home soon, actually," Tallulah said. "Just going to have one more drink with Chloe."

His smile remained glued. "Where is home?"

A sour taste spread in her mouth. "Beacon Hill."

"I'm going in that direction, if you want to split a cab."

The chill on her skin traveled inward. Splitting a cab shouldn't be that big of a deal, right? She'd be seeing a lot of this guy at school. Outside of school, too, since they were partners on an assignment. Probably end up on more nights out together. But what if he got out of the cab at her building and decided to walk her to the door? What if he sent the cab on its way? It was nearing one o'clock in the morning.

No one would be around. Just them.

Still, she'd been living in fear so long. She just wanted to break out of it.

"Maybe. Sure."

Finn's smile widened.

"One amaretto sour for the lady," Chloe sang, coming up on Tallulah's right, pressing a cold drink into her hand. The blonde's gaze bounced between Tallulah and Finn, lighting up with interest, and she leaned in close to speak near Tallulah's ear. "Should I make myself scarce?"

"No."

"Gotcha. Should he?"

"Uh. Yeah, I think so."

"Double gotcha." Chloe hooked her arm through Tallulah's and stuck her bottom lip out at Finn. "Sorry, babe, I'm stealing her for drunk girl talk."

"It's the best kind," Tallulah tacked on with a tight smile, grateful when Chloe steered her toward the bar. "Thanks. He wasn't being excessively creepy or anything. I'm just . . ."

"You don't have to explain. It's just a no."

"You're right. I don't have to explain." They found a sliver of space at the bar and wedged themselves in, propping their elbows on the wood and facing one another. "Maybe I just think a marine biologist named Finn is a little too convenient."

Chloe's head fell back on a laugh. "Far too convenient."

"I used to be way less discriminating with men. So long as they weren't holding a bloody meat cleaver, I'd consider making out with them."

"Oh man. I miss making out," Chloe whined.

"I can help you out with that," a young man shouted from behind Tallulah.

Chloe waved both hands at him. "Trust me, you don't know what you're getting yourself into. I am a huge problem."

"What about you?" Tallulah looked over her shoulder to find a backward ball capped frat boy grinning at her. "Need any help making out? I happen to be available."

"Rain check," Tallulah responded, facing Chloe again with a scoff, the quick head movement making her vision swim just a tad. Yup. This was definitely her last drink. "You're not a problem. Why would you say that?"

Tallulah's friend went up on her toes, craning her neck to see over the top of the crowd toward the club entrance. "Oh, you'll see."

"Cryptic."

Chloe dropped back down. "I'm so glad we did this." She gripped Tallulah's arm. "Thank you for not holding my part in the whole seven hundred dollar rent deception against me. If I'd been given more than a few hours to prepare, I would have realized it was a girl code violation."

"Please, stop apologizing." Tallulah squinted an eye. "To be honest, it was kind of satisfying to see straight through Burgess's plan in point eight seconds."

"Did you rip him a new one?"

"Oh. You bet I did." Tallulah took a quick sip of her drink and set it down where she could see it, keeping it within the circle of her hand. "Well . . . not really. But I was *very* sarcastic."

"Sarcasm can cut deep. *Very* deep."

"Right? I know."

"People underestimate its power."

"It occurs to me that we're a little drunk, Chloe."

"I'm *so* drunk." They shared a laugh. "So you're officially moved in with Sir Savage?"

"As of today. Yes."

"What is he like in real life?" Chloe asked after a handful of seconds, her question followed by a mock shiver. "Seriously, he's so mean looking. I sat behind the bench for all of the home games last season and it's pretty much just him ripping off his helmet and shouting at everyone. I can't even hear what he's saying, and I want to wet my pants."

Tallulah thought of his earlier invitation to attend the home opener.

Maybe it was best to avoid it.

Although . . .

"I'm still figuring him out, but I can tell you he's . . . passionate and yeah, kind of quick-tempered, but also . . . reasonable? On occasion." She thought of him in the kitchen, chopping onions and peppers, his forearm flexing with every movement of the knife, allowing himself to be temporarily managed. "I told him I had some doubts about moving in with a man that I don't know very well and he didn't treat me like I was over-reacting. He loves his daughter, and he isn't afraid to say it. He's protective."

"He's hot."

"He is," Tallulah blurted. "He's extremely hot."

"In like a mean Daddy way."

"I know. I know." Tallulah drained her drink. "Not that it matters. I work for him."

"I know, right?" She stage-whispered over the music. "Why does that make it hotter?"

Your call, Tallulah. Had he already issued her an invitation? Why couldn't she stop thinking about it? "Chloe, you're a terrible influence."

"No! I'm not!" She shook the ice in her glass. "It's the vodka talking."

"Likely story. Next, you'll tell me you're a marine biologist named Finn."

Chloe spit out her drink onto Tallulah's shoes, laughing. Tallulah joined her, both of them leaning against the bar for support. Approximately six men jumped to offer them bar napkins, waving little white squares in their faces, which only made them laugh harder.

And that is the exact moment the air changed in the club.

Chloe must have felt the ripple in the air, because the mirth abruptly fled from her pretty features and she went back onto her tiptoes, her chest expanding on a breath at whatever she saw. "Don't look now, babe," Chloe said. "But my huge problem is here."

The words *don't look* didn't fully register with Tallulah, thanks to the alcohol-induced brain fuzz, and she joined Chloe in peering out over the top of the crowd. A man was weaving his way in their direction, a forward-facing ball cap pulled down low on his forehead. Still, that didn't stop people from turning in his wake with their mouths hanging open. Were they shocked by his height? Because he wasn't quite as tall as Burgess, but he was within a couple of inches and the width of his shoulders only amplified the size difference between him and everyone else in the club.

"Who is that?"

"That's Sig. My future stepbrother."

"The third member of the cheap room rental dark triad?"

"Yes." Chloe sighed.

"Sig *Gauthier*?" shouted one of the guys offering them a napkin.

"Yes," Chloe said, louder, finally taking one of the napkins and stooping down to quickly mop the spilled drink off Tallulah's feet, before Tallulah could tell her not to worry about it. By the time Chloe stood up again, Sig had reached the bar—and he didn't look happy. At all. His icy glare traveled over the bevy of men surrounding Tallulah and Chloe, growing colder by the second. At least until Chloe said, "Sig!" and threw her arms around his neck.

The hockey player blinked a few times, the ice thawing slightly, before he drew her in with one thick arm. "Time to go, Chloe."

"I was going to call an Uber."

"I'm your Uber. Where's your purse?"

"Ummm. I think I only brought my phone and my debit card."

"You *think*?" He started to brush a hand down the back of Chloe's head, but stopped before he could complete the action, curling his hand into a fist and stepping away. "This is why I can't relax when you go out."

"You *can* relax, actually. I'm a fully functional adult."

"I told your mother I would keep an eye on you." He returned to frowning at the men in the vicinity, clearly not moved by the hero worship they were projecting in his direction. "Obviously she asked for a good reason."

Chloe's expression grew shuttered.

Very pointedly, she turned her back on Sig.

He threw up his hands and rolled his eyes.

"Can I get you to autograph this napkin, man?" asked the frat guy behind Tallulah.

"No," Sig replied, without missing a beat.

Chloe's lips pressed into a line for a tense second, but she brightened almost just as quickly. "It's okay." She smiled sweetly at the frat guy. "I'll write my number on it, instead."

Sig snorted and crossed his arms.

Until the guy happily produced a pen, extending it toward Chloe.

The hockey player intercepted it. "Fine, an autograph. You want it personalized?"

While the autograph transaction took place, Chloe gave Tallulah a look of clear exasperation and pointed at Sig. "Huge problem," she mouthed.

Tallulah was starting to worry the relationship between these future stepsiblings might be an even bigger problem than Chloe seemed to realize, but she was distracted by that thought when Sig finished his autograph and hit her with a scrutinizing glance. "You're Tallulah?"

"You're the guy who tried to trick me into renting a room for next to nothing with Chloe?"

He reared back slightly. "Hold up. I'm not the only one."

"You're the only one who hasn't apologized."

He looked kind of impressed, not that she was trying to impress this man who thought he could barge into the club and order his adult future stepsister around. "Consider this my formal apology, then."

Tallulah inclined her head. "I'll let you know when I formally accept."

Sig's lips twisted in something that came close to a smile. "You need a ride, too?"

This was fine. Chloe would be there. "Are you going in the direction of Beacon Hill?"

"Not really, but it's not a problem." Sig tipped his head toward the exit. "There's no traffic this time of night."

She couldn't do it. Couldn't accept them going out of their way for her. "I'm going to grab a cab, but thanks for asking."

"You sure? It would earn me some points with Sir Savage."

"All the more reason to pass."

Sig laughed at that, but his mirth came to a quick halt when one of the men at the bar tried to scoot a bar napkin and a pen in front of Chloe while he was distracted.

He picked up the pen and pitched it across the room.

"Let's go," he growled, turning Chloe around and ushering her out of the club.

Tallulah laughed into her empty glass and slid it back onto the bar, intending to follow in their wake, but when she turned around again, Finn stood between her and the exit and a frisson of alarm climbed her spine. "Hey," she blurted, startled. "I'm just about to leave. I'll see you—"

"I thought we were sharing a cab," Finn said, boyish half smile in place. Was he standing too close or was she imagining things? "I'd love to talk strategy for our project."

"We haven't even been given the assignment yet," Tallulah pointed out, beginning to get more than a little peeved. Nervous, too, dammit. She couldn't see Chloe or Sig anymore and suddenly it didn't feel so good to be surrounded by strangers. Or this classmate who seemed to be overly fixated on her. Desperately, she glanced over Finn's shoulder, hoping to make eye contact with Tisha or Evan, but they were no longer at the table. "Did everyone leave?"

"Yeah." He followed her line of sight. "Looks like it's just you and me." He held up his phone, shook it a little. "I'll call an Uber."

"Actually, my boyfriend is on the way," she blurted, without flinching. It was unclear what instinct propelled those words out of her mouth, only that she felt better immediately.

This guy was being too pushy. Eager to be alone with her.

It wasn't her imagination.

Right?

If you get stuck or something happens, you can call me. Two A.M. Whatever.

Burgess. He would come.

Finn's mouth pressed into a flat line. "I didn't realize you had a boyfriend."

"Yes. I do. We . . . live together. Excuse me." Tallulah skirted past Finn while looking down at her phone, swiping into her most recent calls. As soon as she was out of earshot, she raised the phone to her ear. Sir Savage answered on the first ring, gruff and alert.

"What happened?"

"Can you come get me? I'll explain when you—"

"Address."

"It's a club called Down."

"I'll find it. Are you okay, Tallulah?"

"Yes."

Something about her tone must have inspired doubt, because a drawn-out pause ensued. "Share your location with me, all right? I'm already in the elevator."

CHAPTER NINE

Burgess left a quick note for Lissa explaining he'd be back soon, just in case she woke up while he was gone, then asked the doorman to make doubly sure no nonresidents entered the building in his absence. Then he sped toward the harbor like a Formula One racer at Monaco, arriving ready to leap out of the car and kick in the front door of the club. He slumped backward in the driver's seat, however, when Tallulah emerged onto the sidewalk and ended his crusade before it started. She was fine. Alive, well, and unharmed, at least to the naked eye. Had she just lost her wallet or something? A total possibility, because, yeah . . .

His au pair was toasted, teetering toward him on her heels. Not sloppy or fall-down drunk, just bright-eyed with her makeup smudged drunk. And still mind-blowingly beautiful.

Burgess checked for oncoming traffic in his rearview before getting out to open her door for her. When he gripped the handle before she had the chance, her lips parted on a breath and she looked up at him, blinking. Then?

She checked him out. Blatantly and openly. Right there on the side of the street.

With her tiny purse clutched between her tits, her brown gaze carved a path from his chest to his biceps, down to his thighs and yeah, right at his crotch. She didn't even seem to realize she was doing it, either, and Burgess decided he liked drunk Tallulah very much.

"Hi. Thanks for coming. Hi," she said, all husky and warm, making his abdomen tighten up. She stepped into his space, close enough for her knee to bump the top of his shin, her head angling back so they could keep eye contact. And damn, his hands wanted to reach out and grip her hips or shoulders to keep her steady, but he was painfully aware that it would overstep their boundaries of her employment, especially considering the trauma she'd confided in him. "Isn't it funny that I'm glad to see you?"

He turned that statement over in his head around nine times. "Why is that funny?"

"A few days ago, you made me nervous."

"I don't anymore?" he asked, holding his breath.

Nose wrinkled, she examined his chin, his throat. "Not in a bad way."

"There's a good way to make someone nervous?"

She scoffed, fell silent, before visibly shaking herself. "I can climb into this vehicle without assistance, I promise. I'm not intoxicated."

Burgess hid his skepticism. "Okay, Tallulah. I'll stand here just in case."

She held up her thumb and forefinger, pinching them together. "That's a little patronizing, don't you think?"

He battled a smile. "Some might call it chivalrous."

"Chivalrous." She tested out the word, like she'd never heard it before. "You are kind of old-fashioned, aren't you? Opening the door for me, installing locks, standing there just in case my delicate lady legs can't handle the climb . . ."

"You could say I'm old-fashioned, sure."

"It's very mean Daddy of you," she whispered.

Burgess's eyebrows shot to his hairline. "It's what?"

"Ooh." She winced. "I shouldn't have said that."

"Now that you have, though, you need to explain."

She shook her head.

He nodded.

One of her shoulders drooped. "Well. Chloe and I were talking about you and . . . it was sort of decided that you were hot in a mean Daddy kind of way."

"*Mean* Daddy."

"Don't be offended—it's a good thing. For *you*, not me. I don't have a horse in this race, you know?" She squeezed her eyes closed. "I'm going to regret every second of this conversation in the morning."

"I have news for you, it's already morning."

"You know what I mean, the morning that comes with sunlight attached."

Burgess hummed, trying to memorize her softened features up close, the dusting of sparkles on her cheekbones, the black smudge in the outer corner of her right eye. She was going to say something else, but seemed to remember a more pressing issue all at once, her attention darting back toward the front of the club.

"Anyway, we should go."

He followed her line of sight, his senses going on high alert. "All right," he said slowly. "Where is Chloe? Does she need a ride?"

"No, Sig picked her up."

"Sig was here? And he left you behind?" He felt a shout coming on and couldn't quite control it. "Why the hell didn't he drive you home, too?"

"I told him I'd get a cab on my own—look, it's complicated. Sort of like Chloe and Sig's relationship? What is even *happening* with them?" She waved her hands around. "Come on, I'll explain on the way."

Burgess ground his back teeth together, moving in close behind Tallulah out of caution as she stepped onto the running board of the SUV and boosted herself up. He was momentarily hypnotized by the little flip of her skirt and flash of thigh, but thankfully not so much that he wasn't prepared to catch her if she lost her balance—which, of course, she did. The heel of her shoe didn't quite fit on the running board and it slipped. She almost corrected herself by grabbing for the seat belt dispenser, but by then, it was too late.

She was already dropping straight down.

In a flash, Burgess crowded in behind Tallulah, using his body to interrupt her descent toward the pavement, slinging an arm around the front of her hips and drawing her back against his chest, catching Tallulah before her feet could make contact with the ground. There was no way to stifle the gruff sound that came out of his mouth when her ass dragged downward over his fly and pressed, her curves locking into place against him, her scent wrestling his senses to the mat.

Holy shit.

Had anyone ever been this soft and strong at the same time?

There was power to her, but she was pliant now, her breath catching from the shock of falling, her head dropping back to rest on his shoulder. It had been a long time since he'd touched a woman, yeah, but even longer since he'd held one like this—and he couldn't remember it feeling this way. Like his nerve endings were on the verge of explosion, his pulse cranking at a thousand miles an hour.

The effort it took not to kiss the side of her neck was absorbing all of Burgess's willpower when voices reached them from the front of the club and Tallulah's head turned in that direction, obvious tension building in her spine. She wiggled against him in a clear request to get down and he reluctantly complied, adjusting his growing erection with a wince before she could face him fully.

"Burgess?"

"Yeah."

"I know I already asked you for a huge favor tonight, but I'm about to ask one more. No questions asked, okay? I'll explain after?"

It was a struggle to follow her whispered speech, because he was still processing the experience of holding her, mainly the way the backs of her thighs felt against the fronts of his, the sexy shape of her backside. Now . . . wait, what was she asking him for? Another favor?

Did she realize he'd say yes to anything right now?

Gator wrestling. Base jumping. Dying his hair neon pink. *Let's go.*

Now that his brain was coming back online—somewhat—he couldn't ignore the way her eyes continued to stray toward the small group of men and women that had just emerged from the club. The man in glasses broke from the group, moving in the direction of where Burgess was parked. And the closer he came, the jumpier Tallulah seemed to get.

Heat flooded his bloodstream, muscles hardening. "Did this guy *bother* you?"

"The thing is, I don't know." Hastily, she tucked some loose hair behind her ear. "I don't know if he was just being nice. Or flirting. Or if he came on too strong. Because I assume the worst now. I just assume the worst in every man. But I know I'm not interested. That I know." The guy was about fifteen yards away now. "But I'm going to see him at school on a daily basis and I didn't want to make things awkward, so I impulsively told him my boyfriend was coming to pick me up. He's going to think that's you. Could you maybe . . . be convincing?"

Burgess's whole body was beginning to thrum. "Convincing how?"

"Could you kiss me? One time. I'll never ask again—"

He went into the kiss like a bear being handed a pot of honey after a winter in hibernation. Stiffness, sweat, lust—these things all drilled him at once, like a reverberating blow. And his body, his hands, his mouth, just moved. Found and took. He gathered Tallulah against him with a forearm, drawing her up onto her tiptoes, and he growled into his first taste of her mouth. It was a kiss born of the hunger he'd been harboring since meeting her, hell yes it was, but her explanation had added two hugely potent ingredients to the mix—protectiveness and jealousy. In other words, he was a fucking powder keg.

Calm down.

You're going to scare her.

Easier said than done.

A peck on the mouth would have been enough to accomplish what she needed, and the footsteps were already moving past them on the sidewalk, hesitating slightly, but continuing down the road until Burgess couldn't hear them anymore. Couldn't hear anything but the raw pump of his heart, the gasps of air she dragged in between his slick invasions of her mouth. And maybe he shouldn't have, but the fact that she kept opening her mouth for his tongue, her hands twisting in the front of his shirt and pulling him closer, closer, caused Burgess to take it a few steps too far. In one swift action, he lifted Tallulah off the ground, took a lunge, and settled her ass on the passenger seat, reclining her back with his chest, leaning over her to keep tongue fucking that pretty mouth, panting brokenly into her neck when she allowed it, her inner thighs brushing his hips. Squeezing. Mother-*fucker*, his cock was hard.

"Burgess," she gasped, patting him on the shoulder with a shaky hand. "O-okay. Okay."

"Okay what, gorgeous?" he muttered thickly.

She moaned as he licked up the side of her neck. "This is . . . we're getting c-carried away."

"I'll carry you anywhere you want to go."

"I'm . . . that sounds . . . oh, God." They attacked each other's mouths in a frenzy of suction and open lips; long, moaning tastes that made his hands shake where they tangled in the hem of her skirt. "I haven't gone out drinking like this in a while and I'm . . . I'm making rash decisions . . ."

Drinking.

She'd been drinking.

What the hell was he doing?

She'd called him, trusting him to get her home safely. Now he was mauling her on the side of a very public street, trying to remember if he still had that condom in his wallet.

Seriously, man?

Get your fucking act together or it's the last time she'll ever call you for anything.

"I'm sorry." He untangled his hands from her skirt, pressing his fists to the ceiling of the SUV, remaining hovered above her while he caught his breath. Stopping wasn't easy by any means. In fact, it was utter torture, especially when she still had her thighs open for his hips, her tits rifling up and down while she struggled to breathe. "Fuck. I'm sorry. I . . ."

I've been thinking about you nonstop for months.

You make me so horny, I am breathing through my ears.

"No, it's okay, I asked you to kiss me."

"Went a little further than kissing. And you've been drinking. There's no excuse." Burgess garnered the deep inner strength it took to haul himself off his au pair, a girl eleven years his junior who'd asked him for help. Wow. What a bastard. He kept his eyes trained on a point above her shoulder while he pushed her legs back together. She quickly turned in the seat at the same time, staring straight ahead through the windshield, and Burgess took that as a sign to give her a moment to collect herself.

Closing the passenger door, he skirted around the front bumper to the driver's side, opened it, and climbed in. He went to turn the key in the ignition and cursed, realizing that one, his hands were shaking and two, he'd left the engine running. Tallulah was still looking off into the distance. Because she'd been equally affected by the kiss or because she'd made a terrible mistake asking for his help? Hoping for the former was probably absurd.

Burgess put the car in Drive and pulled away from the club, judging he had approximately twelve minutes until they reached his building and that definitely wasn't going to be enough time to make her comfortable with him again. "I'm sorry, Tallulah."

"You can stop apologizing. I encouraged you."

The confirmation that he hadn't imagined her willing participation was hell on his dick. It swelled at the proof that she *had* yanked on his shirt. Her tongue *had* been inside of his mouth. Those moans were real. Still. "I knew you'd been drinking. I just . . ." He stopped at a red light, raked a set of fingers through his hair, and decided to go with a modified version of the truth, which was that he'd been in lust with her since they met. She was already freaked-out enough. He just wanted to give her an explanation that would get that deer in headlights expression off her face. "It's just that I haven't been with a woman in a while, Tallulah, and you're fucking beautiful. It's still not an excuse. And it won't happen again."

She turned wide eyes on Burgess.

Said nothing.

"What?" he prompted.

"You're *so* intense," she finally sputtered. "Have you ever made small talk in your life?"

"About what?"

"That's the thing about small talk. It's not *about* anything. It's small."

"What's the goddamn point?"

She implored the ceiling for patience. "It's preliminary conversation. You have to gauge the other person to see if they're in the mood to discuss anything deeper. It's like kissing—"

His zipper turned suffocating. "Please don't bring up kissing." *While your legs are crossed two feet away in that little leather skirt and stockings. Dear* God.

"You're right, that's a bad example. You don't ease into kissing, either. Holy *moly.*"

He took a right turn a little too sharply. "Is that a complaint?"

"Nope. Just an observation."

"Okay then." *Let it drop. You should one hundred percent let it drop or you'll sound insecure or pathetic.* "You would have liked it differently?"

"I didn't say that." She waved her hands in a crisscross motion. "I guess I'm just wondering if your inability to make small talk has anything to do with . . ."

"What?"

"Not being with a woman for a while." She winced a little, as if embarrassed by her own bluntness, yet she still continued. "Small talk is a significant part of dating."

"Dating?" He cringed involuntarily. "Who said anything about that?"

Understanding dawned on her face. "Oh, I see. No beating around the bush there, either, so to speak. Just straight to the main event."

"If you're implying I don't know how to make a woman wet, I'd be happy to disprove your theory, gorgeous. I only need one hand to drive this car."

A split second before she looked away, her eyes turned unmistakably smoky, her exposed thigh muscles shifting right there in the moonlight. While he was berating himself for slipping again into an inappropriate place with her, Tallulah was visibly regrouping. And if she had to regroup with him, she was uncomfortable, right? He wasn't having that.

Change the subject.

"What did that geek do to make you upset?"

"Don't say geek. It's mean." She sighed. "He is kind of a geek, though."

Burgess's expression remained stony. "What'd he do?"

She tapped her fingers against her knee and Burgess got the impression she was weighing what and how much to tell him. *Everything. Come on.* "He wanted to share an Uber," she said finally. "I said yes, even though I didn't want to. Then I panicked and told him my boyfriend was coming to collect me."

"Good. Why did you say yes to sharing a ride, even if you didn't want to?"

"It's complicated. Part of it is that I'm going to see him at school and why make things awkward. But mainly . . ."

"Mainly?"

"I want to stop feeling like this," she murmured. "Distrustful and helpless. It's not me. I hate it and I don't seem to have any control over how it makes me . . . react. I guess I'm just being impatient with myself. Forcing myself to behave like who I was *before*. But I'm learning over and over again that I'm not the same person." She said the last part almost to herself. "I'm not bold and fearless anymore."

"Really? I think you're twice as fearless. Most people have the benefit of putting on blinders, walking around thinking *that will never happen to me.* You don't have blinders and you're still going. Still *doing.*" When she turned to stare at him in silence, he wondered if he'd said the dead wrong thing. "I can't imagine someone coming out on the other side of something like that . . . unaffected. But I disagree that you're not bold and fearless. Now that I know what you went through, when I think of the way you came into my apartment while I was yelling because you wanted to help out with Lissa . . ." He cleared his throat. "You're plenty goddamn bold, all right?"

She let out a hitched breath. Paused. "Thank you for saying that."

The back of his neck felt suddenly hot and all he could manage was a grunt.

"Now that I'm here in Boston and I'm reluctant to do new things, the difference in me is a lot more obvious than it was in Antarctica. As much as I loved hanging out with Chloe, I can't lean on her company every time. I just don't want to reach that place where I start staying home and forgoing risks. There's nothing wrong with that, it's just not who I am. Was."

Her explanation made something hard form in his throat and he couldn't get it down with a swallow. "What things are you reluctant to do?"

She inhaled and let the breath seep out slowly. "I want to go to a show at Paradise Rock Club. I want to climb up beneath the Citgo sign on campus and watch a Red Sox game. I want to go skinny-dipping in Jamaica Pond."

"Jesus. And you won't even say yes to a hockey game?"

"I'm thinking about it!"

"What is there to think about?"

"I don't know. At first, I was hesitant to witness the wrath of Sir Savage. Now . . . I don't know." Her voice dropped to a grumble. "It might be a bad idea to see you in your element."

Something that felt suspiciously like hope sparked in his midsection. "Why is that?"

"Well. I already know you're good at kissing. Throwing in a second skill seems like it could get . . . distracting. Too much capability porn muddles the mind." Her wince told him she already regretted saying that out loud. But hell if that revelation wasn't making him sit a little taller. Fine, a lot taller. "And anyway, I don't have time to be a sports fan. Too time consuming." She made a face. "Josephine tried to make me like golf and I almost had to kick her to the curb."

"You wouldn't do that."

"I know." She covered her face and groaned. "I love her so

much it's painful. I can't believe she's marrying Wells Whitaker. Once, on a particularly wild weekend in New Orleans, I had to talk her out of getting his name tattooed on her bikini line. That was before they even met. Now they're going to have a bunch of little golfer babies. It's too much weight on my heart." She sat up straighter on a gasp. "Do you think we're going to be god-parents?"

Being connected to Tallulah in any way that included the word "parents" made him feel weirdly giddy. And he didn't do giddy. In fact, this might have been the first time. And last. "They haven't even set a wedding date yet and you're mentally checking them into a delivery room."

"I know." She uncrossed her legs and slumped back in the leather seat. "I know."

Don't look at her thighs. Distract yourself with something. Anything.

Burgess cleared his throat hard. "So. Skinny dipping, huh?"

Perfect, man. Nailed it.

Now he was thinking of her naked.

"Would you ever skinny dip?" Tallulah asked. "Or does that fall into the same category as small talk? As in, there is no point."

"There really isn't."

"Spoken like a person who has never done it before. It's ex-hilarating. The excitement of getting caught alone is worth it." She stayed quiet for a few beats. "Or it used to be, anyway. I don't know that I have the courage anymore. To take risks or be adventurous. To do new things without knowing the outcome. It's all different now."

That hard object lodged in his throat was expanding by the moment. He didn't like this. He didn't like her scared to do the things she loved. Strangling the person who'd done this to her might have helped temporarily, but what he really wanted was her to be fulfilled. Not hiding. That man who'd hurt her wasn't available for punching now or ever. What Burgess could do, however, was beat down the fear that monster had put inside of her.

"What if you had someone there to protect you?" Shit. First giddy, now vulnerable. All in one night. What was going on with him? She could so easily turn him down. "While you . . . did these batshit things you believe are entertaining?"

Without taking his eyes off the road, he sensed her head turning in his direction, felt the surprise and curiosity radiating from her. "What do you mean?"

"I mean me. I mean, I'll come along and make sure nothing bad happens to you." Already the potential privilege was becoming something he wanted. Needed. "I'm a defenseman, that's kind of my specialty."

"Yeah, but . . . you would do that?"

Burgess grunted.

Tallulah sat forward abruptly, gasped. "I have an even better idea."

CHAPTER TEN

To clarify, she had a *terrible* idea.

Just terrible.

Or was it freaking genius?

Tallulah was tipsy to begin with, but then. Oh then. Her brain had been flipped upside down and punted like a football by this man's kiss. Who knew Burgess had that kind of . . . passion lurking inside of that big warlord body? She'd never been kissed so soundly in her life, especially not while fully clothed. Like, the man had serious skills. And the part she was having the hardest time forgetting was that he seemed to understand *sensuality*.

Though her memories of men were growing foggy, she remembered how they usually went straight for the ass during a kiss. Their hands were drawn there like homing pigeons returning to their lofts. Inevitably, a girl ended up with a tongue tickling her tonsils and greedy hands exploring her crack without permission.

But Burgess.

Their kiss was only supposed to be a tactic to divert Finn's interest, but she'd gotten a lot more than she bargained for. He'd massaged her hips with those big hands, dragged his knuckles up the curve of her waist, *licked* her. She might have teased him about having his foot on the accelerator, but the big guy obviously knew what he was doing. Maybe because he'd been married? Why did that correlation make her mouth taste like bad milk?

Must be the alcohol.

Bottom line, he was her boss. They couldn't have a replay.

However, all sorts of plans were weaving themselves together in her brain, despite the amaretto sour fog. She could help this man get back out into the world, right? As a tradeoff for watching her back while she found her footing?

Burgess put an arm across her seat back and leaned over. Thinking he was going to kiss her again, Tallulah opened her mouth to scold him. Just kidding, she moistened her lips and prepared to have her mind blown. But although he watched her tongue skate across the seam of her mouth, he continued to twist his thick body, one hand on the steering wheel—and she realized he was parallel parking in front of the building. They were home.

Cool. She really needed to sober up.

"What's your idea?" Burgess asked while straightening out the SUV.

Now would be the time to say "never mind" and forget the whole thing. Maybe it was a really bad idea to spend more time with this man, considering she found him troublingly attractive. She definitely wasn't looking for a relationship, so what could the fascination amount to? Living with her hookup? No. What a grand disaster that would be. Especially with Burgess who was old-fashioned. He'd probably expect her to stay home and cook, even on her nights off. She'd be locked down by a grumpy, set-in-his-ways hockey player before she could blink—and that wasn't the life full of freedom and new experiences that she wanted.

But. Maybe she could play Ted Lasso and leave this family better off than she found them. She could help Burgess revive his social life, thus making him happier and a better father. In return, she could go on her adventures securely.

Just say it, before you lose your nerve.

"Okay." Tallulah unbuckled and turned to face Burgess in the seat. "First of all, thank you for your offer to come with me on my batshit journeys. I accept."

He cut her a sidelong glance. "Really?"

"Yes."

The man seemed to be having a hard time stifling a smile.

"Oh my gosh, you love this, don't you?" Tallulah laughed. "You get to come along with me and scare people off. That's your sweet spot. That's where you thrive."

"Correct."

"Weird."

He shifted in the driver's seat. "I'm also . . . relieved. I don't have to lie awake and wonder where you are and if you're safe—"

"Okay, that's more *Father* than Daddy. Don't get the two twisted."

"Jesus. I can be protective without it being . . . paternal."

"Would you be like this with any au pair that you'd hired?"

"No."

Wow. Really, it was Tallulah's fault for asking. She'd walked right into that sticky web of knowledge and now the SUV was filled with a charged silence, although if she listened closely, she could hear the muscle ticking in Burgess's cheek. *Move on. Pretend he was kidding.*

"Um, wait. You haven't heard the rest of my idea," Tallulah said, her voice sounding more than a touch reedy. "You admitted that you haven't been social in a while. It's hockey and home. Hockey and home. But what if this is your chance to get back out there?"

"What do you mean?"

"I mean, you might have the disposition of a cranky old man, but in reality, you're only thirty-seven. There are students in my masters program who are older than you, my guy. Instead of coming along on my outings with the express intention of putting the fear of God into other men, we could use this as an opportunity to resocialize you."

"Christ, Tallulah. You make it sound like I've been living among the wolves. I *choose* not to be social. People are fucking annoying."

"Maybe you just haven't met the right one yet."

His expression sharpened. "Is that what this is about? You're going to take me on a quest for a mate—"

"More wolf talk. Are you sure you're not missing your pack?"

"Funny." He dropped a fist on the steering wheel. "Listen, I'm a rich professional athlete. If I wanted a relationship, I could find one. I wouldn't need any help."

That bad milk taste made a strong comeback. "Going out and learning to have fun is less about finding a relationship and more about . . . having some excitement to offer when you *do* meet the right one."

He actually seemed to consider that, studying her closely as the statement sank in. "So what you're saying is my life is boring. What woman would want to get involved?"

"That's harsher than I would have put it, but the sentiment is accurate."

"Huh."

He took his hand off the steering wheel in order to stroke his beard. Disturbingly, Tallulah's fingers twitched in her lap, remembering what that bristle had felt like against her jaw. Wondering what it would be like to tug it gently with her fingers. "What do you think of my plan, boss?" Tallulah said, forcing herself to stop speculating about the sensitivity of his facial hair. "You come with me on my excursions. I teach you how to meet new people. Have fun again. And *be* fun again. Assuming you ever were in the first place."

"I was," he said gruffly, looking slightly self-conscious. "If you consider raising hell fun. Growing up, I was known as the kid who never turned down a dare. I got older, though. Started collecting responsibilities—and I like those responsibilities. But maybe I went too far in this direction. If nothing else, maybe . . . I don't know. Maybe I'll learn how to be fun for Lissa."

Tallulah's heart went *whommm*, electricity snapping in her brain.

A man who recognized his own faults. A man who wanted to be better.

Apparently she found that incredibly appealing.

In that moment, she warned herself to be careful. To think of Burgess as a boss. A friend. But nothing more. Or her ties to him could get a lot stickier.

And she didn't want to get stuck. She was just learning to fly again.

"For what it's worth, she adores you."

Burgess scoffed, turned his face away.

"She does. It's hidden under a bunch of angst, but . . ." Tallulah smiled to herself. "When Lissa says something at the dinner table, she always looks at you first to get your reaction. Did you notice that?"

He looked back at Tallulah, a groove between his brows. "Does she?"

"Yes."

A long pause. "Huh."

"I bet the rookies on your team do the same thing."

"The Orgasm Donor Twins?" Burgess rolled his eyes. "They don't care about what anyone is saying unless it's coming out of their mouths."

"Oh yeah? Watch them next time."

"No."

Tallulah laughed.

"You've gotten me to agree to too many things tonight. You've hit your quota."

"That's fair. Thanks for coming to get me. I really appreciate it." Before she could register her own movements, her hand reached across the center console and squeezed his bicep—and honestly, she'd intended a friendly lil squeeze, but when she encountered pure concrete in the shape of an arm, Tallulah frowned, thinking she must have grabbed onto something else by mistake, because this arm didn't feel human.

Frowning, she molded the grapefruit-sized lump in her hand, only partially aware of the amused twitch of Burgess's lips.

"I guess this is another thing I'm going to regret in the morning," Tallulah muttered.

"Probably."

Still touching. Why was she still touching? Her fingertips traced the rainbow-shaped bulge, top to bottom, like a kid riding a slide at the park. *Wheee.* "So this is . . . a result of the high-protein diet. Good to know. Good. To. Know."

"Tallulah?"

"Yes?"

Slowly, he leaned in. And oh-so-casually flexed his arm. "I'm like this all over."

"Oh."

Their eyes met, locked, their breath accelerating in tandem. "You want to bring me around Boston on your adventures, good. Let's go." His face came closer, close enough to feel his warm breath painting her mouth. "You let me know if you want my bed to be one of them."

Burgess hadn't been exaggerating.

He really did know how to make a woman wet.

Tallulah had no problem becoming aroused by her own mental fantasies or the occasional trip to the X-rated section of the internet, but it had been a really, *really* long time since a real-life man had inspired that warm spread of moisture between her thighs. That hot, reckless flutter in the lowest regions of her belly. Her pulse thickened and sped up at the same time, that long absent ache of need, the one that required skin on skin, turning sharp and greedy in places that made her squirm . . . closer. She *was* squirming closer, her hand sliding from Burgess's troublesome bicep to the collar of his shirt, twisting to drag him closer—

Both of their phones rang at the same time.

The riot of sound was so unexpected in the quiet intimacy of the SUV that Tallulah immediately thought they were being arrested. Surely those were sirens to signal a SWAT team descending on them to demand why she was about to kiss her boss for the *second* time tonight.

But no. Phones.

Who was calling them?

"Lissa," they said at the same time, scrambling apart to find their respective devices.

Burgess fumbled his out of the cup holder first, letting out a blast of breath when he saw the screen. "Oh, thank God. It's Wells." He bolted upright. "What the fuck is he doing calling me at two thirty in the morning?"

Tallulah turned her screen in his direction. "Probably for the same reason Josephine is calling me." Her pulse was racing now for an entirely new reason. "I hope something isn't wrong."

They both answered.

"Hello?"

Josephine's dear and familiar face beamed back at her, a welcome vision of auburn hair and clever green eyes. "Hey! I knew you'd be awake. Where are you?"

Tallulah shifted guiltily. "Never mind where I am. What's going on?"

Instead of answering, Josephine shot a perplexed look at someone off-screen, and Wells appeared beside his fiancée suddenly, holding his phone in his hand. "Hold up, hold up." His lips spread into a cocky grin. "Are you two together?"

"I'm hanging up," Burgess snapped, doing just that.

"What are you doing together at two thirty in the morning?" Wells asked.

"She needed a ride," Burgess near shouted from the driver's side.

Josephine was failing to smother a laugh. "Ohhh. She needed a *ride*, did she?"

Wells and Josephine fist bumped.

"Okay, you two. Very funny. Burgess was gracious enough to put his beauty sleep on hold to come pick me up." Tallulah turned so that she and Burgess would both be visible on their screen. "Long story short, you've got us both. Now what is the meaning of this?"

"Well . . ." Josephine looked at Wells with heart-shaped eyes. "We finally picked a wedding venue. And the wedding . . . it feels like it's really happening now. I got so excited that I had to call and ask you to be my maid of honor. I knew you'd be out and I thought it would be even better—read, funnier—if you were tipsy. Obviously, I'm screen recording this."

"I'm not that predictable, am I?" Tallulah stared at the screen through a gathering veil of tears. "You're really asking me to be your maid of honor?"

"Yes."

A couple of tears popped free and rolled down her cheeks. "Oh my gosh. Oh my gosh."

"Is that a yes?"

"Of course, it's a yes."

Something bumped Tallulah's knee and she looked down to find Burgess had opened the glove compartment. He lifted the manual, shifted some paperwork aside, and found a small pack of tissues, taking one out and handing it to her.

"Thanks," Tallulah sniffed.

He frowned at her, but it wasn't an irritable one; it was more helpless than anything.

"I'm fine," she mouthed at him.

A grunt was his response, surprising no one.

A lightbulb went off above Tallulah's head and a weird lightness invaded all four of her limbs. "Wait, are you calling Burgess, too, because . . ."

"Yeah, hey." Wells coughed into a fist, looking distinctly uncomfortable, but he also seemed grateful for the circles Josephine started rubbing into his back. "Do you want to be my best man, B?"

It was a true pleasure to watch the hulking hockey player do a double take. "Me?"

"Please don't make me repeat myself."

Silence landed like a splat.

Josephine raised her eyebrows at Tallulah.

"Uh . . ." She hurried to fill the void left by Burgess's stunned reaction. "Wait! You didn't even tell us which venue you landed on."

Wells executed a finger drum roll on his fiancée's knee. "Costa Rica. This December."

"*December?* That's . . . just over two months away. Josephine!" Tallulah bounced in her seat. "I'm screaming!"

"Pack your bathing suit," Josephine sang. "Especially if you still have that baby blue one from college, because that's one of our wedding colors."

"I do! I still have it! Might be a little tight, but—"

"I'll do it," Burgess said, abruptly. "I'll be the best man."

"The timing of that agreement was a little transparent, man," Wells said, dryly. "But I have no choice but to take it. Thank you."

"You're welcome," Burgess said, crossing his arms.

This fucking guy, Wells mouthed to Josephine.

"We'll let you guys get back to . . . whatever you were doing when we interrupted." Josephine's grin broadened. "I just couldn't wait until morning to pop the question."

"I'm so excited for you guys! I can't wait!"

"Me either," Wells muttered, planting slow kisses on Josephine's neck that were quickly turning the phone call un–family friendly. Not to mention Josephine's eyes were beginning to grow suspiciously glassy. "All I want is to call you my wife . . ." came the golfer's muffled voice.

"Okay, talk tomorrow!" Tallulah said quickly, severing the connection. "Wow. Costa Rica. Wedding colors. Venues. It's like . . . on."

"Yeah."

Tallulah and Burgess looked at each other so long, the air started to crackle. It was clear from Burgess's tight expression that he remembered exactly what was on the verge of happening when those phone calls came through. And he wanted to get back to it.

But while Tallulah could still feel the deep pull of need in her lower body, the reckless impulse to venture into muddied waters with her boss, the conversation with Wells and Josephine had only served as a reminder of what she didn't want. At least, for herself.

To be tied down.

And this man who waited up to make sure she got home safe, this single dad, this old-fashioned man . . . he was the commitment type. No question about it.

"I'm going to head up. I rescheduled some of my weekday classes for Saturday ones, so I can be free for Lissa during the week. They're kicking off tomorrow afternoon."

"Right."

They exited the car, entered the building, and rode the elevator in silence that screamed with electricity. Tomorrow, when she was fully sober, she wouldn't ache with the need to abandon her caution with Burgess. She'd have herself under control and her priorities in line.

But when she turned at her bedroom door and found him watching with hooded hunger from the living room, she wondered if she'd overestimated her willpower.

With a burst of determination, Tallulah closed herself in the bedroom.

And slowly engaged the lock.

CHAPTER ELEVEN

Burgess gritted his teeth and growled his way through the final three squats in his set before settling the weighted-down metal bar into its cradle. After getting Lissa off to school this morning, he'd had an early press panel and a lunch meeting with the team owners, followed by a three-hour practice. No one would have looked at Burgess sideways if he'd decided to skip weightlifting, but he'd never cut corners before and he wasn't going to start now, even if his body was demanding he do just that.

He slapped a hand onto the white cinder block wall and twisted, trying to alleviate the severe throb in his lower back by stretching. Didn't help. One more set and he'd let himself go home. It wasn't the grueling workout he used to put himself through, but he'd done enough to maintain his strength.

Maintain?

Since when was that enough?

A memory from a week and a half earlier drifted to the forefront of his mind. Tallulah in the passenger side of his SUV feeling his bicep with a look of astonishment on her incredible face. Although in his version, she dragged her hand downward, giving his thighs the same thorough treatment, gasping over the hard ridges and sinew, teasing him before eventually stroking her palm into his lap and feeling how thick he was there. For her.

Three. He'd do three more sets before he went home.

Burgess swiped a towel over his sweaty hair and tossed it onto

a nearby bench, pacing with hands on hips. While putting himself through another three rounds of squats, he didn't see his image in the mirror at all. Just Tallulah. She'd lived for ten days in
his home. All of her things were kept confined to that bedroom.
No shoes by the door. No coat on the peg. Yet her presence was
everywhere.

In the air.

In his lungs.

Sometimes he caught her staring at him across the apartment
and his blood would heat to a fucking boiling point. He'd swear
hers was doing the same and tonight was the night she came to
his room, stripped at his bedside, and they gave in. But despite
those hungry looks, they kept things professional. And by professional, he meant Tallulah was transforming their very lives one
genius fix at a time. She didn't merely talk Lissa down from a
ledge when she came home from school after a bad day, she explained to Burgess afterward why her method had worked. She
had the inside track to the teenage brain.

Burgess had stumbled on the Holy flipping Grail.

And yeah, she said she'd never cook again, but she continued
to make dinner almost every weeknight and enlist their help in
the kitchen. A couple of days ago, she'd had too much homework to prepare the meal, so he'd done it with Lissa. Just the
two of them. They'd prepared a stir fry from memory and it
hadn't tasted like hot garbage.

In ten short days, life felt different. His kid was happier. He
was learning to communicate with her, simply by watching
Tallulah. So he should probably be happy with what he had. A
harmonious household. A wildly competent au pair.

Though he couldn't help but wonder what might have happened if they hadn't been interrupted by a phone call the night
he picked her up from the club. When he'd almost kissed her a
second time in the cab of his truck, her hand fisted in the front of

his shirt. Maybe that kiss would have gotten out of hand. Maybe she would have taken off her lacy black panties, climbed onto his lap, and ridden him in the front seat while the windows fogged up. Hard, fast, letting out urgent little whimpers at the ceiling—

"You seem kind of distracted today, man," Sig said, leaning against the mirrored wall in front of Burgess. Where the hell had he come from? "What are you thinking about?"

"Next week's game," Burgess snapped. "That's where everyone's focus should be."

Sig smirked at him. "You're forgetting that I met your au pair last Friday."

Burgess gave him a pointed look. "We'll talk about it later."

"Why? Now seems like as good a time as any."

"Hold the fuck up. Burgess has an *au pair*?" Mailer emerged from the other side of a partial cinder block wall that separated the weight area from cardio equipment. Of course, Corrigan followed directly in his wake, two sharks homing in on the scent of blood. "Is she French?"

Burgess stared blankly at Sig.

Sig rubbed the center of his forehead. "Sorry, man. That's why you didn't want to talk about her. I forgot the rookies hover around you at all times."

Corrigan slapped a hand down on Burgess's shoulder. "Like vultures around a rotting carcass."

"Don't make me rip your fucking arm off," Burgess said as calmly as possible.

The rookie took his hand back, snickering nervously.

"So?" Mailer rubbed his hands together. "Is she French?"

Sig groaned up at the ceiling. "You don't have to be French to be an au pair, you absolute dumbass."

"Fine," Mailer said. "What is she? Hot?"

"Yes, Mailer," Sig replied dryly. "She's from the Republic of Hotness. Just *below* France."

Corrigan slapped his friend in the chest. "Hotness isn't a nationality."

"It is in my book," Mailer said, letting his tongue hang out.

"Your book is just a notepad with a bunch of dick drawings," Burgess commented.

Mailer and Corrigan doubled over laughing.

Burgess's back let out a particularly sharp throb and he ground his molars together. "Can you fuck off now and let me finish my workout—"

"I had a nanny for a while growing up," Corrigan interrupted. "She was in her sixties. But there were some days she looked pretty good. Those were confusing days for me."

"Every day is a confusing day for you," Sig quipped.

But the rookie was looking at Burgess.

Both of them were.

As a matter of fact, any time either one of them said something, they turned to get his reaction. Every. Single. Time. Tallulah was right. What exactly did that mean? She'd implied that Lissa did it because his opinion mattered the most, and he'd been . . . honored to know that. That couldn't be the case here with Orgasm Donor One and Two, though. They didn't give a shit about anyone's opinions but their own. Right?

He wasn't sure what made him test out the possibility. Maybe he was genuinely curious. Or maybe he simply wanted an excuse to knock on Tallulah's bedroom door later to tell her she'd been wrong. Whatever the reason, he jerked his chin at the pair and asked, "What do you think of the 1–2–2 forecheck we've been using?"

To Burgess's utter astonishment, Corrigan and Mailer traded an excited glance and snapped to attention, all traces of humor vanished from their faces. "Honestly, we've been talking, and it's too passive for the speed we've got now."

"We're wasting an extra defenseman when you've got the goal covered. We could be forcing more turnovers at the blue line with a 1–3–1."

Burgess started to give the response he'd been planning before the two doofuses had even given their answer . . . but he never expected their point of view to have some actual merit. Enough to snap his mouth shut and make him consider what they said. "That's not a terrible point. I'll mention it to the coach."

They looked like they'd just been given the opportunity to drink a beer from the Stanley Cup. "Nice. Thanks. Cool," Mailer said, visibly with no idea what to do with his hands.

"Thanks, Sir Savage."

He started to slap Burgess on the shoulder.

Burgess shut it down with a "Nope."

But when the rookies disappeared back into the cardio area, their heads bent together in a whirlwind of whispers, Burgess couldn't help but feel a little . . . humbled.

"Wow." Sig sauntered closer. "That was off-brand. Are you feeling all right?"

No. The base of his spine was in a vise that grew tighter by the second. "When did we become friends?" Burgess asked, assuming Sig's question had been rhetorical. "Like at what point did I stop treating you like a rookie asshole?"

Sig answered without hesitating. "My second year in the league. We were on the road in Pittsburgh and the game went to penalties." Sig shook his head. "I was off that night. I missed my shot by a mile and I guess you were feeling generous because you told me to shake it off. And I told you to get fucked. We were cool after that."

Burgess barked a rare laugh. "That sounds about right."

"Doesn't it?" His brow quirked. "Imagine my surprise a few minutes ago when you gave the Orgasm Donors the time of day."

"Tallulah . . ." he started without thinking.

Sig clasped his hands beneath his chin and gasped. "Tallulah, what?"

Burgess sighed at the theatrics. "Nothing, she just said something that made me think."

"I liked her. Two seconds after meeting her, she was breaking my balls. That's a hockey player's dream." He raised an eyebrow. "How fast are you trying to lock her down?"

"It's complicated."

"Uncomplicate it."

"Says the guy who was out at two A.M. picking up his future stepsister."

"That topic is off the table." A muscle leapt in Sig's jaw. "Go back to the nanny. Why is it complicated?"

"You want me to give you a list? One: she works for me, so I'm paying her, plus I'm essentially her landlord, too. There's a whole issue with that power dynamic. Two: she's not only younger than me by eleven years, but . . . she's young on a whole different level. She's still excited about life. To me, life is just something I'm being forced to get through." At least, until Tallulah arrived in Boston. This morning, he'd woken up and *wanted* to get out of bed. Been eager to find out what the day would bring. "Three . . . She's been through some shit that I'm not sensitive enough or equipped to . . . navigate."

"Says who? Your ex-wife?" Sig snorted. "Fuck that."

Burgess did a double take. "Wow. How long have you been waiting to say that?"

"Few years, actually."

He caught sight of his expression in the mirrored wall, unsurprised to find confusion written all over his face. Where was this coming from? "The divorce was amicable. We're friendly."

Sig grumbled something.

Burgess shoved him in the shoulder. "What was that? Speak up."

"I said, it might have been amicable . . ." He crossed his arms, beginning to look pissed. "But you're the one who walked away shouldering all of the blame."

"I was always occupied with hockey. All the media attention. The split was my fault."

"Nah, I don't see it that way."

"What?" Burgess was beginning to raise his voice. "You weren't there."

"I've been here to see the before and after version of you. I don't think you two were meant to be, but the divorce itself pulled the rug out from under you." Sig two-hand shoved Burgess in the chest. "Where's your fucking confidence, man? Burgess before the divorce would have gone and pulled that hot nanny without breaking a sweat."

"You sound like one of the Orgasm Donors." Fire scaled his spine. "Call her hot again and I'll put your head through the wall."

Sig laughed, visibly delighted by his outburst. "Okay, I won't." His friend gave him a slow grin, obviously meant to incite him— and it was working. "I'll just think about it."

"You have a death wish."

"Look. I'm just saying . . ." Sig made a flippant hand gesture, indicating Burgess's body. "You've still got it. She's already living with you, right? So you don't even have to invent reasons to see her. That's half the battle. Now let's say you forget to wear a shirt to breakfast. Oops! Suddenly she's got two hundred and eighty pounds of defenseman of the year looking back at her over a bowl of Cheerios." Sig picked up a kettle bell. "Just saying, it could be compelling."

"I promised to take her skinny dipping in Jamaica Pond," Burgess grumbled, sneaking Sig a measuring look. "Is that something?"

Sig dropped the kettle bell. *What?*

Burgess feigned nonchalance. "Nothing."

"Fuck you, nothing. Explain."

"No."

Sig stared at him hard. "She better not invite Chloe."

"I'll make sure to suggest it."

"God, you're a prick." Sig considered him through a squinted eye. "I'm starting to think this au pair affair is going to be fun to watch."

Burgess didn't know if "fun" was a word that could be attached to anything related to him.

But he did know he was looking forward to getting home tonight. More than ever.

Again, the memory of Tallulah stroking his bicep skipped like a stone across the pond of his mind. Not that he would admit this to Sig, but . . .

Maybe the whole shirtless thing had some merit?

CHAPTER TWELVE

Tallulah clutched her chest with one hand, the script in the other. "I fear too early, for my mind misgives. Some consequences yet hanging in the stars shall bitterly begin."

Lissa flopped onto the couch, throwing a dramatic arm across her eyes. "How do they expect a bunch of twelve-year-olds to know what this stuff means?"

Not for the first time, Tallulah wondered if Lissa was an adult trapped in a tween body. "You read my mind, kid," Tallulah said, plopping down beside her. "I think the point might be that you *try* to figure out what it means. Sometimes that's what learning comes down to. Making your mind stretch."

Lissa groaned. "You sound like Mrs. DeSoto, my language arts teacher."

"Mrs. DeSoto sounds like a wise and stylish woman," Tallulah sniffed.

The girl humphed. "We're going to get assigned roles in class, so we can act out *Romeo and Juliet*. We don't have to memorize the script or anything, you get to hold your book while you do it. But . . . all the girls want to be Juliet."

"Including you?"

Lissa picked at the edge of the couch. "Maybe."

In other words, *yes, desperately.*

"Thad Durst is probably going to get picked for Romeo." Lissa's face started to turn pink. "He's, like, the best reader and he's Mrs. DeSoto's favorite, even though he goofs off in class. He never raises his hand, he just blurts things out and everyone laughs. It's not even fair."

"Every class has a Thad, I think. Mine was named Nolan. Let me guess, he's constantly fixing his hair. Like this." Tallulah did a microscopic head flick. "Over and over again."

Lissa burst out laughing. "He does do that!"

"They all do. It's in the cool guy DNA."

"A bunch of girls like him."

"Hmm."

"*I* don't."

"Okay." Tallulah surreptitiously studied the flush coloring Lissa's usually pale complexion and decided they would be turning the corner into crushes soon. Maybe they already had, but she wouldn't push Lissa to talk about it. Instead, Tallulah cleared her throat and raised the script up in front of her face. "You're up, Benvolio."

"I want to play Juliet, too," Lissa said quietly.

Tallulah put her arm around Lissa's shoulders. "Then I hope you get picked, but no matter what happens, you'll always be my Juliet."

A thoughtful smile plucked at Lissa's lips. "My parents are kind of like Romeo and Juliet, I think. They were meant to be together."

That statement dropped into Tallulah's stomach like a brick into a swimming pool.

Just over a week ago, she'd made out with Romeo outside of a club. Who did that make her? Rosaline? Some other off-script side chick? "What do you mean?"

"Sort of like Romeo and Juliet, they were just star-crossed. The timing was wrong. My dad was more famous when they were married, so he was always doing interviews and filming commercials. Now he has more time. They just have to figure it out." She slumped a little. "I've been begging my mom to bring me to the opening night game, so they can see each other, but she said no."

Probably because Mom was busy with her new fiancé.

Or maybe they simply weren't the type of divorced couple who could make a friendship work. Conscious uncoupling wasn't for everyone. Sometimes a split was clean, without a second act friendship. Whatever the reason, it worried Tallulah that Lissa wanted a reconciliation so badly and it didn't seem to be remotely in the cards.

Was it her place to discuss it with Lissa, though? Not even close.

Especially considering the idea of a reconciliation between Burgess and his ex-wife made Tallulah feel pretty . . . weird. And jumpy. A touch jealous?

Certainly not, she mentally scoffed.

But when she heard the key turn in the apartment door and her pulse took off like a racehorse, the possibility of getting jealous over Burgess didn't seem that far-fetched.

Great.

"Dad's home," Lissa said, bounding off the couch with her script in hand, skidding to a stop in front of the door as her father walked through. "Hey, Dad."

"Hey, kid." With an equipment bag slung over his shoulder, Burgess pulled Lissa over and dropped a kiss on the crown of her head. "How was your day?" he asked while his eyes searched out Tallulah across the room. Nodded once at her.

She nodded back.

They stared for a moment, then averted their gazes at the exact same time.

Tallulah dried suddenly damp palms on the thighs of her yoga pants. This was how it had been going for the ten days since she'd moved in. A lot of staring and trying not to get caught, but getting caught repeatedly. And by the end of the night, they gave up altogether.

Openly staring, his gaze a silent challenge. As if to say, *you know where to find me.*

Although, his stony countenance wasn't giving big, hungry alpha at the moment. It gave nothing away at all. But the way he massaged his lower back after setting down the bag . . . that was rather telling. As were the white brackets that appeared at the corners of his mouth.

"Dad. We're doing *Romeo and Juliet* in class. Mrs. DeSoto is going to assign parts next week."

"Oh yeah?"

"Yup." She danced on the balls of her feet. "Tallulah is helping me get used to the lines."

Burgess was visibly distracted by the pain in his back. "That's great."

Lissa looked down at the script in her hands, then at Tallulah. Back at her dad. "I hope I get Juliet. Everyone wants to be Juliet."

Daughter stared at father, holding her breath. Waiting for a reaction.

Tallulah's hands snuck together in her lap and clutched. *Say something*, she begged Burgess. *Say anything.* To her disappointment, Burgess grunted and started to walk past his daughter, but he slowed down on his way to the kitchen, his chin coming up a notch, something seeming to occur to him. He turned and looked back at Lissa. "You'd be good at playing Juliet, kid."

Lissa fumbled the script, pure joy sprinting across her features before she hid it. "Thanks." She didn't seem to know what to do with herself, but eventually she jogged toward her bedroom. "I'm going to go practice."

"Wait. What about dinner?"

"I ate with Tallulah!" The bedroom door slammed.

Burgess shot Tallulah a raised eyebrow.

She was busy trying not to swallow the heart in her mouth. "Um . . . yeah. Yeah, sorry, I broiled her some sole with lemon and capers. Threw it on top of some broccoli rabe." She tried to be casual about saying, "There's a plate for you in fridge."

"I thought you weren't going to cook anymore."

"I'm not. This was the last time."

Burgess hummed on his way to the kitchen, but there was a distinct hitch in his step.

Tallulah sat half-turned on the couch, watching him, trying to put a name to the fluttery sensation in the dead center of her belly. Maybe it was his overall freshly showered athletic sexiness that made it impossible to not peruse him. Or perhaps it was the way he'd clearly been listening to her advice. He'd obviously realized how much Lissa valued his opinion . . . and he'd incorporated it into his behavior. That. That was . . .

Very appealing.

Too appealing, really.

Now she had the nonsensical urge to reward him for it in some way, which was so *ridiculous*. Why should she reward him for being an attentive dad? That wasn't her job. His attentiveness should be a given! Yet she was already rising to her feet, making excuses for the sudden need to make sure he knew he'd made an impact with one little sentence. Maybe because it wasn't a small thing for someone set in their ways to learn a new way to be. It wasn't small at all.

Tallulah entered the kitchen slowly, telling herself to turn back every step of the way. Burgess stood at the counter, looking down at the plate of food she'd left, garnished and all, appearing kind of bemused. Her entrance distracted him, though, his head turning sharply to the left. "Hey," he rumbled. "How were your classes today?"

"Fun."

He smirked at her. "Dork."

The smile just kind of blossomed across her face. "Damn right. I'm even excited for the homework I have ahead of me tonight."

"Appalling." He dipped his chin toward the plate. "Thanks for this."

"You're welcome." She ventured closer, despite her common sense telling her to go lock herself in the bedroom again. Common sense and her sense of self-preservation. The activity she had in mind was incredibly unprofessional, but she couldn't seem to stop herself from coming to a stop directly behind Burgess and going up on her tiptoes, reaching past him to take the olive oil out of the cabinet. "You were great with Lissa just now."

"Yeah?" He shifted on his feet. "Thanks. Remembering to say the thing . . . it takes focus, right? You have to be ready at all times."

Her hands paused in the act of uncapping the olive oil. Why was her heart beating so fast? Because he'd listened to her? "Parenting and hockey are more similar than you realized?"

"Yeah," he said on a rushing exhale that didn't sound all that steady. "I gotta ask. What are you doing back there, Tallulah?"

Good question. "I noticed your back is bothering you," she said, pouring a dollop of olive oil onto the pad of her thumb, rubbing it together with her index finger.

He'd stiffened at her explanation. Now he picked up the plate and stuck it in the microwave in front of him, closing the door soundly. "It's fine."

Before he could move away, Tallulah lifted the back of his T-shirt and dug her thumb into the base of his spine, running it firmly upward. And the man all but collapsed forward onto the counter, moaning. It was actually far more dramatic a reaction than she'd expected—and she'd expected him to release a satisfied male groan at the very least.

This? This was a man who'd just sailed past the pearly gates.

"Do that again," he ground out. "Please."

She dug deeper and pressed a horizonal line up the base of his spine, before moving right and rubbing a circular pattern into the hard muscle of his rear hip.

"Oh my God," he said raggedly, fully propped on his forearms now.

Oh my God was accurate. That's what he was. A marble-slabbed God with a firm ass that was now fully displayed in mesh athletic shorts a foot below her face. And she'd brought him to his proverbial knees with a stroke of her thumb. Which was wildly empowering. Also . . . very worrisome.

"How long has it been hurting like this?"

"I can't remember a time when it didn't hurt," he breathed.

"How are you treating it?"

"Over-the-counter painkillers."

"Burgess."

Momentarily, he straightened. Hesitated. And stripped off his T-shirt, tossing it onto the kitchen floor. Then he dropped forward once more against the counter with a mesmerizing ripple of muscle. "Yell at me all you want, gorgeous, just keep doing the thing."

She'd never actually felt her pelvic floor so acutely, but wow, there it was, tightening up like shrink wrap around a doorknob. Holy mother, this massage had been the worst idea of her life. His back muscles were . . . *prolific*. Primal. Flexed. He had a tattoo on his right shoulder that went all the way down to the center of his back, the existence of which she was unaware of until this moment. The inked skin/thick butt/muscle trifecta was really bringing home the fact that she was not simply working for a single father. She was working for a snack. A DILF. A big boy.

The most eligible of bachelors.

How was this man—this hot, rugged professional athlete—not dating?

She knew firsthand that he was a skilled kisser. Now he'd

broken out the body to end all bodies. The fact that he wasn't out being chatted up by single women was a crime.

He needed a push. She'd obviously been sent here for the job. Even if the image of him surrounded by women caused a heat rash to break out under her clothes.

"You okay back there, Tallulah?"

"Yes," she blurted, digging her thumb into him once more, forced to close her eyes against the deep burr of his satisfaction, the way it rumbled in his torso and vibrated her fingertips. Ugh, he was so warm and hard and taut. Everywhere. How would a man like this make love? Probably fast and furious. Or maybe he knew how to take his time?

Stop wondering. You're not going to find out.

She cleared her throat of gravel. "So . . . I don't really know how this type of thing works, but shouldn't you tell a team doctor? Or trainer?"

"Yes." She probably shouldn't have made him talk, because the gratification was evident in his tone, causing regions of goose bumps to prickle into existence all over her body. "In fact, I'm contractually obligated to tell them about any injuries, so if we're splitting hairs, I'm in violation of my contract."

"Why not tell them?"

"It's not that easy."

"I imagine they have more advanced ways than Motrin for dealing with injuries."

"They do. Shots and pills and physical therapy." His muscles tensed beneath her fingers and she instinctively tried to rub away the tension. "I don't want any of that shit."

Frowning, Tallulah stayed quiet. She didn't have to ask him why out loud for him to know she was wondering why.

After a drawn-out sigh, he continued. "I don't want to be one of those veteran workhorses out on the ice being held together by tape. I used to pity those players. On their last legs, battling nine different injuries, getting shots to numb this or that. Once I go down that road, I'll never be able to turn off. Once my body knows there are remedies for everything, it'll start falling apart."

"Wow."

"Wow?"

She slid her thumb up his spine and he hissed. "I'm not a doctor, but I'm relatively sure that's not how medicine works. Or the human body. Like, I don't think the various parts of our bodies are conspiring against us."

"Of course not, you're twenty-six."

Tallulah rolled her eyes. "Stop acting like being thirty-seven makes you the crypt keeper. I'm going to tug your shorts down a couple inches, okay?" He grunted. Flexed. "Can I let you in on a secret? Thirty-five and up is the golden age for men." She tucked her fingers into the waistband of his shorts and shimmied them down, revealing twin dimples at the very base of his spine . . . and the breathtaking top swell of his butt. Just the very beginning of it, only the shadow of his crack appearing, but it was enough to make her wonder if the part of her brain that made good decisions had been severely compromised. Why was she subjecting herself to this flesh fest when she couldn't be the one to really enjoy it? "As I was saying, thirty-five is prime time. Women are looking for men in your age bracket, because you're done douching it up. Maturity is appealing."

"I thought we were talking about my age in terms of hockey." He looked back at her over his shoulder, eyebrow up. "Sort of took a left turn there, didn't you?"

Whoops. Be a little more obvious that you're objectifying him.

Mentally floundering, she pushed her thumbs into the newly exposed plane of his back and he turned around in a flash, groaning and clutching at the counter. *"Son of a bitch."*

"Back to hockey," Tallulah said briskly. "Is that really the only reason you're not telling the team about your injury? You're afraid treating it will have a domino effect?"

"I *know* it will. And . . . yeah. That's the only reason."

"You hedged."

"I didn't hedge."

"I know a hedge when I hear one."

Another long-suffering sigh. "Fine. I . . . refuse to be seen as weak. I'm not supposed to have weaknesses. And it had to be a fucking back injury, too? I might as well bring a cane out onto the ice, instead of a stick."

"Oh my gosh, Burgess. Anyone can have a back injury."

"It's a signal to everyone that I'm on borrowed time. It's blood in the water. You would understand more if you'd played professional sports for a decade and a half, like I have. It's cutthroat and unforgiving and . . . image is important."

She considered his words. "Maybe you're right, maybe I don't fully understand the mentality of athletes, specifically hockey players. But I know if you don't treat this injury, it's going to get worse. *That* I know." She slid her flat palms up his back and went to work on his shoulders, sort of absently, forgetting for the moment that his injury wasn't up there. "You have a life to live outside of hockey. You'll need your back for that."

"Do I have a life outside of hockey? I'm not so sure." His sides expanded and relaxed. "At one time, I did. I was a husband and a dad. I thought I was doing everything I was supposed to do. Providing. Showing up at birthday parties. But there's a missing ingredient. Whatever it is, I don't have it."

"I disagree. I'm watching the way you're growing and changing with Lissa. Maybe you just didn't have it mastered back then. And who does? I'm not even a parent and I know being one is a learning process."

"Hockey is safe. I know hockey."

"Maybe it's okay to feel unsafe," she said quietly, internalizing the sentiment as she went along, because it didn't only apply to him, did it? "Maybe it's okay for the both of us to start reaching for . . . more."

Burgess stayed quiet, though he tilted his head right so she could stroke up the side of his tense neck, his sides dipping and expanding faster than before.

Hers were doing the same.

In fact, she was grinding her back teeth to allay the impulse to press her breasts to his hard back. *Imagine your bare skin against his muscle.* Slipping and sliding—

No. Don't *imagine that.*

She needed to stay the course. This conversation was about a lot more than she'd anticipated. There was pain and insecurity lurking inside this Hercules of a man . . . and he'd been shouldering it alone. Hiding it from everyone. It wasn't a small thing that he'd chosen to open up to her, and she couldn't help but feel privileged.

"My father had a favorite athlete growing up—do you know Pedro Martinez?"

"Tallulah, he played for the Red Sox. Of course, I know him. I've *met* him."

"Really?"

A pause ensued while he shook his head. "You are totally clueless about anything sports related, aren't you?"

"I'm only there for the snacks." She laughed under her breath at the sheer indignation she could sense radiating from the man. "But I do know that Martinez played for the Red Sox. It's part of the reason I looked for a grad school in Boston, apart from BU having a stellar marine biology program. Boston was this glamorized place in our household growing up."

"Because of Pedro Martinez."

"Yes. So since you're his best friend, you must know that he had a lot of injuries during his final season. But my dad never saw him as anything but a baseball god. Pedro never stopped being his favorite player. His triumphs didn't stop counting because he strained his calf or tore his rotator cuff. That's just a human being a human. Sometimes we break a little." She dragged all ten of her fingers down the rocky terrain of his back and pressed her thumbs into those twin dimples, savoring the way his breath shook free at her touch. "Will you at least go see a private doctor?" she near whispered.

"Nope."

Her nose wrinkled in disappointment. "Not even if I promise to do this for you every once in a while?"

"Promise to do it every night and you've got a deal."

"Done. Wait, what?" Tallulah's hands dropped away, accompanied by a disbelieving gasp. "Why does it feel like I just got maneuvered?"

He turned around, sporting a grin. "I'll make the appointment tomorrow."

Respond. Say something. Fast.

Stop looking at his mighty, Zeus-like chest.

And his stomach. Was it even a stomach? It was more like a flesh-colored egg carton.

Our Father, who art in Heaven . . .

Apparently flip-flopping between Greek mythology and Christianity was the final proof that she'd been overwhelmed by the sight of him. The six foot three inches of brawn and masculine beauty that was Burgess Abraham stood before her looking like he should be holding a boulder over his head. Or crushing a village beneath his feet.

"What does your tattoo mean?" she said, winded, sounding like a sorority girl who accidentally stumbled into a biker bar. Humiliating with a capital *H*.

Burgess didn't answer right away, because he appeared to be

scrutinizing her reaction to his naked chest with . . . surprise? Had no one clued this man in that he was a panty dropper? "It's uh . . . yeah." He shook himself slightly. "Syracuse team logo. We all got it after winning state." He rolled the shoulder in question and she could see, in her mind's eye, how that ink on his back was rippling. "Seemed like a great idea at the time."

"It's good. I think it's good."

"Are you feeling all right, Tallulah?" His gaze ran down to her throat, up and over her cheeks. "You're a little flushed."

"No. I mean, *yes*. I am feeling all right. I get a little emotional talking about Pedro Martinez." She ignored his lip twitch. *Pull it together, girl.* "So you're going to call a doctor tomorrow and make an appointment to have them look at your back?"

He ran his tongue along the inside of his bottom lip. "Are you going to use those hands on me every night?"

Mark this as the second time Burgess had made her panties wet. Like, *wet* wet. Last time hadn't been a one-off. This guy got her hot and bothered, no use denying it. But who wouldn't get worked up around a man in peak physical condition? She was excused! "If that's the only way to make you healthy," she murmured, still feeling the delicious ridges of his back against her palms. "I suppose I can learn to sacrifice."

Mirth twinkled briefly in his eyes. "Then I'll call the doctor." He sauntered forward slowly, so slowly that she could feel her stomach tendons knitting tighter with every inch of space he eliminated between them, until his mouth and her forehead were separated by the barest of spaces. "But only for you."

A flare went off in her chest, like someone signaling for a rescue. Which couldn't have been more accurate. "Only for my massages, you mean."

His warm breath bathed her forehead, a bull preparing for the gate to open. "*Is* that what I mean?"

They remained like that, time suspending itself while they

started to breathe faster. He wasn't moving, though, was he? No, he was waiting for her to do it. To . . . engage. And what else was she supposed to do when her hands were warm from his skin and he was carved from granite, going around saying things like "but only for you." Was she *not* supposed to kiss him?

"One weekend has already passed us by," he said, his focus very intent on her mouth. "Are we going to make plans for the next one?"

"Who? Me and my bodyguard?" she murmured.

"That's me." He looked her up and down. "I'll guard it well."

"Better than you guard your goalie?" she managed choppily.

"Yes. And that's saying something, considering I'm a beast on defense." He dragged his bottom lip through his teeth, a low sound leaving him. "I'm a beast everywhere, Tallulah."

"Oh. Everywhere." Her pulse was going to beat out of her veins. "Like offense?"

"Nah."

"Hmm." Her core tightened so much that her voice went up an octave. "You're saying it's time to start our adventures. I learn to let loose again while we prepare you for the dating scene…"

Their mouths inched closer. "Name the time and place."

She ransacked her mind, searching for the reasons she shouldn't tilt her head back and see what happened. But all she wanted to come up with were reasons she should.

It'll boost his confidence with women! He'll realize he's still got it!

Really, *not* kissing him was kind of selfish, no?

Well aware her reasoning wasn't sound, she felt the slightest brush of his lips against her forehead and all manner of sense went out the window. She dropped her head back, inviting him with searching eyes. He made a gruff sound of hunger, propped his hand on the wall above her head, wet his mouth and leaned down slowly—

"*Tallulah!*" Lissa called, her bedroom door busting open.

Burgess and Tallulah jumped apart like two guilty teenagers, Burgess spinning around, snatching up a rag and pretending to mop the counter down. Meanwhile, Tallulah was frozen in place. "Huh?" Wake up. "Yes?"

"Dad, why is your shirt off?"

A line hopped in his cheek. "I . . . spilled something."

What a coincidence. Tallulah's common sense had spilled out of her ears.

Did she honestly just agree to *nightly massages*?

Why was she looking forward to the next one?

Oddly enough, the anticipation didn't only stem from the joy of having skin-to-skin contact with a man who made her feel safe. She looked forward to talking to him. That latter seemed to be a bigger problem than the former.

"Oh." Lissa was halfway across the living room. "Can you come do the lines with me? I think I'm pronouncing the words better now."

"Sure, of course."

"I think Tallulah has homework, kid. I'll do them with you."

"Oh! Okay." Visibly shocked, Lissa stayed still for a moment, before dashing back to her room. "Come on."

Burgess set down the rag and dropped his head forward for a few beats. Then he turned to leave the kitchen. But not before stopping beside Tallulah and letting out a jagged exhale in the space above her shoulder. "Just want to mention that I'm happy to give, not just receive. In fact, I fucking love giving, Tallulah."

She blinked up at him, shock spearing down to her toes. *"Excuse me?"*

"Massages." He winked at her. "I'm talking about massages. What did you think I meant?" Then he continued on his merry way, whistling. *Whistling.* "See you tomorrow."

Tallulah stared after her giant roommate/employer as he entered his bedroom and emerged wearing a shirt, vanishing into Lissa's room a few seconds later. And she wondered what in the heck she'd just gotten herself into . . . and possibly a lot more concerning . . .

Why she didn't want to get out of it.

CHAPTER THIRTEEN

Muscle strain.

That's all.

Burgess had a strained muscle in his lower back.

He'd expected the doctor to walk in after the series of X-rays and tests to tell him he'd fractured a vertebra or torn a ligament. The diagnosis was nothing that serious, though. Strain he could deal with. Strain wasn't a career ender.

Until the moment the doctor said those two magical words to him—"muscle strain"—Burgess had no idea of the ton of bricks he'd been carrying around on his shoulders. Holy fuck. His back still ached like nobody's business, but knowing he wouldn't require some bullshit surgery or a magic concoction to numb the pain, the relief made him feel like a new man. And there was no better timing than finding out the day before the Bearcats season opener.

He had Tallulah to thank.

Instead of being in the dark and worrying that a single hit was going to put him down for the count, confidence was already beginning to flow back into his veins.

Although, his former confidence had definitely begun its triumphant return last night in the kitchen when his au pair had very nearly jumped his bones.

Hard as it was to admit, Sig was right.

It paid to go shirtless.

Burgess slid off the doctor's table, both of them laughing over the way it groaned beneath his weight, and reached out to shake the man's hand. "Thanks for the great news, doc. I appreciate you seeing me on such short notice."

"Anything for my favorite Bearcat." Why was the guy frowning after delivering the world's most welcome diagnosis? "Listen, Burgess. I feel the need to inform you that this isn't *great* news, although it might seem that way compared to, say, a herniated disc. But if you don't rest the injury, it could get worse. You're going to compensate for the pain out on the ice and that could lead to injuries to other parts of your body. Knee, shoulder . . ."

"No, I hear you."

Spoiler: he wasn't really hearing him.

Muscle strain was all Burgess heard. *Halle-fucking-lujah.*

"I highly suggest you speak to the team's trainers about physical therapy to keep the muscle from stiffening and to strengthen the ligaments surrounding it," continued the doctor. "In the meantime, I can prescribe something to lessen the pain—"

"No thanks, doc. I appreciate the offer, but I'll handle it." He shook the man's hand again, ignoring the concern etched into the man's forehead. Doctors were paid to be overly cautious, that was all. They didn't understand an athlete's capacity to overcome minor shit like this with the power of adrenaline and will. Burgess had those things by the bucketload, especially now that he knew his body wasn't falling apart. "Thanks again."

Burgess walked out of the building in Back Bay and found himself . . .

Extremely interested in getting eyes on Tallulah.

It was just after lunchtime. Lissa was still in school and he didn't have practice tonight, meaning he didn't have to rush home and change. He was free.

He slipped his phone out of his coat pocket and looked at it, wondering if it was wise to call Tallulah. Maybe a better idea would be to let things happen the way they'd been happening. As in, taking his shirt off in front of her in the kitchen. That seemed to be the way to go. Let her get used to him. Let her come to him.

But nah, he was a fucking hockey player.

She'd given him an opening and it went against his nature not to take it. Despite Tallulah's claims that she wanted to help him get back out on the social scene and meet new people, she'd offered him her mouth in the kitchen. And he might not be an expert on the opposite sex, but an unsolicited massage from *this* woman seemed like a good sign?

Before he could talk himself out of it, Burgess shot Tallulah a text.

Burgess: Good news from the doctor.

Tallulah: WHAT? TELL ME.

Shit, he was smiling like a goddamn clown. Someone passing by in a white sedan rolled down the passenger window and stuck their head out, yelling, "Sir Savage!"

He lost the smile and put on the most terrifying expression he could muster, earning him a furious round of honks and cheers from the occupants of the vehicle.

Bostonians, man.

They loved a villain.

Burgess: Just a muscle strain. I'm golden.

Tallulah: That's amazing. SO MUCH YAY.
No more massages needed, I guess?

Burgess: Actually, the doctor said massages were vital to my recovery.

Tallulah: Sounds sketch.

Burgess: Nope. He's one of the best.

Tallulah: Hmmm. HMMM.

All caps coming from anyone else was annoying.
Why was it funny and adorable coming from Tallulah?

Burgess: Was thinking, if you want to go on one of your Boston adventures today before Lissa gets home, I'm available to be a badass.

Tallulah: GASP.

Tallulah: I'm in class right now, but . . . I could go for an adventure in about an hour?

Burgess: Do you have something specific in mind?

Tallulah: . . . I might.

Burgess: Tell me where to meet you.

Tallulah: Amory Park?

Burgess: I'll be there.

BURGESS STOPPED OUTSIDE of the coffee shop across from the park, making sure no one was looking before leaning close to the glass and fixing what the September wind had done to his hair, licking his fingers and smoothing down a section on top.

Any other time, he might go a full day without checking his reflection or the state of his hair once, but he was about to meet Tallulah. In the park. In the middle of the afternoon.

Not a date.

He had to keep telling himself that.

No number of reminders made him any less tense, unfortunately. Whether or not this was a date, he was spending his free time with a beautiful woman. She was spending her free time with him. It might have been over a decade since he went on an actual date, but didn't hanging out in the park together fit the criteria?

Based on the drivel he'd overheard from the Orgasm Donors, Tallulah's generation didn't like to put labels on anything romantic. They called each other partners, instead of boyfriend and girlfriend. They dated in groups. Just because two people were sleeping together didn't make it exclusive. In other words, the kind of vagaries that would give him a brain bleed . . . if they concerned *her.*

He'd deal with it, though. For now.

She'd taken time out of her day to come meet him. Trusted him to come along as she explored his city. The unknowns were a fair trade-off for feeling his pulse pounding for something other than a hockey game. Yeah. Fine. He'd let it be vague. For now.

Burgess checked his watch. Fifteen minutes early.

Maybe he should call Sig. His teammate might be able to help him figure out how to handle the fact that the girl he wanted to sleep with was trying to prepare him for the dating scene. *Other* women. Sig dated, right? They didn't really discuss their love lives, but Sig always claimed to be busy these days when the young guys went out to clubs or parties.

His other option was Wells.

Yeah, he'd call Wells. The golfer had gone through some recent turmoil trying to lock down his caddie, which was probably the same level of difficulty as trying to land his grad student au pair. Jesus Christ, was that really what he was trying to do?

He thought of her braiding Lissa's hair.

Glaring at him over a peanut butter smoothie.

The way she'd blushed when he leaned in to kiss her.

The first night she'd lived in his place and he'd come home to find her bent over the kitchen table in a leather skirt.

Yup.

Land her. That was the game plan.

Burgess took out his phone, sighing as he tapped Wells's name in his contacts. This was going to be insufferable, so he'd damn well better get some insight out of it.

"Burgess. What's up."

"Wells." He paced the sidewalk in front of the coffee shop window, dismayed to see his hair was back to being out of place. What he wouldn't give to slap a hockey helmet down over the whole mess. "How is wedding planning going?"

A pause ensued. "You called me to talk wedding plans?"

"No. But I'm working up to the real reason I called."

"The reason wouldn't happen to have a name that rhymes with awooga, would it?"

"Awooga barely comes close to rhyming with Tallulah."

"Ahhh, but you are calling about her. See what I did there?"

"This was a mistake."

"Don't hang up. Don't. Josephine will kill me if I miss a chance to get the tea."

"The . . . what?"

"The *gossip*, man."

Ohhh. Tea was *gossip*. A couple of Lissa's recent statements were suddenly making sense. "Are you in charge of planning any part of the wedding or are you just showing up looking smug?"

"I'm going to show up looking smug *and* I'm in charge of music. It's called multitasking."

"Band or DJ?"

"DJ. But I was thinking of surprising Josephine with something a little extra during the ceremony. Like . . . a choir? Or a harp. I don't know. Something fucking romantic."

"Harp." Burgess quit his pacing, taking a moment to recall why that instrument stood out in his mind. "Sig Gauthier's future stepsister, Chloe, plays the harp. She's supposed to be really good. Like a prodigy or something. Let me know if you're interested."

"Wow. Look at you coming through with harpist recommendations. Send me the info."

"Fair warning, if Chloe goes to the wedding, Sig goes."

"Why?"

"I don't know, and I don't ask. But if you end up hiring her, make sure you add two to the guest list." All right, that was enough small talk. He had less than ten minutes now before Tallulah showed up. "I'm meeting Tallulah in the park."

"Now we're getting somewhere. When?"

Burgess removed the phone from his ear briefly to see the time. "Eight minutes."

"Is this a date?"

"No. I don't know."

"That's two different answers."

"Fine. No. It's complicated."

"Let me tell you, I've been there."

"That's why I called you." Burgess let out a long breath, scanning the park across the street, just in case Tallulah had arrived early. "I'd like to make her my girlfriend."

A nostalgic chuckle from Wells. "I've been there, too."

"Yes, I know. With Josephine. How did you do it?"

"I fired her. Don't do that. That was very specific to our situation, okay? I repeat, *do not* fire Tallulah." The rattle of golf clubs could be heard in the background. "Does she like you?"

"How would I know?" Burgess growled.

"Is she giving you any signs?"

"She gave me a massage last night in the kitchen."

"Then I'd say you've got a fighting chance, my man. Especially if it was a dick massage."

"It was a back massage, shithead. Jesus." He licked his hand again and furiously tried to smooth down the piece of hair that had chosen today to stand straight up. "What does it mean that she wants to help me get back on the dating scene?"

Wells didn't answer for several seconds. "You know, you could have led with that. It's kind of the crux of the issue, wouldn't you say?"

Burgess grunted.

"I'm out of my depth here, Sir Savage, but I'll tell you one thing I know purely from a standpoint of self-preservation." His friend seemed to be pausing for dramatic effect. "Do not *actually* let her get you back on the dating scene, do you hear me? If she has even the slightest ounce of interest in you and you go on a date with someone else, it'll sink faster than one of my putts."

"Okay. Yeah." Burgess slowly started to nod. "This is the kind of advice I came for."

"Glad I could help. Godspeed."

Burgess hung up, put the phone back in the pocket of his coat and crossed the street toward the park, relieved to know what *not* to do. It wasn't a plan, necessarily. Still, it was more than he'd had ten minutes ago. But when he saw Tallulah coming up the sidewalk in an open trench coat that blew out behind her to reveal a short skirt and boots that went all the way to her knees, everything he'd just been told drained straight out of his head.

Un-fucking-real.

She saw him and a glow spread across her face, her hand lifting in a fluttery wave, turning heads as she walked. Was he actually trying to make something serious happen between him and this woman? On the wild chance he could have some kind of relationship with Tallulah, how long until his cantankerous nature wore thin and she got sick of him, like his ex-wife had? Was there even any point in trying?

Tallulah did a little skip as she reached him, and his heart followed suit.

Yeah.

Yeah, she was worth trying for.

"Congratulations on your good news."

"Thank you."

They agreed tacitly to turn and walk beneath the wrought iron arches into the park—and Burgess immediately did a double take. He'd expected the park to be empty of anyone but children and parents at this time of day, but there was a whole gathering of what looked to be young professionals milling around on the grass, holding cups of lemonade in their hands.

"Must be a company picnic or something," he remarked.

"Yes," Tallulah murmured back, vacillating briefly on the stone path. "Or something."

He studied her out of curiosity, but whatever had her hesitating seemed to have taken care of itself. "What made you want to come to this park?"

"Um." She rolled her lips inward. "The water, of course."

"Lead the way."

They continued down the pathway until they reached the edge of the pond, Burgess watching as Tallulah hunkered down to observe the brief shoreline, her gaze sweeping the rock, grass, and dirt landscape in one fell swoop and warming with fondness. "Isn't she pretty?"

"I'm guessing you see a lot more than I do when you look at a pond."

"My heart belongs to the ocean, but I do love knowing there is a structured ecosystem on the shores of a pond that isn't always visible to the human eye." She dragged a finger through the still surface of the water. "You have your producers, like algae. Consumers, such as fish, insects, occasionally crustaceans. And your decomposers, who are basically like nature's Roomba, just cleaning up all the waste. Light and heat act as the engine for everything. It's all running like clockwork, even if we can't see it."

"It's like a team. Everyone has a job to do?"

"Exactly."

The need to know more about what she loved was too pressing to deny, even though he had to battle through the imposter syndrome that came from being out with a girl this compelling and gorgeous. "Are you enjoying the graduate program so far?"

She made a wishy-washy sound. "Yes and no. I love learning and the information we're being taught is necessary and valuable. For instance, today we learned about coastal law and policy. But going from exciting internships on four major research studies to . . . a classroom . . ."

"You like being in the field more."

She wiped away a fake tear. "So much more."

Burgess chuckled. "You, uh . . . never said what made you choose marine biology."

When she stood up again, a gust of air carried across the water and sent her hair flying, so he angled his body to block the wind, grunting to himself when the dark strands settled back down around her shoulders. He assumed she wouldn't notice, but she blinked at him, her eyes tracked upward from his chest to his face. "Did you just block the wind?"

He jerked a shoulder. "I'm a defenseman."

"Uh-huh." She continued to regard him thoughtfully with those incredible lips pressed together. "I grew up in a noisy house. I think that's why marine biology appealed to me."

Thank God they were off the topic of him defending her

against the elements. Could he be any more obvious that he was crazy about her? "I don't really see how one corresponds to the other."

Tallulah looked out over the surface of the pond. "My parents love each other, but their mode of communication is bickering at the top of their lungs. My sister was always playing loud music. Like, I developed a spot-on impression of DJ Khaled, because he was just constantly dropping intros in our home. The house was just loud. So freaking loud.

"But in fourth grade, I took a field trip to the zoo. I wandered off from the rest of the class and ended up in the winter animal section of the park. There was one of those underground walkways that allowed me to see underwater as the polar bears swam." She gestured with her hands, as if trying to portray the shape of the structure. "On the other side were the penguins, diving in and zooming by like little torpedoes. And it was so quiet. It was like that comfortable muffled sound when you go underwater in the bath, you know? Just a glacial hush. I always associated the cold with quiet after that. I wanted to be in the cold quiet."

Burgess had asked the question with the intention of learning more about what made this woman tick, but he hadn't expected to relate so hard. "I get that. Feeling more comfortable in the cold. I have that, too."

"Oh. Yeah. I can see that." A dimple appeared in her cheek. "This might be the first and last time I've ever had something in common with an athlete."

"It can't be the only thing we have in common."

"Should we find out?"

He gave a firm nod.

She hummed. "I like trying new things."

"I don't."

"I like making new friends."

"Hard pass."

"I could dance for hours."

"Pure torture."

Her laugh echoed over the surface of the pond, in direct contradiction to Burgess's wince. "Still not getting along with the rookies, I assume?"

"Actually," he drew out, relieved to have a reason to interrupt the list of things that made them incompatible. "I let the rookies talk to me at practice recently."

"You *let* them talk to you?"

"Correct. I asked them for their thoughts on our strategy against the team we're playing opening night and . . ." He shrugged, gave his beard a scratch. "Their opinions weren't as piss-poor as I was expecting."

After a short pause, she tilted her head. "Did you so graciously allow them to converse with you . . . because of what I said?"

He made a gruff sound that served as affirmation. "I guess you could say I'm a good listener. Do we have that in common?"

"I suppose . . ."

"I'm good at working on teams. How about that?"

"Yes, that, too."

"We're getting somewhere. Now if you'd just do something about your terrible choice in smoothies, we'd have three things."

Making Tallulah laugh was like taking a shower in sunshine. It just rained down in the form of warmth at the top of his head, coating him down to his toes. The sound and sight was already perfect, yet somehow she made the moment exponentially better by reaching out and giving him a shoulder shove. His hand moved involuntarily, catching her wrist, which she wasn't expecting—and it did something to her balance. She faltered and tried to right herself, but ended up stepping on the embankment leading down to the pond.

Burgess saved her from taking a swim in the nick of time, hooking an arm around her waist and catching her up against his body, where she landed hard, her breath puffing out on a startled exhale. And he felt her everywhere. *Everywhere.* The bare thighs that pressed to his longer, denim-clad ones, her tits flattening against that region below his pecs.

Their mouths were close enough to trade breath, his coming faster by the second, because goddamn, she fit him like a glove. One single bat of her eyelashes and he'd ask her to wrap those thighs around his waist. Just to hold her like that, bear her weight, feel her from above.

It was his fault the spell was broken.

He made a hungry sound in his throat and crushed her closer—

But that telling noise seemed to snap her out of her apparent trance and she wiggled out of his hold, pushing a handful of fingers through her hair and letting out a gulping laugh. "Sorry." She struggled through a breath and he curled his fingers into fists to keep from reaching for her again. "But, um . . . see? You're better at small talk than you think."

"Maybe I'm just good at it with you."

Color spread up her neck in that way he pictured in his sleep. "You'll never know unless you try it with other people, though, right?"

A chorus of alarm bells rang in the back of his head. "Is that so?"

She squared her shoulders, but he could tell from her expression that she was confused about something. Maybe by her reaction to him? Still, she said, "Yes." Those bells clanging in the back of Burgess's head grew even louder when Tallulah's gaze flickered at the crowd of people just beyond his shoulder. "That's why I thought it would be fun to bring you to a singles mixer."

Fuck my life.

CHAPTER FOURTEEN

All right, so taking the man she was lusting after to a singles mixer could probably be categorized as self-sabotage, but there was no turning back now. She'd heard about the "young professionals meet-up" (code for *find a gainfully employed hookup that doesn't have roommates*) from some of her classmates this morning. She'd sort of mentally laughed it off as nightmare fodder and gone back to taking lecture notes. Then Burgess texted and his name popping up on her phone made goose bumps spread down her arms, her pulse ticking in triple time . . . and she'd blindly tapped out the invitation, acting purely on her survival instinct.

Well, as they neared the group of young people dressed in varieties of business casual, she found herself panicking, trying to pinpoint which one would be Burgess's type and gulping heavily over the imminent handoff to somebody else. Because no doubt about it, Burgess was going to be all *their* type. Heads were already turning, elbows digging into rib cages, lemonade being swigged so the paper cups could be discarded, thus freeing up two hands with which to wrestle her boss into their possession.

"Wow, you're already causing quite a stir."

"Great," he said, flatly.

"*Isn't it?*" she agreed with a high-pitched laugh.

"What exactly am I supposed to do here, Tallulah?"

"Just get used to mingling with women again, you know? You might not be interested in anyone here and that's okay. *Totally* okay. But at the very least, you'll get some practice."

He grunted. "I don't want any fucking lemonade."

"Do you hate all the good drinks?"

"There's no need for anything but water."

"When you're making small talk, don't open with that."

He stopped walking suddenly, eyebrows slashing together. "Hold on. What are you going to do while I'm practice mingling?" His voice dropped. "You're not mingling, too."

"Nope. I'm just here to be your wing woman."

Burgess eyeballed the group over the top of her head, a tick beginning in his cheek. "What if one of them wants to mingle with you?"

"I'll give clipped responses and a tight-lipped smile to deter them."

"That can't be foolproof."

"It is." She gave him a tight-lipped smile.

He shivered. "Jesus. You're right. That's cold."

"Pray you're never on the receiving end." She hooked their elbows together and dragged him forward. "Now, stop stalling. It's going to be educational. We can identify what you need to work on."

"If you talk to any of these guys, we're leaving."

The pulse in her neck went utterly bananas. "That's not helpful."

"I don't care."

Every single person at the mixer was facing them now, watching as they approached, half of them frozen in shock, the other half verging closer to fascination. "Hi, everyone! Sorry we're late." She extended a hand toward the person wearing an Organizer badge, smiling as they shook. "I'm Tallulah. This is my friend, Burgess."

"I knew that was him," someone whispered.

"Sir Savage," growled one of the men, pounding a fist to his pink pinstriped chest.

Burgess beat his own chest once without missing a beat. "How's it going?"

Pink Pinstripes stepped forward, apparently taking the role as group spokesman. "Are you really here for this singles mixer?"

"It's a Young Professionals Meetup," droned the Organizer.

"Sure, dude." Pinstripes sent the group a smirk. "My question is, what is Sir Savage doing here?"

"I'm asking myself the same question," Burgess said.

"You're an NHL legend. Can't you just date whoever you want?"

Burgess frowned at Tallulah. "Apparently not."

"As you were, everyone," Tallulah said quickly, praying her cheeks weren't as red as they felt. "Just pretend he's a regular Joe, okay?"

"Do you want a lemonade?" asked the Organizer.

"*No*," Burgess shouted.

"He hates joy in all forms," Tallulah explained in a whisper.

A young woman in a blue wrap dress slipped in front of Burgess with her hand out and Tallulah watched in slow motion, stomach gurgling, as Burgess raised his paw and grasped the offered hand, spreading a smile across the lady's face. "Hi, I'm Jeanine."

"Nice to meet you, Jeanine."

Tallulah realized her arm was still linked with Burgess's and tried to slip free, but he trapped her without so much as a blink. Jeanine watched the action with a bemused smile . . . that was mirrored by the other two women—Samara and Annie—who joined their small offshoot group. Burgess shook all their hands with the enthusiasm of a man meeting the Grim Reaper.

"So how do you two know each other?" Annie asked, gesturing with her lemonade.

Tallulah nudged Burgess to answer, in the interest of him taking the conversational center stage. Her throat wasn't shrinking to the size of a swizzle stick *at all*.

"She's my daughter's au pair," Burgess said, finally.

"Wow." Annie drew out the word, exchanging knowing glances with Samara and Jeanine. "Interesting."

Burgess made a gruff sound. "You could say that."

"It's a little unusual for a man to be such good friends with his au pair, isn't it?" Samara asked, her mouth on the rim of her lemonade cup. "Accompanying you on something of a romantic outing . . . ?"

The Organizer cleared his throat. "The object is to make professional connections—"

"Bro." This, from Pinstripes. "Stop trying to make fetch happen."

Burgess tilted his head at Tallulah, obviously waiting for her response to Samara's question. Did he look a bit too interested in her answer? And why was everyone standing so *close* to Burgess? A few more inches and all three women were going to attach like barnacles to the underside of a boat. "He's a single father and a professional hockey player, as you know. And, well . . . when one has no time for dating, they might be tempted to give up altogether, but he's only thirty-seven and has so much to offer—"

"Like that wicked body check," roared Pinstripes, fist to the sky. "You saw what he did to that fucker from the Pittsburgh Huskies—splintered his schnoz. Do *not* cross Sir Savage. Do not even—"

"That fucker from the Huskies is fine," Burgess interrupted roughly, squeezing Tallulah's arm tighter to his rib cage. "*We're* fine. I sent him two six packs."

Tallulah glanced up at him sharply. "Two?"

He shifted right to left, no longer looking at her. "After our conversation, I might have . . . sent him another one."

The swizzle stick that was her throat was almost completely sealed up now. "Was it Sam Adams again?"

"No, it was Yuengling. Brewed in Pennsylvania. I'm sure he's telling everyone I've gone soft. I hope you're happy."

"I am," she breathed, pressing her cheek to his shoulder. "That was so sweet of you. Were you even going to tell me you did that?"

"No. And don't ever expect me to do it again."

Tallulah beamed up at Burgess. He grunted and brushed a finger against her nose.

His eyes are so beautiful. And is his beard extra full looking today?

Everyone around them had gone very silent.

How long had she been staring at her boss, who she was supposed to be reintroducing to the dating scene? With a nervous laugh, Tallulah removed her cheek from his brawny shoulder. "As I was saying, Burgess has so much to offer—"

"Pardon my frankness, but . . ." Annie started, one eye squinted. "Is there anything going on between you two?"

"No," Tallulah said, empathically. "For one, he's my boss. And two, we're *very* different."

Jeanine wagged a finger between Tallulah and Burgess. "So, just to be clear, nothing has ever *happened* here?"

"Define happened," Burgess said, appearing to be enjoying himself.

Because of the attention he was getting from the women?

Why did that possibility make her sweat? This had been *her* idea.

"Has anything happened . . . physically," Samara supplied.

"That's a little forward!" Tallulah laughed/winced.

"She gives me back massages," Burgess said, downright jovial now. "Does that count?"

Tallulah pinched his elbow, frowning when he only grinned at her. "You're supposed to be making small talk," she whispered, before zipping her attention back to the trio of women, which had now expanded to . . . everyone at the mixer. Roughly a dozen. "Just a friendly massage. Totally innocent."

He looked up at the sky, lips pursed. "There was also that time we made out in front of the club. You remember that night, don't you, Tallulah? It was a measly two weeks ago."

"I was trying to shake off some unwanted attention from another guy," Tallulah explained, fire climbing her face. "Burgess was just helping me out."

"I'd be happy to help you out next time," laughed Pinstripes.

Burgess's head turned so slowly, time seemed to be moving backward. Birds flew overhead, children laughed and cried on the playground, cars honked, the earth rotated around the sun, and *still* he was in the process of turning his head. "What do you mean by that, buddy?" Burgess asked, his tone dripping with malice.

Only, the way he said "buddy" sounded more like "future corpse."

Pinstripes looked like he was choking on a human arm. "Ah, Jesus, I don't know why I said that. I don't know why I say anything. That's why I'm single, I guess." He scrubbed at the back of his neck. "I'm sorry, Sir Savage."

A muscle popped in his jaw. "Why? You didn't imply you'd like to make out with *me*."

"You're right." He looked at Tallulah, hands clasped in prayer. "I'm sorry, ma'am."

"Please. It's *fine*," Tallulah laughed, wanting to defuse the situation. "It's fine."

"But going back to what we were discussing . . ." Annie and Samara were elbowing each other. "There's nothing going on between you?"

"You're just a rich, eligible, attractive man living with his hot au pair, getting back rubs and occasionally making out with her." This from Annie. "As friends."

Burgess looked at Tallulah with mock thoughtfulness. "It does sound a little suspicious when you put it all together like that," Burgess mused happily.

"Okay. Well, this has been nice—" Tallulah started.

"I'm still willing to give him my number," piped up a woman in back.

"Me too." Samara wiped an imaginary tear. "It's slim pickings out here."

Annie stuck out a business card, followed by three more business cards being stacked on top. "Call me if this"—air quotes—"'friendship' doesn't work out."

Burgess smiled at Tallulah while the colorful rectangles were piled into his palm.

Tallulah watched them grow in number with a spike in her throat.

"Are we done here?" Burgess asked, voice low.

"Yes," Tallulah said, weakly.

"Goodbye to everyone except that guy," Burgess called, hitting Pinstripes with one final glare, before turning Tallulah around and escorting her back the way they'd come. When they reached the path that would lead them to the exit, however, he steered her around the pond and she went, incapable of gathering the wherewithal to separate from the rich, eligible, attractive man who was filling her with a whole lot of confusing emotions. Every one of those phone numbers was like a kebab skewer to the jugular.

"Well." He nudged her gently in the ribs. "How'd I do?"

"Great," she said, trying to sound upbeat. "You were just yourself. No pretenses. Which is . . . which is good, because, you know, you want people to like you for *you*—"

"Tallulah."

"Yes?"

"Look at me."

She stopped walking.

Burgess stared her right in the eye while ripping the stack of business cards in half and holding them up, letting the wind take them in eighty directions. "We clear?"

"Oh," she whispered, feeling suddenly and dizzyingly light. "I don't know—"

"The only woman I'm calling is you."

The world just kind of doused itself in lavender. "For au pair reasons. And because I'm your friend."

He cupped the back of her skull, bringing her forward to kiss her forehead. "Whatever you say, gorgeous." Her eyelashes fluttered when his lips lingered at her hairline. "You got more classes today?"

"Yes. This whole week is going to be busy. Homework, Lissa . . ." There went the daylight. Her eyes were now closed completely. "And Saturday afternoon, I have the first session of my study group. I figured the timing worked because Lissa is with her mom. But after that, I don't have plans . . ."

"Maybe we need to change that." Burgess's arm crowded her in tight to his body, so he could speak beside her ear. "Until then, who is the only man you'll call if you need a ride? If you need any damn thing this week?"

"You."

His exhale bathed her ear. "Exactly."

Oh. Wow. Tallulah's eyes were open again, but she was seeing double. "Huh."

A chuckle was his response to her puffed monosyllable, but he got serious pretty fast. "Are you getting closer to letting me spend time with you? Just us?"

"Yes," she whispered, almost to herself. "I think I am."

"Time for skinny dipping, Tallulah." Another press of his lips, accompanied by a rumble in his chest. "Don't you think?"

"It's supposed to be unseasonably warm this weekend," she murmured, sounding dazed.

His mouth grazed her ear. "Can't wait."

Burgess progressively released her, giving her a long final once-over before turning and striding from the park, his gait more purposeful and cocky than usual, if she wasn't mistaken. Were those new jeans or did his butt just look incredible in every pair he owned? Tallulah didn't realize she watched him go the entire way to the exit, until he vanished around the brick pillar.

She tore her eyes from the spot where Burgess had once been, furiously smoothing her hair to distract from the wild, winged butterflies besieging her middle. Her hopes that no one had witnessed her starry-eyed booty appreciation were dashed when she glanced over at the Young Professionals Meetup . . . and they were all grinning back at her, some of them even saluting her with empty lemonade glasses.

Wonderful.

She clearly hadn't sold them on her and Burgess being just friends.

And she was beginning to wonder if she'd even sold herself.

CHAPTER FIFTEEN

Burgess handed Lissa's overnight bag to Ashleigh the follow-ing Saturday morning, trading a grimace with his ex-wife as Lissa climbed into the passenger side of the car and immediately cranked Raskulls at full volume.

"Is it too late to write into the custody agreement that you're required to bring Lissa to her first Raskulls concert?" she asked, pretending to cry.

"Yes," he said, emphatically.

She laughed, the sound fading as she gave him a considering look. "Maybe you can sucker your au pair into earning some overtime," she suggested primly. "According to Lissa, she's young enough to enjoy Raskulls."

Burgess grunted at the reminder that Tallulah was on his pay-roll. And young.

Especially considering he planned to take her skinny dipping tonight.

He also knew his ex-wife well enough to know she was fish-ing. "Is there something you want to ask me?"

"Who, *me*? No." She pursed her lips. "Does she stay here on the weekends, too?"

"Yeah, Ashleigh. She does. This is where she lives." *Thank God.* "Obviously, she doesn't move out every weekend."

Her nod was exaggerated. "Of *course* not."

Burgess sighed. He liked his ex. He did. She was a great mother. She'd been supportive of him when his hockey career had yet to take off. They had a good enough relationship to make co-parenting work for Lissa's sake, but he didn't like the passive-aggressive game she seemed to be playing with him this morning. It wasn't typical of her, though, so he was going to let it roll off his back. "You want me to pick Lissa up Sunday night or will you drop her off?"

"I'll drop her off." She pried open the driver's side door, winking at him before she ducked inside the car. "Enjoy your plans. Whoever they might be."

Burgess frowned as the car drove away from the curb, waving at Lissa through the rear windshield until they turned the corner. During their marriage, there had been times while he'd been on the road for weeks at a time that Ashleigh had gotten understandably insecure, though she never asked him outright if he was being faithful. If she'd asked, he would have told her the truth—he never strayed. But she'd just kind of . . . *poked* at the possibility. A lot like she'd done just now. There was no way Ashleigh was jealous of Tallulah, though, right? She'd never even met Tallulah. Her wedding was set to take place next year and Burgess was *invited*.

The undercurrent of jealousy had to be his imagination.

On his way back into the building, Burgess happened to glance toward the top floor window and caught the wooden blinds swinging back into place. In the window that belonged to Tallulah's bedroom. Had she been watching the exchange between him and Ashleigh?

Deep in thought, Burgess took the elevator back up to the penthouse floor and strode the short distance to his door, which he'd left unlocked, knowing that bringing Lissa down to her mother would only take a few minutes. Inside, the living room and kitchen were empty. He had practice in an hour and he needed to get his gear together, but despite the time crunch, Burgess found himself in front of Tallulah's bedroom door.

Was it locked? He wondered, but he wouldn't test the knob. She'd have to let him in.

He rapped a knuckle against the wood.

Two seconds ticked by, followed by a creak of the bed and some muffled footsteps. The door opened to reveal Tallulah in tank top and rolled-up shorts, her hair in a haphazard knot on the top of her head. No bra. Fuck. He should have just gone to practice. That way he could have worked off some energy before seeing her tonight. Right now, he was fully charged, more than capable of picking her up, throwing her on the bed where her study materials were spread out, and licking the orange and basil scent off every inch of her skin.

"Hey," he rumbled.

"Hey," she echoed brightly. Too brightly.

Burgess propped a forearm on the top of the doorjamb, pleased to see her attention zip over to his right bicep. "Did I see you watching from the window?"

"What?" She sounded dazed. "Oh, I was just . . . making sure Lissa got into the car okay."

"Were you worried I'd put her into the wrong car?"

"No." Laughing, she slapped him on the left shoulder. "That would be silly!"

"I agree." He tucked his tongue into the inside of his cheek. "So why were you *actually* watching?"

Tallulah seemed to be deciding whether or not to keep up the pretense, finally deciding against it, letting the ruse drop and rolling her eyes. "It's natural to be curious about my . . . friend's ex. Totally normal."

"Okay."

"Don't say 'okay' like that," she complained adorably, crossing her arms and dropping one of those sexy hips. "Why else would I be watching?"

"I don't know. I guess I want to know how you feel about the fact that I've been married before. That my ex still comes around. I, Burgess, want to know what you think, Tallulah."

"Why?" she whispered.

"Because you're in my life. In whatever capacity you decide, you're in it." He blew out a breath. "And fuck, I would pay a million dollars to get inside of your head. That's why."

She threw a quick glance at the window, as if remembering what she'd seen. "I think . . ."

When she didn't continue, he dropped his hand from the door, but remained on the threshold. "Can I come in?"

Face beginning to flush, she nodded. "Yes."

The satisfaction of being trusted by this woman made him feel like he had a hundred medals pinned to his chest. "Thank you." He kept walking until the backs of her legs met the bed, bringing his face down to hers, so he could study her every blink, every breath. "You think what?"

"I think . . . no, I know that Lissa is holding out hope you'll reconcile. She told me."

"Jesus." Burgess hadn't seen that coming. Had they missed having an important conversation with her? If so, they needed to remedy that as soon as possible. "I don't need to tell you that's never going to happen, do I?"

Tallulah hummed.

"What does that sound mean?" he growled.

"It's just a sound."

"No, it's not."

"Is."

"Dammit, Tallulah."

"I think I wouldn't like it if you got back together!" The force of her outburst knocked her into a sitting position on the bed, putting her face level with his stomach, head tipped back so they could maintain eye contact. "Okay?"

"Because you might be out of a job?" He framed her jaw in his hand, brushing his thumb slowly down her cheekbone, dragging along her full bottom lip. And then going on instinct, he pushed his thumb into her mouth, a sound breaking off in his throat when she let him. She let him press that thumb all the way in, her pupils expanding until her eyes were darker than usual, her fingers twisting slowly on the comforter. "Or is there another reason you wouldn't want me back with someone else?" he rasped, drawing the digit back out, rubbing spit on her beautiful lips and leaving them shiny. Slowly pressing it back in. Deep. "Suck on it if the answer is yes."

A beat passed.

And then she drew on it hard, cheeks hollowing, dragging a moan from the deepest recesses of his body, the sound growing stuttered when the suction increased, more, more.

Tallulah let go of the bedding and flattened her palms on his stomach, observing her hands move in fascination, as if they had a mind of their own. Meanwhile, Burgess watched her with his lungs seized, waiting on her next action. Reeling from the very fact that she was touching him. Making admissions. Thank God he'd knocked on the fucking door.

When she lifted the cotton material of his white T-shirt, let his thumb leave her mouth in a wet slide, and pressed her moist lips to his bare stomach, her breath warming his happy trail, Burgess shuddered, his balls turning the weight of brass. His cock was hard as a motherfucker, obviously, tenting the front of his sweatpants, just hoping for a stroke. And his vocal cords were rubbed raw by his groan when she laved her tongue against his exposed skin, before moving in a southwest journey over the ridge of his dick, licking him root to tip through the garment.

Disbelief gave way to pure awe and his every brain cell went sideways over a cliff.

"I don't think there is a woman alive who wouldn't give this up and miss it from time to time." Another torturous lap of his bulge, her hand coming up to grip his root, hold him steady while she sucked him through the sweatpants, setting his mind on fucking fire. "Or more likely . . . all the time. Every." Lick. "Single." A gentle bite that made him roar behind clenched teeth. "Night."

Was this happening?

This was happening.

"You want my cock, Tallulah?" he panted. "Fuck practice. I'll keep my hips bucking for the next thirty-six hours. But you better be sure."

"Be sure about what?" she breathed, suctioning his tip through the cotton.

It took him a moment to answer because he was moaning for God. "Me."

Panic zigzagged across her face. "Sure how?"

Knowing he was about to take a huge risk, Burgess nonetheless knelt down in front of her, his mouth slanting over hers before his knees even hit the floor, the kiss tumultuous and frantic as he leaned over her pliant body, his fingers plowing into her hair and upsetting her bun. "I'm not doing this with no strings attached," he said, before taking her mouth in another ferocious kiss, his forearm scooting her ass to the edge of the bed so he could feel her ultrasoft inner thighs slide along his rib cage, her pussy warm against his chest. *God, so perfect.* Worth the risk of asking for too much? A million percent, yes. "I *want* to get attached, Tallulah," he said on top of her mouth. "Nah, I'm already more than a little obsessed with you, aren't I? You start babbling my name while I spoon-feed you orgasms, I *will* get attached. Happily. Just like I'll happily knock out anyone else who tries. Be. Sure."

Face full of conflict, she kneaded the muscles of his chest, as if deciding whether to push him away or draw him down on top of her. "I'm not sure," she whispered in a burst.

Frustration clawed at Burgess, but he kept it to himself, as much as he could. Dropping his head forward, he breathed in through his nose, out through his mouth, forcing himself to remove his hands from Tallulah's spread thighs. This was pain. Knowing she'd welcome a good, hard fuck. He could probably flip her over, pull down her shorts and panties to get access to her pussy. Eat it out until she'd come, then hammer her tight body from the back.

God. Was Burgess foolish to make demands on her, instead? He was *definitely* out of his mind to stop when she was so worked up, nipples stiff against the front of her tank top.

Ready. Willing. Flushed and beautiful and his. That was the problem; something inside of Burgess had been chanting *mine*. *Mine. Mine.* Since the first day they'd met. He couldn't do casual. And he wouldn't pretend to, either, because it did them both a disservice.

He rolled their foreheads together. "I'm too old to play games, Tallulah."

"I'm not," she murmured, still breathing hard.

"I know." He licked into her mouth, enjoying the sound of her breath catching, the way her neck lost power after one stroke of his tongue, how she kissed him back like she couldn't help it. "For now, I take you to watch the Red Sox. Take you skinny dipping. Whatever else you want to do. And you keep getting to know me and see if you want strings, too."

"I—I'm warning you," she stuttered. "I . . . won't."

"Okay."

"Don't say okay like that. Like you're skeptical." She turned solemn, looking him in the eye. "It's not just the fact that I'm learning to be . . . unencumbered again. It's just going to take me a long time before I stop worrying that there's a different person lurking under everyone's surface. I might never shake the fear, whether it's rational or not. You could be wasting your time on me."

"Time with you could never be a waste. Only a privilege."

Tallulah closed her eyes and leaned back on both hands, giving him a lust-inducing view of her bare thighs, her braless tits swaying like a taunt. "Speaking of spending time together . . ." She suddenly looked anxious. "I might have to push adventure hour back a little bit."

"Why?"

"I have a meeting."

"A meeting."

"Yes. I have to meet with a classmate, because he's my partner on an assignment. And he's going out of town next week, so we won't get another chance to outline. After that, we can collaborate remotely. But I'm meeting him at a coffee shop later this afternoon."

Burgess tipped her chin up, studying her face and trying to determine why she sounded so anxious. "Sounds normal. What's the problem?"

"My partner is the geek from the club who was pushy about splitting a ride."

"Nope," he shouted, protectiveness sinking and twisting in his gut like a freshly sharpened blade. "Fuck that."

"I can't fuck that. And we'll be in public, so there's no reason I should be jumpy."

"But you *are*."

She squeezed her eyes closed. "I hate that I am. It makes me feel pathetic."

"Hey. You are *not* pathetic." She needed more from him. He could see it. So he tried to put himself in her shoes, which was nearly impossible, because he'd never been scared of another human being in his life. He didn't have to be. Why had he never thought about the unfairness of that before? He took his safety for granted. But what if he couldn't? "Tallulah?"

"Yes?"

It took him a moment to locate the right words. "How do you feel about telling this clown that he's making you uncomfortable and he needs to back the fuck off?"

She hissed a breath. "Oh, I don't know. I'd rather just get through it."

"Is getting through it working?" When she only blinked at him, he searched for a different tactic. "When someone encroaches on my territory on the ice, I let them know it's not okay. And I guess it's . . . I never thought about it, because it's just my job, but I guess it's empowering. To demand somebody backs off. You have that right, too."

"I know I do. But enacting it is harder."

He got that. "What if I'm there?"

Twin lights went on in her eyes. "You're going to come on my study date with me?"

"Hold up. Why are you suddenly calling it a date? It was a fucking meeting before."

"Fine. Meeting. Sheesh." She searched his face, her chest dipping deeply, before rising. "You'll really be there?"

"I'm your bodyguard, aren't I?" He dropped a reassuring kiss onto her mouth. "And you won't always need one."

She puffed a humorless laugh. "Are you sure about that?"

"Positive."

They looked at each other for long moments. The sound of traffic hummed outside the window, the ceiling fan whirred, and they just sort of melted together, chests meeting as his mouth worked hers from above, the kiss wet and breathless, boundary-less, her palms moving over his pecs and shoulders like a sculptor. Need accelerated into pain and his tongue went particularly deep, Burgess tasting her hungry whimper, her hips beginning to rock restlessly on the edge of the bed—and he knew they had to stop. Because this was so much more than lust, as potent as it was. He was kissing her to comfort her, reassure her, bolster her courage . . . because he fucking liked her. A lot.

So he was trying to allow his heart and gut to make the decisions here. Not his dick.

He broke off with a curse, their panting breaths colliding. Could he realistically resist this woman who drew him in in ways he didn't know were possible?

"Text me the place and time," he said hoarsely, standing up and leaving the room, before his control deserted him completely. Thank God he'd have ample opportunity to blow off some steam before he saw her again. But even as the thought formed, he knew no amount of time would ever be enough. Could he convince her to take a chance on him before the steam finally blew his top off and he gave in?

CHAPTER SIXTEEN

To be fair, Burgess tried to be inconspicuous. He really did.

Tallulah was sitting across from Finn in the coffee shop, their notes spread out between them on the table, when her legendary boss walked in—and the air was promptly sucked out of the establishment.

"Holy fucking shit, that's Sir Savage," someone blurted at the table beside her.

Phones came out immediately and started snapping pictures of Burgess where he'd hunkered down in a booth, baseball cap pulled down low over his eyes. He'd chosen a spot in her line of vision, but not so close that he was hovering.

Gratitude pooled in her belly immediately, the glands in her throat starting to ache from the force of her gladness to see him. To have an ally. One who believed in her, even though she didn't quite believe in herself yet or her ability to simply live normally again. But she'd had the day to think about what he'd said while kneeling in front of her in the bedroom with an erection the size of a tree trunk . . . and he was right. She needed to stop hiding and empower herself. If she was going to start being present in her own life again, she would encounter ugliness along the way, because ugly happened.

But how she handled it this time would determine how she handled it in the future.

Maybe she wouldn't even have to put Finn in his place. Maybe he'd gotten the message when he'd seen her kissing Burgess outside of Down.

No matter what happened, though, Burgess would be there.

And you won't always need me.

That was the part of his speech this morning that hit her the hardest. Burgess liked playing protector. Yet he still wanted to help Tallulah stand on her own two feet again. That said a lot about his character.

Dammit. Dammit, she liked him. On top of wanting to roll around beneath him naked.

Not enough to be his girlfriend, though. Or anyone's girlfriend.

Right?

Tallulah absorbed some reassuring eye contact from Burgess and took a deep breath, focusing on the outline they were making. The Bostonians in the coffee shop were trying to play it cool about Sir Savage being in their midst, but the buzz around the room was growing and a couple of kids had run over for autographs, the hubbub finally drawing Finn's attention, his shaggy brown head popping up from its tilt over the notebook.

"Did I miss something?" He started to twist in his seat. "What's going on—"

"We should keep going," Tallulah said quickly. "The role acoustic signals play in the courtship of fish. Riveting stuff, right?"

"Yes, but do acoustic signals increase the likelihood of reproductive success . . ." he muttered. "I think we should split this up. You analyze the acoustic playback experiments linked in the article. I'll . . ."

Someone stopped right in front of their table, holding up their phone and filming, a dazed smile frozen on their face.

"Seriously," Finn said, casting a look over his shoulder. Thankfully, a crowd was forming and no matter how he craned his neck, he couldn't see through them to Burgess. "What is the fuss about?"

"For me? The fuss is about sound variability," Tallulah laughed, unearthing a paper from the stack and flapping it in the air. "I'll take it. Should be an easy enough collaboration."

"Uh, yes." Still distracted, he faced her again regardless, seeming to realize their meeting was coming to an end. "Although, I would have loved to meet one more time, at least." He settled a hand on the back of her chair while flipping the pages of his notebook with the opposite hand, as if the move was absentminded and she wouldn't notice. "Maybe when I get back from my trip, we can meet up again."

Her stomach filled with weight. "If it's necessary to the assignment."

Finn looked up, shrugged, that impish smile playing around his mouth. "Or just for fun."

Tallulah opened her mouth to remind Finn she had a boyfriend. But . . . she didn't *want* to lie. She shouldn't have to lie or make an excuse not to be interested. She was allowed to simply not be interested and didn't owe him an explanation about it. Her fear stemmed from how he would react if she turned him down. Would he cease to be this mild-mannered guy? Would his features become unrecognizable, all pretenses out the window?

Her chest started to tighten.

"Although, I guess I should be afraid of your big jock boyfriend coming to beat me up, shouldn't I?" Finn snickered. "Tisha mentioned you're working as an au pair for one of the Bearcats. Is that who I saw you kissing outside of Down?"

Heat scaled the back of her neck . . . and with it, a dose of irritation. Something about his condescension when speaking about Burgess was weakening her fear. "I'm not sure this conversation is appropriate. We're here to talk about the assignment."

"Right." He flipped the notebook page more forcefully than necessary. "You need to run home to your Neanderthal."

Indignation turned her spine to steel.

It clogged into her throat and made her eyes sting.

Curious that it should be an insult leveled at someone she cared about that would finally bring back her bravery, but she wasn't going to question it. Not when it felt so good.

"Listen, motherfucker," she growled, turning and slapping his hand off the back of her chair. "If you say another negative word about Burgess I will snap your designer glasses in half. Maybe I *do* want to go home to him. Mainly to get away from you. I've made it clear I'm not interested—if you're too dense to notice, I think that makes you the Neanderthal. If you *did* notice, you're something way worse." This worm had the nerve to insult Burgess? When he made her so uncomfortable, she was sitting there in a cold sweat? "Say one more thing about him, I dare you. Or ask me out again when I already said no. Those glasses are DOA."

Finn stared at her in openmouthed shock for several seconds, before beginning to gather his things. And she was pleased to see he was the one sweating now.

"I'll take an apology, too, before you go."

"Sorry."

"One for Burgess, too."

"Sorry."

"Uh-huh."

Tallulah had to cross her arms to prevent herself from snatching the glasses off his face. If only to celebrate the fact that she could. She wasn't arrogant enough to believe she'd fully cured herself of the trauma and fear. She'd made a big stride today, though. If Lara could see her, would she be proud? Tallulah desperately hoped so. In that moment, however, there was one person she wanted to share her triumph with, and he was sitting in the rear booth of the coffee shop, probably restraining himself from intervening.

Tallulah kept a cautious eye on Finn as he got up and scrambled out of the coffee shop, just in case, but once he'd vanished out the front door, Tallulah stood up on shaky legs. She left all her things on the table and wove through customers toward the back booth, only to find that Burgess was already standing, too, watching her with tension bracketing his features. She wasn't sure what compelled her to break into a jog, only that she wanted to be in those strong arms as quickly as possible—and he was already opening them for her.

She ran, jumped, and was enfolded in the warmest, safest hug of all time.

All she had to do was dangle there, surrounded in strength.

People were taking pictures and she didn't care. Let them.

"Are you okay, Tallulah?" He clutched her to his body like a giant holding a stuffed bear, his rib cage dipping and expanding on heavy breaths. "Did he—"

"Yes. He did. So I called him a motherfucker and threatened to break his glasses."

Slowly, a rumble started to spread in Burgess's chest, his arms squeezing her even closer, his lips pressing to her hairline. "That's my girl."

CHAPTER SEVENTEEN

Burgess couldn't stop staring at Tallulah.

She'd already had a lively sparkle in her eye, but after what happened in the coffee shop, he could see that spark had always been slightly subdued. Until now. They stood on the rooftop of a building that overlooked Fenway, the famous Citgo sign buzzing fifty yards over their heads, and she was brighter than any star in the sky. More brilliant than the nighttime lights illuminating the field. She put the Citgo sign to shame. She fucking glowed.

Remaining seated in that coffee shop booth had nearly killed him. At one point, he'd been positive his hand was going to rip a chunk out of the Formica table. Especially when that slimeball touched the back of her chair and leaned in. Every instinct inside of Burgess screamed for him to go rampaging through the establishment, flipping tables as he went, roaring for the geek to back up off his girl, but thank God, he'd controlled himself. Stayed put, even though his ribs felt as though they were being crushed by a boulder.

Tallulah had overcome something.

And he could see she was better for it. Proud of herself.

Still hopped up on adrenaline, too, which made her very flirtatious—and Burgess wasn't mad at that. Quite the opposite, actually. He loved how comfortable she'd grown touching him, almost like it came as second nature since hugging him in the coffee shop.

At the moment, she was leaning back against his chest watching the sliver of Fenway they could see from their vantage point on the roof, the crown of her head tucked beneath his chin. She'd tuned in to the live feed of the Red Sox game on her phone, so the sound of the announcer's voice mingled with the cool night breeze.

Tallulah's resulting shiver had Burgess wrapping his arms around her, resting them just beneath her collarbone, letting out a breath when she didn't protest, relaxing against him even more. Enough to rest the back of her head on his chest.

God. He didn't want to be anywhere else in the world.

There was a cracking sound, followed by the announcer's excited voice. The distant roar of the crowd. Tallulah smiled up at him. "I think they've got this one in the bag."

Having this woman smile up at him was almost too much, so his response was preceded by a lot of gruff sounds. "You know, I could have gotten us tickets to the actual game."

"No way, this is so much better," she murmured.

Burgess had to agree wholeheartedly. Even if he'd gotten them seats in one of the air-conditioned boxes, there would have been other people around. And honestly, fuck other people right now, he just needed this one.

"What are you thinking about?" he asked her, pressing his lips to her hair.

She made a soft sound and snuggled back against him, steeping him in oranges and basil and contentment. "I was thinking about the stir you created in the coffee shop. You're kind of a big deal around here. In Boston. But you haven't always been here, right? Where's home?"

The fact that she wanted to know more about him had to be a good sign, right? His pulse seemed to think so. "Syracuse. New York. My mother retired from her position at the university last year. She was a creative writing professor."

"Wow. Is she the one who molded you into a hockey player?"

"No, although I attended and played for Syracuse. She definitely had some influence over that decision." Burgess laughed quietly. "But when I was young, she didn't know what to make of me. My father was never in the picture, but he must have been a big dude, because my mother barely clears five feet. She's a tea-drinking connoisseur of the arts. Classical music was always playing in the house, book clubs held weekly. But suddenly she's got this six foot tall eleven-year-old asking to try out for the hockey team. So anyway, I kind of had to mold myself into a player, with the help of my coaches." He huffed a laugh. "And thank God for those coaches, because when I hit my teens and started to rebel, they stepped in and helped her out there, too. Surrogate dads."

"You mentioned before that you used to raise hell," she said, squinting up at him thoughtfully. "I'm having a hard time picturing that. What's the worst thing you ever did?"

"Worst or craziest?"

"Oh. Craziest. For sure."

He took in a breath and let it out. "Probably the time I broke the ice at both ends of my local pond and swam underneath from one end to the other. All in one breath. On a dare."

Tallulah gaped up at his chin. "Okay, that is *bone-chilling*."

"I know. Imagining Lissa doing something like that makes me break out in hives." He was silent for a moment. "My mom compensated for my father's absence in so many ways, but sometimes I think all the risks I took were to punish him for not being around. Which is ridiculous. He couldn't have known what I was doing."

A sympathetic spasm took place in her breast. "Not ridiculous. A way of expressing a need. Pain." She rubbed his arm. "That can look so many different ways."

"Yeah. Looking back, I wish I would have appreciated my mom more. How hard she tried to understand hockey. She even brought her book club to a game once. That effort was more than enough. I didn't need anything else."

Her throat squeezed. "Do you visit her? She must love Lissa."

"Lissa is definitely more her speed. We get together at Christmas and they dork out."

Tallulah's throat muscles loosened with a laugh, her body starting to shake with mirth. "What does your mother think about your nickname?"

"She said the alliteration is pleasing."

"Oh yeah. That's definitely a creative writing instructor."

"Through and through."

Tallulah was quiet for a beat. "Does it bother you that you never met your father?"

Burgess rested his chin on her head and thought, briefly. "When I was younger, it did. Yeah. I had no one to watch hockey games with on television in my living room. I'd sit there silently, trying not to interrupt my mom's reading."

"Oh, *that's* where you learned to be the strong, silent type."

"Maybe so. Is that how you've categorized me?"

"You don't have a category," she said tilting her head back to bat her eyelashes at him. "You need two of something to make a category and I doubt there's more than one Burgess."

See?

Flirtatious.

Or was she just being playful so he wouldn't read too much into her words? They carried weight with him, either way. Everything she said and did carried weight. Just this morning, though, she'd told him she didn't want anything serious. For now, he needed to let her feel free to say whatever she wanted to him, touch him however she wanted, without worrying he was going to press the issue of a relationship. That would only cause her to back off and damn, he really didn't want that.

Not when he was holding her in the moonlight, listening to her telling him he was one of a kind.

"There's only one you, too," he said, his right hand sliding down to her hip, massaging it in his hand and watching her lashes flutter. "Are you going to tell me what he said to you in the coffee shop?"

"I don't think I should."

Wires wound slowly around his jugular. "That bad?" he managed.

"Yes."

Burgess was starting to breathe hard, using the hand on Tallulah's hip to pull her closer, protecting her after the fact. Maybe he shouldn't have stayed put in the booth after all. Maybe he should have gone over there and tossed the cretin through the plate glass window. "What did he say? I can handle it."

Tallulah took a deep breath.

Oh God, this was going to be bad.

"He called you a Neanderthal," Tallulah whispered, anger crackling in her voice. "I'd told one of our mutual friends I worked for you and he assumed correctly you were the man I was kissing outside of the club. And he called you . . . that."

The hot magma that had been flowing in his veins, prepared to erupt over a vile insult toward Tallulah, cooled immediately. "Wait, that's it?"

She spun around in his arms. "What do you mean, 'that's it'?"

"I mean, he insulted *me*, not you? That's what pissed you off enough to call him a motherfucker and threaten to break his glasses?"

"Yes!" She scrubbed circles on his chest with her palms. "He doesn't even know you!"

Holy shit, she was really, honest-to-God upset. And . . . was she attempting to soothe him by rubbing his chest? The very possibility made him feel immortal. He usually defended other people, but . . . she'd come to *his* defense? That meant a lot. But number one on his priority list was making her feel better. Immediately. "Tallulah."

"What?"

"Do you have any idea what kind of names I've been called on the road? Hell, I've been called worse by my own teammates."

She blinked up at him. "So?"

He stroked the side of her face. "'Neanderthal' doesn't even rate, gorgeous."

"Oh yeah? Then why did I want to stab him in the throat?"

I'm going to marry this girl someday. "I don't know," he said, winded by the vow he'd just made to himself. "You tell me."

Possibly realizing she'd revealed too much, Tallulah bit her lip and turned back around, allowing him to gather her back against his chest, not even protesting when he started planting kisses on her hairline. She'd found her voice today . . . all because some geek insulted him? What did that mean and why did it make him feel like his chest was disintegrating?

"If someone insulted you," he said, taking a handful of her hair and tugging, looking down into her upturned face. "I would do a lot worse than break their fucking glasses."

"I know," she whispered.

"Good."

He could kiss her right now. She wanted to be kissed. But whatever pandemonium was taking place inside of him all but guaranteed he wouldn't be able to stop—and she wasn't ready to sleep together without a no-strings disclaimer attached. Therefore, even though it pained him, he let go of her hair, allowing them to regroup while the baseball game played out in the distance.

"Whatever caused you to stand up to someone who made you uneasy, Tallulah, I'm proud of you for doing it. I hope you're proud of yourself, too."

"I am . . ." She shifted against him. "I am, but I still have a long way to go. I think I'll know I've overcome what happened when . . ."

"When what?"

"I don't necessarily want to go on adventures alone all the time—I just want to know that I *can*. Without being afraid. Once I'm strong enough for that, I'll call my family. In Istanbul. I'll be able to speak to my sister and know I kept my word."

He couldn't swallow around the goose egg stuck in his throat. "I think that day is closer than you think."

"Yeah. In the meantime, I have the postcards."

"Postcards?"

She nodded, reaching down to unzip the purse that was strapped diagonally on her body, resting against the front of her left hip. After the briefest of hesitations, she removed a ziplock baggie containing a stack of postcards. He could only see the top one, which was an aerial shot of Boston Harbor.

"I've been sending home postcards for four years. On all of my stops. Most of them go to Lara. I tell her I'm having a great time and enjoying myself—and maybe I was, in a way, but . . . I wasn't out trying new things and refusing to be held back by the fear, like I promised her I would. The postcards are kind of a placeholder for what I'd hoped to do eventually. I'm sure she knows that I was stalling. She could always read me."

Being allowed into this person's head would forever be his life's biggest honor. It was a beautiful, complicated place and he couldn't wait to explore it. As much as he could for as long as he was allowed. "Then she also knows you'll keep your promise when you can."

"Thanks," she whispered, nuzzling his shoulder with her nose. They remained that way in the silence, Tallulah wrapped in his arms, the back of her head on his chest, the breeze occasionally traveling along the rooftop to lift her hair, the pounding of his heart drowning out the announcer's voice.

TALLULAH THOUGHT SHE'D be a lot more nervous about skinny dipping, once time for the main event arrived, but as Burgess put the SUV in park approximately fifty yards from Jamaica Pond, a sort of giddiness stole over her. Maybe what had taken place earlier that day had bolstered her confidence or maybe it was the man sitting beside her, stern and unshakable, that allowed her to feel pure excitement, as opposed to concern. Or perhaps it was the thick darkness that allowed only Burgess's headlights to penetrate it and knowing the black sky would cloak her nefarious adventure.

Whatever the reason, she all but threw herself out of the passenger side, almost forgetting to grab the beach towel she'd borrowed from Burgess. Immediately, crickets chirped on all sides of her, the sound mingling with the whispering wind. Night cloaked her.

Excited her.

"Are you sure you don't want to do this with me?"

"You're the thrill seeker, not me. I'm just here for backup."

Tallulah pursed her lips thoughtfully. "I'm not sure if I should be insulted or comforted that you're passing on the chance to see me naked."

Burgess came around the front bumper of the SUV, his hefty frame passing through the beams of his headlights one by one. When he drew closer, she could see his expression, which read something along the lines of *are you being serious right now?* "Tallulah, I'm passing on the chance for you to see *me* naked after a dip in that freezing cold pond."

His meaning dawned on her. "Really? You're missing out because of shrinkage?" She wrapped the towel around her shoulders and tucked the corner in between her breasts, starting to disrobe beneath the barrier. Off came her shoes and sneakers, followed by her skirt and panties—and she couldn't help but notice the way Burgess swallowed what looked like a goose egg, the object getting stuck in his throat as he watched her every move. "You're forgetting I've already met the man downstairs."

"Not the way I'd like you meet him."

Tallulah was grateful for the darkness that hid her blush. "I'm just saying, I already know it's . . . you know."

He sauntered toward her with a raised eyebrow, stopping just inches away. "It's what?"

"Substantial." It took an effort, but she ignored the closeness of his chiseled mouth, wiggling around so she could unsnap her bra, dropping the black demi cup into the pile of clothes forming beneath her. "Is that what you wanted to hear, Sir Savage?"

"Find me a man who doesn't like the word 'substantial' in reference to his junk."

She trapped a laugh. "But?"

"But . . ." He tipped her chin up, rubbed the pad of his thumb in the indent at the center of her bottom lip. "After you meet me down there, you won't be laughing when you talk about it. You'll whisper about my cock like you're in church."

The playfulness of the moment came to a screeching halt. Prickles of awareness carried down her torso, tightening her nipples as they went, sensitizing her thighs and shooting sparks in her nerve endings, her toes digging into the ground, the only things keeping her locked to the earth. Suddenly the cover of night gave permission for a lot more than a single nefarious act. They were alone out there, she was naked, him fully clothed, and he'd let her know his dick would be a turning point in her life. And God, he smelled good, looked good, towering over her, radiating competence and protectiveness, an open invitation in his eyes.

"Maybe you should have a little think while I'm skinny dipping." She walked her fingertips up his chest and gently tugged on his beard. "About your reasons for not sleeping with me. And whether calling yourself my boyfriend is really necessary when you're already getting to do the *most fun* part of being someone's boyfriend."

He tucked his tongue into his cheek, laughing in a way that suggested physical pain. "You make a compelling argument, but it's not going to work."

"Why not?"

"A few reasons. One, you work for me. You're the nanny, Tallulah. It sounds like some ridiculous porn category and nothing about the way I feel about you is ridiculous. Two . . ." He rubbed at the back of his neck. "I guess I want to be important to you. It'll be easier for you to pretend I'm not important once I become the man you're hooking up with. Instead of the man you could . . . maybe fall for someday. When I take you to bed for the first time, I want you looking back at me like you might. Like you could, you know. Fall for me." He cleared his throat extra hard. "And three, I won't relax until I know some punk ass college kid isn't going to come steal you out from under me."

Tallulah stood mostly naked, in a towel that flapped in the cool wind, but she didn't feel a hint of the cold. In fact, she couldn't feel a single thing, save the heart that was absolutely rioting in her rib cage. *I want to be important to you.* Those seven words stood out in a sea of similarly incredible words, bobbing up and down like happy little buoys. Sure, those buoys were surrounded by man-eating sharks, but they still stole her breath. They made her think . . . *what if this man could be the one and I've just met him sooner than I expected?*

Would there be other men who came along and made her feel like this?

It didn't seem likely, but what did she know? She was only finding her legs again.

"I don't know what to say to . . . all of those big and vulnerable things you just said—"

"You don't have to say anything."

"But I know you're already important to me." Whoa, making that admission out loud was like dangling over a ravine with one hand on a loose rock, and yet, his expression, the way his eyes snapped up and his jaw popped, kept her going. She wanted to make him feel the way his honesty had made her feel. Like someone's first choice. "I think I knew you were important a lot earlier than now, I just can't remember when it happened. Second, I think if some punk ass college kid asked me out, I think saying yes to him would feel . . . wrong. Because of how we, you know, carry on. But I can't do anything about us being a porn category."

Burgess looked away, then down at the ground while stroking his chin. When he looked back up at Tallulah, he was fighting a smile. "I guess it's a start."

"Maybe," she whispered. "I'm going to go jump in some freezing cold water now."

"How about you *walk* into some freezing cold water, Tallulah? I'm not going to be happy if you land on a rock and get hurt."

She turned on the ball of her foot, throwing him an inviting look over her shoulder on her way to the pond's edge. "It's not too late to join me," she called. "Forever is composed of nows. Dickinson said that. It's the one time English Lit piqued my interest."

He smirked. "I'll be ready and waiting to warm you back up."

"I thought you just said warming me up was against the rules."

"I meant I'd wrap you up in towel. Like a burrito."

"I bet that's a porn category, too."

His deep chuckle inspired a raw tug between her thighs and

she almost—almost—blew off skinny dipping, so she could turn around, run to Burgess, leap into his arms and agree to be his girlfriend. He'd reward her so well for committing, but her mind and gut weren't fully convinced yet that being someone's girlfriend was the right thing to do at this precarious stage in her life. Her heart was another story, but she'd ignore that traitor for now.

Tallulah stopped a few feet from the water and took a deep breath. She looked back to find Burgess pacing in the headlights of his truck, arms crossed. Wouldn't the man meant to be with her forever . . . want to take these adventures, too? Would he really remain on the shore?

This moment is for you. Be in the moment.

Before she could think too hard about the water temperature, Tallulah set aside the worry for another time and dropped the towel, walking straight into the pond. "Oh. Oh God," she gasped, even as she plowed forward. "Oh God. Oh God. I just have to get my shoulders under. That's when it'll stop feeling like death."

She kept going, focusing on the rush of adrenaline, the shock to her system. Her pulse raced a million miles an hour, a sort of giddiness steeling up the walls of her throat and gluing her back teeth together. She embraced the feeling of freedom and mischief and simply being out in the open, living, breathing the night air and leaving fear to wither on the shore alone.

Fully submerged now, she turned over onto her back and let herself float in the moonlight, imagining herself from above, looking peaceful, free of the constraints of trauma. What Brett had done to her. In that moment, she didn't feel like a hypocrite who made promises and didn't keep them. She felt more awake than she had in a long time.

Tallulah let herself sink beneath the surface, the water muffling everything except the heartbeat in her ears, and rejoiced in the simple fact that it was working. That she was alive to jump into a pond or watch a baseball game. Dance and learn and travel.

She wouldn't take that for granted anymore.

A few moments later, Tallulah surfaced and looked over at the bank to find Burgess waiting there, his arms crossed over her towel. While his stance was casual, something told her he was preparing to jump in and save her at a moment's notice. This man. Whatever shape their relationship ended up taking, he'd joined her on these first steps to finding her sense of adventure again. Based on the way her heart kicked into triple time at the sight of him, so regal and large and reassuring and supportive in the moonlight, Tallulah started to wonder if maybe, just maybe, he was one of the destinations on her journey.

Was he the right one, though?

Every fluttering nerve ending in her body seemed to believe so. The organ caged inside of her ribs, as well, and how it knocked louder and faster as she swam in his direction was telling. So telling.

"You look like a mermaid out there," he said, gruffly, then seemed to decide his statement sounded ridiculous, looking down and toeing the earth with his boot.

"Do you believe in mermaids, Burgess?"

"I believe I've *watched The Little Mermaid* four hundred times." He shivered. "The real thing, though? No. You?"

She made a considering sound. "Ninety-five percent of the ocean hasn't been explored. I think that's a lot of room for secrets." Slowly, Tallulah started to swim back to the shore, enjoying every ripple of water against her bare skin. "But more than anything, I think they were designed so that men had women to blame for shipwrecks or bad luck at sea. Surely these accidents couldn't be a man's doing. It *must* be a fish woman."

A corner of his mouth jumped. "Some explorer refused to pull over and ask for directions. That's what really happened."

"Bingo." Tallulah's feet found the bottom on the pond, but she didn't stand. "That being said, I do find the idea of mermaids very romantic. These beautiful creatures appearing to sailors." She dragged her fingertips through the water in front of her. "Enchanting them so thoroughly they go totally off course."

Burgess blew out a slow breath. "Right about now, I can commiserate."

"Would I cause you to crash your ship, Burgess?"

"Into a million pieces."

"Mmmm." It wasn't lost on Tallulah that his admission excited her even more than skinny dipping. More than . . . anything in recent memory. "Are you going to be a gentleman and close your eyes while I get out of the water?"

"Yes," he said with conviction, but his chest was beginning to rise and fall.

"What would you be willing to do for a peek?"

"Fuck it," he muttered, like a sailor accepting that he'd been tempted into steering his vessel toward the rocks. *"Anything."*

That guttural confession caused an electric current to move through Tallulah. "If you had to pick something of mine to look at," she murmured. "What would it be?"

"You mean, which part of you?"

Tallulah nodded.

Several charged seconds ticked by. "You realize that's an impossible choice."

She started whistling the *Jeopardy* theme song.

He dragged a hand down his face. "Jesus Christ."

"Walk me through your decision-making process," Tallulah suggested, having an inordinate amount of fun, every inch of her tingling, anticipating, her whole body seeming to hold its breath.

"Obviously it's down to . . . two. Parts."

"Tits and ass."

"Oh yeah," he growled, his gaze seemingly attempting to cut through the water. "I mean, for a minute there, I was considering something else. But I'm pretty sure that would end with you on all fours in the grass."

The body part she *assumed* was in question clenched involuntarily, causing her breath to hitch. "You're even blunter in the dark."

"You have no idea."

"Consider me warned." Without waiting for him to respond, she swam in a meandering circle. "Which part of me?"

His chest dipped so low, she wasn't sure it would ever rise again. "Let me see your tits."

Either her body temperature had elevated, or the pond had turned into a hot tub. "Close your eyes while I'm getting out. I can't have you getting a peek at *everything*."

"You worried I might discover you have a fish tail?"

She honest to God giggled. "I think you would have noticed by now. You stare enough."

"You make it impossible not to." With a quick twist of his neck, he got into position, holding the towel open and closing his eyes. "Come out of there now. I'm tired of pretending it's not making me anxious to watch you shiver. Get in these arms."

"As you wish, Sir Savage."

Fully trusting him to keep his eyes closed, Tallulah splashed and dashed out of the water, running straight into the open towel, groaning loudly when the warmth of the terry cloth, accompanied by the crush of Burgess's arms, closed around her, rubbing to create friction and warmth on her skin. And the adrenaline rush burned a path up to her throat, turning her into a weightless jumble, a livelier, more daring version of herself that she loved and wanted to lean into. Explore.

Burgess had wrapped the towel around Tallulah in such a

way that the opening was at the back, so she turned around and gathered it around her body, tucking the corners between her breasts. Then she brushed past a stone-silent and utterly rapt Burgess, their arms grazing together as she picked her way back toward the SUV, tossing him a come-hither glance over her shoulder, her blood pumping hotter when he followed.

She reached the vehicle first and opened the passenger side door the entire way, using the runner as an impetus to push herself up onto the seat and twist around, so her bare legs were dangling outside of the car. A lot like they'd been the night they kissed outside of Down. Burgess came closer, studying her with the kind of intensity that said he wanted the deal they'd made fulfilled. But that wasn't going to happen. Not quite yet.

"Remember, I asked you what you would be *willing* to do for a peek?"

He kept coming until her knees were pressed against his stomach, his gaze riveted on the knot between her breasts. "It's not enough that as soon as you lower that towel, I'll probably have to call a doctor about an erection that won't subside?"

"Funny you should mention doctors . . ."

His eyes shot to hers. "Tallulah. I already went."

"And it's still bothering you." Slowly, she raised her arms up over her head like a ballerina. "If you promise to talk to the team trainer about treating the muscle strain . . . you can look."

"This is the epitome of playing dirty."

"Let's call it incentivizing."

He pressed a fist to his mouth and groaned. "Fuck. Fine. Done. Call it whatever you want, I'm not noble enough to turn it down."

She arched her back slightly, planting her hands behind her on the seat. "Whenever you're ready, Mr. Savage." Very slightly, she slid her knees apart. "Unless you've changed your mind about what you want to see."

Burgess swiped a wrist over his upper lip to collect the sweat forming. "I told you how that would end."

"I know," she whispered.

"Goddamn." She actually heard the grind of his jaw. "You *are* a mermaid." Both of his hands lifted, fingertips settling on the terry cloth knot, slowly beginning to loosen it and her nipples hardened so eagerly, pinpricks of light danced in her vision. "Because this is definitely going to wreck me."

"And yet you can't stop yourself."

"God no."

She gave him a slow wink. "Sorry, sailor."

Expression rife with lust, he shook his head and tugged the towel open, exposing her breasts. He made a low, stifled sound, leaning down to explore them with a long look, his mouth falling open, as if he couldn't believe what his eyes were telling him. It took him several moments to look his fill, before letting go of the towel and slamming both hands onto the roof of the SUV, dropping his head forward as if gathering his control.

Maybe a few weeks ago, that kind of animalistic response would have scared her, but not with Burgess. He allowed her to feel safe while also vulnerable to her body's needs and wants. And so she didn't cover herself or feel an ounce of reservation. No, she leaned back and shook her breasts for him, excited by the way he started to pant, his right hand dropping, hesitating against the zipper of his jeans, before tearing it down and reaching inside.

Fisting himself.

Groaning up at the moon.

Beginning to stroke.

"I wouldn't do this unless it was necessary," he said, the words catching on rough inhales, grunts as his hand moved faster. Faster. "But it's either fuck myself or fuck you before we have an understanding, so keep shaking them."

It was like a dream, this scandalous moment in the pitch black, bouncing her breasts for her boss while he masturbated in his jeans, and she never wanted it to end. Her body had gone from cold to hot so fast, she was feverish, the flesh between her legs soaking wet—and not from swimming. From the continual seizing of her intimate muscles, the appeal of this giant man who made her feel naughty and cherished, in the space of one breath. She'd forced this tightly controlled man to relieve himself in front of her and the thrill was like a chemical eruption going off inside of her, wrecking her, too. Not just Burgess.

They never broke eye contact as her hand found its way beneath the bottom of the towel, her moan swallowed up by the nighttime sounds and Burgess's grunts, fingers sliding through that moist, swollen part of her, refusing to tease herself for even a second, finding her clit instead and petting up, down, up down, then breaking into a firm rub of the spot, her mouth parting on gasp after gasp.

"You want to finger yourself, gorgeous, go ahead. But don't you dare let me see that pussy or I'll have to add ten more locks to your bedroom door."

"You could still break the door down," she managed, though her back teeth were glued together. "Couldn't you?"

"Yeah. I could." His hips moved, wedging between her knees, the muscle of his right arm flexing in the moonlight as he worked, worked, veins beating in his neck and he leaned down, pressing their foreheads together, his hot breaths battering her lips. "But I want you to unlock it for me, Tallulah. Open it and let me in."

Pressure landed on her chest. Good or bad, she couldn't tell, only that it was a lot. It called for a big decision when her head was in the clouds, propelled upward by arousal so potent she could hardly get a decent breath. "Open it?" She licked at his mouth, doing it a second time when he bared his teeth and growled. "Like this?"

She opened her thighs and drew back the towel, watching his eyes go molten as she sank two fingers inside of herself, pressed deep and lifted herself on top of those digits, grinding her hips, riding them with a whine of his name, her orgasm cresting and delivering.

"Burgess," she gasped.

"Fucking . . . *fuck!*" Burgess roared.

His body lurched forward, his hand moving in disjointed jerks, those huge hips shoving her legs wider, so wide, while her bare sex was bathed in his come, rope after rope of wet warmth landing on her there while he panted brokenly into her neck.

"More," she whispered, licking the side of his face. "Cover me in it."

"We both want more," he said, turning his head so he could speak right on top of her mouth. "You ready to admit it's the same type of more?"

That pressure returned to her chest, the weight of indecision. "Oh. I . . ."

Seconds passed and she couldn't fill them.

"Uh-huh." He looked her right in the eye while reaching down to grip her sex in a big hand. "When you're ready to call me your man, I'm going to spit on this hot little cunt and call it mine before I fuck it. Go ahead. Lie and tell me you don't want that."

Yearning like she'd never experienced in her life powered through her system. It was unexpected and consuming, cleanly knocking the wind out of her. The chance that she might go without his full claim caused her stomach to shrink in on itself. "Do it," she sobbed.

"When you're mine." Blue eyes blazed, before he slammed his lids shut. "For now, I want you to agree to come to my game. It's not a lot to ask. I want to look into the stands and know you're there because of me."

"Fine. I'll go. I'll go. Just spit on me—"

"Soon."

Tallulah made a sound of protest as Burgess drew himself up and off her, stumbling back a little while refastening his jeans, his forehead covered in sweat. They retreated to their corners for several minutes to recover from what had started as playful, but turned into something bigger. Something deeper, more permanent.

A pond she didn't know if she was ready to wade into.

CHAPTER EIGHTEEN

Oh. The energy in the arena was wild. These people were *enthusiastic*.

Tallulah had gone into the evening well aware that Bostonians didn't do sports halfway. After all, her dad was a Red Sox fan. During baseball season, the games had served as background music to homework time. Thus, she knew that every Red Sox game was a matter of life or death. But hockey? She simply hadn't known. The fans were not there to friggin' play.

Everyone was wearing team colors. Like . . . *everyone.*

The dress code hadn't been optional.

But here she was in jeans, a white long-sleeved shirt, and a coat. And she couldn't even blend anonymously into the crowd, because the tickets they'd just picked up at the box office were in the front row. She and Lissa were heading there now, weaving in and out of fans holding loaded chili dogs and giant beers.

Nervous somersaults were happening in her tummy. Why?

Maybe because the last time she'd been alone with Burgess, she'd been asking him to spit on her? Her skin flamed just thinking about it. For the entire week that followed, he'd been busy preparing for the season opener, most of his waking hours spent at the arena in team meetings, doing press, and practicing. Tallulah had been splitting her time between caring for Lissa and working on her half of the collaborative assignment with Finn. Every time she'd been in the same room with Burgess, Lissa had been there. Which had done nothing to stifle the charged glances and brushes of his lips across the back of her neck in the kitchen.

This time, her shiver had nothing to do with the temperature.

"Do you think I should go buy a sweatshirt or something?" she leaned down and asked Lissa, who had been a little too quiet on the ride over. Hopefully there wasn't something new going on with the girls at school. "I feel . . . underdressed or over-dressed, I can't decide."

Lissa looked down at her phone and scrolled through a feed of colorful pictures, somehow managing to avoid bumping into foot traffic. "Um. No, I think it's fine."

"Sure, easy for you to say." She hip bumped the twelve-year-old. "You're in a cool Bearcats shirt, complete with claw marks on the sleeve. Did your dad get that for you?"

"Yeah." Lissa paled, her mouth falling open. "Oh no, I forgot my sweatshirt in the cab."

"Oh. Shoot. I can call the car service and see if they're still nearby? Or I can figure out how to pick it up in the morning."

"We don't have time—the game is starting and I don't want to miss them introducing my dad." Lissa's shoulders slumped. "I'm going to freeze to death."

"It's that cold in the arena? We're indoors."

"Trust me. It's that cold."

"Well, hold on . . ." Tallulah craned her neck to see what each of the stalls was hocking. "Let's just get you a sweatshirt or something."

Three and a half minutes later.

"*Seventy-five dollars?*" Tallulah croaked. "For a sweatshirt?"

"No one has ever been shocked before, I tell you," drawled the bored, red-shirted man with Boston in every syllable. "You're the first. Wow."

"Her dad is on the team. Isn't there some kind of discount?"

His eyes rolled around like a pair of marbles. "Yeah, my mom is the coach. And my schnauzer drives the Zamboni. Next!"

Tallulah ushered Lissa away from the merchandise counter, leveling Red Shirt with a dirty look as long as possible. "Sorry, Liss. I don't get paid for another week. And I grew up in a household where my mother made our clothes. I'd never be able to look her in the eye again." Quickly, she whipped off her coat and draped it around Lissa's shoulders. "You can wear this."

Lissa's hesitation was clear. "What about you?"

"Are you forgetting I lived in Antarctica?" She snorted. "I can survive a hockey game."

They took their seats a few feet from the plexiglass just as the lights went out and blue paw prints were projected onto the ice, moving in a swirl pattern. An announcer's voice swept in and sent the crowd into a frenzy, feet stomping on concrete, voices chanting *cats cats cats*. The referees took the ice first and they were booed, which Tallulah didn't think was fair, since they hadn't made any calls yet, but the negative greeting also seemed kind of . . . good-natured? As did the shouts of *get ready to lose, you fucks*, that were yelled without reservation at the visiting team.

Tallulah raised an eyebrow at Lissa. "Remind me to never piss off a hockey fan."

For the first time since she'd arrived tonight, Lissa cracked a smile. "The game hasn't even started yet. Wait until the fights break out."

"Ominous."

"Yup."

Geez. It was starting to get cold. *Really* cold, actually.

Tallulah tried to be covert about huffing warm air into her palms.

"*And now. Introducing* yoooooour *Boston Bearcats . . .* " said the announcer.

Holy Ice Capades, there was nowhere colder on earth.

Was she *inside* of an air conditioner? It stood to reason that the arena temperature needed to be kept cold enough to keep the ice from melting, but holy shit. Shouldn't there be a warning issued in advance? She was already beginning to shiver, and they'd only gotten through the first few Bearcats players, including Sig Gauthier who was received by thunderous applause. Although . . . was it her imagination or did he continually glance toward the empty seat to the right of Tallulah while the announcer continued the intros?

"Last but not least, Bearcats family . . . you know him as the Blight of Boston, the Menace of Massachusetts. Make some noise for number fifty-nine, *Sir Savage himself*, Burgess Abraham."

Something very funny happened when Burgess skated out onto the ice in pads, looking decidedly gigantic and irritable, despite the rafters shaking on his behalf. Something very funny happened, indeed. Yes, she'd seen Burgess play hockey on television and online, but seeing it happen *in person*, Tallulah momentarily forgot she was freezing to death. A troubling little engine started to hum, a pair of invisible hands stroking up the valleys of her sides.

Huh. Hooo. He looked . . . hmm.

Valiant?

Dangerous?

Sexy.

Okay, he looked really, *really* hot. But why? He was covered in padding, his lips protruded slightly due to his mouthpiece. She'd seen him shirtless. And yet, hooo. There was something attractive about the whole package. The jersey, the grimace, the way he skated as easily as he walked, unaffected by the hero worship being directed at him. Almost . . . blasé.

For some reason, the fact that he could also kiss was high-key occurring to her right now. Like, really, truly kiss. And his hands. They were so big. Capable of holding a hockey stick and chopping onions and ripping up business cards like they were silly little nothings. Not to mention, drying pond water off her body and unknotting towels . . .

She might not be cold anymore, but her nipples hadn't gotten the memo.

They were stiff as nails.

Of course, Tallulah realized she had the equivalent of bullet casings in her bra just as the arena lights blasted back on, the Bearcats skating in a loose formation and separating into a warmup. As casually as possible, Tallulah crossed her arms over her breasts and resumed shivering, but this time, it was more about her cresting estrogen than the cold.

It was snack city out there.

Did everyone know about this?

How did the players manage to swagger while on skates? It seemed like it should be impossible, yet Tallulah was witnessing it with her own eyes. And it was very troubling that despite the entire squad of dishes out there, she could barely manage to rip her attention off Burgess for a second. How did he balance that tremendous weight on two little blades *and* make it look so effortless?

Also, why was he coming toward them?

Probably just a coincidence . . .

Nope. There he was. Three feet away, rapping the end of his stick against the glass, looking grumpy and intimidating and famous. The fans sitting behind them choked on their tongues, rushing to get their camera apps open. Lissa giggled and waved at her dad and received a gloved one in return. Tallulah tried to wave without uncrossing her arms, but they were now frozen to her person, like a tongue on a flagpole in January.

Burgess pinned her with an unholy frown.

You're cold, he mouthed at her.

You think? she said back.

He made a questioning gesture.

Fans were going out of their minds, tripping over themselves to converge on their section. Tallulah opened the notepad app on her phone and quickly typed out a memo, standing up and pressing the device to the plexiglass.

Sweatshirts are $75. She added a head exploding emoji for clarity.

His exasperation was plain.

Then Tallulah was looking at his back, because he was skating away, leaving her with the view of the name Abraham stitched on the flipside of his jersey. Over to the bench, where he shouted something at a man who appeared to be a trainer in his Bearcats blue polo shirt. Burgess returned to warmups, though he seemed more distracted than before, continually glancing over in their direction. Just as the buzzer sounded, a man blocked her view of the ice—the Bearcats trainer, if she wasn't mistaken—holding a bundled up, inside out sweatshirt.

He handed it to her with a curious once-over. "Burgess told me to tell you to please put it on so he can concentrate."

"Oh." Tingles danced up her arms and onto her scalp. Pulses were leaping in all kinds of places. She accepted the garment, once again, without unfolding her arms. "Um . . . thank you. Thank him and thank you."

The man nodded, turning his attention to Burgess's daughter. "Lissa, right?"

She grinned.

The trainer fist bumped her and off he jogged, curving back toward the bench.

Having no choice now but to uncross her arms and reveal her bullet nips, Tallulah turned the sweatshirt right side out as fast as possible, yanking it down over her head, sticking her arms into the holes and sobbing over the rush of warmth.

It wasn't *only* heat that permeated her bones, however. Burgess's scent did that, too.

She'd never registered his scent before, but she knew it as soon as it wrapped around her like a cool forest waterfall. Simply put, he smelled like winter. Her favorite season.

Gulp.

Out on the ice, the Bearcats were poised to begin, the volume of the crowd rising to an earsplitting level as the referee dropped the puck. Activity exploded in front of Tallulah. Within seconds, giant bodies were crashing up against the glass, the puck moving in a black blur from end to end and back again. Burgess's reflexes were swift and exact, every one of them with purpose. He wasn't merely an immovable object, he was fast. *Really* fast. And she couldn't figure out how both were possible. One minute, he would be blocking the path to the net, like a stone monument, and the next, he would be cutting through a sea of opponents to slap the puck back toward the opposite end—

"Is there something going on between you and my dad?"

Tallulah's head moved on a swivel, alarm expanding like a sponge in her stomach. "Is there what?"

Lissa didn't blink. "Are you my dad's girlfriend?"

"No." Tallulah made the denial automatically, because it was the truth. Right? She hadn't agreed to be Burgess's girlfriend, despite what he wanted. Sure, *something* was afoot between them, which would likely prove to be a sexual itch that wanted to be scratched. But they weren't *dating*. Nuh-uh. "I'm not your dad's girlfriend. We're friends. What I am is I'm *your* au pair." She squeezed the girl's arm. "And I hope we're friends, too."

Relief was breaking across Lissa's features. "Yeah. We are."

Tallulah exhaled. "Good."

"Because I can tell he still likes my mom. He was waiting outside the building today and everything, like maybe he misses her. I just wish they would stop being so stubborn."

Not for the first time, Tallulah's heart sank at Lissa's belief that her parents could possibly get back together. It was painfully clear that wasn't happening, but perhaps a twelve-year-old with a big imagination saw what she wanted to see. Breaking the bad news to Lissa would be overstepping, so she wouldn't, but she'd mention it again to Burgess later.

"I bet my mom is watching the game on television," Lissa said, smiling.

Tallulah's gut churned. Lissa's mom was already engaged to someone new. Maybe it wouldn't hurt to gently prepare her for the eventual disappointment of her parents moving on?

"Lissa . . ."

"Hey! Oh my God, I'm so late!" Tallulah turned just in time to watch Chloe bounce into her seat with a ripple of blond hair and a pink jersey with the name Gauthier on the back. She dropped her purse and threw her arms around Tallulah's neck. "I'm so glad you decided to come!"

"I'm still reserving judgment on the sport itself, but I'm happy to see you, too!" She hugged Chloe, laughing fondly over her excitement. "Do you know Burgess's daughter, Lissa?"

"Yes! We met in the team box last season." Chloe leaned forward to look at Lissa, gasping. "Wait, you're like even cuter now. Stop."

Someone bashed up against the glass.

A shrill whistle rent the air.

Chloe lunged from her seat without missing a beat, slamming her fist into the glass where the referee was trying to separate Sig from an opponent. "*Boarding?* Are you kidding me, piss face? Update your eye prescription, ref!" She sat back down with a sweet smile. "Did you guys eat yet?"

"Well. You're definitely not lacking for passion, Chloe."

"I'm just getting warmed up." She rubbed her hands together. "Speaking of getting warmed up, did Burgess tell you his friend hired me to play the harp at your friend's wedding in Costa Rica?"

Tallulah jolted forward, turning to face the blonde at the same time. "Seriously?" They clasped hands and danced in their seats. "That's amazing."

"Girl, the way I am going to shop in preparation. I can already hear Sig sighing in disappointment at me." She kept right on smiling through that statement. "I'll probably have to turn on the waterworks. He can never stay annoyed at me after that."

"Right . . ."

"Seriously, though, I'm starving," Chloe said, reaching to the other side of Tallulah to squeeze Lissa's shoulder. "Eat trash while you talk trash, I always say."

As the game wore on, Tallulah decided hockey fans were nuts. Graciously violent was the only way she could describe them. Good thing she wasn't one of them.

By the end of the second period, Tallulah was screaming at the referee to find a new occupation.

THE BEARCATS WON their home opener 2–1.

Tallulah took a sleepy Lissa home and got her into bed, turning off the lamp and closing the bedroom door behind her. She should have gone to bed, too. There was no reason to wait for Burgess to get home from his postgame press conference.

In fact, it was a bad idea all around.

What she *needed* to do was embark on a cold shower.

But she couldn't bring herself to take off Burgess's sweatshirt. Or stop sniffing the collar.

Keyed up and exasperated with herself, Tallulah went inside her bedroom and firmly closed the door, even engaging the lock. She stripped off her jeans, sweatshirt, socks, shirt, and bra. But instead of retrieving a nightshirt from her drawer, she pulled the sweatshirt back on.

Bad idea.

That soft, fleecy material skimmed down against her naked skin like a lover's fingertips, that winter scent giving her a light-headed feeling. She lay down in bed, stretching her legs under the covers and getting into her preferred side sleeping position, but she couldn't get comfortable, no matter how many times she turned over. And then she realized she was turning over on purpose, so she could feel the rub of material on her sensitive skin. Every time she blinked, she saw Burgess stopping two opponents in their tracks with nothing but his stationary body, and she sighed in surrender, slipping her fingers down the front of her panties.

Unsurprisingly, she was already wet. Warm.

She'd been this way since the game started, hadn't she?

There was no one in bed with her. No reason to lie.

Burgess turned her on—badly—and his effect on her only seemed to grow more potent the longer she stayed out of his bed. The more time she spent around him, the harder it was becoming to maintain a friendly, professional distance and keep her hands to herself. The effort she'd put in had taken a toll, and now? Her body was demanding relief. Her knees drew up under the covers while her fingers worked circles into flesh made slippery by *a hockey game*.

No. A hockey player.

Her chest shuddered up and down as she pressed and rubbed her clit, her heels digging into the mattress, toes flexing, anticipation fluttering in the lowest region of her tummy. Oh. Wow. This was going to be fast. She bit down on her lip and squeezed her eyes closed, picturing Burgess in the locker room, unlacing those padded pants, drawing his sweaty jersey up and over his head. Suddenly she was there, too, obviously having evaded security and he was pinning her to the locker, wreaking havoc on her mouth with his own, his hands on her breasts, dragging lower and riding the curve of her backside into her jeans. Gripping. Lifting her.

The locker rattled.

No. Wait.

That rattle was in real life.

It was the front door of the apartment.

"Shit," she whispered, rolling face down to muffle her panting mouth with the pillow, two fingers delving into her body now, pumping once, twice . . .

But the effectiveness of her fantasy was wearing off, because the real-life man was trudging past her bedroom door, in the flesh.

Flesh.

Don't think of his flesh.

It was too late.

And the truth was, she *wanted* to give in to the demanding attraction. Just once, to stem the restlessness. It was the middle of the night. No one would know. Burgess had made it abundantly clear that he'd like to take her to bed. While that would not be happening, because it wouldn't come without the price of commitment . . . maybe she could get just a taste? It had been approximately nine thousand years since Tallulah found herself hungering for a specific man, and this hunger far surpassed any that she'd experienced before. The rush, the proof she could still trust enough to feel the pull of need, was a relief. An intoxicating, exciting relief . . . and she desperately wanted to explore it.

The entire way to the locked door, she told herself to turn back.

But her body wasn't listening.

CHAPTER NINETEEN

Burgess sat on the end of his bed, his hands clasped between his knees.

He stared at the door, begging it to open.

It wouldn't, but a man could damn well hope, right?

His dick was heavy and hard in his jeans, like it always was the night after a victory. But he'd do what he always did and jerk off in the shower. This time, however, he'd be thinking of Tallulah in his sweatshirt on the sidelines. How he'd caught her in between the second and third period taking a long whiff of the collar. Did she like how he smelled?

Did she . . . like the game? What had she thought about his performance out there?

Did she notice that he'd lost a step, like everyone else in the hockey world?

His throat burned with the possibility.

Could this one woman see him as capable of anything? Ten years ago, he could have been her fucking superhero. Who could he be for her now?

Would she even want him to be someone to her?

Burgess pushed to his feet, his eyes watering over the pull of tendons in his back. He'd kept his end of the bargain with Tallulah and spoken to the team trainer, who'd given him some more powerful painkillers, but they'd worn off slowly throughout the game.

Just a strain. Just a strain. He repeated those reassuring words to himself on the way into the en suite bathroom where he undressed, removing the clothes he'd only donned an hour and a half ago, prior to the press conference, leaving them in a heap on the ground. He looked at himself in the mirror over the sink, shaking his head at the sight of his swollen cock and trying to see himself through Tallulah's eyes. Those silver hairs creeping into his sideburns, beard, and chest hair . . . were they a warning flag to her?

Stay away from this guy. He's past his prime.

He's none of the things you want. Spontaneous. Fun. Adventurous. Young.

Or was she curious about what his experience brought to the table?

Burgess's eyes closed, his fist closing around his cock and beginning to stroke.

Yeah.

He liked that scenario better.

Tallulah was standing in front of him now, imaginary, of course.

Not a fucking stitch of clothing.

Show me what you know, she whispered, guiding his hand between her thighs.

"*Mhhhh,*" he grunted, already panting, his pulse loud in his ears. He wasn't even going to make it to the shower. He'd bust right there in the sink—

He heard the very distinct creak of his bedroom door opening.

His hand froze, the fantasy bursting like a bubble.

"Burgess?"

Son of a bitch, that was Tallulah's voice. She was in his bedroom? Why?

"Yeah?" he said, trying to make his voice sound natural and failing. Hard. He sounded like a buzz saw trying to break through metal. "Everything okay?"

Silence.

Three seconds. Four.

"Don't you want your massage?"

Burgess bit down on his balled fist to stop himself from groaning. Or ejaculating.

Or both.

She was just following through on her promise.

He wouldn't hope for more. Not until he knew for sure.

His movements were almost lethargic with lust as he whipped a towel off the rack and wrapped it around his waist, knotting it in a way that hid his affliction. Taking a deep breath, he opened the bathroom door, keeping his erection hidden behind the jamb as a backup plan.

When his eyes adjusted to the darkness of the bedroom, his flesh started to throb all the harder, so intense he almost couldn't bear it. There she was, in his room.

In nothing but his sweatshirt.

"Tallulah, tell me exactly what you want," he said thickly. "What are you here for?"

"Can we please just call it a massage and see what happens?" she whispered.

This was the difference between them. She could come to him without a game plan, carried by a whim or a momentary break from good decision-making. He wasn't like that. He wanted to have their relationship spelled out. Wanted everything neatly defined, so he could sleep at night, secure in the fact that he had her all to himself.

If they went to bed together, would it be understood they were exclusive, even if she refused to say it out loud? Burgess didn't have a clue and he wanted to push for clarity, but his discipline was wearing thin as fuck and he wouldn't survive Tallulah running back to her room behind the locked door, so he bit his tongue.

His strategy wasn't working. He'd have to try hers for a while.

"Yeah," he said, voice rusted. "We'll call it a massage."

Relief seemed to trickle through Tallulah, her shoulders losing some of their tension. She nodded once, hesitated, then walked to the bed, climbing onto the high king-sized mattress on her hands and knees in a way that made his cock swell. The sweatshirt was so huge on her, he couldn't see much of her body, but he could imagine the curve of her ass, the lithe flex of her thighs. How her panties would cup her between the legs. *Jesus.* He swallowed hard at the sight of her kneeling near the edge with her hands folded on her bent knees, *in his sweatshirt*, obviously waiting for him to come sit down in front of her. It felt like a dream. Only he knew it wasn't, because of the pain weighing down his balls, the way his heart thunked in his throat.

Do you even know how to play it cool anymore?

God, he didn't want his relationship with Tallulah to be casual, because nothing he felt for her was remotely fucking casual, he wasn't going to turn down the chance . . . for whatever was about to happen here.

When it came to this one woman, he was losing the battle with his willpower.

But if she'd come for casual and he walked in there panting like a dog with his heart on his sleeve, she'd recognize they weren't on the same page and put on the brakes. And she might never show up in his bedroom again. No, he'd let go of his need for transparency tonight in the hopes that whatever they did on that bed brought her back for more.

Burgess snagged a bottle of lotion from the bathroom vanity, then made his way slowly into the room, thanking God for the darkness that kept his secret. The low bathroom light spread across the bed, illuminating Tallulah partially, enough that he could see her lips part as he approached, her gaze stroking down his bare chest and stomach, her fingers curling into fists on her bent knees. That proof of her attraction gave Burgess some confidence, but not enough. Not as much as he used to have.

What if there were new ways to hook up that he didn't even know about?

What if she needed to be touched a certain way, and he couldn't read the signs?

Had he thought this through properly?

Calm down, man.

It's a massage.

They were calling it a massage.

With a fist-sized object lodged in his throat, he turned and sat down in front of the most beautiful woman he'd ever seen in his life, handing her the bottle of lotion over his shoulder, before realizing that might be presumptuous. "You don't have to use that . . ."

"No, I want to. It'll make it better."

Her hands were going to be on him. How much better could it get?

At the sound of her squeezing the bottle, he was forced to close his eyes, the anticipation of her touch was so severe. He focused on keeping his breathing deep and even, but if the lights were on, she would see the rapid-fire pulse at the base of his neck, the way his hands were clasped so tightly in between his knees there was no blood left in his knuckles.

The slippery sound of the lotion being warmed in her hands ceased—

And then, her hands were on him. In the center of his back, smoothing the lotion downward where his injury lurked, throbbing sharply like a bad tooth. She found it with the same precision as always, her thumb digging into the meat to the right of his spine and working around, around, causing a shuddering groan to escape his mouth.

"Good?"

"You have no idea," he managed.

"How does the muscle feel?"

"It's just a strain," he evaded automatically.

She hummed a reproof. "Since you won, maybe I'll let you get away with that tonight."

A thank-you got stuck in his throat because *oh fuck*, her buried thumb felt so good. Maybe this *was* only going to be a massage. If so, he needed to stop thinking about turning around and nudging her backward on the bed, finding out if she'd come for more. Giving her more. Giving her everything he knew how to give.

Casual.

Stay casual.

"Speaking of our win tonight, I couldn't help but notice you were heckling the ref like it was your job. Did we make a hockey fan out of you?"

"I'm claiming temporary insanity," she sniffed. "That being said, I might have taken a tiny peek at the website for season ticket info."

He chuckled into the darkness, but the sound dissolved into a hiss when she found a particularly sore spot just beneath his towel. "You don't need season tickets, you've got me. Even when I, uh . . . even when I'm no longer playing, I'll have standing tickets."

She massaged him in silence for a moment. "Do you think that'll be . . . soon?"

"Me not playing anymore?"

"Yes."

He struggled through the uneasy feeling he got whenever the subject of retirement came up. It was more prevalent than usual because Tallulah was there. He wanted this woman to believe he was made of steel, but maybe that hope was as unrealistic as scoring another MVP trophy at thirty-seven. "Tonight . . . did it seem to you like it might be time for me to bow out?"

Gradually, her hands stopped moving.

Here it was. The moment she broke her opinion to him gently. Burgess waited, tensed.

"Are you serious?" She sounded kind of stunned, as if the answer should be obvious. Oh shit, this was going to be worse than he thought. "You were . . . *amazing* out there. I don't know anything about hockey, but I know the other team would have scored a bunch of goals if you weren't standing in front of the goalie like a brick wall. *No one* got past you. I couldn't . . ." He heard her swallow. "I couldn't take my eyes off you. And not just because I know you. I genuinely couldn't figure out how you were anticipating the other players so far in advance. It made me pity Lissa's future significant others."

Burgess couldn't draw breath.

There was a fuzzy ripple passing through his ribs that he didn't know how to handle.

"I mean . . ." He cleared his throat, resisting the urge to rub at the too-light sensation. "One person got past me. They scored a goal."

"Oh wow." The sarcasm was evident. "Your goalie had to do his job one measly time. He should be giving you half his salary."

A crack of laughter got free. "Tallulah . . ."

He didn't know what to do with his hands.

His arms crossed over his chest and dropped, the right one lifting to smooth his beard unnecessarily. "Okay. I . . . okay. It's not your job to fix my ego."

"Who damaged your ego in the first place?" Honestly, now she sounded kind of pissed? Burgess twisted around to look at her over his shoulder and yeah, he could confirm. She looked adorably miffed. His heart pounded harder. "Who, Burgess? Who did this to you?"

"I've lost a step. It's common knowledge."

"Well maybe you had a couple steps to spare!" she sputtered.

His heart pumped in a drawn-out beat. "What?"

"Maybe now everyone is a little closer to your level, but they're not on it." She was rubbing his shoulders almost angrily now. "Like I said, I might not be a sports enthusiast, especially when the sweatshirts are seventy-five dollars, but I have eyes."

Maybe you had a couple steps to spare.

No amount of personal pep talks or coaching had given him as much insight into how his own brain worked as those eight off-the-cuff words. Because that not only made total sense to him, it was the one thing that made him feel . . . relaxed. Like maybe there wasn't a guillotine waiting above his neck, poised to fall. For the first time, he wondered if maybe . . . he was being too hard on himself—and that was difficult to admit, because he made a living being hard on himself.

Right. That's how he'd succeeded.

"Thank you. For saying that. But . . ." He gave a concise headshake. "I'm not going to start taking it easy on myself now, Tallulah."

Again, her hands suspended in their treatment of his back.

Then they left him completely.

Goddammit, he'd spoken too harshly. Cut her off at the knees when she was just trying to help. What was wrong with him? He was in the act of formulating an apology when Tallulah slipped off the bed to his right, paused a moment, then slowly moved to stand in front of him. *Close.* Right there, in between his out-stretched thighs.

He stopped breathing.

"Maybe if you won't take it easy on yourself, you need some-one to do it for you."

Off came the sweatshirt.

Time stood fucking still as he registered the sight of her in nothing but a pair of black silky panties. As in, not a bra in sight. And he'd been more than aware that his au pair was hot as sin. Tallulah, though? The word "hot" didn't begin to do justice to a body that could spoil a man fucking rotten. There wasn't a dude alive that had done enough good in his lifetime to deserve the chance to touch her, but he'd make up for this shortage of goodwill later, because he was too busy staring at her sexy tits, all golden and sweet, like they wanted a bite taken out of them. It was almost painful to tear his attention away from them to memorize the rest of her, the nip of her waist, the flare of her hips and the snug fit of her underwear. Those *thighs*.

God, he wanted to be pumping his cock between them.

"You want to take it easy on me?" he hooked a finger in her panties and drew her closer. "I'm going to be honest, I don't want to take it easy on you at all."

Tallulah's stomach hollowed on an intake of breath, her nipples turning to stiff buds right there in front of his eyes. He held his breath as her hands lifted . . .

And she slowly plowed all ten fingers through his hair.

That scrape of her nails on his scalp was better than any orgasm he'd had in recent memory. In need of an anchor, his hands gripped her hips and yanked her closer, his mouth releasing a shaky exhale between her tits.

"Why do you doubt yourself?" she asked, rubbing leisurely circles onto his head.

"I don't know, I . . ." Her smooth, warm skin that smelled like oranges and basil. His tongue licked out involuntarily, wanting to taste those ingredients, whatever components made her up, made her this perfect, but mostly, that lick clued him in to how hard her heart was pounding. As hard as his own. Holy shit. "The divorce made me realize how flawed I am. It also made me realize how quickly the things I rely on can . . . go away. So I held on tighter to hockey, but the look in the mirror has me noticing flaws everywhere. On the ice. Off. I'm constantly looking for signs that my career is over."

"It's not." Her thumbs traced the shells of his ears, massaging the lobes, and he wondered how long he could survive her touch without melting like hot candlewax. "And everyone has flaws, but they're outweighed by your strengths. Your many . . ." She tugged his hair slowly. "Wonderful." She wound the strands around her fingers, turning him to fucking putty in her hands. "Strengths."

"Thank you," he said, more than a little shaken.

"You're welcome," she murmured back, their eye contact making his throat ache.

What is this happening between us?

Burgess was burning to ask. To demand.

But he was starved. Fucking *starved*. And if she ran away right now, he'd collapse under the weight of unsatisfied hunger. So instead, even though it ate him up inside, he asked, "What do you want from me tonight, gorgeous?"

Those nails scraped him again and his vision wavered, pleasure stiffening the muscles of his abdomen, the sac between his legs growing unbearably heavy. Then she leaned down and kissed him without any restraint, her mouth open and wet, moving over his in a way that made his hand itch to reach beneath his towel. To choke his cock in a tight grip and stroke one out with her delicious mouth as inspiration.

They broke for air, both panting, his palms tracing the valleys of her sides eagerly, moving inward to knead her firm tits. Their foreheads met, eyes searching and his were no doubt swimming with lust, because that's what dominated him. Painful, sharp-toothed lust. And fuck it, maybe some vulnerability, thanks to him being totally and completely overwhelmed by the fact that this woman thought he was still great, couldn't take her eyes off him, touched him like he didn't need a single improvement.

A second before they could dive back into another kiss, she whispered against his mouth, "You can give me what I need tonight . . . by taking."

She went down on her knees.

And his eyes went fucking blind.

TALLULAH LOOKED AT the white flap of the towel in front of her, wondering how she'd missed the gigantic erection pressing up against the knotted fabric, lifting the cloth at an angle. She definitely hadn't missed the lord-have-mercy thighs that had started tensing up the moment she got on her knees. Or that ripped-up stomach. Or the giant mitts that were already holding on to the comforter for dear life.

"Tallulah, please."

"Please, what?"

"I don't fucking know, just please."

Sparkly little prickles danced down the slopes of her shoulders, pushing into her fingertips, the flesh inside of her panties damp and swollen with the excitement of what she'd decided to do. He'd asked what she needed from him tonight—and yeah, she'd been a little caught off guard by the answer, too. But this man . . .

This *man*. She really, *really* wanted to know what he tasted like. How he'd react to flicks of her tongue and draws of her lips. If he would gasp or groan or if he'd fist her hair and push himself deep. She was practically salivating for salt and weight and the flood of pleasure in her mouth. Like, she wanted it now. *Now.*

What far outweighed her yen for his body, though, was a more complicated truth.

She was dying to make him feel incredible.

She wanted him to know he was powerful and amazing.

Which was not her job, of course, but . . .

She wasn't sure he knew his own might. In fact, he'd just revealed that quite a few cracks existed beneath his confident facade, and she was compelled to help fill them in. A blow job wasn't the only way to do that—and dear God, she was about to complicate their relationship by a trillion percent, but in the dark of the bedroom, in the quiet midnight hour, when they were both dressed in very little clothing, tomorrow was an eon away.

Tallulah couldn't slow down her intakes of breath as she unknotted the towel around Burgess's waist and . . . she didn't even get the chance to toss it aside, because her hand quite literally dropped it over the first look at Burgess's sex. Without the burden of the towel, it swelled up toward his belly and stayed there, thick and broad and full. So full. *Frustrated.*

She walked forward on her knees and slowly wrapped him in her fist, watching his face as she stroked him up, down, up . . . and oh. God. Kneeling in front of this man was like kneeling in front of a king to pledge fealty, his thighs were so muscular, his chest heaving and beginning to perspire, his body in general so much bigger than hers. Bold. Striking. Strong.

"Please," he gritted out. "Fuck. Only for a minute."

Unable to wait a second longer, she leaned in and licked up the smooth, veiny side of his shaft, noting the way his thighs shuddered when she swirled her tongue around the bulbous tip. "Why only a minute?"

"My come will end up in your throat, Tallulah. That's why." His face screwed up, in obvious pain, but he didn't take his eyes off her. "Ah Jesus, stop looking at me like that."

"Like what?"

He settled a hand on the top of her head, a sign of surrender, his body leaning back slightly to give her better access. "Like you've been dreaming about putting that beautiful face in my lap."

Slowly, she teased her tongue side to side in his slit. "I have."

"Goddamn. Me too. That's why you need to stop." His head

fell back on a closed mouth moan. "Please, I'm barely holding on and you haven't even sucked it yet."

"Do you want me to?" she whispered, kissing the head. Lathing it with her tongue.

His stomach heaved up and down twice. "Yes," he said through his teeth. "Just a couple of times. Hard and deep. Give me something to think about on the road while I'm beating off in my hotel room."

In response to that guttural request, her clit throbbed. Insistently. It had been sensitive in her panties the entire time she was giving him the back massage, but now . . . ohhh. She couldn't keep her right hand from dropping, rubbing the wet spot that had seeped through her panties. She closed her eyes and pictured Burgess naked in his hotel room bed, his fist slicking up and down his hard inches, his teeth buried in his lower lip, heels digging into the bed. The image turned her on so completely that she wasn't even aware of how hard she'd started pulling on the stiff flesh in her mouth. Her left hand held him steady, her thumb sweeping up and down the underside where that vein lurked, throbbing so tellingly, while her mouth drew him in, in, in, to the back of her throat, moaning as she kept him there, then slowly releasing him, relishing the pop of him as he left the sanctuary of her lips.

"Motherfucker, that's so good." His fingers were tunneling in her hair now, his hips giving punctuated upward thrusts—and she loved him like this. Big, cocky royalty. "I can take one or two more just like that . . . *fuuuuuck*."

"Why?" she whispered, lapping at him, her hand moving in quick strokes, marveling at the size and inflexibility of him. The firm set of his balls that lifted slightly and dropped down every time she pumped her fist. "Why stop at two?"

"You're not leaving my bedroom unsatisfied, Tallulah. If you think I'd let that happen, you haven't been paying attention."

She tilted her hips up, so he could see her fingers massaging circles into the front of her panties. "I can satisfy myself. I just wanted this to be about you."

His thumb brushed the curve of her cheekbone. "Satisfying you is for both of us."

For some reason, that made her throat feel momentarily crowded and she panicked a little, because she'd run the gamut of feelings for this man tonight. Awe, protectiveness, lust. Now there was gratitude, connection . . . and she was scared to add more. Scared where it would lead, so she brought his shaft to the back of her throat again, again, again, continuing even when she choked on him and his fist started to shake in her hair.

"Tallulah, no. No, no, no. *Fuck. Fuck me. Fuck me.*" He had her head in both of his hands now, guiding her down for big swallows of his sex, the strength of him on full display in every rough flex of his hip abductors and chest and biceps. "Fine, you want to swallow me? Swallow me, girl. You don't get to spit after taking me to the balls. God, I love this pretty mouth. Tell me it was made for me."

"Made for you," she gasped, before he pumped deep one final time, his entire body simply breaking, shattering, shaking violently, his muscles flexing and releasing in bunched-up patterns while salty moisture found her throat, her grip continuing to stroke more of him free, home to her where it belonged. Yes, that's how it felt. Like taking some part of Burgess inside of her was long overdue, and she moaned, drawing until her cheeks hollowed, begging with her eyes for every single ounce.

The power of his finish was so intense that when his fingers released her hair just slightly, she pitched back onto her butt, gulping down oxygen like she'd just surfaced from the bottom of Boston Harbor. What in the sweet hell? The room was . . . spinning.

She'd only meant to give him a blow job and let him know she found him wonderful. Now she felt emotional. Like she wanted to be in his arms. And her body was overwhelmed by the height of its own arousal, so much higher than it had ever been. So high that she was almost afraid to reach for it, because it would set the bar too high. Or rip her chest wide open.

Not knowing what else to do but retreat, Tallulah scrambled to her feet and bolted for the door, forgetting the sweatshirt. She forgot her own *name*, really, but before she could actually turn the doorknob, Burgess was standing behind her, planting a hand on the door and closing it with a firm click. His exhale bathed her ear, his mouth latching onto the sensitive skin that connected her shoulder to her neck, and slowly, slowly he pinned her to the door.

"What happened?" His breath continued to come fast. "Did I fucking *hurt* you?"

She shook her head adamantly. "No."

"Thank Christ." He kissed a path into her hair, his hand finding her breasts and kneading them each once, before skating his knuckles down the shuddering plane of her belly. "Is the ache so bad you don't know what to do about it?"

"Yes," she sobbed, flooded with alarm and relief in equal measure. How did he know?

"That's okay, gorgeous. I know what to do." He fingertips lingered at the waistband of her panties. "Are you going to let me?"

She nodded, whispering, "Please."

Holy shit. Her knees were shaking, her breath wheezing in and out, but she felt gathered together, secure even in the storm, when his body pressed the front of hers tight to the door, mouth busy on her neck while he yanked down her panties to midthigh and . . .

And slowly delved two fingers inside of her. Deep, deeper still until she gasped, compelled to rise up onto her toes, curving her butt into his lap and seeing nothing, nothing but stars, hearing only the rush in her ears as he fingered her roughly, the heel of his hand pressing and rubbing her clit every few pumps until she was openmouthed and clawing at the door . . . and then, as if he knew she was getting close, he focused in on her clit and exploited the sensitivity with three finger pads, rubbing so fast that she couldn't have matched him for speed. Not even with her own fingers, her own body.

"Oh my God. *Oh my God.*"

"What happens in my room?"

"I . . . I . . . what?"

"This is where you come to be fed, Tallulah." His magical fingers picked up the pace that much more and she whimpered, squeezing her thighs around his hand. "Nowhere else and no exceptions. *I* tend to you. Especially after you get on your knees and suck my cock raw."

It was the grind in his voice, the explicitness of his words and the sudden pressure of his three fingers back inside of her that caused release to wreck her, mind, body, and soul. She went somewhere. Somewhere beautiful and gleaming and made of rainbows while she shuddered and orgasmed between Burgess's barrier of a body and the door. Sobs broke and broke and broke past her lips, her legs quaking, hands slapping and twisting against the door, immense relief coursing through her, muscles contracting almost in shock.

As soon as it was over, she collapsed, Burgess catching her on the way to the floor, looking down at her in his arms for several beats with an expression of pure animal pride, before carrying her to the bed, tugging up her panties and smoothing them—a little unnecessarily—over the mound of her sex. Getting in beside her, he lay down, drew her into the warmth of his giant body, and made a gruff sound that found its target in her chest.

I'm screwed.

That was her final thought before passing clean out.

CHAPTER TWENTY

Burgess woke up knowing Tallulah wouldn't be in bed beside him.

But he couldn't help but stack his hands beneath his head and smile, perhaps a tad smugly. Because she *had* been there as recently as a couple of hours ago. He'd woken up to find her nose smooshed up against his chest, her eyelashes making fringy, black half-moons on her cheeks. He'd planned on waiting until the last possible second before sunrise to carry her back to her room, because he didn't think she'd want to be discovered in his bed by Lissa, but the warmth of her must have put him back to sleep.

Burgess allowed himself a final, fleeting grin, directing it up toward the ceiling, seeing nothing but memories from last night. Tallulah being so generous on her knees that he was pretty sure he'd died and left his body twice. That slippery clutch of her mouth, the vibration of her throat, those eyes glassy with heat. Walking upright today was going to be a challenge with those images at the forefront of his mind, but the one now making him stiff beneath the top sheet was Tallulah's body shaking, how she'd gone limp between him and the door, falling right into his arms where she belonged.

I've still got it.

He stroked a hand down his face and beard, scrubbing the satisfied smirk off his face.

All right, so maybe he still had it.

Didn't mean he had the girl. Yet.

That thought handily erased the final traces of his smile and he tossed aside the covers, climbing out of bed. His back gave an ominous throb as he stood, a wave of queasiness rolling through him before subsiding, the ache settling into one he could manage. *Would* manage.

You were amazing out there.

Well maybe you had a couple steps to spare.

With Tallulah's voice in his head making him feel ten feet tall, a puny little backache was nothing. It no longer felt like an injury signaling the end of his career; it was a minor worry—and he had a major one that needed his attention.

Tallulah was endgame.

He needed her to get that.

Burgess brushed his teeth, finger combed his hair, and threw on a pair of sweatpants. He started to put on a shirt, then remembered his muscles seemed to be working wonders and left it off, padding out of the bedroom and down the hallway. He heard Lissa and Tallulah before turning the corner into the living room and had to pause, the rightness of it hitting him right in the jugular. He liked their voices together. He liked the gentle sizzle of pancakes and his daughter giggling about something Tallulah said. These things made his apartment seem like a home for the first time since he'd moved into it.

Furthermore, he didn't feel like an intruder as he stepped out into the open. Didn't feel guilty for showing up and trying to fit into the family unit after being absent, thanks to hockey.

He belonged. She'd made him belong.

Now he just needed to convince her she belonged with him.

And when she turned at the stove with a deer in the headlights expression, he knew that probably wasn't going to be easy.

Fine. Fuck easy.

"Hey, Dad," Lissa sang, her bag packed at her feet. A quick check of the clock said Ashleigh would be there in ten minutes to pick up their daughter. Shit, he should have gotten up sooner. Blame the gorgeous grad student who'd melted his bones last night. "Good job, last night. You were extra mean."

Burgess's lips twitched. "Was I?"

"The other team looked so sad at the end."

"Losing is good once in a while," Burgess said. "It makes you try harder."

"Losing is good?" His daughter's eyebrows went up. "For you, too?"

"Hell no. Not for me. *Other* people."

Lissa laughed. He started to walk past her, but decided to lean in for a hug instead, patting her gently on the back. "You're good luck. Told you."

She ducked her head, but he still caught her smile. "Yeah."

Burgess locked eyes with Tallulah when he circled the breakfast bar into the kitchen, suddenly hungry for some acknowledgment that they'd given each other orgasms last night and slept in the same bed. He didn't want to pretend it hadn't happened. "Morning."

"Morning," she said back, pink filtering into the tan of her cheeks. "It's raining."

His attention drifted to the nearest window, taking in the gray sky, the droplets clinging to the glass. "Is it?" His eyes ran a lap around her face. "The sun is shining in here."

She fumbled the spatula slightly, but caught it before it could clatter onto the surface of the stove, a telltale pulse moving at a gallop just above her collarbone. "Do, um . . . do you want pancakes or are you sticking to your Diet of Doom?"

"Have to stick. Especially during the season." Playfully, he flexed a bicep for Lissa. "One pancake or peanut butter smoothie and this deflates like a balloon."

Lissa snorted, digging into the plate of pancakes Tallulah set down in front of her. "No, it wouldn't."

Tallulah poured another circle of batter onto the pan, very obviously pretending not to watch him flex. "You know, half the joy of pancakes is sharing them with someone else. No one wants to watch someone eat egg whites while they're adding a second layer of syrup to their breakfast. You enjoy it more when you get to watch someone else enjoying it, too."

"Maybe in the off season."

Lissa and Tallulah traded an eye roll.

His daughter was halfway finished with her first pancake when the intercom buzzed, the doorman's voice filling the apartment. "Mr. Abraham. Your guest is waiting downstairs."

"That's my mom," Lissa said, jumping down off the stool while in the process of rolling her second pancake up like a taco. "Thanks for the pancakes, Tallulah."

"Anytime, babe. See you Monday."

Lissa started for the door, but stopped and circled back to the kitchen, giving Tallulah a hug where she stood at the stove. "Bye."

Caught off guard, Tallulah recovered quickly and squeezed Lissa in return. "Bye."

Burgess picked up Lissa's bag and followed his daughter to the door, his chest tight as he shoved his feet into the slip-ons he kept by the coat rack. Before he could walk out after Lissa, Tallulah cleared her throat in the kitchen. In a way that implied she had something to say. "Um." She waved the spatula at him. "Aren't you going to put on a shirt?"

"Wasn't planning on it."

She faced the stove again, her chin notched up. "Oh."

"You want me to cover up?"

"It's up to you."

"Are you sure about that? Seems kind of important."

Tallulah let out a high-pitched laugh that didn't sound all that humorous. "I'm sure your ex-wife has seen you shirtless before."

"Yeah." Hiding his smile was growing more difficult by the second. "Honestly, it's hard to remember anything that happened in my life before you moved in."

She wouldn't look at him.

He took a jacket off the coat rack and put it on, buttoning all the way to the top, smiling on the inside when her shoulders relaxed. "I'll be right back. Stay where you are."

She shrugged daintily. "Fine."

A moment later, Burgess got into the elevator with Lissa, trying not to let it show how eager he was to get back up to the apartment, but Jesus, his pulse was slamming in his veins, his mind coming up with ideas on how to wipe that half-confused, half-miffed expression off Tallulah's face. And then later today, he was going to bring her to a place he'd been dreaming of taking her since . . . fuck. Since they'd met in California.

God, he'd been gone for this woman so long.

He wanted rings on fingers. Commitment. Permanency.

All the things she'd told him she *didn't* want. From the beginning.

The closer they got, the more he wanted to pretend she'd never said those words, but that would be unwise. Just like last night, he'd continue to keep their relationship unlabeled. Even if in his head, they were each wearing a label written in black Sharpie.

Tallulah's read MINE.

His read HERS.

Burgess got Lissa safely into Ashleigh's car, stowing her bag in the trunk, before practically jogging back to the elevator and impatiently stamping the button for his floor. Watching the numbers go up on the screen, he pushed five fingers through his hair, reminding himself to be patient. Not to rush her.

While also making it clear he was serious.

Easy.

On his way to the apartment, he was already unbuttoning the

jacket and he dropped it to the ground as soon as he was over the threshold. And he kept walking right to the kitchen where Tallulah was standing at the counter, just about to take her first bite of pancake. She dropped the fork when he was five feet away and that was good, really good, because he went into the kiss hard, spinning her around and lifting her feet clear off the ground, her ass rattling the lower cabinets as he slanted their mouths together, growling in a way that he hoped said *this is how I want to fucking wake up.* After her initial surprise wore off, and it wore off fast, her fingers dove into his hair and pulled, her mewl tasting like heaven on his tongue, his lips twisting over the top of hers, pulses pounding in his temples.

"Tell me you want to be the only one who sees my bare chest, Tallulah, and it's done." He wound her hair around his fist and tugged her head back with just enough force to make her suck in a breath. "Matter of fact, it's done either way. Feel free to add some nail marks to it."

His au pair appeared to be adorably scandalized. *"Burgess."*

"Yeah? Say what you want."

Two shallow breaths. "Right now, I just want you to kiss me again."

This time, when he claimed her mouth, he was growling, a sense of victory spearing him in the dead center of his chest. He hadn't felt this sense of purpose in such a long fucking time, like he had something worth winning right within his reach, and he packed intention into the kiss, using her fisted hair to tilt her left, coming at her like a starving man, keeping it up until she started to shift around restlessly between him and the counter. "What else do you want?" he said against her swollen mouth. "Do you want to see me tonight?"

"Yes."

Thank God. The organ in his chest boomed wildly. "You

want to come to my room again and call it a massage? Just see what happens?"

She was nodding, gratitude softening her features. "Yes."

"Then that's what you're going to get."

"Maybe I'll let you massage *me* this time," she whispered, winding her arms around his neck and very lightly dragging her tongue along the seam of his mouth. "You won't be too rough with me, will you, Sir Savage?"

Son of a—

Heat ransacked his lower body, his hands moving of their own accord, boosting her up so he could pin her to the cabinets, her bare legs wrapping around his hips like silk. Tightening. Taking two handfuls of sweet ass, he thrust up between her legs with a grunt, instantly obsessed with the way her eyes glazed over with need. Excitement. "Gentler? Or rougher?" he asked, massaging that beautiful backside. "Just in case I need to know for later."

Oh, she liked that. Appreciated the lack of firm planning. The lack of pressure. The spontaneity didn't suit him, but the increasing welcome of her body, the euphoria that painted itself on her face when he didn't demand answers? That sure as shit suited him, so they would play this game as long as necessary. "Rougher, gorgeous?"

"*Yes.*"

Burgess pumped again, harder this time, though he was still tempering his strength, and her nails dug into the back of his neck, a shudder going through both of them. At the top of that drive, he ground himself against her warm pussy, remembering everything he'd learned about it last night. How soft and tight it was. How wet it got from blowing him. "Rougher?" he rasped.

Her nod was vigorous. "Stop holding back."

"Ahh. I'll always have to hold back a little, Tallulah. I'm a beast, remember?" His grip turned bruising on her ass, his next thrust causing her ass to pound loudly into the cabinets. "But how's that?"

"Good. Oh my God, so good. So good."

Burgess groaned, burying his face in her neck and drove upward several more times, humping her through their clothes, the sound of her hitched whimpers like music to his ears. "If I didn't have a postgame meeting this morning, I would spend the day like this. Throwing you up against every wall in this apartment and fucking you through your panties until you say you're ready for me to rip them off." He raked his tongue up the side of her neck. "Goddamn, you sucked me off so good last night. I can still feel your mouth working my dick."

Her nails sank deeper into the meat of his neck, her thighs starting to quiver around his hips. "Please. A l-little more. A little more."

"You want to come?"

She bit her lip and said something unintelligible that he interpreted as a yes. Her moisture was beginning to dampen the crotch of his sweatpants, her breaths turning stuttered and erratic. Close. "Tell me you still taste my come in your throat and I'll finish you off."

Tallulah's moan filled the apartment. "I still taste you in my throat."

Lust socked him in the gut. "Good girl."

All it took was three more flexes of his hips to make her eyes glaze over, a violent shiver coursing through her body, her thighs squeezing around him so tight, so tight, like she wanted to close them completely to combat the pleasure, but couldn't because he was blocking the action and now nothing could defend her from the twist of bliss, so she let it pummel her. He watched all that play out on her incredible face, looking right into her eyes, more connected to her than he'd ever been to anyone else in his life.

When her trembles started to lose tension, he turned her sideways and scooped her up against his chest, carrying her through the apartment to his bedroom where he laid her down in the messy sheets. After a moment of thought, he strode to the guest bedroom—hard dick and everything—to retrieve the balled-up sweatshirt she used as a pillow, bringing it in to her, making a gruff sound so she would lift her head, allowing him to slide it under.

"You'll see me later," he said, brushing his knuckles against her cheekbone.

After a beat, she nodded. "You'll see me, too."

"Good."

She blinked, as if suddenly remembering something. "Burgess."

"Yeah."

A beat passed. "I think it might be a good idea to talk to Lissa soon. Not about us," she rushed to qualify. "Not yet. I mean, maybe not ever. This could be a fling or temporary insanity—"

"You're just *asking* to be panty fucked again, Tallulah."

"I'm not. I mean . . . I wouldn't turn it down. But what I'm trying to tell you is . . ." She wet her lips and propped herself up on one elbow. "Last night, she was talking again about you and Ashleigh getting back together. And I'm worried she's getting her hopes up so high, the disappointment could hurt. A lot. That is, if what she wants isn't going to happen—"

"It's not."

She studied his likely thunderous expression for a moment. "I know."

"Good. I'm glad you know." He stroked a thumb down the crease in the middle of her bottom lip. "I'll talk to Lissa about it."

"Okay." She yawned, flopping back down again and curling her arm around the wadded-up sweatshirt. "See you later."

Getting dressed and leaving Tallulah there, soft and a little bewildered looking in his bed, wasn't an easy task. But he left the apartment with a smile on his face.

Because he had a date tonight with the woman he'd fallen in love with.

CHAPTER TWENTY-ONE

Tallulah walked into a dream.

She'd been to the New England Aquarium on a few occasions, and it never failed to stupefy her with its high ceilings and underwater atmosphere. Most of the time, there were crowds blocking the glass or field trip leaders shouting at their charges to stop running, but at nine o'clock at night, there was no one home.

Apart from the nightguard who'd let them in, there wasn't a single other soul at the aquarium. Only Tallulah and Burgess. Free to roam anywhere without so much as a ticket.

"How did you do this?" she breathed, walking through the cavernous space, turning in a slow, awestruck circle to take it all in. It was so quiet, she could hear their footsteps, the sound of the filters running in the giant tanks full of colorful fish, the ripple of water.

"I don't use my name to pull favors very often in Boston, but . . ." He walked along behind her, hands shoved into the pockets of his pants. "Found the most worthy reason."

Tallulah pressed her hands to the sides of her face and squeezed until it kind of hurt. "I can't believe you did this. I can't *believe* it. I don't even know where to start." Spinning around like a kid in a candy store, Tallulah stopped when her attention landed on Burgess and she realized she knew exactly where to begin. Without second-guessing the impulse, she took three big steps and launched herself at him, his now familiar grunt bringing a dreamy smile to her face, especially when those big arms picked her up off the ground, his nose inhaling the scent of her unbound hair. "Thank you, Burgess. We just got here and I already know I'll never forget this."

He kissed her temple. "Take your time, Tallulah. Enjoy it."

Oh boy. What was the intense pressure behind her eyes all about? Was it the fact that this man had thought about what mattered to her and delivered? Or was it the insufferable, cardiovascular tug that was becoming the norm around Burgess? Could she reasonably pretend anymore that she didn't want to be with him? It was too much to think about right now when her emotions were spiking out of pure ecstasy. "You're going to enjoy it with me, because I'm going to show you everything!" She wiggled out of his hold until her feet touched the ground, then grabbed his hand and started pulling him along. "Pretend I'm your tour guide."

He made a low sound in his throat and she could feel his gaze lingering on the backs of her thighs, left exposed by the purple mini dress she'd worn tonight. "Guide me anywhere you want, gorgeous. I can keep up."

Sensitivity crept up her arms, spreading to her breasts and the slopes of her shoulders. She didn't need to turn around to remember how good he looked tonight—the image of him walking into the living room in a black button-down shirt, gray dress pants, and a belt was going to be engraved on her brain for as long as she lived. His hand was large and reassuring around hers, their fingers weaving together naturally. So natural. Just like being around him with her guard down felt now. Perfect. Easy. Like breathing.

"We can't go see the penguins first, because I'll never be able to move on to anything else," she said, not surprised to find her voice sort of feathery. "Let's start with the green sea turtle. Last time I was here, Myrtle was under the weather. I hope she's back—" Tallulah gasped as they turned the corner and the majestic creature came into view, paddling happily through her sizeable habitat. "There she is!"

"Myrtle?" Tallulah could hear the smile in his voice.

"Yes, Myrtle. She's kind of a big deal around here." She guided Burgess all the way to the glass, not giving the slightest resistance when he came up behind her, wrapping his arms around her shoulders and settling her back against his chest. "Um . . ." Oh lord, she was startling to become a little *aroused*. All the touching, the way they gravitated together every chance they got, the proximity becoming more and more intimate, made her panties feel . . .

Like a hindrance.

They were wet already, simply from holding his hand, knowing how his palms felt molding her breasts, stroking her hair encouragingly while she knelt in front of him. Now instead of looking into the glass and seeing beautiful Myrtle, she saw only the way her boss towered over her protectively, his athletic frame dwarfing her.

"You were saying, Tallulah?"

Stop thinking about sex. "Oh. Yes. Myrtle has been at this aquarium for fifty years, isn't that wild? A green sea turtle might weight three hundred pounds on average, but Myrtle weighs in at an impressive five hundred and fifty pounds." A laugh tripped over her lips. "She's, like, the Sir Savage of the New England Aquarium."

Burgess's big chest rumbled behind her, the bristles of his beard finding the curve of her neck and rubbing there. "I wouldn't want to square off against her."

"Smart man," she managed, tilting her neck even further and going up on her toes, sighing when he sucked on a patch of skin. "Good man. Very, very good . . . man."

"As far as tour guides go, Tallulah, you're very easy to distract."

"Maybe we should skip to the penguins," she blurted, tearing herself away while fanning her face, much to Burgess's visible enjoyment. Pursing her lips, she took him by the wrist and continued to pull him along, knowing the route to the penguin colony by heart. It lay in the direction they'd come from, near the giant ocean tank, but up a winding concrete ramp where they could look down into the rocky habitat from above. As soon as she looked over the railing, nostalgia and a sense of connection cranked a handle in her chest. "Oh," she whispered. "There they are."

As if Burgess realized this was an emotional moment for her, he didn't make contact, leaning beside her on the rail, instead. "Are you okay?"

"Yeah." She pressed three fingers to the space beneath her collarbone where the burden had concentrated itself. "Sometimes on a research project, you get really connected to individual animals. We can't touch or interact with them directly or we could upset the balance of the colony, but I did watch a penguin named Kirk extra carefully." She pointed. "He was an Adelie, like that little guy down there."

"I don't call things cute, but if I did . . ." He shrugged. "I'd say he's cute."

Tallulah laughed. "Kirk used to play pranks on the other penguins. At first, I thought I was imagining it, but there were too many coincidences. Skidding in behind his friend on a glacier and knocking him off. Or, there was an Adelie who had a more exaggerated waddle than the others and Kirk imitated him behind his back. I've never seen scientists laugh so hard." She let out a wistful breath. "It's hard not knowing what will happen to him."

"I'm sure he's got some good prank playing years left in him."

"I hope so." She studied Burgess's profile. "Did you have pets growing up?"

"Sure." His expression warmed. "I had a husky named Dunk."

"You *did*?" Tallulah furiously tried to picture a serious giant teenager with his trusty dog and found it made her pulse go out of whack. "Why did you name him Dunk?"

"We gave him a treat the day he came home from the shelter and he dunked it in some water. He was an older dog. Think he'd figured out the water made the treat easier on his teeth."

"Smart boy," crooned Tallulah.

"Yeah. He was. Couldn't bring him to my league games, though. He wouldn't stop barking because he thought everyone was trying to attack me."

"He should have been worried about everyone else."

"That's what I told him. He wouldn't listen."

A smile spread across Tallulah's face and she found herself missing his touch, the curves of his muscles against her softness, his breath on her skin. And so she eased in between him and the concrete wall, savoring the reunion of her breasts on his abdomen, the drag of her hips on his meaty upper thighs, the wind of her arms around his neck. "You have no idea how happy this made me. Bringing me here." She sank her fingers into the back of his hair, razing his scalp with her nails, and just like last night, his eyes glazed over at the treatment.

"Tallulah," he said, his tone a cross between formal and winded. "I'm in a position to make you even happier." He tried to get serious, like he was delivering a business proposal, but her thumbs stroked his ears and he lost the inclination, shuddering. A big bear who just wanted to be petted and scratched. "I'll bring you here every night, if that's what you want."

Tallulah gave a casual head tilt, even though there was dramatic rapping in her chest. "Do you think promising me aquarium trips will make me agree to be your girlfriend?"

"It's worth a shot." He framed her face in his hand, studying her features one at a time. Lips, nose, chin, eyes. "If this doesn't work, I'll try something else. And something else after that . . ."

He'd stolen her breath. She didn't think such a thing was possible, but there she stood, unable to find a single ounce of oxygen floating around.

Tallulah hadn't come to Boston with an eye toward finding a romantic partner. Hadn't even considered it. She was still finding her sea legs, learning how to live in the real world again without distrust and paranoia. Moreover, she never would have paired herself up with a divorced single father, eleven years her senior, who didn't like going out or being spontaneous or embracing the unknown. Burgess was mostly set in his ways, unlike her—or who she *wanted* to be.

Still, even at twenty-six, she knew this feeling wouldn't come around again.

Nor would she find someone so caring and noble and steadfast.

This man was a treasure, and giving up would be something she regretted for a long time. Maybe even the rest of her life. So, she wouldn't. She physically *couldn't*. He'd slowly knit himself into the fabric of her existence.

"What if I agree to be your girlfriend regardless of aquarium trips?" she said quietly, watching his big chest cease to rise and fall. Tallulah ran her hands down those significant pecs, his hard stomach and back up, nearly purring at the access she had to this perfect beast, joining her wrists behind his neck again. *God*, she couldn't stop touching him. "What would you say to that?"

A knot climbed in his throat. "Tallulah, are you being serious?"

"Yes," she said, lifting onto her tiptoes and kissing the underside of his bearded chin. "I want to be your girlfriend. Do you still want to be my boyfriend?"

"Do I—" he growled, jolting a little. *"Yes."*

"I guess it's settled then." She rubbed their mouths together, giving the seam a playful lick. "Do we get official T-shirts or something?"

"Tallulah," he said raggedly, lifting her off the ground without warning, making her yelp. Scratch that, he literally *threw* her up into the air and caught her with a forearm beneath her ass, making it oh so easy to circle his waist with her legs, giving her a very rare chance to look down into the face of a giant, instead of up. And her heart was flooding with so much happiness, her decision was the right one. She knew it down to the tips of her toes. While she planted kisses all over Burgess's face, he marched her right, then left, his gait stilted. "Where the hell are we? I have no sense of direction right now."

"Then why don't we stay right here?" she breathed, pressing their foreheads together and lingering, memorizing the sensation of his breath, how it joined with her own.

"Okay, yeah. Right here. Fine. I can't fucking believe it." He'd gone hoarse. "You're my girlfriend."

"You're my boyfriend." She coaxed his mouth open with brushes of her lips, their tongues meeting in a single touch, a groan shaking through the ample breadth of his body. "Should we talk about what that means?"

"You're really going to give me specifics?" Intensely hopeful eyes searched hers. "No more pretending it's a massage?"

"No more pretending it's a massage." She kissed him through his visible show of relief and gratitude, wishing she'd given it to him sooner. "Being your girlfriend means you're no longer my bodyguard. When we go on adventures together, it's simply a date."

"I'm still going to guard you," he blustered.

"I know."

His chest vibrated against her. "What else does being exclusive mean?"

"Exactly what you said. We're exclusive."

"You're all mine," he rasped, drawing her head to one side and sucking hard on her neck, like a barbarian claiming a mate. And dude, it was really, *really* working for her.

"Uh-huh." She slid down his body a couple of inches until his erection was lodged between her thighs, rocking herself against it once, twice. "And you're all mine."

"Ah, gorgeous. I've been yours since California."

A severe tug of her heart made her slightly dizzy. "I'm going to come to your games."

"And wear my sweatshirt?"

"I might have to spring for a jersey."

He let out a torrent of breath and dropped back a step, as if that possibility was too much for him to handle. "I won't be able to concentrate."

"Maybe it'll be easier after we spend a few nights taking off the edge." She rubbed herself side to side against his arousal, allowing her weight to push down on it more and more until he caught her ass in a bruising grip, keeping her in this one spot, tilting his hips and treating her to little bounces. "Is that the spot?" she whispered in his ear, her nipples and thighs tingling when he moaned in the affirmative. "I'm going to learn all of them tonight. That's what being my boyfriend means." She gave his ear a long, slow lick. "You get to take me home, strip me naked, and fuck me. However you want. As hard as you want."

"*Christ*," he hissed through his teeth, both of his hands up her skirt now, inside her panties to work her buttocks in a frustrated massage. "You're killing me. I'm serious. I won't make it to the car."

"Yes, you will. You're Sir Savage. That stamina is legendary." She kissed him fully on the mouth now, in between pants of breath, her hips hitching up and back now, faster and faster, swallowing the growls he issued from his throat. "I can't wait to test it out."

Burgess's expletive echoed through the aquarium as he started to walk, carrying her in long strides toward the exit. "What do you know? My sense of direction is back."

She buried her face into his neck and giggled, feeling like she was drunk. Or high. Or both. Just completely overcome with jubilation and lust and her connection to this man who touched her so gently one moment, aggressively the next. Her boyfriend.

And holy hell, she'd already fallen for him. Hard.

BURGESS COULD BARELY remember the drive home.

Actually, no. He remembered it in vivid, painful detail, he just didn't remember any landmark they passed or if he'd obeyed a single traffic law. Because Tallulah had her hand on his aching cock, stroking him through his jeans, and he'd harnessed every iota of his willpower to keep himself from coming. Or begging her to suck him.

Do not.

Do not do either of those things.

He had too much to look forward to tonight. Escorting his girlfriend home would have been enough to make his life, but in a matter of minutes, he'd have a one in a million opportunity to be inside of the hottest, most intelligent, passionate, funny, caring, interesting . . .

"Can I unzip you?" she murmured in his ear, sounding . . . Jesus, kind of pouty? Like she would cry if he said no. "I just want to give it a kiss."

Mother of . . .

What had he been saying?

His brain had turned into an actual head of cauliflower. Useless.

"Please God, I want to do this in my bed," he rasped, desperately trying to calculate the amount of time it would take them to get home. *Where are we? Wait, there's the deli.* He knew that deli. They were no less than a minute away. "Tallulah," he growled, snagging her wrist and holding it away from his lap. "I promise, I'm going to have your skirt up around your tits in three minutes. If we're not in my room when time is up, I'll take you on the floor."

Tallulah threw herself back into her seat, eyes closed, gulping in breaths and shuddering them back out. Mind blown. He'd not only convinced this incredible woman to be his girlfriend, but she was down bad for him, too. How the hell had he managed that? And damn, his heart was in this, too. He wanted to look into her eyes while their bodies were connected, wanted to make her feel safe and beautiful and gratified. Wanted to give her everything inside of him, lay it all out there, expose himself, be her best friend. Her addiction.

He wanted so much with her.

These admissions he made to himself were so huge, he almost missed The Beacon. But there it was, along with his reserved parking spot—and his tires screeched as he maneuvered into the space, anticipation clawing at his insides, his hands desperate to undress her slowly and touch every inch of her smooth skin. Kiss it. Bite it. Lick it.

Burgess turned off the ignition, got out, and jogged over to the passenger side, nearly ripping the door off its hinges in order to get her out. She fell into his arms and they stumbled around on the sidewalk, Tallulah on her toes, him leaning down to kiss her like it would be the last time. And—

A horn honked. Twice.

At first, Burgess didn't pay it any attention, because he was used to being honked at in Boston. Good, let him get caught and photographed kissing his girlfriend. Bring it on. He hoped it ended up on the front page of the fucking *Globe*.

But the honk returned. Blaring. It was . . . close. Not simply somebody driving past.

"Burgess," someone called—and his whole body stiffened. He knew that voice.

It was Ashleigh. His ex-wife.

Everything went to utter hell after that. So quickly, he couldn't do anything to stop it.

Burgess looked back over his shoulder to find the absolute last thing he wanted to see, which was his ex-wife standing at the bumper of her car with an exaggerated wince on her face. And Lissa on the other side of the passenger side window with tears streaking down her cheeks.

A warning shot fired in the back of his head.

Something had gotten past the defense. He'd fucked up some-how, but he was too disoriented to figure it out now. Don't worry, though, a few minutes later he would recall what he'd neglected to do—and he'd recall it big time.

"I'm sorry to show up like this. I tried calling. Todd had a family emergency, and we have to drive to Vermont tonight. I need Lissa to stay with you." Ashleigh leaned to the side, waving at a stone-silent Tallulah. "Funny way to meet the new nanny, I guess."

"Do not call her the nanny," Burgess barked on instinct, his hackles rising. "Her name is Tallulah."

Ashleigh crossed her arms. "She's even younger than I was ex-pecting. Don't you think it's a little much to be hooking up with someone under the same roof as your daughter?"

"It's not hooking up. It's not like that. And I don't owe you an explanation."

"You don't? We share a kid. Part of co-parenting is—"

"Ashleigh," Burgess said, seeing how much the argument was upsetting Lissa. "Let's talk about this another time."

His former wife followed his line of vision to the passenger side, her shoulders drooping, resigned and clearly concerned. "Yeah. Okay." She reached the door handle. "Hey, Liss—"

Burgess's daughter launched herself out onto the sidewalk be-fore her mother had a chance to open the door. And when all her twelve-year-old fury was directed solely at Tallulah, not him or his ex, Burgess remembered what he'd missed with stunning clarity and his heart sank down into his boots.

"You promised me you weren't going to steal my dad," Lissa shouted, her voice high-pitched and wobbly. "You are such a liar!"

"Lissa!" Burgess roared out of pure shock. Steal him. Liar? "We're going to calm down and talk about this, but there is *no* reason for you to speak to Tallulah like that. Apologize."

"No."

Burgess turned to apologize to Tallulah himself and found her usual glowing skin had paled, her attention locked on Lissa, and his pulse started to pound in his temples. This was bad. This situation was beyond a point where he could stop it from hurting Tallulah or his daughter. How had he failed so hard? "I'm sorry," Tallulah whispered to Lissa. "When I told you that your father and I weren't . . . I . . . it just happened—"

"I don't care. They'll never get back together now. I *hate* you." Tallulah blanched.

"Lissa, okay, that's enough," Ashleigh said, seeming a little caught off guard herself. "I might have asked about your father's love life a few too many times and given you the wrong impression. Maybe at first there was some leftover jealousy, but now it's pure curiosity. That's all. Lissa, Dad and I are divorced. I'm engaged to Todd."

"Yeah, but you're not married yet." She hit Tallulah with a glare so mean that even Burgess flinched. "If she hadn't come here, there would still be a chance."

Burgess didn't know what else to do; he could only follow his instinct to protect Tallulah from the blow of Lissa's emotional accusations, so he turned and wrapped her in his arms, whispering apologies into her hair, which was probably the absolute wrong thing to do. Lissa started sobbing and Tallulah, God, she was so stiff, her eyes beginning to water.

"Burgess, I'm sorry to do this, but I really have to go." Ashleigh's voice was quiet. "Todd's mother is in the hospital with a complication from her surgery and I have the car. I can't bring Lissa with me."

"I'll go," Tallulah said, trying to pull away from him. "I'll sleep at Chloe's or something."

"Absolutely not," Burgess gritted, cradling her face in his hands, brushing away her tears with the pads of his thumbs. "This is where you live. Stay. You did nothing wrong."

"No, I really think I should go. I'll defuse the situation by leaving. It's for the best."

"Tallulah, please."

But she was already ordering an Uber on her phone, her fingers shaking as she tapped the right buttons, her face stricken the entire time in a way that made him want to lie down and die. Because he couldn't stop her from leaving, and on some level, he knew it was the only way to proceed at that moment. But as she climbed into the back of a black sedan moments later, misery clogged his throat while he watched her drive away, wondering if their relationship was too new, too fragile to survive the blow it had just been dealt.

CHAPTER TWENTY-TWO

The following evening, Tallulah sat on Chloe's couch, staring through gritty eyes at her friend over the mug of her hot chocolate, her chest churned up and raw. Last night, she'd arrived on Chloe's doorstep with nothing but her purse, but she'd been too overwrought to explain what happened. Sweet as ever, Chloe had simply led Tallulah to the still unoccupied guest bedroom and urged her into bed, saying they would talk in the morning. Only, Tallulah must have blacked out from pure abject misery, because she didn't wake up until the afternoon, when Chloe was already at harp practice.

This was her first chance to speak to anyone about what happened. She hadn't even spoken to Burgess, although he'd called several times. Tallulah desperately wanted to know if Lissa was all right. She was also very afraid to find out she wasn't. The numerous calls were yet to be returned, but she would get to that. Maybe. Probably.

As soon as she fully absorbed what happened.

And what *was* happening. Continuously.

"I think I might be in love with Burgess," she stage-whispered into the quiet.

Chloe nearly spat out her hot chocolate. As soon as the shock wore off, a giant smile bloomed across her face. "Oh, my goodness. Really?"

"Don't look so happy about it."

"I can't help it. I'm a terrible romantic." Her grin dimmed in degrees. "Are you telling me this is a bad thing?"

"Let me start at the beginning." Briefly, she explained to Chloe how Lissa had been hopeful for a reconciliation between her parents and brought it up several times since the beginning of her employment. "Last night, we were in the car coming home from . . ." She expelled a breath. "Honestly, it was the best night of my life. He rented out the aquarium, Chloe. The *whole thing*. There was some, um . . . interesting foreplay in the works. We were kissing on the sidewalk, like *really* going for it, and . . . there they were. Lissa and her mother. There'd been an emergency and they'd been waiting for us to come back, so Lissa could stay while Ashleigh and her fiancé dealt with it. Lissa just freaked out. Worse than I was expecting she might. I couldn't stay in the apartment with them."

Chloe's mouth dropped wider as the story went on. "Holy shit biscuits."

"You can say that again."

"Holy shit biscuits."

Tallulah's snort turned into a groan, her head falling backward onto the arm of the couch. "The worst part is, I had told Lissa there was nothing going on between me and Burgess. When she asked me, I was still trying to convince myself there wasn't. Now she feels like I lied to her, which I kind of did . . . but only because I was lying to myself."

"You know what? It's all going to work out." Chloe squeezed her knee beneath the fleece blanket that was currently draped over them both. "Everything is life or death to kids that age. I was the queen of drama queens. Still am, sometimes," she said, taking a thoughtful sip of her cocoa. "I remember when my mother divorced my father and we had to move—again—and leave all my friends behind—*again*—I ran away the first day in our new house. I lived in a tree for six hours. My mother had to call the police and everything."

Tallulah's mug paused halfway to her mouth. "Wow. Did they find you or did you just eventually go home?"

"I went home." She shrugged. "I'm scared of the dark."

"Really. Do you sleep with a nightlight?"

"No. I leave the TV on the Home Shopping Network."

"A criminally underrated channel," Tallulah said, briefly raising her mug.

"It *is*." Chloe glanced toward the coffee table where their phones sat, side by side, each of them lighting up periodically. "I think we should call Sig. He'll know how to fix this."

Tallulah jolted upright. "What? How?"

"Sig fixes everything," Chloe said simply.

"What does he know about a twelve-year-old's psyche?"

"Probably not a lot, but I've gone running to him with far weirder problems."

"Such as?"

"Well." Chloe pursed her lips, thinking for a few beats. "I didn't know how to clean when he rented me this apartment. I'd never cleaned anything before, so he gave me cleaning lessons. He even created a homemade formula for hard water stains. He's a *genius*."

"Hold on, I'm trying to picture this professional hockey player giving cleaning lessons."

"I picture it a lot." Twin red stains bloomed on her cheeks. "Because it's funny, I mean."

"Uh-huh." Tallulah watched Chloe's reaction closely. "When did you say your mother was marrying his father?"

"I don't know. Next year sometime." The words came out in a rush and sitting forward, she quickly set down her mug on the coffee table. "But back to the problem at hand . . .

don't you think you should give Burgess a call? He's probably worried."

"He knows I'm here."

"I mean, he's probably worried you're going to end things."

"I don't know if I have any other choice. I don't want to be the person who Lissa believes is preventing her parents from remarrying. The things she said to me . . ." A pang struck Tallulah in the chest. "How do we come back from that?"

"Maybe . . . you don't. Maybe you go somewhere different." Chloe pointed at her own mouth, looking very pleased with herself. "That was pretty good."

"It was. Foot high five?"

They tapped feet beneath the blanket.

Mostly in the interest of distracting herself, Tallulah was just preparing to launch into a speech in defense of the Home Shopping Network when someone knocked on the door.

"Chlo?" came a deep male voice from the other side. "You home?"

Chloe's mouth formed an O. "That's Sig," she whispered.

"*What?*" Tallulah whispered back. "Did you know he was coming?"

"No!" Her eyes widened. "But he has a key."

Both women tensed, their heads turning slowly at the sound of a key turning in the lock of the door. Simultaneously, they got the idea to hide underneath the blanket, both of them yanking it over their heads, just as the apartment door creaked open . . .

And not one, but two sets of footsteps thudded in.

Oh lord. Tallulah knew those footfalls anywhere. Burgess.

He'd gotten sick of calling and now he was there.

Why hadn't she expected this?

And why were her toes curling up in anticipation?

Sig chuckled. Sighed. "Do you think the blanket makes you invisible, Chlo?"

"Maybe."

"It doesn't."

The blanket was torn away, revealing two very large, very annoyed hockey players.

Tallulah's gaze swung to Burgess, absorbing him like a houseplant that hadn't been watered in a week. Had it really been less than twenty-four hours since the last time she'd seen him? How had he managed to look so terrible in such a short space of time? Black circles hugged the bottom rims of his eyes, his worry and exhaustion evident in a way that made her want to lie down beside him and kiss him better. Guilt over not answering his calls drilled her in the stomach like a line drive from Pedro Martinez.

And the fact that she was casually making sports references made her want to cry even harder.

"Can we talk?" Burgess asked Tallulah, hoarsely.

"I don't know what to say," she croaked. "I'm sorry."

"Jesus." His brows drew together. "I'm the one who needs to apologize, Tallulah. Not you."

Tallulah's chest hollowed itself out, making her ache to bound off the couch and throw herself into his arms where she knew, without a doubt, she'd feel a thousand percent better.

Burgess's chest rose and fell heavily, as if he knew what she was thinking.

And wanted—needed—the same thing.

Sig reached down and snagged Chloe's wrist, hauling her off the couch. "Come on, let's go sit in my car while they work this out."

"No, Sig," Chloe said, reaching a hand toward Tallulah. "I can't abandon my friend!"

Tallulah shook herself out of her Burgess trance. "Yeah! You guys can't just walk in here and ambush us like this."

Chloe pointed at the mugs of cocoa. "Look! We're doing emotional recon."

"Do it later," Sig and Burgess said at the same time.

"Wow." This from Tallulah.

"*Wow*," Chloe echoed. "Don't get any toxic masculinity in my hot chocolate."

Sig tapped her nose. "I have a five-hundred-dollar Sephora gift card waiting in the car and a banana acai bowl for you to eat on the drive over."

Chloe turned on a heel and started walking. "Good luck, Tallulah."

Tallulah watched in shocked fascination as Sig ushered his future stepsister out of the apartment, the door closing neatly behind them, but not before Sig could shoot them a smirk. "Sold out for acai," she muttered. "I guess it really is a superfruit."

The words were barely out of her mouth when Burgess took a seat beside her on the couch, wasting no time before pulling her into his arms. Tallulah went so fast, she even surprised herself, climbing right onto him like a clinging monkey, legs circling his waist, her head lodging into the notch of his neck, his strong arms wrapped around her like a physical promise. "I'm sorry, Tallulah. I'm so fucking sorry for what was said to you." He kissed the crown of her head, her temple. "You didn't deserve that. I've been sick to my stomach."

"I'm sorry I didn't answer your calls. I think . . . I'm embarrassed, maybe."

"No. Don't be. *Please.*"

"How is Lissa?"

She lifted her head in time to see a shadow pass through his eyes. "She'll understand eventually. But . . . it might take some time."

Those two sentences landed like blows to her solar plexus. "She's . . . still really upset?"

Several seconds passed, each one heavier than the next. "Yeah.

I'm not going to lie to you. She is." His tone was grave. "It's my fault for not talking to her sooner."

"It's okay. It's a hard conversation."

"One that could have saved your feelings, Tallulah. One I could have had months ago and you'd still be home with me where you belong." He spoke through his teeth, stroking her hair and fisting it, pulling until he could look down at her upturned face. "I know this, us, is new. But I'm asking you to ride this out with me. Come home and do this. She'll accept it with time."

Oh my God.

Burgess was asking for something monumental. Not only to be in a relationship with him, which was enough of a leap for her, in itself. But to essentially . . . co-parent. Be the equivalent of a stepmom to a kid who actively resented her. That was a massive jump from being his fun, new girlfriend. Was it only a matter of days ago they were still pretending she was in his room to give him a sports massage?

"Burgess."

"I know," he said gruffly, against her lips.

"That's a lot. That's scary."

"I know." With the use of her gathered hair, he pulled her head back even more, raking his mouth up the slope of her throat. "God, I miss the way you smell and taste and fucking feel." Looking into her eyes, he shifted his hips forward so she could feel the growing thickness between his thighs and she openly sobbed. "I've been going out of my mind."

Tallulah slid her knees open wider on the couch and rocked forward, shuddering over the friction of panties on denim. "It's only been one day."

"One day in hell feels a lot worse after spending weeks in heaven, Tallulah."

"I'm heaven?"

"My heaven, yeah."

The scary unknown might have been a third party in the room, but the need to touch him, revel in his huge, reassuring presence, overruled everything in that moment. "One kiss and we'll talk this out," she said, mesmerized by the sculpted shape of his lips. The mint he breathed from his mouth onto hers, the calloused hands that moved so possessively up her thighs and around to her butt, sliding into her panties and gripping her cheeks like he owned them. Because he did.

"Yeah," he said, his breath beginning to labor against her mouth. "One kiss. Let's go."

"I mean, maybe we shouldn't. What if it turns into more? This is Chloe's *couch*."

"I'll fuck your mouth anywhere I want. You're mine."

"Whoa, yeah, okay."

Their lips joined hungrily, but so seamlessly, the soft clash felt like rough poetry, and a sense of rightness spouted in the center of her chest and spilled in every direction. Down her thighs, to her fingertips, up behind her eyes like hot pressure. They wolfed each other down—she believed that was the technical description—her body melting into the strength of him, writhing on top of his hardness in pure mimicry of her mouth, which couldn't get enough of his taste, who he was, the fact that he was there, the bridge that had been built between their chests from nothing into something sturdy that couldn't be walked across.

Could it be walked across?

There was no thinking about it now, because she was having her neck sucked, her backside molded like clay, moist heat beginning to dampen her underwear in that place they connected, soft rubbing on top of hard. They separated less than a millimeter to ply themselves with oxygen and didn't bother consulting each other if another kiss was in order, it simply was, but the act of throwing their one-kiss plan out the window stole the rest of their inhibitions, and Tallulah's hands were suddenly moving on their own, raking down the rough, mountainous terrain of his chest, lower to the fly of his jeans, twisting the button open and opening his zipper as much as she could in their positions.

Burgess broke the kiss, looked down, panting. "What are you doing?"

"I have to touch you," she said on a rushing exhale.

Briefly, he tipped his head back, making a low sound in his throat. "Tallulah, we were going to fuck as soon as we made it inside the apartment last night. I'm warning you that I'm in a bad, bad way."

"I'll take care of you," she whispered, nipping at his jaw while making more headway with his zipper, lowering it until she could finally slip her hand inside and find the source of his hunger, wrapping her fist around it and stroking, kissing into his guttural groan, their mouths moving in a messy tangle, his flesh swelling and pulsing in her palm. "Better?"

"No."

"What do you want?"

"You know goddamn well what I want."

"Here?"

She couldn't even remember where *here* was anymore, really. Not with his urgency filling her fist, their connection on the verge of exploding, the debris falling into a new, more permanent and meaningful landscape, their bodies nearly frenzied with the need to pick up where they'd left off last night, when it seemed like they would die unless they had dirty, messy sex.

No, she *was* going to die if that didn't happen.

Her inner thighs were ticklish things, her core pulsating so insistently that she was beginning to ache without something to fill it, her breath beginning to hiccup in and out, hand moving faster, faster until Burgess's head fell back, his teeth gritted, his agony clear. Agony she could put an end to, while eliminating her own in the process.

Deal with the fallout later. There was no stopping this.

Their scorching eye contact causing her heart to pitch and race, Tallulah rose up on her knees over his lap and used his stiffness to push aside her panties, gasping at the drag of smooth steel through her wetness, the drag of his head over and around her clit.

"Don't fuck with me, girl," Burgess panted, landing a sharp slap to her ass.

And her atmosphere turned wildly colorful, enjoyable stings racing up and down her arms, back, through her tummy. That slap caused her to react in a way she never could have predicted, drop-kicking her need into the next galaxy, making her feel like a scolded brat, and she would have expected to hate that, but oh no, no, her body was of an opposite mind, her sex contracting like a flower blooming in reverse, her hand shaking with the desperation to guide Burgess inside, to put him there—and she did, she did, absorbing that thick helmet of flesh into her body and wiggling her hips in an attempt to take the rest.

"Tallulah."

"Yes?" she whimpered.

"I want to get it in, too, but we need to slow down."

"*No.*"

His laughter was pained as he brought his hand around, strumming a quartet of knuckles over the front of her panties, making her mewl. "We've got some work to do before I get it in here. I've fingered you, remember, gorgeous?" He issued a grunt. "You're tight as a motherfucker."

Heat cascaded down her sensitive skin in waves, the vibrating hum between her legs turning almost monstrous. "I can't believe I like being spanked and told that I'm tight. Like, I can't *believe* it—"

Burgess stood up in one lightning movement, easily keeping her legs wrapped around his waist and striding toward the rear hallway where the bedrooms were located. "Burgess, your back—"

"My back hurts when I collide with musclebound athletes." He kicked open the door to the guest room and looked around, as if to determine if they were in the right place. Something on the bed must have confirmed it was, indeed, the right place, before he slammed the door shut with a bump of his hip and continued toward the bed. "My back can more than handle a pretty little thing like you."

The gruff delivery of that sentiment made her feel pliant, hot. For lack of a better term, fuckable. Sexy. "I can't believe I like being called a pretty little thing."

"If it makes you feel better, I got a semi that time you called me Mean Daddy. Now, get your damn clothes off." Burgess dropped her onto the bed and stripped the T-shirt over his head, messing up his hair in the process, the enticing power of shirtless Burgess making her hands tremble while she pushed down her panties, arching her back in order to remove the night shirt she wore. And then she was lying, completely naked, on the bed in front of him. In front of this rough-hewn hockey god whose erection was all but tumbling out through the open V of his jeans, his forearms a series of muscles and veins, chest heaving up and down, eyes glittering with an almost dangerous amount of lust.

Wow. Wow. Wow.

"Is that your way of telling me you want to be called Daddy?" she whispered, letting her knees inch apart so he could see how wet he'd already made her.

"Don't you dare."

"I might dare," she whispered.

Shaking his head, despite the affection turning his eyes a mesmerizing shade of blue, Burgess dropped his jeans completely and planted a knee on the bed, his beard tickling her inner thighs as he went down, down, down on her . . .

Looking her in the eye, he spit on her slit and licked it up. "Mine."

She almost blacked out. But she didn't want to because he kept going, his mouth a vessel for magic and it was so good. So perfect. He lubricated her clit in one animalistic drag of his tongue, before absolutely positively going to town on the most sensitive, vulnerable, neglected place on her body, his hungry laps of her flesh accompanied by low rumbles from his chest.

"*Fuck*," he growled, meeting Tallulah's eyes from his face-down position, his gaze glassy, jaw tight. "Thighs open, pussy drenched. That's how I know it's mine. Now I need to come home to you every night, get you hot, and make you grateful you date a big motherfucker." He delved his tongue downward between her folds and teased her bundle of nerves with the very tip. "Make *me* grateful I found my beautiful girl who knows how to take it."

"I'm ready," she sobbed, brain in the spin cycle. On some level, she'd known Burgess would be like an alpha conqueror in bed, but she'd never expected to respond like a shaking, impatient peasant, her body thrilling to the pure domination of him. But here she was, opening her thighs like a big box store on the morning of Black Friday, her nails scoring his scalp, his massive shoulders, her own hips, anything she could reach. "I'm ready, I'm ready!" she screamed through her teeth, but he continued to move his tongue in the most unique and confident way, like, like, in a snake pattern, pressing down the hardest on her clit, rubbing relentlessly, and her spine quite literally bowed without her permission, stars frolicking in front of her eyes. "Burgess, please! Please, please, please."

Instead of stopping, instead of weighing her down into the mattress with his heavy body, as she was craving, he gently filled her with two fingers and dragged his puckered lips side to side over her nub, humming as he went. And then he looked at her, his upper lip tugging slightly in a snarl, and added a third finger, pushing it deep until she cried out. Spat on her again. Pumped his fingers once, twice, twisting them, while bathing her with the flat of his tongue, over and over and over until she was ripping at the strands of his hair, pressing her hips up and begging, out loud. Begging for the end of her own life, because she couldn't take the incredible pressure anymore. Couldn't withstand it without breaking.

And that's when she shattered.

Screaming.

His lips ground down against her clit, pushing down and holding tight while she came, like how, *how* did he know exactly what to do? How was this real? Her sex clenched and quivered and pulsed in excruciatingly perfect waves of gold, sweat rolling down the slopes of her temples, toes digging into the mattress, bliss radiating outward, inward, everywhere.

She was still lost in the glory of it all when Burgess came up over her, wedged his hips between her trembling thighs and brought his fisted shaft to her entrance, his expression one of palpable starvation. "Still saying yes to this dick, Tallulah?"

"*Yes*," she managed, still unable to pry her molars apart.

Burgess's muscles locked up and he pumped home, deep, his balls smacking off her bottom, a fractured yell coming from his mouth, the headboard slamming off the wall. "Oh God. Oh God, yes. *Fuck* yes." He suctioned their mouths together, kissing her once roughly, before giving her a series of soft, gentle ones. "Look at me. Tell me you've never been filled up as full as I'm doing it right now. I need to know."

How could he even wonder? Her nails were sinking into the fleshy curve of his buttocks, urging him to scramble her like eggs. "Never," she moaned, lifting her hips. "I'm so full."

Still, his gaze took a few laps around her face, even as sweat started to form on his upper lip from the effort of holding still.

Until . . . "Yeah, I can see you like it." Relief flickered in his expression a second before he licked into her mouth, flexing his hips a couple of times, before beginning to rock, pulling himself out slightly and pressing back in. "Been wanting inside of you so long, I can't believe I'm there. Can't believe you're so fucking perfect. Goddamn."

"You've been inside my mouth before," she purred against his lips.

He groaned through a slow thrust. "Don't remind me of how well you suck my dick when I'm trying not to come in eight seconds."

Tallulah could actually feel herself grow more slippery where their bodies joined. Could feel every minute expansion of her lungs, his lungs, could pinpoint every atom in the air, her senses were so heightened from being connected to this man. "I suck your dick so well," she whispered in his ear, against his wishes, tightening her flesh around him cruelly, wanting him to join her on the cloud of pleasure where she'd been dropped, thanks to his tongue, floating and luxuriating in the scent of his sweat, the firm shape of him inside of her. "I suck it so hard because I love it."

In response, Burgess's breath shuddered out, eyes clenching shut momentarily. "Jesus, that's a hot squeeze." He reared back and slammed home. One, two, three, four, five times, his mouth open with enjoyment. "Fuck!" He slowed down, panting, visibly trying to rein back the need for relief. "The day we met, you could have asked me to bring you the moon on a platter and I'd have done it," he said raggedly. "Ask me for galaxies now. You get anything you want, gorgeous. Just let me be the one to spread these legs."

"I'll spread them so wide for you," she whined against his mouth, her body eagerly absorbing the blows that followed, the punch of his powerful hips, the rough ride of his erection over the sensitivity of her clit, rubbing and teasing her a little, before taking some hard thrusts all for himself, his tongue busy on her neck, in her mouth, his eyes feverish while watching her breasts jiggle while he took her. "Nobody's cock but yours."

The bed started to creak faster. "Say that again."

"Only yours."

His groan was almost earsplitting. "Good girl. Good fucking girl."

He enjoyed her body for everything it was worth and watching it happen, *feeling* it happen, was like an aphrodisiac. He pummeled her a while and pulled back, repositioning her legs to experience a different angle, before falling on top of her and straight fucking like an animal—and she grew painfully turned on in the unrehearsed, frantic face of it all, her nipples spiking once again, that ripple and flex reigniting between her legs. Oh. Oh. *Oh my goodness.* And it was like he sensed it, sensed the moment Tallulah's second orgasm started to build, because his gaze turned sharper on her face, watching, a muscle popping in his cheek.

"Yeah. That's right." He trapped her jaw in his hand. "You grateful for your big motherfucker yet, gorgeous?"

"*Yes*," Tallulah gasped, mentally and verbally, his confidence in her body, the way he knew just the right amount of force to use, made her feel safe and free and prized, so much so that she bit her lip and let loose, her hips smacking up against his thrusts, rigid flesh entering wet, their mouths loudly exchanging breaths while they worked themselves into a frenzy in search of that peak, that sharp, perfect, mutual peak so they could jump off together.

"Put your legs over my shoulders and let me finish rough."

How did he make an order sound like a request for permission? She didn't know, but his manner was so uniquely Burgess and she . . . was grateful. Grateful in so many more ways than one, because she could feel his gratitude in the air between them, in the blaze of his eyes and worship of his big body. And *God*, he was . . .

"So big," she moaned, accepting his first drive after propping her calves on his shoulders, watching his features become engulfed by lust, white teeth clenched together while his hips kicked into a purposeful gallop, his angle giving her the contact she needed on top of her clit to twist the comforter in her hands and search for an exit from the breathtaking quickening, the telltale pulsing of her muscles. And that total blackout of reservations, combined with the drugging effect of Burgess, made her mouth form words that didn't require approval from her brain. "That's so good, it's so good. Hurt me."

"Never."

"Make it hurt," she screamed.

He hesitated. And broke. *"Fuck!"*

That's when she realized he'd only been using half his strength on her—and the second half was raw and brutal and delicious. She heard the headboard crack, the groans of the bedsprings running together into one long, continuous protest, a shout stirring in his chest as he gave in to his nature and took her crudely, her body bent in half, his lips peeled back in a snarl, sweat coating his expansive chest, muscles straining.

The sight of him blew her right out of the comfort zone she didn't even realize she'd been living in, turned her almost feral as she slashed her nails down his muscular back and orgasmed beneath his punishing body, nothing but a shaking, satisfied mess, wet heat rolling down the cheeks of her backside.

And all she wanted was to be his relief. To see him break. To be the reason for it.

With that desire blocking out every other thought in Tallulah's head, she constricted her sex around his, drawing on all those delicate muscles and bit down on his ear. *"Mean Daddy,"* she whispered, and he spent inside of her, almost like she'd sucked it clean out with two single words, his Goliath form shaking her body and the entire bed with it, deafening groans releasing against her ear, and she only pressed closer, hoping the deep, growling sound of his pleasure would be the final thing she ever heard.

"Mean, so mean, so mean," she pouted, writhing on his stiffness to rid him of those final ounces and he flattened her, pumping several more times, before collapsing, the mess they made together dripping down her inner thighs and butt—and she couldn't have cared less. Didn't even rustle up enough wherewithal when her head was drowsy, body sated beyond belief, and she had this warrior as her own personal blanket. "Wow," she breathed, head spinning, the ceiling above resembling white puffy clouds.

"My God," Burgess said hoarsely into her neck. "My God, Tallulah."

"Yeah."

The muscles in his shoulders bunched. "I didn't hurt you, right? Please, I'll—"

"I am the opposite of hurt. It was . . . I can't . . ."

He lifted his head and hit her with so much affection, rubbing their lips together softly, slowly, that she lost the ability to breathe. "You can't what?"

Live . . . without you.

"I can't believe I . . . twice."

His mouth twisted to subdue a smile and he glanced quickly to the side. "Oh yeah?"

Mirth danced up into her throat. "Are you being smug?"

He shrugged a shoulder, pitched onto his side and drew her into a giant, warm bear hug. "Maybe I'm a little relieved I still know what I'm doing." He dropped a hard kiss on her forehead. Then another. "Twice, huh?" A grunt. "Hell yeah."

"No fair. I can only make you come once."

Burgess scoffed, running his hands down her back, giving her butt a nice squeeze. "Believe me, gorgeous, I could make you come a hundred times and getting to experience you once would still make it fucking fair."

"That's so romantic," she whispered, but it dissolved into an intimate laugh against his mouth, his big hand traveling up her back to stroke her hair.

"Tallulah."

"Yes?" she whispered, rolling their foreheads together.

"It's not a home without you." He pulled her close. "Not anymore. Come back."

CHAPTER TWENTY-THREE

Burgess hadn't been this clearheaded on the ice in years, especially on the road.

Tonight: Pittsburgh. As he collided with two opponents and a battle for the puck ensued, ending in him chipping it to one of the rookies, he was clear on his mission. Energized and focused. He wasn't thinking about his problematic back. Nor was he thinking about how his every movement would be perceived by the people occupying the seats. If they'd already written him off as a player who'd seen better days. If they were right.

Yeah, he was focused, although for the first time in his professional career, there was an underlying sense of *I can't fucking wait to go home.* Perhaps home needed some repairing, but it *would* happen. He, Tallulah, and Lissa had figured out something good and he'd fight to get it back. Harder than he'd ever fought for anything.

Thank God he had the perspective of someone in their late thirties—because the view from thirty-seven was valuable as hell. Happiness didn't just appear out of thin air; a man had to search for it, cultivate it, and guard it with their life. Someone like Tallulah wouldn't come along again. Ever. He'd found someone who slowed down time and made him feel immortal. Someone who believed in him. Someone *he* believed in, too. He'd been going through the motions for years; now suddenly there was determination in his chest to take her places, show her things . . .

Be alive with her.

Love her.

As if he could do anything but. Love and Tallulah were interconnected. There couldn't be one without the other. Love was her. She was love.

Someday, he'd walk through the door of the apartment, drop his bag. There would be an amazing aroma hanging in the air, whether it was takeout or Tallulah broke her rule again about not cooking. Tallulah and Lissa would look up from the kitchen table and smile at him, both of their homework spread out all over the place. He'd kiss Lissa on the top of the head, drop another on Tallulah's perfect shoulder, and he'd watch and listen and absorb them.

His home.

Someday.

The opposing offense sliced down the ice and Burgess forcibly got his head in the game, registering the spreading formation of a center and two wings bearing down on him. Keeping his eye on the puck as it was passed, positioning himself between the net and the left winger, who was already taking the shot. No time to stop it, but Burgess blocked the progress with his body, the puck rebounding off his pads onto the ice. His back was only a foot from the goal now and everyone swarmed at once, the Bearcats trying to get the puck out of the danger zone, the other team trying to press their advantage of already having gotten past the defense.

Burgess found the puck among the sea of skates and sticks, looking for a sliver of daylight through which to fire it—and there it was. He blasted it out, away from the net. The crowd's collective roar of disappointment only fed his aggression, and he skated after the puck, his job far from over. He had a rare moment of being out in the open with no one around him, the puck sliding toward the boards, bouncing off. He reared back with his stick, Sig approaching in his periphery. That was his target.

Burgess's stick never connected with the puck.

The moment the left wing slammed into him from behind and bashed him up against the boards, a blinding pain streaked through his lower back. Not a twinge, not a throb or a twist. This was a rip. A dislocation. A satanic level of misery that tore the breath out of his lungs and numbed his legs so completely that he couldn't stop himself from dropping. At first, the opponent provided enough support to keep him upright, but as soon as they skated back toward the other end of the ice, there was nothing to prevent gravity from doing its job.

Burgess landed in a kneel, and though he automatically struggled to get back up and keep going, because that's what he'd been taught, he couldn't. He couldn't fucking get up.

A very specific sound filled his ears. That desolate rush of winter wind he'd loved as a kid, when he was the only one out on the frozen pond in the morning. Heavy, reverent silence, snow absorbing the slicing of his blades. He could feel the welcoming cold on his face.

Then there was warmth, because Tallulah's hands were on his face, her smile right there in front of him. He'd pictured the pond from his youth a thousand times, the perfect solitude of those mornings being the part that appealed to him most. He'd never visualized anyone there with him. Never wanted to. But she was now included in his idea of heaven. She was heaven.

And she was watching this whole nightmare happen on television.

She was seeing this moment of weakness live—and that fucking burned.

Let the whole world witness this, except for her. That would have been fine.

Impossible, though.

Get the hell up.

"Burgess," Sig shouted to his right, but he couldn't even turn his head; the pain was so debilitating it tensed every muscle in his body, clenched his teeth together until he could taste blood. "Stay down, man. Don't make it worse. The trainer is on the way."

"No," he ground out, trying and failing once again to get back on his skates.

Christ, it was so quiet in the arena, every eye on him.

Horrifyingly quiet. They all knew. They knew it was over for him.

He knew, too, didn't he? That spreading pain beneath his collar that rose slowly and choked him left no room for doubt. This was the widow-maker. The career ender. His spine was being twisted in the hand of the devil, around and around, until black started to bleed into the edges of his vision, freezing sweat coating every inch of his body.

And he had no choice but to stop trying to stand up.

Humiliation stabbed into him from all sides. Denial. Anger. Resentment.

Tallulah's concerned face appeared in his mind, her clear pity pissing him off all the more, his fist coming down and slamming into the ice while the trainer asked him questions he couldn't process or acknowledge. Not while she remained, so young and free-spirited and optimistic, looking down at him, a broken heap. A man who was once someone great.

But could no longer be that for her.

As SOON AS she watched the injury happen on television, Tallulah started to move. She was still staying in Chloe's apartment, but all her stuff remained at Burgess's place, forcing her to go there in a blur and pack essentials even though she could barely focus. Could hardly summon the brain power to text Ashleigh and confirm Lissa would stay with her mother until Tallulah returned. Booking a flight to Pittsburgh when the tears wouldn't stop forming in her eyes was not easy, but she did it, her hands shaking as she ordered an Uber and organized a flight on the way to the airport, the phone slipping out of her hands and into her lap several times. She didn't stop to consider flying to be by his side might not be her place . . . yet. She just went.

Her heart demanded nearness to Burgess, and she obeyed blindly, dread breathing fire like a dragon in her chest.

When Tallulah reached the airport, she got through security as quickly as possible and jogged to the gate, since her flight was already boarding. And there, on every television screen she passed, was the moment Burgess went down. People grouped together, watching in silence, muttering things into their phones. This was Boston after all. This was his town. But seeing their obvious grief did nothing to comfort her. No. Only the opposite.

If they believed Burgess was done . . . did he believe that, as well?

Was it true?

If so . . . oh God, Burgess was going to be devastated.

Of course, he would.

He loved hockey more than anything in the world. The sport was interwoven with his identity. And he was spectacular at it. On some level, she'd foreseen more problems arising with his back injury, but this? So public and brutal and painful to watch. He didn't deserve that.

The flight time was only ninety minutes, but it might as well have been five hours. Tallulah stared straight ahead the whole way, cobbling together a speech to deliver as soon as she reached . . . wherever he was. The hospital, the hotel, the arena. She'd already texted Chloe to find out from Sig where Burgess had been taken and hoped to have that information as soon as the plane landed. And she'd be ready. She'd wrap her arms around him and assure him that he wasn't finished with hockey forever. If he wanted to keep playing, he'd go to rehab and come out stronger. On the flip side, if he needed to stop playing, so much life was waiting to be lived.

With her.

With them. Together.

She'd made the decision to move back in with Burgess and Lissa as soon as she'd seen him take the ice tonight. He'd stood there during warmups, so mean and forbidding, always adjusting his gloves. And she'd thought . . .

Life doesn't happen on her timeline.

She'd found her people before she was ready, but if she didn't seize this moment with them, there might not be another one. Her plan had been to surprise Burgess when he got home from Pittsburgh by coming back to live with him and Lissa. For good.

It's still going to happen.

She wanted to be there with Burgess more than ever now. If seeing him in pain could rend her heart in two, something huge was there. Running from her feelings for this man wasn't going to make them any less real.

The plane landed and she exhaled the breath she'd seemingly been holding the entire flight. There was a text from Chloe that contained the name of a hospital and a crying emoji, but Tallulah refused to dwell on emoji choices, ordering an Uber, instead, and throwing herself into the back of it, carry-on bag clutched in her arms.

Thirty minutes later, she walked down a squeaky, disinfectant-scented hallway toward Burgess's hospital room. She'd been directed to the orthopedic surgery wing, and the word "surgery" pealed like a chorus of broken bells in her head. Okay. Surgery. If she'd stopped to think, she would have known that course had to be taken. It was inevitable. But the road to recovery after any surgery was hard. Painful. Frustrating.

If anyone could get through it, though, Burgess could.

He was strong, powerful, resilient. A giant.

"My giant," she whispered, pausing at the sight of five men in suits outside of his room, all of them wearing grim expressions, some of them speaking into phones. They were likely from the Bearcats, relaying news to the powers that be, the media. None of that mattered to her, however. She was only there for the man.

Tallulah coughed into her fist as she approached the gathering of suits, gesturing to the door. "Hi, I'm Tallulah . . . Burgess's . . ."

A couple of them stared at her blankly, waiting for her to continue, but one of the men stepped up and extended his hand. The trainer. She recognized him from the game she'd attended. "Hey. Good to see you again, Tallulah, even if the circumstances aren't great."

"Good to see you again, too," she said, her throat dry as a Saltine. "Is he . . . up?"

Something that could only be described as ominous traveled across his expression. "Yeah, he's up. They're prepping him for surgery."

Even expecting to hear the word "surgery," the reality winded her. "What happened?"

· The trainer sighed heavily. "Slipped disc. He's having an artificial one put in. I'd like to say he'll be out for the rest of the season, but given how long he's been in the league and how tricky recovery can be, not to mention sustaining that recovery . . ." He looked at the door. "I don't know if we'll see him out on the ice again."

Denial raced through her bloodstream, accompanied by fear. But above all, she had confidence. In Burgess. "If he decides to get back out there, he will."

A quick flash of a smile. "You know him well."

Damp heat crowded in behind her eyes. "Yes. I do."

He studied her for a moment. "He's such a private person, I couldn't believe it when he asked me to bring his sweatshirt to his *girlfriend*." The trainer chuckled. "I asked him where you were sitting and he said, just 'look for the most beautiful woman in the place.'"

"Oh," she said, her voice sounding watery. "If you don't mind, I need to see him."

"Of course." The trainer hesitated, looking between Tallulah and the door. "Look, he's obviously not himself right now. Maybe . . . just be prepared."

With that dire warning ringing in her head, Tallulah pushed open the hospital room door and closed it behind her, eyes adjusting to the startling lack of light. Normally the cold comforted her, but just then, it only caused goose bumps to streak up her arms, her nerves to multiply. Burgess didn't even look at her when she stopped beside his bed—and he was wide awake. As large and commanding and extraordinary as usual, only now he was wearing a hospital gown that probably proclaimed the opposite, in his mind.

Ten seconds ticked by and still he didn't turn his head, a line leaping in his jaw.

This is bad.

This is so much worse than I was expecting.

Fine. She could handle it. He'd just lost the most treasured part of his life. His anger was understandable. She wouldn't let it beat her. Him. Them.

"Are you just going to pretend I'm not here?"

"You shouldn't have come," he snapped, turning hard, glittering eyes on her. Unrecognizable eyes. "There's nothing you or anyone can do. Go back to Boston."

Stones struck her breast, one by one, but she didn't allow the impact to show on her face. He'd never spoken to her so coldly. Not ever. *This isn't him.* "I'm sorry this happened. I'm sorry." She reached for his hand, slipping their fingers together. For the briefest of seconds, his grip tightened, eyes closing, nostrils flaring, but then he abruptly let go.

"I told you this would happen, Tallulah. Once I got medicine and doctors and trainers involved, instead of toughing it out on my own, like I always have, that there would be a domino effect. That those things would *ruin* me." His tone was harsh, so harsh, and it cut into her like a scalpel. "But you knew better, didn't you?"

Stay strong. "You're hurting and taking it out on me, but that's fine. Go ahead."

"Yeah, you're real tough now." He looked at the wall, not her, his right hand fisting in the sheet, like speaking was costing him an effort. Or maybe it was the words themselves. "Wasn't it just a few days ago you walked away because a twelve-year-old was mad at you?"

How long had she been inside this hospital room? Two minutes and she already felt punched full of holes. What kind of pain would ten more minutes bring? "I did what I thought was best. I still think I made the right decision."

"Good for you, gorgeous. The right decision is to *stay* away." He flicked a look at the door. "Go. Please. Go."

"Why?"

"Because I fucking hate you seeing me like this," he growled. "Get out."

"No."

The hurt was only going to escalate until she gave up and left. Maybe . . . she should go and come back later? Once he'd had a chance to digest the present and future? Maybe she'd come at too raw of a time? Maybe all that could be accomplished tonight was saying words he couldn't take back and she should leave before that happened—

"Did you think you would fly here and say something inspirational to make all the difference? That's not happening." His throat worked with a swallow. "I'm done with hockey and we both know it, Tallulah. It has never been more pathetically obvious that you're too young for me. If you think I'm going to have my college student girlfriend help me walk again after this surgery, you're dead wrong. I would have rather died out on the ice."

"Do you think my impression of you . . . or my belief in you has changed, because au're hurt? That's ridiculous. People get hurt."

"I don't. I'm not supposed to," he shouted. "I can't even *look* at you when I'm like this. I'm fucking *begging* you to leave."

"No."

His upper lip curled, cogs turning behind his bloodshot eyes and she could see it, the death blow was coming. Her feet stuck to the ground like cement, an almost morbid curiosity toward what he could cook up to make her go keeping her in place.

"I don't want you here."

"I need to be here," she whispered, unable to keep the tremor out of her voice.

He looked away sharply at that, jaw flexing furiously.

Burgess was not unaffected. He didn't mean the terrible things coming out of his mouth. She was close to getting through to him, and that belief caused courage to well in her chest. She had no idea of the source, only that she was grateful for it. Clinging to it with both hands. "I came here to tell you I love you." Her heart got stuck in her throat halfway through that sentence, making her words run together, high-pitched and breathy. Speaking that truth was freeing. The greatest adventure of all. And at the moment, the scariest. "Don't shut me out. We'll get through this."

He started at her confession, his blue gaze deepening in color, that large chest starting to pulse up and down. He opened his mouth to speak, then snapped it shut.

Another handful of seconds passed.

"You think you're strong enough to get me through this? You're not a coward who walks away, right?" His voice turned almost unnatural, like he was rushing to get the words out or he'd lose his nerve. "But there's a ziplock full of postcards in your purse that say different."

Those words rang so loudly in her ears that she didn't even hear the nurses entering the room, didn't see them until they were surrounding Burgess, checking his blood pressure and asking him questions. He didn't answer them, continuing to stare at Tallulah as she backed toward the door, hardly able to feel her feet on the linoleum.

Cold shock swallowed her in one bite. This wasn't the Burgess she'd fallen in love with. He was unrecognizable. A different man altogether. He'd fooled her. Tricked her into thinking he was different. Lulled her into a sense of complacency, before ripping off the mask. Perhaps not as bad as the man who'd locked her in a closet with the intention of killing her, but emotional cruelty brought its own brand of injuries. And as she continued to back toward the exit, those open wounds started to hemorrhage.

The farther she got from Burgess's bed, the more drastically his chest heaved, panic making dents in his hard resolve.

"Tallulah, my God, I'm so fucking sorry," he said, right before she stepped backward into the hallway. He pushed off the nurses' hands and attempted to climb out of bed, but roared over the pain it caused his back and landed on the bed again, face white. If it was a fraction of the agony detonating on repeat in her heart, it had to be excruciating. *"Tallulah."*

Those increasingly desperate calls of her name fell on deaf ears.

She turned and walked away.

CHAPTER TWENTY-FOUR

Burgess had no idea what day it was. After seeing the replay of his injury once, he'd banned the television from being turned on and refused repeated attempts by the nurses to open the window shades. If the sun was shining outside, he didn't want to fucking know about it. Anything less than a postapocalypse would be unacceptable. And confusing. It didn't seem possible that the world could carry on as usual when his chest had been reduced to a smoking crater.

He stared into the darkness now, the latest painkiller beginning to wear off, no longer targeting the hellish pain in his freshly repaired back, but he didn't ring for the nurse, like he'd been instructed. Nor did he press the button to release more morphine. No, he just lay there and let it grow increasingly worse, praying the pain would expand until it swallowed him whole.

His mindset was garbage. As an athlete, he was painfully aware of that. This defeatist attitude was pathetic. He should be meeting with the team physicians and trainers, plotting out his recovery time. Scheduling rehabilitation. He should be in touch with his teammates, assuring them they wouldn't miss a beat in his absence. As the captain, that was his duty.

Then there was Lissa. Apart from a brief phone call to assure her that he was okay, there'd been no communication. She'd be worried. He'd learned over the course of the last month how much their relationship benefitted from simply talking and he shouldn't backslide now. But he just lay there in the darkness and willed himself to die, instead.

I just want to die. Let me die.

Having all the time in the world to think was turning out to be a curse. Because he could see the events of the last month so clearly now. Knowing his duty as a captain extended to emotional support of his teammates . . . that was all Tallulah. Realizing his daughter needed a more open line of communication. That was Tallulah, too. All these worthy things he worried about now, even while his world was burning down, were worries because she'd heightened his awareness of the people around him. His relationships, his legacy, his outlook.

She'd altered everything for the better.

This woman had come into his life and flooded it with light.

And he'd kicked her out.

Time had stood still since the second she walked away. He'd let the doctors numb his body and steal his consciousness, rearrange his spine, talk to him in medical jargon that went in one ear and out the other. But Burgess was still living in the second Tallulah disappeared into the hallway. He was still there, replaying it repeatedly, growing increasingly sick with grief.

Jesus Christ, how could he say something so fucking horrible to the best thing that ever happened to him?

He could see it now, like a projection screen playing on the wall of the hospital room, the way she'd paled and stumbled backward a little, totally unprepared for him to lash out with that particular weapon—and oh, he was a bastard for using that against her. She was right to leave. She was right to keep walking while he shouted her name. Ignore his calls and texts.

She was right to never want to see him again.

He'd been wounded, devastated to have hockey taken away from him. But ironically, he'd stopped mourning the loss of his career as soon as she walked out.

That was a special kind of fucked up.

Because he might be able to recover from this back injury, but he would never, ever, get over the loss of Tallulah. No, he'd be living without oxygen for the rest of his miserable life.

The hospital room door creaked open, allowing artificial light to illuminate the room and he turned his head away from it, closing his eyes. "What now?" he barked. "I don't want the painkiller. You might as well shut off the goddamn machine."

"Wow. You speak to your nurses that way?"

"They're superheroes, you know."

Burgess turned his head sharply at the entrance of Sig and Wells. One of them slapped on a light and he squinted into the sudden and unwelcome assault on his eye sockets. "What the fuck are you two doing here?"

"What *are* we doing here?" Wells asked, shooting Sig a raised brow. "I have a beautiful fiancée back in Florida who gets turned on by wedding planning. I should really be there."

Sig crossed his arms, regarding Burgess in the hospital bed without a single trace of sympathy. More like disgust. And even in his rock-solid state of self-pity and misery, Burgess felt a spark of appreciation for that. "You remember why we're here, golf man. Tell him."

"Ah. That's right." Wells swept off his hat and slapped it to the center of his chest. "Welcome to your intervention."

"Intervention, my ass." The roar burned his throat. "Get the hell out."

"Sorry, but no," Sig replied calmly. "Normally, I would heed that warning from the legendary Sir Savage, but this is my one chance to tell you you're acting like a piece of fossilized shit without getting my nose broken."

Burgess's pulse started rapping in his temples. He didn't like this. He just wanted to go back to staring into the darkness. "You realize I'll be healed one day, right?"

"*We* realize that," Wells drawled. "Do *you*?"

A twitch started behind his eye. "What's that supposed to mean?"

Wells and Sig traded a look. "It means, you've been out of surgery for a week and you're refusing to be transferred to the rehab facility. You're sitting here rotting away like yesterday's trash." The golfer waved a hand in front of his nose. "And there's fish in it."

"We're here to tell you to pull your head out of your ass."

A whole week had passed?

Burgess had assumed it'd only been a couple of days since the surgery . . . but a week?

Apparently shunning sunrises and sunsets had taken a toll on him.

No. Losing her. That's why time no longer mattered.

"I'll go eventually. Just not today."

"Sorry, man, it's going to be today. They're getting the paperwork ready."

"I won't sign it."

"Why not?"

"Because I don't give a fuck if I heal or not!" Burgess shouted at their annoyingly placid faces. "That's why. All right? Should I go through rehab to buy myself one more year in the league? Two, at best? I've already slowed down, but how useful am I going to be out there, postsurgery? And what the hell does any of it matter now, anyway? She's . . ."

A few seconds ticked by. "She's what?" Wells prompted.

Saying the words out loud was like having his esophagus raked with a claw hammer. "She left me. I . . . hurt her feelings. Badly. I *forced* her out of my life. So I don't care if I ever leave this room again. I don't want to go back to a world where she's walking around hurt because of me. Just let me lie here and die."

That statement landed in the center of the room like a ten-ton boulder, the crash followed by a charged silence.

"Burgess—" Sig started.

"You don't understand."

"I understand more than you think," Sig snapped, briefly taking off his ball cap to rake five fingers through his hair and slapping it back down. "You were in a bad place. Tallulah is an understanding, compassionate person—"

"Stop talking about her. Please. It hurts worse than the injury." Burgess let his head fall back against the pillow while he pulled himself together, as much as possible. "Is she okay? Is she staying with Chloe?"

Sig's voice was gruff when he responded. "Yeah. She's with Chlo, although . . ."

"Although *what*?"

His teammate looked hesitant to tell him something and it was causing craters to form on his arteries. "She's been out. A lot," he said. "Last I heard, she'd gone kayaking on the Charles. Chloe also mentioned Tallulah taking a bus to New Hampshire for a hot air balloon ride tomorrow, but I don't have all the details. Bottom line, she hasn't been home much."

That news hit him like an uppercut.

Too many emotions to process inundated him at once.

Fear of her doing those activities alone, possibly scared. Definitely nervous.

Without him to protect her. That panic momentarily robbed him of breath.

Mostly, though, there was pride. In Tallulah. And it tripled and quadrupled. She'd grown strong and confident enough to take her adventures alone. The message was clear. She didn't need him at her side anymore. As much as that gutted him, he was proud. So fucking proud.

Wells stepped forward. "As you know, Burgess, I literally fired my girlfriend as my caddie. *Fired* her. Believe me, I wanted to drink myself to death afterward, because . . ." He shot a glare toward Sig. "You didn't tell me this intervention was going to require me to relive my own emotional trauma."

"Why didn't you?" Burgess said hoarsely, still thinking of Tallulah soaring in a hot-air balloon.

Wells squinted an eye. "Why didn't I what?"

Focus. "Why not drink yourself to death instead of coming here and annoying me?"

"Love you too, man. I didn't drink myself to death because there was a sliver of a chance Josephine would come back. And it was worth living for. Now we're planning a wedding in Costa Rica." He cleared his throat hard. "That's it for me on sharing. I'm out."

"Nice job," Sig commented.

"Thanks."

His teammate refocused his attention on the hospital bed. "This isn't you. Lying here, feeling bad for yourself. Get better and go apologize. Tell her everything you just said to us."

"It's not going to work. I really . . . did a number on her." A fresh wave of agony tripped and fell in his sternum. "I fucked up."

"The game isn't over. There's still another period left to play."

"This isn't hockey."

"Is it golf?" Wells asked. "We have a lot of holes, if you're looking for metaphors."

Sig shook his head at Wells. "You know, the thing about this intervention, Sir Savage, is we knew you were going to be stubborn. Hence, we prepared layers."

That tick behind Burgess's eye accelerated. "What do you mean by layers?"

Wells put two fingers in his mouth and whistled.

The rookies walked in.

"Oh, Jesus Christ," Burgess complained, wishing he was closer to the window, so he could jump out. Maybe get lucky and become impaled by a flagpole. "Are you serious?"

"Hey, Captain."

"Sup, Cap."

"What the hell are you smiling about?"

"Just relieved to see you alive."

"Even though, if I'm being honest, you smell like fish."

Wells pressed his lips into a straight line. "Told you."

"No one asked you to come," Burgess growled at the rookies.

"Sig and Wells did," Mailer and Corrigan said, simultaneously.

"Is there food here? Like a cafeteria?" Mailer asked. "My sister had a baby last year and the cafeteria food was top tier. Came for the baby, stayed for the banana pudding."

Burgess split a look between Wells and Sig. "I hope you're happy."

Sig snorted. "I'll be happy when you're out of this motorized bed, you big fucking baby."

The rookies' mouths dropped open.

"I don't like it when Mom and Dad fight."

"Me either."

Anger and pressure and resentment built in Burgess's veins until he swore they were going to burst. "What did you call me?"

"A big fucking baby. What are you going to do about it?" Sig held up his phone, and without breaking eye contact with Burgess, he tapped a green icon on the screen. The ringing sound filled the too-crowded hospital room. "I'm breaking out the big guns."

Burgess couldn't swallow, sweat forming on his palms. "Who are you calling?"

A familiar voice answered on the third ring. "Sig. They didn't have strawberry Pop-Tarts at the store," said Chloe, audibly crestfallen. "What am I going to eat for breakfast?"

"I'll track some down when I get back and bring them by."

"You will?" She sighed.

"Of course, I will." Sig shifted, coughed into his fist. "Hey, Chlo, you're on speaker. Remember when I told you we were doing Burgess's intervention today?"

Burgess rolled his eyes so hard, they almost exited through the back of his skull.

"Yes, I remember," Chloe said brightly. "Hi, Burgess!"

He grunted.

Sig kicked the bed, as if to say *be nice to her or die.*

Burgess gave him a withering look. "Hi, Chloe."

One of the rookies popped up behind Sig's shoulder. "Hey, Chloe," Corrigan drawled, adding a wink. "Allow me to formally introduce myself—"

Sig shoved him back across the room into his seat, which rocked ominously before settling back into place. "Absolutely not." He kept the rookie pinned with a death glare. "Not happening. Never. Don't even think about it."

"Sig," Chloe scolded him. "Don't be such a meanie."

"Yeah, Sig," Mailer complained. "Don't be a meanie."

Sig picked up a full box of tissues from the tray attached to Burgess's bed and threw it at the rookie, who blocked it at the last second with a defensive forearm.

"This intervention sucks," Burgess declared.

"Really?" Wells asked, settling into a lean against the wall. "I thought it was just beginning to get interesting."

"I'm sorry my pain isn't entertaining enough."

"You're forgiven."

"Chlo," Sig said, hitting Burgess with some truly ominous eye contact. "How is Tallulah doing?"

"Stop," Burgess managed, his chest already on the verge of cracking open like an egg.

"Umm." Chloe paused long enough that Burgess felt the threads of his sanity thinning, fraying, nearly snapping. "She's just okay."

"What does that mean?" Burgess shouted.

"It means, she's . . . going to class and staying busy with her outings, but not really . . . present, I guess. She's pretty checked out."

Pretty checked out. Put those words on his grave, because they were going to bury him. He could already smell the freshly turned earth. "Why are you doing this to me?"

"Why are you doing this to *me*?" Wells raked a hand down his face. "I'm getting flashbacks."

Sig clucked his tongue. "Because you need a reason to get out of this bed. What would you do if someone *else* hurt Tallulah like this?"

Burgess's hands turned to fists. "Slaughter them."

"Yeah, but *after* that."

"I'd . . . go make her feel better."

"Exactly. You'd do everything you could to fix what's broken."

"Lying here isn't going to do that," Corrigan pointed out.

"Do you think they still have banana pudding?" whispered Mailer to his friend.

"I'll concede that inviting them here was a bad idea," Sig said.

Burgess hoisted a brow. "You think?"

"Burgess," Chloe said. "I managed to get her out shopping yesterday, so we could both buy some bathing suits and sandals for Costa Rica. Not easy to find in Boston during the winter, but prevail we did! Anyway—"

Sig almost dropped the phone. "What do you mean you *both* had to buy bathing suits? You're not going to Costa Rica."

"Yes, I am."

"Yes, she is," Wells interjected. "I hired her to play the harp during the wedding ceremony. On Burgess's recommendation."

"Was anyone going to tell me?" Sig sputtered.

"I was a little busy wrecking my back."

"He *did* suggest we add you to the guest list, too," Wells continued. "And we did. Although, I'm sorry to relay the news that you're sitting with Josephine's uncle Herb. Aptly named because he smokes a lot of medicinal herb. Glaucoma."

"We should have brought you shopping with us, Sig!" Chloe lamented. "You always know what colors look best on me."

"That's easy. Every color looks—" Sig broke off, took a centering breath. "Back on track, Chlo. What did you tell me about that guy giving Tallulah his phone number?"

Burgess's chin snapped up so fast, his neck popped. Jealousy went through his chest like a bull in a china shop, smashing plates and teacups as it went. *"What?"*

"Yup!" Chloe sang brightly. "A professor, actually. But he teaches undergrad, so it's cool. She's not sure whether or not she's going to call him, but I told her to go for it. He's yummy."

Burgess and Sig were staring at the phone, like they wanted to bite it in half.

"I told her she should invite him to the wedding, too. She gets a plus one!"

"No, the hell she doesn't." Burgess ignored the sting in his back as he sat up slightly, pointing a stern finger at the golfer masquerading as his friend. "Wells. Take back the plus one. Now."

"The invitations are sent." He faked a wince. "It's out of my hands."

His head was on the verge of exploding. There wouldn't be enough doctors to repair him if Tallulah showed up at this wedding with a professor. How old was this guy anyway? He didn't want to know. "How old is this professor, Chloe?"

"Um . . . like, forties? Yeah. And a Sagittarius, so he *loves* an adventure."

Burgess could barely see straight, the throb in his head had intensified so much. Forties? Adventure? This had all happened in the space of *one week*? Was she . . . moving on already? Because he never would. Ever. It was Tallulah or no one—end of story. And suddenly, he was more helpless and panicked than he'd ever been in his entire life. This would never have happened if they'd just let him remain in the darkness, numb and angry and protected from further pain. "As soon as I'm better, I'm kicking everyone's ass!"

"Aha!" Sig widened his eyes. "Does that mean you're going to rehab?"

Burgess crossed his arms over his chest. "I didn't say that."

"You stubborn motherfucker."

"Sig!" Chloe gasped.

"Sorry." He tapped his finger on the back of the phone. "I'll see you later with some Pop-Tarts. Frosting, right?"

"My *hero*!"

A line appeared between Sig's brows. "*You* don't have a plus one to this wedding, right, Chlo?"

"Yes, I do."

His left eye twitched. "Okay. See you later."

Sig hung up the phone.

The rookies were elbowing each other.

Burgess and Sig traded a silent communication that could only come between two athletes that had spent the last six years predicting each other's moves on the ice. Sig's jaw flexed. Burgess shook his head almost imperceptibly. Sig's upper lip curled. Burgess sighed.

"What was that?" Wells said, sounding almost awed.

"We'll tell you in a minute. But we have one more intervention guest and she's been waiting very patiently with an iPad and a Big Gulp." Sig jerked his chin at one of the rookies and they stood, opening the door.

And in walked Lissa.

Burgess's throat seized up so suddenly, he briefly looked away to get himself under control. His chest burned like the surface of the sun. *My kid. My kid is here. Seeing me like this.* It was unbearable and yet, he was almost knocked over by the relief and joy of her presence.

"Hey, Liss."

She'd stopped at the side of the bed. "Hi."

He reached out and ruffled her hair. "I'm okay, kid."

Was he, though? He should be up trying. To move. To heal.

If anything could be deemed motivation . . . it was his daughter. She needed him. Tallulah had made him see that, hadn't she?

Lissa remained stoic for several beats of time, before her chin started to wobble. "Dad?"

"Yes?"

It took her a long time to speak. "I messed everything up," she whispered finally. "I keep thinking about how happy you looked with Tallulah before . . . I said those horrible things to her. I didn't even mean them, I was just sad."

"She knows that, Liss."

Hope traveled like a shooting star across her face. "How do you know? Have you talked to her?"

Burgess took a moment to breathe. "Not in a while. But she knows you love her, Lissa."

"You love her, too. And I made her leave."

"I'm just as guilty of making her leave, kid. Believe me."

"When is she coming back?" She looked down at her fingers as she twisted them together. "I didn't even get to tell her I got picked to play Juliet in English class."

"You did?" he managed to say. "Damn. Congratulations, kid. I'm proud of you." The next part burned his esophagus, because it was so true. So heavily true. "Tallulah would be proud of you, too. You know that."

"Please. I wouldn't have done it without her. I want to tell her in person."

All Burgess could do was shake his head. She wasn't going to come back. He'd blown it. Not only for himself, but for Lissa. If he'd let her stay and help him through surgery and recovery, the family unit they'd formed would still be intact. *God*, that burned. He would kill to have her there right now, smelling like blood oranges and basil, her calming energy lifting everyone else around her like a steady wind. Instead, he had stale air and desolation.

"She's coming *back*, right?" Lissa asked again, pools of tears forming in her eyes.

Burgess glanced at Sig and Wells, even the knucklehead rookies, for help, but they only looked back at him expectantly. And he knew that expression. It was *go hard or go home*. What else could he expect from a room full of professional athletes? And maybe, as fucking obnoxious as this intervention had been . . . he'd needed it. As galling as it was to admit.

He could remain lying in this hospital bed, letting life carry on outside without him, Tallulah eventually—or maybe *already*— moving on from him. Dating a professor. Wearing bathing suits in Costa Rica. Going on adventures without him.

He could hide from his mistake, instead of confronting it. Apologizing. Making it right.

He could explain to his daughter that Tallulah wasn't coming back and hope she eventually got over the loss.

Or he could get up and fight. Rehab his back, get whole again . . .

And go to that wedding and get his woman.

Burgess flicked a look at Sig.

Sig nodded.

Burgess pointed at Wells. "I'll go to rehab if you take back their plus ones. Tallulah *and* Chloe. No dates allowed."

Wells rocked back on his heels. "Is that what that whole silent communication thing was about earlier?"

They gave a synchronized shrug.

One of the Orgasm Donors smacked the other one in the shoulder. "Why don't we communicate silently like that?"

"We do. What am I thinking about right now?"

"Banana pudding."

"Holy shit!"

"Fine." Wells sighed, but the corner of his mouth ticked up. "Worked like a charm."

"I hate you," Burgess deadpanned.

"Josephine thought we needed a fail-safe. That's why she was the best caddie I've ever had." He pressed a fist to his mouth. "God, I'm going to marry the shit out of her."

"What's everyone talking about, Dad?"

"Sorry, Lissa." He hesitated to say the next part, but if he really thought about it, there could be no *other* outcome. Not without him losing his will to live. Did that mean . . . he had one now? Yeah. He looked at his daughter, who meant so much more to him than hockey. He thought of Tallulah and how she felt in his arms, how her voice sounded like it had been missing from his ears his whole life. "Go get the paperwork, Sig." He stroked a hand down the back of Lissa's hair. "I'm going down to Costa Rica to get Tallulah back. But I've got some work to do first."

CHAPTER TWENTY-FIVE

Tallulah looked down at the orange and golden leaves of New Hampshire from fifteen hundred feet in the air, the cool wind drying tear tracks on her cheeks. They weren't tears of devastation, like the ones she'd been crying for over a week, even while going through the motions. School, sleep, activities. Go go go. Not sitting with the heartbreak long enough for it to consume her. No, these were tears of appreciation for the stunning world below.

The landscape rolled forever, disappearing into a bright blue sky. So much bigger than her. Bigger than anything, right? But just like a lot of the platitudes she'd been feeding herself since Pittsburgh, telling herself that her problems were tiny in comparison to the world . . . didn't help the pain so much. Now the fact that she'd rekindled her courage alone? Put it to use by kayaking, hot air ballooning, trying new restaurants, existing with a broken heart?

That helped. A lot.

Truthfully, Tallulah wasn't as nervous to be fifteen hundred feet in the air as she'd expected to be. For one, she'd kept her promise to herself. To stop hiding. Ejected herself from the safety of quiet research labs in remote areas, away from people and reminders of what happened with Brett, and she'd forced herself back among the living. She'd danced, she'd skinny dipped, gone back to school, made friends, taken a chance on love.

She'd had her heart shattered for her efforts, but look. Look. She was still walking, talking, and breathing. She'd reasoned that if she could survive what happened in that hospital room with Burgess, she could do just about anything, couldn't she?

Even call her family. Hear their voices without being ashamed of herself for retreating into the safety of solitude, like she'd sworn to them she wouldn't.

No more postcards.

No more pretense.

She'd reached the end of that lifeline.

Burgess might have been wrong to call her a coward, to wound her like that when she was offering only love and care and support. But his words had rung true, nonetheless. Before she took the final step of calling Istanbul, she wanted to do something big. Something to tear her safety zone wide open once and for all, so here she was. Floating above the tree line, as high and unfettered as a bird. Vulnerable to the wind. And she wasn't scared.

Burgess had been right about more than one thing. He'd told her she wouldn't need a bodyguard forever, hadn't he? Yes. Here she was proving him right. Proving herself capable. She couldn't help aching to share the moment with him. It was an ache that wouldn't quit.

Tallulah braced a hand on the tightly woven basket, her heart performing one of those dramatic nose dives into her stomach that it insisted on doing every time she thought of the hockey player too much. Was his back getting better? Was he in pain? Should she have screamed at him for being a dick, but ultimately stayed?

No.

No, he'd lost her.

He'd shown his true colors and abandoned the trust they'd built.

She would never allow him to get close enough to hurt her again.

Ever.

Bolstered by her resolve, Tallulah took her hand off the basket and reached down into its depths for her purse. She took out the ziplock bag containing the postcards she'd been collecting, holding them to her chest for several moments. Finally, with a quick intake of breath that she held until her lungs started to burn, she opened the baggie and turned it over outside of the basket, letting the wind take the dozen or so cards and carry them away, bringing a fresh wave of tears to her eyes. They fluttered toward the ground in spins of color, eventually growing so small they disappeared from view.

Letting go of those postcards, her crutch, was hard, but obviously necessary, because as soon as they were gone, she felt higher than the balloon. Like she could float all on her own.

Before setting down her purse again, she removed her phone.

And with her heart knocking in her ears, she called Istanbul.

"Hey, Lara, it's me." She listened for a moment, warmth flooding into her limbs, her face, and heart as exclamations and questions filled her ears. "Yes, I'm fine. I'm . . . going to be fine."

FIVE WEEKS LATER, Tallulah stood in the reception area of the resort thinking of those postcards and how they'd looked fluttering to the ground. How momentous that moment had been and how she'd grown a little stronger every day since beginning to communicate with her family again.

There was nothing that could rattle Tallulah now. So her ex-boyfriend/boss was attending the same wedding? And due to them being the only members of the bridal party, they were going to be spending *a lot* of time together? Bring it on, bub. She was wearing an invisible breastplate of steel, reinforced by the closure she'd gotten in New Hampshire. Some hockey player wasn't going to penetrate it.

Tallulah was one hundred percent confident in the belief that seeing Burgess again wouldn't rattle her. She'd even vowed it to herself on the plane ride from Boston, during which Chloe chatted her ear off about her secret wish to own a dog grooming company because who wouldn't want to clip those *widdle biddy* paws all day? Sig sat beside his future stepsibling reading a book about financial investment strategies, an interesting choice for a professional hockey player, but she didn't comment.

Once again in the resort shuttle, Tallulah reminded herself that she'd faced harder obstacles than a hulking athlete who'd chosen to cut her off at the knees, instead of accepting her love. Her help. She wasn't nervous about seeing a man who didn't even like to dance. A man who didn't seize his chance to skinny dip or meet new people. A man that didn't suit her—at all. He could be staring down at her right now and she'd be unaffected. Unmoved.

Thank you, next.

I'm over you, Burgess Abraham.

She believed that right up until she saw him at the resort reception desk—

And her heart tried to swan dive out of her mouth.

Oh. God.

All it took was an instant for the pain of his rejection to come flooding back. The pain that had bloomed in the center of her body as she walked away from his hospital room roared to life now, only it was in more than one spot. It was behind her eyes, in her wrists, the pit of her stomach.

Everywhere.

He looked incredible—that was the main problem.

There was no trace of the defeated, bristling ogre she'd encountered in that hospital bed six weeks ago in Pittsburgh. None whatsoever. He accepted a key from the woman behind the desk and picked up his suitcase with no effort, the muscles of his shoulders rippling like a lake on a windy day. Had they gotten bigger? Had getting twice as jacked been part of the process for rehabbing his back?

Wow. And he had on shorts. Of course he did. They were in the tropical climate of Costa Rica, the humidity cut by a sea breeze, but still decidedly balmy. Those navy blue shorts stopped at the top of his calves and time truly slowed down as he walked through reception, the undersides of those chiseled calves flexing.

All of him, the full package, was . . . even better than before.

Great. Can't wait to see him in a tux.

Tallulah remained cemented in place, hoping and praying Burgess wouldn't spot her a few spots behind him in line, but obviously Sig couldn't keep his big mouth shut, giving his friend a two-finger whistle, followed by a grunt. "Cap."

Burgess turned, his blue gaze darting toward Sig, but only remaining there momentarily before it trained on Tallulah, his chest dipping and rising slowly, the hand around his suitcase handle tightening into a fist. The casual conversations taking place around her grew muffled, the glands on the side of her throat swelling. She needed to look away from him, but she couldn't seem to stop cataloguing new and familiar things about his appearance. His beard was trimmed, closer cropped. No longer did he have the pale hockey complexion. There was actually some color in his face, as if he'd been spending time outside. Maybe in the roof garden.

The only thing about him that didn't look good were his eyes.

They were sunken. Hollow. As though he hadn't slept in months.

"Are you doing okay, roomie?" Chloe whispered covertly.

"I don't know," Tallulah answered, sounding dazed. "I didn't expect to see him so soon. I would have preferred to shower first."

"Shower and put on your revenge dress, you mean."

"Exactly."

"What is a revenge dress?" Sig asked, warily.

"It's a dress you wear when you want someone to regret losing you."

"Even more than he already does?" Sig waved Burgess over. "Doubt that's possible."

A bolt twisted in between Tallulah's breasts at the implication that Burgess had been suffering, but she refused to acknowledge it. She'd dealt with more than her fair share of heartache for the last six weeks. She'd loved this man, gone to him and confessed it, despite her arsenal of fears. In return, he'd doused her feelings in kerosene, set them on fire, and told her to split. If he regretted his behavior now? Then *good*. He should.

That indignation and resolve didn't stop her legs from shaking as Burgess got closer, his gaze never leaving her once. "Tallulah." Her name was a rattle in his chest. "You look beautiful."

Oh, I get it now. This is going to be the hardest three days of my life.

It hurt to speak, so she gave a jerky nod. "Hi."

Several seconds passed while his eyes ran the length of her, back up, then started at the beginning to do it all over again. And all she could do was stand there and pretend she didn't feel safe and warm for the first time in a month and a half. Not quite whole, thanks to the chunk missing from her heart, but more . . . assembled. More alive.

Which was *dangerous.*

Letting him get to her, letting him back in even an iota, would only lead to more pain the next time he was hurt. The next time he got wounded and took it out on her.

"We're here, too, man," Sig snorted, finally.

Burgess shook himself and reached over Tallulah's shoulder to shake Sig's hand, but his attention remained on Tallulah's face. "Sig." His voice was hoarse. "Chloe."

"Hi, Burgess," sang the blonde. "It looks like rehab was successful."

He acknowledged that with a dip of his chin. "Yeah." He paused, as if it suddenly hurt to talk. "Surgery and rehab fixed my back. But there's a lot left to be repaired."

Tallulah wasn't sure what she'd been expecting upon seeing Burgess again. Awkwardness. Mea culpa. Another round of fighting. But this . . . open and obvious air of regret had to be the worst possible scenario. He wanted to take back what he'd said. That much was clear. Over the last six weeks, however, she'd concluded that their breakup was about more than one sharply delivered line during a bad moment. Although, her fear of settling down with someone only to find they were hiding an ugly side had been exacerbated in the hospital. The trust she'd built in him was damaged, oh yes, but their rift went beyond that.

They were too different.

She wanted adventure. He didn't take blind leaps.

While she danced in the kitchen, he sat out the song.

When she jumped into the pond naked, he waited on the shore.

Whatever magic they'd made together was in the past, and that's where it would remain. She wouldn't lie to herself and pretend the spell they'd woven had dissipated completely, but she'd spent the last forty-odd days learning to suppress it and she would continue to do so.

Surgery and rehab fixed my back. But there's a lot left to be repaired.

"If you're talking about our relationship, as short-lived as it was . . ." she said quietly, putting out her hand, terrified he would take it, that his touch would disrupt the stillness she'd worked so hard to achieve. "Why don't we just agree to . . . forgive and forget."

Slowly, Burgess's gaze tracked down to her hand, before reestablishing the relentless eye contact that was battering her nervous system. "Forget?"

"Yes."

"I couldn't forget a fucking minute of you if I tried."

With a sharp intake of breath, she took her hand back. "Burgess—"

"Welcome!" A man in khaki shorts and a cream-colored polo stepped into view. "I have it on good authority that you're here for the Whitaker-Doyle wedding. My name is Carlos and I'm the head of guest services for the event. If you wouldn't mind stepping out of the check-in line, I'd love to go over the itinerary while you're all in one place."

"Itinerary?" Sig echoed.

"Has my harp arrived?" Chloe asked, holding her breath.

"Ah, you're the harpist." Carlos smiled indulgently. "Yes, it arrived last night and we've placed it in storage until the morning of the ceremony."

"Will it be safe there?" Sig asked, earning him a grateful look from Chloe.

"Yes, of course."

While all these details were being discussed, Burgess and Tallulah continued staring at each other without so much as a blink. *I couldn't forget a fucking minute of you if I tried?* What was going on here? Was he trying to . . . to win her back or something? In *hotel reception?*

"Try harder," Tallulah suggested sweetly.

"I'm sorry, ma'am?" Carlos hedged.

She poked the air in front of Burgess's pecs. "I'm talking to this guy."

"Thank God," Burgess said gruffly. "That's one battle down."

"One? How many are there?"

"As many as it takes."

"Should I be made aware of a small rift in the wedding party?" Carlos asked, nervously.

Chloe squared her shoulders. "They dated. Sort of."

"It was a hell of a lot more than dating," Burgess said without taking his attention off Tallulah.

"It hardly matters now." Tallulah turned a smile on their host. "It's in the past."

"I see." Carlos trailed off momentarily, then came back twice as enthused. "Well, I can't wait to see how this ruins everything." Briskly, he produced a stack of laminated schedules from the folder that had been wedged beneath his arm, handing them out. "The wedding is in two and a half days and obviously there will be rehearsals, but folks, we are in Costa Rica!" He gestured to the lush greenery surrounding the open-air lobby. "Josephine and Wells wanted to make sure to supply everyone with enough entertainment—optional, of course. You're free to sit by the pool and drink mojitos, as well. If you would like to take advantage of the resort's wide selection of outdoor activities, however, we'd love to send you home with some unforgettable memories."

"Where are Wells and Josephine?" Burgess wanted to know.

Carlos launched into an explanation without a moment's hesitation. "They are taking this time before the vow exchange to connect as a couple—"

"They're golfing, aren't they?" Burgess and Tallulah said, at the exact same time.

"Since sunrise," Carlos confirmed with a sigh.

Still, intrigued, Tallulah pursed her lips. "What kind of outdoor activities are you referring to?"

"Ah, I see we have piqued your interest," Carlos said, rubbing his hands together. "Tomorrow morning, we have sunrise ziplining planned, followed by cliff diving. And—"

"Count me in. All of it." Tallulah knew a lifeline when she saw one. Staying busy and active would keep her away from Burgess, too many mojitos, and access to a hotel bed. Not to mention, the activities sounded like amazing, once-in-a-lifetime opportunities that she couldn't even fathom turning down. "Where should we meet for—"

"I'm in, too," Burgess said. "All of it."

"You're going t-to go zip-lining?" Tallulah sputtered. "And jump off a cliff?"

"That's right."

Her heart kicked into a trot, then a gallop. Something was happening here. She'd never seen him look so determined. Not even while playing hockey.

"What about your back? You just had surgery!" Tallulah sputtered.

"I had surgery almost two months ago. I've been rehabbing with the best physical therapists in the country since then. Day and night. My back is stronger than it has ever been." He cocked his head. "Guess I'll be proving it in the morning."

Oh. Okay. This man had a plan.

And it involved her somehow, that much was obvious.

I don't want you here. Go.

His words from the hospital came back to her, stiffening her spine.

Bolstering her resolve.

"Is anyone else game for the excursion?" Carlos asked with a wily expression.

Sig shook his head at Chloe. "Please, Chlo. You'll give me a heart attack."

The harpist shrugged. "Mojitos it is."

"Two participants so far, then. Fantastic," Carlos said, clapping his hands together and focusing on Burgess and Tallulah. "You will meet your guide here tomorrow morning at six A.M. sharp."

"Great," Tallulah said, smile tight.

"Great," Burgess echoed, picking up his suitcase and backing away, keeping her in his sights until he'd turned the corner onto the walkway leading to his room, apparently.

"What just happened?" Tallulah asked, still staring dazedly at the spot where he disappeared, excitement warring with foreboding in her belly.

"I think it's pretty clear," Chloe answered.

"Is it?"

"Yup. It appears that Sir Savage is ready for a fight." Sig ushered Chloe back into line, a smile dancing around the edges of his mouth. "And at the risk of stating the obvious, fighting is sort of what he does best, so . . ."

"Uh-oh, roomie," Chloe whispered. "You might need more than one revenge dress."

Tallulah swallowed hard. If Burgess had decided to come to Costa Rica and show her they weren't so different after all, and he planned to prove that by thrill seeking alongside of her . . . she feared there might not be enough revenge dresses in the world.

Or worse still, that each and every one of them could end up on his floor.

CHAPTER TWENTY-SIX

Burgess strode along the stone walkway leading to the patio where the welcome dinner was being held, his heart still located in his fucking mouth since his encounter with Tallulah at hotel reception. Encounter? Yeah. More like an ambush.

He was not off to a good start.

Some vine-like greenery blocked his view of the lit-up outdoor space ahead and he smacked it out of his way, berating himself once again for being too impulsive. He'd meticulously written and planned a speech declaring his love, bullet pointing the reasons he could not live without her. He'd intended to deliver it the first time he saw Tallulah again, but as soon as he laid eyes on her, the words he'd practiced in rehab, in the shower and on the plane became nothing but scratches of noise, utterly and completely unworthy of her.

Mother of God, he'd actually let the most beautiful woman alive walk out of his life.

She'd gotten even prettier, too, started doing something different with her eye makeup. She'd bought a new pair of sandals he'd never seen before. A mere six weeks and he'd missed a whole host of little things he could have noticed *as* they took place, instead of after the fact. How did he screw up so badly? And then double down this afternoon by challenging her, instead of kneeling down in front of the girl and asking for mercy?

These had to be adverse effects of anesthesia.

And God, he could use a shot of the stuff in his chest right now, because the whole thing was a throbbing wound that begged to be numbed, just so he could breathe. Focus.

Focus on what he needed to do.

Apologize. Prove to Tallulah he could be the right man to love her.

Maybe even prove it to himself in the process.

Get her back.

Love her until his heart gave its final beat.

Burgess slowed to a stop on the path when the party materialized in front of him. Approximately three dozen guests mingled beneath a half-moon, sipping champagne from flutes, candles flickering among greenery dotted with white hibiscus. The Beach Boys drifted softly in the humid night air . . . and all he could see was Tallulah.

In a pink dress.

Not just any pink, though. It was hot pink—and he only knew the exact name of the color from back in the day when Lissa used to play with Barbies. There was nothing plastic about Tallulah, though. Jesus, he'd never seen anyone look softer or more natural, her hair left loose and kind of curly due to the tropical air. Her dress was like a swift knee to the balls. Looking at her actually, physically hurt. Like a son of a bitch.

And the message was clear as crystal. *Look at what you're missing.*

Despite the misery it would cost Burgess to get closer, he couldn't help gravitating toward the party, the need to be near her fiercer than ever. But hell if keeping his jaw off the floor didn't grow impossible. Goddamn. Her ass and thighs in that tight hot-pink dress were going to be listed as the cause of death at his autopsy. Dew glistened on her skin from the humidity. Her lips were painted to match her outfit. And men were noticing. *Golfers.*

Fuck. That.

Burgess made a face and stomped into the moonlight, cutting across the grass toward the gate that would let him onto the patio. He closed it behind him with an intentional clang, hitting every golfer at the party with a look that said *touch her and die*. And he meant it.

Get yourself under control.

He'd lost her by acting like an asshole. He definitely wouldn't win her back that way.

"Hey, man," Wells said, appearing in front of him in a crisp white polo shirt, a glass of scotch in hand. "You're looking a lot better since the last time I saw you. Mostly."

Burgess stared at Tallulah over his friend's shoulder. "Mostly?"

"You still look like you're being tortured on one of those medieval stretcher tables, but at least you're up and walking around. I call that progress."

"Not the kind I'm looking for right now." Sighing, he clapped Wells on the shoulder. "Congratulations on the wedding, by the way."

"Heartfelt. I'm misting." Wells chuckled dryly, before leaning in and lowering his voice. "I hear you're signed up for cliff diving and zip-lining tomorrow."

"Yeah." Finally, Tallulah paused in her conversation with a group of women and made eye contact with Burgess, the sudden fulness in his throat making it necessary to pull hard on his collar. "Hopefully we'll get a chance to talk."

"That shouldn't be difficult, since you're the only ones who signed up."

"We are?"

"I mean, yeah." Wells took a sip of his scotch. "You're also the only ones Carlos was told to schedule for the outdoor activities. If Chloe and Sig had asked to participate, he was going to give them a false time and location, then blame it on me. You're welcome."

Burgess found himself at a loss. "Thanks, man."

"You need the help. Josephine said something about a revenge dress." Wells shivered. "I've never been happier to be getting married."

Revenge dress.

Burgess eyeballed the sleek curve of Tallulah's ass, the way the hem hugged the smackable undercurve of her backside.

Yeah.

The phrase "revenge dress" made a lot of sense.

And he deserved every second of the torture.

Reluctantly, he dragged his attention back to Wells. "You don't think married women can wear revenge dresses?"

Wells paled slightly. "I'm not going to give Josephine a reason to wear one."

"Uh-huh," Burgess drawled.

The golfer narrowed his eyes. "Maybe it's not too late to add a clause to our vows."

"Good luck with that."

"Hang on to that luck." Wells took a glass of champagne off a passing tray and handed it to Burgess. "You need it more than me."

On his way across the party, Burgess grimaced down at the tiny glass flute in his giant hand, eventually setting it down on a high-top table without taking a sip. He had a lot to get off his chest tonight and wanted to be sober for every word, because the mere presence of Tallulah after six weeks without her was enough to make him feel drunk, as it was. Currently, his former au pair was watching him approach with a wary expression, shifting right to left in her sparkly pink heels. Matching shoes?

Fuck. She really wanted him to suffer.

He passed Chloe and Sig who were arguing quietly about God knows what, but his destination was Tallulah. When he reached the group of women in which she stood, he cleared his throat and the chatter cut off immediately, the strangers splitting their curiosity between him and Tallulah. "Can we talk?" he asked.

"Um. Later would be great," she said, giving him a flat smile.

Also known as her signature brush-off. He remembered it all too well from the afternoon of the singles mixer in Amory Park. Well, it wouldn't work with him.

"Later? Sure. Your room or mine?"

"Actually, now sounds good," she rushed out, complexion turning pink. "Ladies, if you'll excuse me . . ."

Burgess stepped aside for Tallulah to precede him, his mouth literally watering as she breezed by, stupefyingly sexy in her pink dress, leaving the scent that had been haunting his dreams in the air behind her. Blood orange and basil. How many times over the last month had he gone into her room and tried to resurrect that smell from her sheets and the air itself? She had no idea how close she was right now to being eaten in one bite.

Tallulah kept walking until they left the glow cast by the candlelight, out onto the stone path that traveled around the back of the resort building. Alone. Finally, alone with his girl again. He wanted to melt them into the side of the clapboard structure like butter, get his mouth on her neck and work that skirt up to her waist, but that wasn't happening yet. They weren't even in the vicinity of a reconciliation. And he wanted to get straight to apologizing, but once he started, he wasn't sure he'd stop until she accepted, so he needed to slow his roll.

"Heard you've been on some adventures since the last time I saw you."

"That's right," she said briskly, turning to face him. Looking at him, but not seeing.

"Were you okay going alone?" he asked, hoarse. Unable to hide his leftover worry.

Some of the stiffness left her frame, a muscle working in her delicate throat. "It got easier. And then I was fine. I was proud of myself. I'm . . . back to where I wanted to be."

Relief and pride in her joined forces inside of him. "You're so brave."

Now she was seeing him. They were both seeing him. In the hospital bed.

Calling her a coward.

He wanted to rip the past down out of the atmosphere and crush it in his fist, but he couldn't. That was impossible. Time could only move forward.

"Tallulah . . ." Burgess said, clearing the rust from his throat. "I shouldn't have come on so strong . . . earlier. In the lobby. I had a whole apology worked out, but the second I could see you and smell you, my speech didn't seem worth a damn."

His apology seemed to surprise her, her mouth opening and closing before she recovered. "Good. You can save it. I'm here for my best friend's wedding. Rehashing everything that happened six weeks ago isn't on the agenda."

"Was it only six weeks ago?" he rasped, his eyes tracing her features. "Feels like a year."

"Could you just stop . . ." Was she flustered? Her hands were shaking. "We don't have to reopen the wound, Burgess. Just let it stay closed."

"Mine never closed. It will never fucking close." He couldn't help it, he took a huge step forward and leaned down to drag in a beggar's portion of her scent, his hands aching to yank her up against him, to hold her. "If you tell me yours is closed already, I won't believe you. We need to talk about what happened."

"Why don't I just save us both time and tell you we aren't getting back together? We weren't even together for five *minutes* when you threw me out." He winced at that—regret carving into his chest like a knife—and whatever she saw on his face caused her words to trip over each other. "I just . . . I think it's for the b-best if we just try and be friends for the sake of Wells and Josephine. It's only three days."

"Friends," he growled like an epithet.

"That's right."

He took a step closer, forcing her head to tip back, relieved when her determination waned in the face of his proximity—and he let out the truth in his heart without tempering a single syllable. If she was suggesting they become friends, he didn't have the luxury of caution. Or time. "I would give up everything I own to go back to that day and tell you I love you, too, Tallulah. I'd smile while handing over my soul to the devil for that chance." He touched their foreheads together and her lips parted, in shock or protest over his words, he had no idea. "I love you. And I'm sorry I was heartless with you. I felt weak and I only wanted you to see me as strong. When I couldn't give you strong, I lashed out. I thought I was doing you a favor, but I fucked up the best part of my life. I'm sorry."

Several beats passed. "Was that your speech?" she whispered, eyes closed.

"You think I could remember a speech with your mouth this close to mine?" Christ, his voice was unsteady. "I couldn't even tell you the name of the sitting president."

Tallulah stumbled back as though someone had cut the invisible strings holding them together, trying to keep her features stoic. Breathing until she succeeded. Had she hardened herself against him already? After a week of calling her with no answer, he'd stopped, vowing to get back on his feet and try again, in person. Once he was able-bodied again.

But maybe he was too late?

"Why is this coming out of the blue?" she finally said, her words jumbled and breathy.

Burgess followed her as she backed up, his steps measured.

Determined to get them back on the same page. It couldn't be too late for them. He wouldn't survive that reality. "You think this is coming out of the blue? I live, eat, and breathe you, Tallulah. You're what got me through every grueling hour of rehab. I just needed to heal me, before I could heal us."

"In other words, you needed me gone. You didn't want me there. But you can't kick people out and bring them back in at will. You'll do it again."

"I won't."

"You're contradicting yourself."

"If there is ever a next time, I will hold on to you with both hands. Believe me. But this time, I knew I'd have work to do when I saw you again. To fix what I broke. If you ran away from me, I needed to be capable of running after you. I needed to be able to lift my arms to hold you and tell you how fucking sorry I am. I needed to be able to stand up while fighting off your doubts. Next time, if there is one, we'll be a team."

"It won't mean you didn't rob me of being on your team this time," she whispered.

His chest dove inward. "I'm *sorry*."

"I believe that. I do. But I'm not putting myself out there again."

"That's not what I've been told." Broken glass scraped the inner walls of his chest, ravaging him at having to say this out loud. "I hear there's some Sagittarius professor interested in you? Is that true? Are you . . . dating him? Because I've been waking up from nightmares about seeing you with another man for over a month." He ground his molars together so hard, he swore he could taste blood. "God help me, if you'd brought him, I'd have killed him."

Genuine perplexity created a crease between her brows. "A professor gave me his number, yes, but I didn't use it. Do you think I could just jump into something else after . . ." A line drive of relief clocked him in the center of his forehead and he wanted more, wanted to hear she was still stuck on him, the way he'd always be stuck on her, but she gave a jagged shrug, her next words escaping in a rush. "Look, I don't owe you an explanation. I appreciate your apology and I . . . hear everything you're saying, but I think we'll be better as friends."

Burgess observed her with so much intensity, it was a wonder she didn't drop. After several moments of silence, he nodded slowly. "Guess you need to be proven wrong." He continued forward until she was sandwiched between him and the building, his nerve endings stretching and groaning back to life just to be touching her again. "And forgive me for saying so, gorgeous," he rasped against her ear. "But if you didn't want to be proven wrong, if you just wanted to be my *friend*, I don't think you'd have worn a dress so short I barely need to lift the hem to get my cock inside of you."

I LOVE YOU. And I'm sorry I was heartless with you.

I felt weak and I only wanted you to see me as strong.

That confession sent moisture rushing to her eyes, even as the filth he spoke into her ear made her inner thighs draw together, squeezing. It was too much at once. He was too much at once, and the tide of emotions she'd been furiously stemming for a month and a half came breaking through the dam, busting the sucker wide open.

His breath on the side of her face sent heat snaking down the sensitive side of her neck, making her breasts fuller, achy, so painfully sensitive that her back arched on its own, her stiffening nipples rubbing side to side against his thickly muscled chest, her breath stuttering in thanksgiving over the friction she'd been seeking without finding for interminable weeks. Oh God, the grief and desperation of it sucked her under like a riptide and she gasped for air, calling for his mouth without saying actual words. But he knew.

Burgess rubbed his open lips right to left on top of hers, leaving a wet mess, and she moaned over the carnality of it, the kind she'd never had with anyone else. The animal freedom of clawing and taking and straining and whining. How could she have ignored the need for it for a whole six weeks? The broken heart must have wiped away her ability to do anything but survive.

"I love you, Tallulah," he said, kissing her hard and looking her in the eye with enough intensity to seize her lungs. "I'm just making sure you heard me."

"I heard you," she breathed.

"How do you feel about that?"

"I don't know. I'm overwhelmed."

Those two words made his forehead pucker, eyes clenching as if in pain. "No. No, gorgeous. Overwhelmed by what?"

"How much I missed you touching me. I can't breathe. I can't . . . I need you, but I don't want to have to decide what it means."

He made a grating sound, like her admission had bought him a stay of execution, but he wasn't sure if he should take it. "You've got me. I'm here to give you what you need. Tell me what it is," he demanded, licking a moist path up the side of her neck, following the trail back down with a rake of teeth that made her inner walls cinch up like a drawn shoelace. "Do you want me to fuck you?"

Tallulah's body moved on instinct, turning to face the wall and flattening her palms against it, moving her backside on top of the hardness that had been growing since their lips touched. Maybe before. "Yes, yes, I want that."

She moaned as her panties were wrenched down to midthigh, his palm skimming roughly up and down the fronts of her legs. Higher.

Slowly, his middle finger pushed down through the soaked valley of her flesh, a second finger joining immediately, pleasing her in thorough circles, his breath hot against her right temple. "Going to use my fingers to get you ready for cock, Tallulah."

"Yes," she wheezed, her fingernails turning to claws on the wall. "Please."

He released a pained groan into the side of her neck. "You're a noisy little fuck, but I'll happily take the risk of getting caught to hear you whine my name again." He tucked two big fingers inside of her sex and jiggled them hard, as if attempting to loosen her up. "Taking it rough from behind is exactly what you wanted when you wore this fucking dress, isn't it?"

Lust popped wheelies in her middle. Gone. She was so far gone, the possibility of getting caught came secondary to untying the knot that had been growing tighter inside of her since the last time Burgess was inside of her. "Yes. Yes. I wore it to make you ache."

"It worked. I'm probably going to come on your ass, before I even get it in."

The coarseness of his tone, the lack of control made her push up on both sets of toes, fitting her bare bottom into his lap and asking for fulfillment with a telltale whimper.

"Even on your toes, you're shorter than me." His fingers alternated between strumming her clit and delving two fingers inside of her, pushing them deep enough to make her slap the wall, her eyes watering, before he pulled back out and rubbed that bud faster, faster, faster, until her thighs started to tremble. "Going to pick you up, okay, girl?"

"Yes. Yes."

Tallulah stared at the wall, panting, as Burgess stooped down and came up fisting his cock, guiding it between her legs while his legs were still bent. But oh God, oh God, as soon as he was halfway inside of her, he rose to his full height, lifting Tallulah a full ten inches off the ground, impaled on his stiffness. "Oh. *FUCK*." He let out a gravelly sound while rolling his hips in a methodical circle. "Only had it once, but I remember this pussy like the back of my goddamn hand. It's wet and tight and it's mine." He bounced her with a savage upward slap of his hips, growling into the top of her head. "You need a good, hard bang, gorgeous, isn't that right? No strings?"

"Please. Yes, *please!*"

"You're going to get it. Exactly what you need from me." He dragged his open mouth down to her ear, his hands planted on the wall, leaving her fully supported by the rough drives of his hips. "You knew you'd catch this cock in your dick-tease dress. Sit there and fucking enjoy it." Those teeth razed her lobe, before baring against the side of her neck. "But you're not going to get me out of your system, if that's what you think is happening here."

Her heart lurched at the accusation, not because it offended, but because . . .

On some level, that's exactly what she'd been trying to do. To scratch the itch he'd left her with so she could try and move on, really, truly move on. And he felt it. She was attuned to him enough that she noticed Burgess recognize her intent. He cursed at the way she briefly froze, caught red-handed trying to have him one last time, before walking away with the remnants of her heart.

No way was he going to let her get away with that.

His hips continued a slow, thorough upward grind that touched her in places that made her blush, made her face bake. Her heels had long since fallen to the ground, her toes flexing helplessly above the shadowed stone walkway and she was already moaning when his right hand dropped from the side of the building, because she knew it was coming and yet she screamed behind her teeth when he started to play with her clit, grunting and grinding, hips bobbing her up, up, up, those blunt fingers busy drawing her orgasm home.

"Let go, Tallulah. Get me out of your system. Go ahead. Scream and shake until I'm gone. Come on, girl." He drove into her faster, her backside slapping loudly on his thighs, his mouth open and panting on her neck. "I love you, though. I love you. I fucking love you and you're going to feel that until I'm dead and gone. The love isn't going anywhere. Come on my dick while I'm telling you I love you. I dare you to kick me out after that."

There was no use trying to stop the buildup; the pressure was too great and every organ in her body seemed to be involved, singing in harmony, carrying her toward an emotional and physical impact that would never allow her to be the same. *"Burgess . . ."*

"Come."

"I . . ."

"You're already there. Ride it out."

Burgess was right, the light-headedness was stealing over her, the lowest, most sensitive regions of her stomach braiding tight, loosening, and braiding again. She started to rut her hips up and back in his lap, making him growl into the nape of her neck, release hitting her with a knockout blow, and she bore down, tiny muscles clenching, her body trembling like the last leaf on a tree in the winter . . . and her body slumped, turned to jelly, but only for a moment to enjoy the replete sensation, the total lack of tension, but then she tightened up again, waiting for Burgess to follow her.

He didn't.

Gently, he set Tallulah back on her feet, kissing her shoulder while pulling her panties back up and securing the hem of the dress over her backside.

"What . . . about you?" she whispered, still winded. Confusion beginning to creep in.

"Me?" He turned her around, framing her jaw and lifting it so she could see the lust-laced regret in his eyes, traces of the hurt she'd inflicted by trying to eradicate him. "I don't want you out of my system." He kissed her hard, once, twice, lingering the second time. "You're staying there forever. Period." She reached for him, but he backed up out of her reach, fastening his erection back into his pants with a sharp hiss. "But if you want me out of yours? You're welcome to try again tomorrow. I'm not going anywhere."

"Burgess."

He gave her a final pained look, heavy with regret and unsatisfied hunger, before continuing down the path. "Good night, Tallulah."

CHAPTER TWENTY-SEVEN

Burgess paced in hotel reception, the humidity already causing him to sweat through his shirt. They'd been told to meet the zip-lining instructor here at 6:00 A.M. sharp, but apparently, he was the only one with a functioning watch. Neither the instructor nor Tallulah had arrived yet.

And he needed to get a handle on his dark mood real quick or this whole day, this finite chunk of time he'd been given to win back Tallulah, would be a waste. But excuse the hell out of him if being chipper was a challenge the morning after the love of his life had tried to fuck him out of her system. While she'd been attempting to purge him, he'd been so completely lost in the feel of her body, the scent of her skin, the hitch in her voice, he couldn't see straight. On the verge of the most blinding orgasm of his life . . . and he'd denied himself the relief his body was still screaming for twelve hours later.

His blue balls were pitch-black at this stage.

So, yeah. He wasn't so much pacing as he was stomping and occasionally shooting a murderous glance at the front desk guy.

A thought occurred to him and ceased his progress across the polished floor.

Was she backing out?

What if she'd decided not to go zip-lining and cliff diving because he would be there?

Maybe last night, after he'd left, Josephine had spilled the beans that Tallulah and Burgess were the only two participants and she'd balked, not wanting to be alone with him.

Without a second thought, Burgess started walking in the direction of her room. If she didn't want to spend the day with him, he'd be disappointed—and that was an understatement. But there was no way he'd let Tallulah miss her adventures because of him. Not happening. She'd worked too hard to regain the confidence to try new things and he wasn't going to be the cause of her taking a step backward. It would kill him to give up the chance to have her to himself all day, but denying her the experiences would be worse.

Burgess reached her door and stood there quietly, listening to definite movement on the other side. She was awake, at least. Maybe just running behind? He raised his hand to knock and dropped it, grimacing at the sweat bleeding through the shirt at the center of his pecs. He looked like he'd just exited the ice after the third period.

Take your shirt off.

It had worked before, right?

Hands on hips, Burgess stepped back from the door and tipped his head back, wondering how his life had come to this. Once again, he felt like one of the Orgasm Donors, taking his shirt off to flex for a woman. He couldn't deny that stripping from the waist up had worked pretty damn well the first time around, however.

Burgess ran five quick fingers through his hair, gripped the back of his T-shirt collar and pulled—just as the door of Tallulah's room opened. When Burgess heard the quiet click of the door unlocking and the whoosh of it opening wide, he inwardly sighed, but it was too late to stop. And frankly, when the garment no longer obstructed his view, the mesmerized expression on Tallulah's face told him he'd done the right thing by getting half naked.

"Good morning," he said gruffly, his balls giving a hard tug at the sight of her in ripped jean shorts and a bright yellow bikini top, sandals. Granted, she had a loose white tank top over the top of the bathing suit, but the cover-up might as well have been invisible for all the attention he paid it. In an instant, his goal in life was to see Tallulah in that yellow fucking bikini.

"Good m-morning," she said, staring dazedly at his bare torso, then down at the floor, back at his abdomen, up at the ceiling, before giving up and running the length of him, throat to happy trail. "Why are you taking your clothes off outside my room? If beefcake was on the room service menu, I didn't order it."

It physically hurt to laugh at one of her jokes, because it had been so long, but he did, the gruff boom bouncing off the stone facade of the building. "Oh, you should. This place is known for having the best beefcake in town."

She sniffed. "I don't like meat, remember?"

"You loved it last night."

Twin spots of color appeared on her cheeks, her attention—if he wasn't mistaken—dropping to his crotch, before zipping back upward. "If this is an indication of how the day is going to go, I think it's best if I skip."

Tallulah took a step backward, retreating into her room, and the invisible hand of panic wrapped around his jugular, causing him to lunge forward involuntarily, catching the door before she could close it. The move brought them inches apart and for a moment, all he could do was marvel over her skin in the light of the sunrise, the luscious shape of her mouth and the rich brown of her eyes. *God, I fucking miss you, Tallulah.*

He opened his mouth to apologize for starting off on the wrong foot. In his defense, there were yellow bikini strings sticking out of her denim waistband and they'd pureed his brain. But before he could speak a word, his focus was drawn to the unmade bed—and that's when he saw the royal blue balled-up sweatshirt. His Bearcats sweatshirt.

She'd brought it to Costa Rica to use as a pillow?

Had she . . . been using it the *whole time* they'd been apart?

Burgess swallowed thickly, unable to speak for a solid ten seconds, his throat working and working until it was sore. With relief. Arousal. Appreciation. Shock.

Tallulah followed his line of sight, the color deepening on her cheeks. "It's the biggest sweatshirt I own. Obviously, it makes the, um . . . most ideal pillow."

With his dark mood evaporated, Burgess decided to let Tallulah get away with that bullshit. The sweatshirt meant something. It had to. And so he found a deep down reserve of patience and drew on it with everything he had. "How would *you* like the day to go, instead, Tallulah?" He struggled against the urge to tuck a piece of stray hair behind her ear, his fingers twitching near the outside of his thigh. "Tell me—and I'll make it happen."

Her shoulder rose and fell on a breath, and he could sense her relief that he hadn't pursued a conversation about his sweatshirt being spotted in her bed. Little did she know he'd be thinking about it nonstop all day. "I don't need protection anymore," she said finally. "I'm more . . . steady now. On my own."

"I'll say." He tilted his head to study her. "A hot air balloon ride and everything."

Tallulah blinked, lips parting. "You know about that?"

Burgess nodded once. "Just because you haven't seen me doesn't mean I haven't been checking in. Constantly. At this point, I've offered to buy Chloe nine new harps and the entire skincare section at Sephora."

She sniffed, rolled a shoulder. "I suppose you think what you said to me, in the hospital . . . I suppose you think that's what gave me that final push to start trying new things without a bodyguard. Maybe it was. Or maybe I was just ready, but . . ."

She stopped for a breath. "Calling my family for the first time in years? Hearing their voices? That was all me."

A bolt turned in his jugular. "You called them."

"Yes." Tallulah snuck a look up at him, just a small one, but it was such a powerful glance, because she let him see, albeit briefly, how much that phone call had meant to her. She generously let him share in the relief, and God, he'd never experienced more thankfulness in his life. She'd opened up to him about her family, the postcards, and he'd thrown it in her face. Yet with one flick of her eyes, she'd let him know their past moments together still stood. They hadn't been erased by his callousness. Not completely.

That didn't mean the present wasn't still a giant fucking question mark.

"You're so fucking brave, Tallulah." His chest was being sucked inward toward his spine. Gratitude rained down on him, just to be given the chance to say these things to her out loud and have her listen, whether he deserved to be heard or not. "I was dead wrong to imply the postcards meant you aren't brave or capable. I was the one being a coward that day."

Without realizing it, Burgess had moved closer, positioning them both in the doorframe, her back pressed to one side, his to the other. He propped a forearm over her head and leaned down, taking a serious chance by rolling their foreheads together, letting her feel the release of breath from his lungs against her lips and hope, hope like hell she knew every ounce of it was for her.

"Burgess . . ."

"Yeah."

"You didn't finish last night," she said on a laughing exhale. "It makes me feel like I didn't, either."

He wrestled back a groan. "You did. The way you shook—"

"Are you really just trying to make me cave in again?" she interrupted. "If so, that's fully evil."

"I'm not going to lie, I hope you'll want me again. But mostly . . ."

When the truth dawned on him, it was so unexpected, he couldn't get the words out.

Tallulah searched his expression with a line between her brows. "What?"

The back of his neck heated. "I guess, uh . . . I couldn't let myself go with you, Tallulah, when your heart wasn't in it. I don't . . . I've never been that weak for or with anyone, the way I am with you. It would have hurt to be weak while you were . . . resisting feeling anything and everything for me. Jesus, I don't even know if that makes fucking sense."

For just a beat, she appeared stricken. "It does," she whispered, tilting her face up.

Bringing their mouths a hairsbreadth apart.

Burgess's heart started pounding so loudly in his chest they both heard it. Guests probably heard their mangled palpitations from the other side of the resort. Was she going to kiss him? Without him initiating? *God, please let it be happening.* Let his rambling explanation of why he couldn't get off last night mean something coherent to her.

His body moved on instinct, pressing her up against the door and she moaned, her hips tilting forward against his, and that was all the encouragement he needed to dip his mouth to her neck and suck a pathway up to her ear, his right hand sliding down the back of her jean shorts. If he got her onto that bed with her legs open, with his balled-up sweatshirt in plain view, nothing was going to stop him from coming this time—

"There you are!"

A familiar voice, belonging to Carlos, shattered the moment like a baseball through a pane of glass. Tallulah lurched back so suddenly, she hit her head on the doorframe and Burgess's stomach dropped through the floorboards. His right palm was cradling the back of her skull before he knew his own intentions. "Oh, gorgeous," he murmured, scrutinizing her face for signs of pain. "You okay?"

"I don't think today is a good idea," she blurted.

"Why?"

"You're being so . . . wonderful. And I'm . . ." She shut her eyes. "I moved *on*. I did."

He ignored the meat cleaver burying in the middle of his chest. "Let me ask you again, how do you want the day to go?"

"Hey, folks!" Carlos was standing beside them, waving both hands. "All aboard the adventure train. Your guide is waiting at reception."

Tallulah never took her eyes off Burgess and vice versa. "Can we just share the experience without any expectations, maybe? Please?" She wet her lips. "Every time you get close to me, like this, I panic. And the worst part is, you used to be the reason I *didn't* panic. You really hurt me, okay?" Her eyes drifted shut. "Obviously, I still have feelings for you, they didn't just disappear overnight, but I don't . . . I—I don't think we're getting back together."

"I'll just wait over there," Carlos muttered, zipping away.

Until that moment, Burgess wasn't sure he'd realized how deeply he'd wounded her. The extent of the damage, the trust he'd mangled like a car wreck. And all at once, he felt like the King Asshole. So arrogant, coming to this wedding thinking he could flash his pecs and win this perfect person back over. After what he'd said?

After so callously severing the bond they'd built?

I'm a complete idiot.

His closeness was hurting her. The damage he'd inflicted must be irreversible.

And the only thing he could think of that was worse than

living without Tallulah was hurting her any more than he already had.

It took all of Burgess's strength to speak, but when he did, he meant every word like he'd chiseled them into a stone tablet. "We can have today with no expectations."

You can stop panicking now, Tallulah. I'm setting you free.

CHAPTER TWENTY-EIGHT

"Who wants to go first?"

For the first time since they'd left the resort, Burgess and Tallulah looked at each other. The van ride had been brief, but quiet, even if their guide—Apollo—had kept up a steady stream of chatter about the local flora and fauna while they bumped their way through the rainforest to the zip-lining center. Burgess had appeared to be reeling while she'd sat beside him swallowing apologies, reminding herself over and over that she had nothing to feel sorry for.

And she didn't.

Allowing herself to bond with Burgess had been scary, but she'd learned to trust him and she could still feel the hole he'd verbally punched into her chest. Every time they touched now, her fight-or-flight response was triggered. Unfortunately, not even the hunger she still felt for Burgess could overcome her instinct to survive, to avoid being hurt again.

They stood on the top of a platform overlooking the endless green canopy of trees that seemed to continue right on through the horizon, the thick black wires stretching out and down, before vanishing into a clearing . . . and she could feel it.

She could *feel* it.

He'd decided to respect her wishes and let her go.

Her legs were so weak over that realization that a gentle breeze could have carried her clean off the platform. She'd drift down into the trees like a badly folded paper airplane. And the thing was, she'd meant what she said, wholeheartedly.

As soon as the truth was off her chest, however, healing became a possibility for the first time since everything crashed down. The panic she'd felt over his touch this morning was nothing compared to the panic that erupted when he shot her a questioning glance, then away just as quickly, as if forcing himself to detach.

"I'd like Tallulah to go first, so I can be here to make sure she's strapped in tightly and the damn thing is safe," he said gruffly, without looking at her.

Tallulah's heart squeezed.

Burgess was still protecting her. He couldn't help it.

But he wouldn't be around to consider her safety much longer, would he?

She'd choked off his air supply of hope.

"Come to think of it, Burgess should probably go first," said Apollo, still chipper despite the tension blanketing the platform. "I'm going to have to loosen the harness to fit someone his size and it will be easier for me to tighten it around Tallulah afterward."

That explanation brought her scattered thoughts screeching to a stop. "Wait. Hold on." She brushed a look across the ample breadth of Burgess's shoulders. "What is the weight limit for the harness?"

"Two seventy-five."

"Wow." Burgess gestured absently to himself. "Just about made the cutoff."

Who had set Tallulah's esophagus on fire? "Wait. Is it safe? For him, I mean?"

"I *always* triple-check the equipment."

"Yes, but when was the last time you put someone his size on a zip line?"

Apollo laughed. "That would be never."

"Burgess," she breathed, narrowly avoiding a dramatic chest clutch.

Her former boss's mouth kicked up at one end. "What, are you *my* bodyguard now?" He visibly hid his affection for her, stuffed it right down. "If something happens to me, you can have my sweatshirt collection, Tallulah."

Heat blasted the backs of her eyes. "That is *not* funny."

Burgess nodded at the harness Apollo held in his hands. "I'd like her to go first. I need to see for myself that she's secure."

"Well, *I* would like to wait for a bigger harness," Tallulah said, crossing her arms. "For him."

Apollo shook his head. "They don't make them any bigger."

Burgess winked at her. "Where have I heard that before?"

"Funny." It was a weird place to be—trapped between tears and laughter. "I think I want him to go first. I won't enjoy myself until I know he made it to the other side."

Apollo's head was moving on a swivel. "Why don't we flip a coin?"

Tallulah calculated her odds of winning against Burgess's stubborn nature versus her chances of winning against a coin. Fifty-fifty it was. "Fine, let's flip," Tallulah said, rocking side to side on the balls of her feet. "Tails I go first. Heads he goes first. Burgess, you have to abide by the outcome, though. Okay?"

A growl crackled in his throat. "The only reason I'm agreeing to a coin flip is that I'm equally unnerved by the cable. I can't decide if it's better to test the harness or the cable first to make sure you're safe."

Apollo threw up his hands. "I'm telling you, it's safe!"

"I need to be positive when it comes to her." Burgess tore his eyes off her with seeming difficulty, a line snapping in his cheek. "Flip it."

The instructor produced a coin from his pocket, tossing it up into the air and smacking it down on his wrist. "Heads."

Tallulah's legs almost gave out.

The air became very thin around her. Was she making the right decision having him go first? Or should it be the other way around? Suddenly she wasn't so sure.

Apollo was already holding open the harness for Burgess to step into, the beige strips of fabric cutting heavily into his muscled back. This was happening. She was going to have to watch Burgess sail down through the trees. And he was only there in the first place because of her. He wanted to prove he could be as adventurous as her. Wanted to prove they could work.

"Burgess, you don't have to do this."

"Yeah? I . . . think I want to." He looked out at the horizon for a moment, before eliminating the gap between him and Tallulah, stopping before they could touch, but close enough that she could read a new determination dawning on his face. "No, I do. I want to. I think maybe if I'd lived more, experienced more, like you do, I wouldn't have been so scared to lose hockey. I wouldn't have thrown you out and ruined my—" He cut himself off with a clenched jaw. "You're worried something is going to happen and you'll be responsible, since you're the reason I'm up here. Don't be. I make my own decisions. I just wish I would have made the right ones sooner. I should have gone skinny dipping with you. I should have danced in the kitchen, no matter how bad it looked." He swallowed, glancing back to watch Apollo tighten the final straps across his shoulders. "I might not have you anymore. I might have thrown away my chance, but I'm *not* going to throw away the lesson you tried to teach me. If it's the only piece of you I'm allowed, I'm keeping it."

"All right, man," Apollo said. "You're double- and triple-checked. The harness is holding your weight just fine. You're going to lean back like you're sitting in a chair. Hold on to the line, just like I showed you, and most importantly, enjoy yourself. My colleague, Ozzie, will be at the other side to help you get down—"

"Make sure Tallulah is secure before you let her go or you'll wish you were never born, Apollo," Burgess said, hitting the instructor with a death stare. And then he went.

He didn't even let Apollo respond, *he just went*, his beautifully athletic body slicing through the misty air at what seemed like a thousand miles an hour over the lush rainforest—and the breath honestly just evaporated from her body, lungs filling with cement in her chest. Because it was the most painfully inconvenient moment to realize she was still wildly in love with the man. She hadn't moved on at all, as she'd thought. She'd been existing, going through the motions, pretending not to look for his face in every crowd. Hadn't she?

But his speech, followed by his pointed leap from the platform made it obvious that . . . now *he* was the one moving on. Out of respect for her wishes, her pain.

Which was exactly what she wanted.

Right.

IN THE DISTANCE, Tallulah leapt from the platform and Burgess curled his fingernails into his palms, squeezing until he could feel blood being drawn. His heart rifled in his chest, the humid air growing even soupier and harder to inhale. She'd be on the ground in ten seconds. Eight. If the line could hold his weight, hers would be a piece of cake. Unless he'd weakened it by going first.

Oh Jesus.

He planted his hands on his knees, cold sweat breaking out on every inch of his body, the feelings completely gone from his hands and feet. *Get your shit together.* She'd be landing soon and she could *not* see him like this, hyperventilating over the possibility of her being harmed. The enormous and tragic and unyielding way he felt about Tallulah could no longer be his responsibility. Not when his touch made her feel *panicked*.

Loving her up close was no longer an option. He'd have to do it from afar.

Later, when he was alone, he'd let the longing and regret burn him alive. But he wouldn't make Tallulah feel guilty on top of everything else he'd inflicted on her. Not today, probably the last time they would ever be alone again.

The whooshing sound of the zip line cut off abruptly, followed by the most beautiful laughter to ever exist, and Burgess straightened, pasting a serene expression onto his face and quickly swiping at the sweat on his brow. There she was, alive, safe, having her helmet removed by Ozzie, the young man with a long braid who'd just done the same for him. Burgess's fingers itched with the need to take over the task. He hated anyone being that close to the woman he still considered his own, touching her even in a perfunctory way, but this was the hell he'd signed up for by failing to recognize the treasure he'd once held in his hands.

"Wasn't it amazing?" Tallulah breathed, looking over at him.

"Yeah." His voice sounded like a rusted door hinge. "It was."

Finally, she was freed from the harness, and she bounded over to him, obviously on an adrenaline high, ready to throw herself into his arms. And his heart shot up into his mouth, the anticipation so heavy that his legs turned to concrete. When she was only a couple of steps away, however, the exultant expression bled from her face and she slowed, holding up her hand for a high five instead. Burgess absorbed the contact like a beggar.

"I saw a monkey while I was up there, peeking out over the tops of the trees," Tallulah said. "Did you see anything?"

"Birds," he lied. He'd seen nothing but point B.

Was he really learning from Tallulah, then? As he'd claimed on the platform?

No, he wasn't. He needed to do better.

Like he'd said, if all she left him with was a will to do more, experience life beyond hockey, he needed to focus on that. Needed to cherish what she'd tried to teach him.

"I felt the wind," he said, mentally putting himself back up on the zip line. "I'm used to the wind, but not it being so warm."

Some of the tension left her shoulders. "No, we like our cold, don't we?"

"Yeah. I'm not sure Josephine and Wells took us into consideration with this wedding."

"I'm not sure, either," she said, humor dancing in her eyes. "It's December. We're supposed to be in coats and mittens."

"Do you wear mittens?"

Way to sound like a wistful fool.

He couldn't help it, though. He'd been caught off guard by the image of her walking through a snowy morning in Beacon Hill, wearing his sweatshirt under a parka, breathing warm air into a pair of woolen mittens.

"Yes, I wear mittens," she said. "They're superior to gloves."

"How? There's no finger mobility. You're basically a lobster."

Did she have any idea that her smile was causing a volcanic eruption in his chest?

"Because you can wave like this," she responded, demonstrating a four-finger wave that was so fucking cute, he needed to lie down.

"That's the only reason?" he rasped. "Waving?"

"And your fingers stay warmer, because of the body heat. They're like little people in there, huddling together to survive a storm."

"I don't want to think of my fingers as people."

Her giggle ripped a hole in his throat. "You're missing out," she said firmly. "You *need* to try mittens, Burgess." His grumble only made her smile broaden. "I can't believe we're talking about outerwear while standing in the middle of a Central American jungle."

"We're not built for this climate. I sweated through my shirt before I even made it to your room this morning."

Tallulah's gaze tracked down his bare chest and stomach, unmistakable lust flaring in the depths of her eyes before she shot them down to the ground. "Oh, that's why you were disrobing when I opened the door? I thought it was to tempt me."

Burgess firmed in his board shorts, the moisture drying up in his mouth. So, she still wanted to fuck him, even though it made moving on harder? That might excite him, ply him with satisfaction and gratitude, but he wouldn't be laying a finger on her. He wouldn't be the reason she turned into her own worst enemy. Still, he couldn't quite stop himself from making the situation worse, because he wanted to be inside her more than he wanted to live for tomorrow's sunrise. And that would be his continuous state until his dying day. "I'm pretty sure you're the temptation with those little yellow strings hanging out of your shorts, gorgeous."

A long slide of muscle worked in her graceful throat as she swallowed, eyes closing, as if to savor the intimate turn of the conversation. "It occurred to me on the ride here that this bathing suit is probably not built for cliff diving, but in my defense, I didn't know we were having an outdoor adventure day when I packed. And it's the only one I brought with me."

"I'll go first. If it comes off when you jump, I'll shield you and we'll find the bathing suit together. Shouldn't be that hard since it's bright yellow, right?" Something possessive and heavy welled in his chest and it wouldn't remain trapped inside. "I don't give a fuck if we're together or not," he rasped. "No one but me is seeing you naked."

Burgess never found out how she might have responded, because Apollo rode into the clearing on an ATV, the churn of the engine splitting the morning serenity in half. "Well, what do you know? You both survived."

It seemed to cost Tallulah an effort to drag her attention off Burgess, but he wasn't going to read into that. Or anything she'd said about bikinis or temptation. He'd hurt her too much for her to recover. That's what she'd said, plainly, and that sentiment was echoing in his ears even now. His possessiveness of this woman had caused him to slip, but that wouldn't be happening again. Unless, of course, someone else tried to see her naked. In which case, he'd rip the sun down out of the sky, so it would be too dark for anyone to see her.

"Yes, we did," Tallulah said, giving Apollo a quick smile. "I guess we'll be adding to your collection of five-star Tripadvisor reviews."

"Of course they're all five stars," Burgess said. "The people who didn't survive aren't alive to leave one-star ratings."

Apollo threw back his head and laughed. "Dead men tell no tales."

Tallulah coughed. "Feeling less confident in this cliff jump."

"Ah, come on, it's going to be just as safe as the zip line." Ozzie rode up on another ATV. "Let's get to the jump spot early. Around lunchtime, it gets too busy. Each of you hop on the back of—"

"Nope," Burgess clipped. So much for keeping his possessiveness at bay. "She rides with me. I made it through her turn on the zip line, but I need to build back some mental stamina before she jumps off a fucking cliff." He shook his head. "That's not going to happen if she's on the back of a different ATV."

Ozzie and Apollo traded an amused glance.

"Do you know how to drive one of these things, boss?" Apollo asked.

"I know how to drive a snowmobile. Same principle."

"If you say so." Ozzie sighed, climbing off his ATV and getting on behind Apollo. "Are you coming, Tallulah?"

Burgess looked down at Tallulah to find her staring at him strangely.

Of course she was. They'd broken up and he was still acting like he had some kind of claim on her. "Protecting you is a habit," he said, the back of his neck extra warm. "I guess I'm not going to be able to break it so easily."

Not wanting to hear her reprimand, Burgess strode for the empty ATV and got on, his attention split between the control panel and Tallulah. Was she going to come after his over-the-top display of protectiveness?

When she appeared at his elbow, sliding her leg over the back seat of the ATV and wrapping her arms around his middle, he tipped his head forward and let out a pent-up breath, relief flowing down to his fingers, toes, even as her bare thighs around his hips made the laces of his board shorts feel uncomfortable.

"Ready," she murmured against his back.

That made one of them.

If he got through the rest of this morning, it would be a miracle.

CHAPTER TWENTY-NINE

The cliff was a lot higher than Tallulah had anticipated.

But she wasn't scared.

Nothing seemed scary, anymore . . . except for maybe the possibility that she'd pushed Burgess away before she was sure it was the right thing to do. He'd helped her off the ATV with all the caution of a baker carrying a wedding cake to his van and now? Now he stood looking out over the lagoon, visibly assessing the danger with his arms crossed, those powerful muscles captured in sunlight, his dark hair with the smattering of gray being picked up and tossed every which way by the wind, jaw tight.

Burgess was the most beautiful man in the world, full stop.

He'd always been a certified stud—hello Mean Daddy—but her attraction to him had reached a point that was almost . . . unendurable. Like she'd had to restrain herself from licking his sun-heated back on the ride to the cliff. Or dropping her hand into his lap to feel the shape of his penis against her palm. Stroke it stiff. And the surge of horniness wasn't only physical in nature. She was . . . emotionally horny. Was that even a thing?

Could be.

No, it was. Because as soon as he'd withdrawn from her, the desperation to feel their connection again came on like a magnitude ten earthquake. She'd soaked up his protectiveness like a greedy sponge, because it seemed . . . that's all there was left.

That's all he was allowing her now that she'd made the potentially premature mistake of ending things.

So what was stopping her from turning to Burgess right now and asking him if they could just rewind? Back up to earlier this morning when she'd been venting and scared and unsteady. Panicked at the thought of being burned again. Maybe if she knew he'd take such immediate action to end things, she'd have kept her mouth shut . . . but keeping her feelings to herself wasn't right, either. Was it?

"Listen, folks," Apollo said, "When you get down there, don't forget to explore. There are various shorelines and mini beaches. There is a cave behind that waterfall—"

"I'm going down first again, Tallulah," Burgess said, pressing his tongue to the inside of his cheek. "I have to judge the depth for myself before you jump."

Ozzie and Apollo both threw up their hands. "Mister Abraham," Apollo said. "You are the most distrustful person I've ever met in my life."

"So be it. I don't—"

"You don't take chances with her. We know." Ozzie sighed and started to kick off his flip-flops, muttering to himself about how hundreds of tourists leap from that exact spot every single day. "I'll jump first so you can see how safe it is."

Before Burgess or Tallulah could protest, Ozzie backed up several steps, let out a yell, and did a pencil jump that kept him in the air one, two, three seconds before he plunged into the aquamarine water below. Tallulah held her breath until he surfaced a moment later, waving his hand—and possibly his middle finger.

"And you're sure we can't jump together," Burgess said to Apollo.

"No. Now that is unsafe."

Burgess nodded, that line bobbing and weaving in his cheek. "Okay."

He closed his eyes. Didn't move.

A full twenty seconds passed.

"Burgess," she prompted. "Are you okay?"

"Yeah, I'm trying to remember what you said that night I took you skinny dipping."

"The pond was ice cold. I'm pretty sure I was just chanting *oh God* over and over again."

His lips tugged. "Before that."

Tallulah thought back, letting the rich velvet memories of that night sail into her mind like unfurling ribbons. A moment stopped like a freeze-frame, and she zoomed in, hearing her own voice drift back from weeks earlier. "Forever is composed of nows," she said. "Dickinson. I told you it was the one time English Lit piqued my interest."

"That's it. Yeah."

"Why are you thinking of that now?"

"Probably because I'm about to jump off a cliff."

Tallulah laughed.

"I don't know, I'm trying to enjoy this, not just get through it alive. The quote . . . it's just making more sense now. If you live merely to get through everything, what parts are you enjoying, right?"

His interpretation made her chest pang. "That's exactly right."

"Okay." He took a few steps back and looked at her. "You aim for the exact spot I land on, okay? *If* I resurface."

Why did her heart feel like one of those movie theater popcorn machines, just crackling and popping and overflowing? "I will. Promise. I'll see you down there."

It was that promise—and that promise only—that made Tallulah watch. As she'd discovered with the zip line, it wasn't easy to watch this man do something even slightly dangerous outside of her reach and the helplessness kicked in now, again, but she was so glad she watched because Burgess released a shout of pure enjoyment, his huge, sculpted body creating the biggest splash she'd ever seen. When his face broke the surface with a reluctant smile and he flipped back his wet hair, the floor dropped out from beneath her feet and she went plunging into another, deeper, cavern of love.

Yeah, you're real tough now. Wasn't it just a few days ago you walked away because a twelve-year-old was mad at you?

How could this be the same man who said those callous words to her?

The fear of *that* man hurting her again lingered, ruining the moment—and she resented it like hell. Resented it so much that it eclipsed the trepidation to leap and so she went, her feet leaving the hard stone, gravity yanking her body down so fast, she almost didn't have time to suck in a proper breath. But she did have time to watch Burgess's face while she was still in the air. To watch him bare his teeth against the terror of watching her fall.

He loved her, too.

Big, boundless love.

That was the truth that was occurring to her as she sank into the warm water, bubbles dancing around her body and carrying her back up to the surface where she sucked in a breath and laughed, loud and shaky at the same time . . . but the sound broke off on a whimper as soon as she realized the water was a little too present on her nipples. And elsewhere.

She couldn't feel the cloth of her bathing suit. At all.

"Burgess," she gasped. "It happened."

"Fuck." He swam in her direction while looking around for Ozzie, glad to see the man was climbing the steep path back to the top of the cliff with his back turned. "Come here."

Nodding, she swam to meet him. Beneath the surface, he took her bare hips in his hands and turned her around to face him, crowding her front to his warmth, the familiar texture of his hard, hair-covered chest. "Didn't he say there was a cave behind the waterfall?"

"Yes."

"Okay, let's head that direction." He looked around, both of them did, but there was no yellow in the immediate area. "You can hide while I find the suit."

"That was *amazing*," she breathed, her head tilting back so she could see the cliff from which they'd jumped, smiling to acknowledge Apollo's wave. "I want to do it again."

"Me too, actually," Burgess said slowly, surprising her. "But maybe we should get you a wet suit for next time."

She snorted into his wet shoulder. "What were you thinking about on the way down?"

Too briefly, he looked uncharacteristically shy. "I was thinking I wish Lissa could see me. She wouldn't believe it."

Tallulah smiled to hide the fact that heat was crowding behind her eyes. "I think she would. I think she would even expect you to fly. You're her superhero."

His Adam's apple slid up and down as they continue their progress toward the waterfall. "What were you thinking about on the way down?"

Apparently, cliff diving made everything clearer, or perhaps it just dislodged her filter, because the truth came spilling out in a big old, waterlogged confession. The truth as well as she knew it, anyway. Where she stood in relation to Burgess . . . the ground wasn't firm, she only knew she wasn't ready to say goodbye completely. "I was thinking I don't know if I want to break up," she blurted, her whole body turning to jelly. Wobbly, insubstantial jelly. "I was thinking . . . this morning I just needed to vent and get my frustration off my chest. I didn't need an immediate solution, you know? I just wanted you to know what I've been going through. You didn't have to try and fix it in two seconds, Burgess."

They'd reached the edge of the waterfall and so she was yelling to be heard over the noise. Meanwhile, Burgess was staring down at her with an unreadable mask, but very clearly not breathing, not a single breath. "Are you saying you want to be with me, Tallulah?"

"I'm saying I . . ." *Yes*, screamed her head and her gut. Her heart, however, which had sustained the most damage, balked. "I'm saying I don't know yet," she said, sounding winded. Because she was. Mortally winded. "But it's too soon to let you go. I can't."

Burgess's chest rose and fell in a plummet. He ducked beneath the waterfall into the hollow behind it and Tallulah followed, the world turning darker and more muffled in an instant.

"Why?" he said, raggedly, taking her by the meat of her arms, his intensity yawning the pit in her stomach wider. Wider.

Once again, her wounded heart intervened, lassoing the words *I love you* and dragging them back into her mouth. The disappointment of her not saying those words were a visible blow to him. He closed his eyes and she closed hers, too, even while sliding her arms around his neck, her thighs wrapping tight to his hips, water lapping around them. "Can I show you, instead of tell you?"

"You're not all here with me, Tallulah." Their foreheads met, his hands slipping down her wet back to clutch her buttocks and rock her closer, his hips tilting in a way that drew a whimper from her throat. "Please, gorgeous, don't break me like this."

"I need you."

Those three words weren't fair, because she knew he'd cave.

Knew she could get what she desperately needed—to be connected to him again. It had only been a few hours since he'd started to shift away and her entire being bled as a result. Couldn't he see that? Couldn't intimacy be enough for now?

"You *need* me? Is that all?" Burgess waded out of the water, carrying her into the opening of the cave with his teeth bared against her mouth. "My survival *depends* on you."

"I'm giving myself to you," she whispered, rubbing her bare sex on the ridge inside his shorts, eager to be filled by his strength, his heat and hunger and urgency.

"You're not giving yourself to me completely. You don't think I can read you by now?" Even as frustration rippled through that harshly delivered statement, he was reaching down to untie his board shorts. "Fuck it, though, right? We'll call it a massage."

"No." Slowly, she parted his lips with a lap of her tongue, suctioning him gently, before sinking into a long, wet kiss, their tongues meeting and retreating, going deeper, deeper until he was groaning, slapping her sex with the hard inches of his, stroking himself, his fist knocking into her inner thighs as he moved it, fast and rough. "It was making love and we both knew it," she breathed against his mouth. "Every time we touched, that's what it was."

Burgess made a sound, a shiver wracking his big body. His voice was thick with rust when he spoke. "And now?"

"Now I'm scared to trust what I'm feeling."

"How do I fix it?" he demanded, pressing the head of his arousal inside of her. Thrusting his hips in an upward drive and seating her in one savage move, leaving them both panting against each other's mouth. "Tell me how to make you love me again," he rasped, gripping her butt hard and working her up and down the stiff jut of his erection, his breath pelting her lips. "I will never, ever, hurt you again, Tallulah. I'll jump off a much higher cliff first."

He didn't give her a chance to respond, because his mouth found hers and ruined it forever, kissing her with so much passion, tears formed in her eyes and her hips eagerly demanded more, more, bucking in time with the jerks of his hands, his thickness finding the deepest angles of her core, their wet bodies slip-sliding together, their groans steadily growing louder until the waterfall was no longer drowning them out and he had to keep his mouth stamped over Tallulah's while he fucked her, raw and hard, while her toes dangled somewhere in the vicinity of his bent knees.

"God, Tallulah, baby, I need to come so bad."

"I want it. Let me have it." She rained kisses all over his perfect face, her hips hinging up and back, thighs beginning to tremble, along with the rest of her. From the intensity of the act, the riot of emotions breaking free and running like escaped felons inside of her chest. "Don't keep it from me again, please."

"I can't. I'm not strong enough." His eyes met hers, glazed, his tongue licking the side of her neck in a wonderfully obscene way, before finding her lips and weaponizing himself against them, lapping the inside of her mouth with a growl. "I'm hungry and your body is the only one that feeds me."

"Devour me, then." She constricted her inner walls, watching his face transform with the agony of pleasure, her own following suit with great pulses and the locking of muscles, the rocketing of her hips. "I'm going to eat you up, too. You feel that?"

"Feel it?" Burgess's pumps grew disordered, his breath turning shallow, fingers digging harder into the flesh of her backside. "You smile at me, Tallulah, and I know I'll feel it for centuries. You have no idea what this does to me. Fucking you. Making love to you. Watching my cock turn your mind blank. No. *Idea*." He growled one final word. *"Mine."*

She bit at his mouth. "Mine."

"Mine."

The imminency of release was transforming both of their expressions, knowledge that the end, the beginning, the everything had arrived, their mouths surged together and fused, Tallulah's sex tightening up around his shaft in an almost unbearable, prolonged ripple, and Burgess erupted inside and out, liquid heat flooding inside of her while he pressed a guttural shout into the side of her neck, his hands grinding her down violently and intuitively on his hardness in a way that was necessary and right and also agonizing, because it prolonged her orgasm until she was slapping his shoulders and writhing on that rigid pike, exciting him further, exciting herself further while stickiness ran down the insides of her thighs and the waterfall made them the sole humans on the face of the earth. In that moment, that's exactly what she wanted.

To have no choices to make.

No feelings to deal with.

Just to . . . be. To stay and be and lose herself in what only this man made her feel.

But as soon as they finished crashing, down, down, down and recovering with gulps of air and calming hands, Burgess read her mind before she even had a chance, letting her down carefully and pulling her into his embrace, his lips pressing a kiss to her temples, her cheeks, her eyelids. "Yeah. We belong to each other. Period. No matter what. You just have to decide if you want to be each other's together or apart, Tallulah." He studied her face for a long moment, adoration etched into every one of his features, before kissing her mouth long and firm, stroking back her wet hair and pressing their foreheads together one final time, making eye contact that left her knees shaking. "I'll go find your bathing suit."

CHAPTER THIRTY

Burgess sat on a bench overlooking the aquamarine water of the Caribbean, shielding his eyes as the sun slowly dipped below the horizon. When it had disappeared completely, he fell back against the wooden backrest, his gaze sweeping left to the trellis adorned in white gauze that would serve as the ceremony site for Wells and Josephine's wedding the next day. He'd arrived an hour early for the rehearsal, because he flat out had no idea what to do with himself and being confined inside his room had only made him twice as restless.

A brief check of his watch told him ten minutes remained until the wedding party was due to meet Carlos for a quick run-through of the ceremony, after which they would head to the rehearsal dinner. That meant he'd be seeing Tallulah soon.

His pulse beat out of time, like an unwound clock.

He could safely say he'd never felt this way in his life. A strange mixture of clearheaded and broken. High and low. Originally, he'd agreed to zip-line and cliff jump so he could spend time with Tallulah, but hell if something inside of him hadn't changed today. He'd let go. He'd learned he could still do something outside of his comfort zone and it wouldn't kill him. No, he'd actually loved the rush of hurling himself toward the water, the sense of satisfaction that spread through his limbs afterward, like he'd satisfied something inside of himself that hadn't existed in a long time. Maybe his sense of adventure had been lurking under the surface the whole time, waiting for her to come coax it back to life.

At the very least, Burgess was more than just Sir Savage.

He had a second act in him.

But he couldn't visualize it just then. Not without her.

Burgess flicked open the top button on his dress shirt, yanking on the knot of his tie to loosen it slightly. Damn the formal dress code for tonight's dinner. Did Wells and Josephine somehow miss the memo that they in Central America? He'd sweated more in the last two days than he had during his entire hockey career. Although, the perspiration beginning to form on his upper lip had a lot to do with knowing Tallulah would be there in less than five minutes now.

Yeah, he wasn't seeing the pristine waters of the Caribbean anymore. He was seeing her completely naked, legs around his hips, begging him not to deprive her of his come. He was seeing the wide, invigorated smile on her face after she'd finished her jump into the lagoon, how his heart had flown up into his mouth in response. Her conflicted expression after they made love behind the waterfall. The pain of that was still with him now, like shrapnel from a bomb that had burrowed beneath his skin and would need a surgeon to take it all out.

He'd fought a war over the last two days . . . and it was possible he'd lost.

More than possible, really. Hadn't he lost Tallulah that day in the hospital?

Getting her back might have never been realistic at all.

The thought of going home and coping with the reality of life without her . . . it scared the shit out of him. For the last six weeks, he'd pushed himself to heal, drove himself to train and fight through pain and discomfort, propelled by one goal: get Tallulah back in his life. And Lissa's.

If he failed . . . what then? Wake up every morning knowing she was out there . . . just not *with* him? And that she never would be, because he'd taken her for granted once in a moment of weakness? That sounded like hell on earth. And yet, somehow, he'd have to take the lessons he'd learned from Tallulah and continue to apply them, because they made him a better man. A better father. He'd live for her in his words and deeds, even if she wasn't physically there. Every second of it would be excruciating, but he wouldn't go backward.

Only forward.

Even if he only had the memory of her to propel him.

When he heard footsteps approaching, Burgess swallowed the burn in his throat and stood, turning to find Wells, Josephine, Tallulah, and Carlos coming down the lit stone pathway, and immediately his pulse started hammering in triple time.

"Jesus," Burgess muttered. Every time he thought Tallulah couldn't get more beautiful, she found a way to prove him wrong. Instead of the tight, short revenge dress she'd worn on the first night, she had on a long dark purple one that blew in the breeze, a golden cuff around her upper arm, her hair loose, wavy, possibly still full of salt water from their excursion. She looked soft and sun-kissed and perfect. In every way.

"Hey, man," Wells said, gripping his hand to bring him in for a quick hug and a back slap. "You been out here long?"

Burgess shrugged, leaned down to kiss Josephine's cheek. "Thought I'd watch the sun go down."

The redhead laughed up at him with her eyes. "Were there no hockey games rerunning on television?"

"Hockey isn't everything," he said, without thinking, realizing he meant it. He meant it even more with Tallulah standing in front of him with an apology swimming in her eyes—and Burgess knew instantly that it was over. She'd decided to walk away. She'd taken the hours they'd spent apart this afternoon to think and her conclusion was . . . no. No to him. No to the life they'd fashioned together, a staid single father, a lively and wise au pair, a confused twelve-year-old. They weren't going to find out what happened next.

It was right there on her face.

His stomach sank down between his feet, fingers numbing, heart giving up altogether.

He couldn't even feel it beating anymore.

"Can we talk?" Tallulah whispered.

"After," Burgess forced out around the object in his throat, knowing he needed time to get his head on straight, his own emotions under control. He needed to brace himself, prepare. Although he'd never be prepared to hear she'd chosen to make him a part of her past, would he?

"Oh. Okay, sure," she murmured, hesitating, then skirting past him to join Wells and Josephine at the white trellis overlooking the coastline. Burgess closed his eyes as Tallulah walked by, inhaling a lungful of her scent and wondering if she could be persuaded to pass on the name of her perfume before they went their separate ways.

He'd buy as many bottles as it took to last him until his last day on earth.

"Okay, everyone, we'll make rehearsal short and sweet, since we're due at dinner shortly. There are only two of you in the bridal party, so it shouldn't take long at all," Carlos said, positioning beneath the trellis, as though standing in for the priest. He motioned to the area in front of them, drawing an invisible rectangle in the air. "There will be white chairs here in the morning. Two sides. Josephine, I showed you the bridal suite earlier where you will be waiting with your father. We've already walked him through his duties in guiding you down the aisle, where Wells will be standing. Burgess, you will be on his right."

Carlos took a few steps forward, guiding Burgess by the crook of his elbow to the spot he'd indicated. "This is where you'll be."

"You could have just asked me to move."

The coordinator ignored him. "Tallulah, you will be on the opposite side, right beside the glowing bride. But of course, before any of *this* happens, Burgess and Tallulah will begin the procession by walking down the aisle together."

That statement hit Burgess in the chest like a torpedo.

"What's that now?" he asked, noticing Tallulah looking at him funny.

Why hadn't it occurred to Burgess that he'd be walking down the aisle next to Tallulah? Of course, he would. He was the best man. She was the maid of honor. That's how a wedding worked. Christ, the act was going to gut him.

"You were both away this afternoon," Carlos carried on, seemingly unaware of the chaos he'd ignited in Burgess's sternum. "I couldn't show you the room where you'll wait for my cue, so I'll show you now. Come with me, please."

In his periphery, he could feel Tallulah staring at him, but he couldn't bring himself to look at her. From this moment on, he wouldn't be able to so much as glance over. Having the memory of walking her down the aisle in his head was going to be bad enough without being able to recall her eyes, how her hair moved in the tropical wind, how the weight of her arm felt while hooked through his. No. He'd entered self-preservation mode.

"Burgess," Tallulah said, as they followed Carlos up the path toward the small outbuilding adjacent to the main resort. "Are you . . . okay?"

He kept walking.

Was he okay?

Was she serious?

"All right, here we are." Carlos took out a set of keys and unlocked a door marked "Reserved" with an efficient twist of his wrist, turning on the light inside. "This is where you will be expected to arrive at three thirty P.M. tomorrow. On my signal, you will exit the door and walk arm in arm toward the ceremony area. Like so . . ." He waved them toward each other, but they didn't budge. "Like so."

"We don't have to act the whole thing out. Three thirty, arm in arm, go stand under the gazebo thing. We get it."

Tallulah frowned. Probably. He couldn't see her, but there was surprise and disapproval in her tone when she said, "Burgess."

Carlos sniffed. "Getting this perfect might not seem like a big deal to you, but it will be a big deal to your friends if you get it wrong."

Fine. That made sense. The last thing he wanted to do was blemish the wedding of two people who'd figured out how to make their relationship work. Two people he kind of loved.

Burgess grunted.

Carlos took that as his cue to shuffle Burgess and Tallulah. "Like. *So.*"

Burgess kept his gaze trained straight ahead as they walked slowly toward the ceremony site, her orange and basil scent wreaking havoc on his senses. When they reached the grass where the seating area would be in the morning, his whole rib cage drew tight, so he switched to replaying his final game at Syracuse, as he often did, but the memory of the roaring crowd did nothing to soothe him now. By the time Burgess reached the end of the "aisle" he felt like he'd been shot full of holes.

"Great," Carlos said, behind them. "Now you two can get into position and wait for the bride and groom to make their way down the aisle, as well. Wells, have you given the ring to Burgess for tomorrow?"

No response.

Wells was too busy staring at Josephine in the moonlight, visibly mesmerized.

Affection radiated back at him from his bride-to-be, their fingers twining together.

For the first time, Burgess ached at the sight of what they had. Coveted it, even.

"Wells," Burgess said, clearing his throat. "The ring?"

"Yeah, I have it, man. I'll give it to you in the morning."

"Great." Burgess backed away from the group, unable to stop himself from giving Tallulah one last look, starved for eye contact with her after going so long without it, but finding her staring down at her hands, instead. "I'll see you at dinner."

TALLULAH DID HER best to keep a smile plastered to her face all through dinner, but she was completely numb from head to toe. Burgess had taken a seat on the other side of the room, even though his name card was right across from hers. There was an older gentleman in his place, an apparent friend of Josephine's parents, and he chatted happily about the Florida weather and how it compared to Costa Rica, but only a third of his words were sinking in.

All she could do was replay the moment she'd walked down the aisle with Burgess.

How distant he'd been.

But Burgess hadn't mentally checked out, had he? Not voluntarily.

She'd forced him to.

Acknowledging that to herself made her heart rattle and dive down into her stomach, the taste of her martini souring in her mouth. He'd told her that making love with her when she wasn't all in, sure of their relationship, would mess him up. And it clearly had. While trying to keep herself protected against being hurt again, she'd hurt *Burgess*.

She'd ignored his request for sensitivity, even though he'd had such a hard time giving it. How could she do that? It wasn't until later, as she lay down on her hotel room bed, that she realized how selfishly she'd behaved. Tonight she'd arrived at the rehearsal planning to apologize, but he'd evaded her. Avoided her.

Especially now, as he sat as far away as possible.

Tallulah reached for her water glass and realized her hand was shaking, so she pushed it into her lap and took a few deep breaths.

"It could very well rain tomorrow morning, I hear. A little sun shower to keep everything green," said the Floridian across the table, while forking some shrimp into his mouth. "But you know what they say, rain on your wedding day is good luck."

"That's true," Tallulah said, trying to appear interested, but her gaze strayed to Burgess at the other table and her whole body throbbed, like a giant heartbeat. She wanted to be sitting next to him so badly, a notch formed in her throat. "They do say that. Rain and weddings."

"It was clear as a bell on my wedding day. That should have tipped me off."

Tallulah made herself laugh. "Oh dear. I'm so sorry."

"I'm the one that's sorry. I let a good one get away." He chuckled. "She's remarried now with a couple of kids. Grown ones. That's the part I can't believe. It feels like we were married yesterday, but that can't be true if she's been remarried long enough to have college-aged children, you know? Time goes by fast, doesn't it?"

The last few months blew by in a series of colors and sounds. "Yes."

A chair scraped on the floor and the tinkle of metal hitting glass quieted the room's conversations. Tallulah followed the source of the sound to find Josephine's father standing up with a glass of champagne in his hand. "Sorry for the interruption folks, but this is my only chance to say something. Tomorrow at the reception will be the best man's turn for a speech and well . . . I can't let the opportunity pass to tell my future son-in-law that I love him. We both do, my wife and me. When you have a child, you never think anyone is going to be good enough for them. But Wells proved me wrong. He's not just good enough for her, he's the *only* one for her." He raised his glass. "And I want to officially welcome him to the family."

A few seats away, Wells pulled Josephine onto his lap and buried his face in her neck while everyone applauded.

"Look at that," said the man across from Tallulah, his face softened by fondness. "I hope they treasure each other. Love doesn't always come around twice. And even if it does, it's going to be different. There are no two exact types of love, you know that? When two people love each other, they create a love snowflake, and it can never be re-created by anyone else."

Tallulah picked up her napkin and dabbed at her eyes, barely able to speak due to the heart cartwheeling in her breast. "Okay, who sent you to ruin me?"

The man paused in the act of spearing a shrimp. "Come again?"

"Who do you work for?"

Blank look.

"Really? Is it just a coincidence that I'm . . . I broke up with the guy I'm still in love with . . . and he's here and everything you say is attacking me?"

Down went his fork. "You broke up with a man you still love? *Why?*"

"It's complicated."

"It's not." He shook his head. "If you think about the problem, really think about it, it's never more complicated than learning to live without someone you love. I promise."

Eyes burning, Tallulah looked across the room at Burgess and found him staring back, yearning etched into his every feature, but he averted his gaze before she could soak it all in. The Floridian followed her line of sight and turned back to her with his mouth dropped open.

"Don't tell me it's the hockey player. *Sir Savage?*"

What was the point in pretending otherwise? "Yeah," she whispered. "It's him."

"You're the woman from the article?"

"I'm . . . who?"

The man rubbed his hands together, then turned, reached into a tote bag that had been hanging on the back of his chair, pulling out a rolled-up, glossy magazine. "I brought my copy of *Sports Illustrated*, hoping Sir Savage would sign it for me. I thought of asking Jim to introduce us, but he's sort of busy giving away his only child."

He dropped the magazine into the center of the table. A soccer player from the US Women's National Team stared up at Tallulah until her dining companion started flipping the pages. "Hold on. I have the article marked . . ."

When the pages were once again spread, Tallulah found herself staring down at a picture of Burgess on the ice, geared up. Chewing on his mouthguard in a way that was endearingly familiar, even if she'd only witnessed him doing it once. There were smaller pictures, still frames of the moment his back injury went from bad to terrible, and she winced over those, heaviness sweeping into her midsection. She started to offer to help get the article signed, but the man turned the page one more time—and there was Burgess in rehab.

Sweating, pale, pulling on a rope while a trainer directed him from behind.

And pinned on the wall in front of Burgess was . . . Tallulah.

A picture of her.

Conversations grew muffled in her ears, the sound of her heartbeat quickening and growing louder until it drowned the whole room out completely. Her whole world narrowed down to the photograph. How he stared at it while he labored.

She'd been his incentive.

"He was interviewed for the article, of course. He doesn't mention the woman by name, but . . . let's see . . ." He used the candle to highlight a passage. "He said, 'Am I motivated by a return to hockey? Sure. But mostly, there's a woman. There's an incredible woman. The thought of her is getting me there. Healing me more than any medicine ever could.'"

Tallulah's air passage was full of cement by the time he finished reading. The candlelit table blurred in front of her, and she quickly swiped at her eyes; if only she could look at Burgess, but he was standing up from the table, phone pressed to his ear. He left the room, exiting onto the patio, and she felt the sudden lack of his presence like a full-body chill.

She stood up on legs that were as insubstantial as air, holding on to the back of the chair for support while she got her bearings. Where was she going? What was she going to do?

If she really thought about it, there was only one answer.

She was in love with a man who'd had a bad day and said something regrettable, but that moment didn't define him. His words might have struck her where it hurt, yes. He'd said so many things to her that made her feel . . . alive and safe and loved, though, too. Right? She didn't want to go any longer, let alone the rest of her life, never hearing his voice, seeing his face, feeling his hands and breath on her body. Loving him. Being loved by him.

"Excuse me," she said, forcing her legs to carry her across the dining room.

Burgess had walked down to the edge of the patio and sat down on one of the lounge chairs, a nearby fire pit highlighting the planes and shadows of his face. There was so much noise from the dining room, he must not have heard her approaching and it took her several steps before she could make out what he was saying into the phone, but she finally did.

"I know, Liss." He massaged the center of his forehead. "I did. I tried."

Tallulah abruptly stopped walking, hands pressed to her chest to keep her heart from leaping out.

"Of course, I told her that I love her. Believe me, she knows." He listened. "It's not that easy. There's not always a way to fix something when it breaks." Whatever his daughter said next caused him to tip his head back and exhale at the night sky. "Yes, of course, I'll tell her you love her. But maybe—"

"Maybe she can tell me herself."

Burgess went still, a beat passing before he turned his head. His eyes were guarded and God, that tore her up. She didn't ever want him to guard himself around her again. Not ever.

"Do you want to speak to Lissa?"

More than anything, she did. But . . . "I was kind of hoping she could tell me in person?" Those words flooded her with so much hope and faith in the future, it almost hurt too much to say them out loud. "Back in Boston?"

A section of the barrier Burgess had erected around himself slipped, a comet of hope streaking across his expression, before it winked out. "You're more than welcome to come over—"

"Burgess," she blurted, heartsick and exasperated. "I'm trying to tell you I want to come back permanently." She took another step forward. And another, until her knee bumped up against the side of his thigh. "I want to come home."

The hand holding the phone dropped like a stone and he struggled bringing it back to his ear, almost like he suddenly lacked the strength. Once he got it there, he listened for a moment, a lump bobbing up and down in his throat as an excited twelve-year-old voice screeched down the line. "She heard you," he said, looking at Tallulah, still slightly guarded but getting closer, getting closer. "Lissa, I'll call you back." He paused. "*We* will call you back."

And then he dropped the phone and lunged off the lounge chair, catching Tallulah in a bear hug and lifting her off the ground with a choked sound, his hands raking all over her, down the back of her head, continuing down to her spine and drawing her impossibly closer, his breath loud in her ear. "I thought you were done with me. I thought you were done."

"I'm not. I never would have been." She wrapped her arms

tighter around his neck, absorbing the homecoming and safety and completion he'd come to represent. That he would always represent to her. "I would have walked around my whole life loving you."

His knees dipped. "You love me. You still love me."

"Of course, I do." Tears ran down her face. "You don't think I'd use just anyone's sweatshirt as a pillow, do you?"

He pulled back slightly, his hand alternating between affectionate strokes of her hair and brushes of his knuckles down the curve of her cheekbone. "I will never make you cry again, Tallulah. I swear to God. I've been half alive since you walked out of that hospital room—"

"Burgess . . ." She searched for the right words, the ones that would put them on the right path. The *same* path. Words that were overflowing from her heart now, like they'd just been waiting for something to knock them free. "Maybe I will cry again. Maybe we'll shout and get angry or push each other's buttons. But our love is going to be bigger than the bad moments. And we know what it's like now. To walk away. To be without each other. So next time we're going to fight together, instead of apart. Next time we'll remember our love comes out on top and we'll skip the indecision . . . and get to making up."

"Sign me up, Tallulah. I never want to be without you again," Burgess said thickly, shaking his head while cataloguing her features, appreciating them one by one. "My God, I don't deserve another chance, but wait until you see what I'm going to do with it." His lips coasted over hers, drawing her into a slow, winding kiss. "I'm going to take you on adventures, because I live to see you happy. And because you taught me to enjoy them, too. But hear me when I tell you, there will never be an adventure that lives up to you." He looked her in the eye. "I want to stay on it forever."

"Sign me up," she whispered. "But I am *not* cooking."

EPILOGUE

Burgess adjusted the AirPod in his ear as his playlist transitioned to the next song. When the familiar whine of Raskulls came on, he rolled his eyes, but he didn't skip. No way. He'd enjoy every minute of the playlist Tallulah and Lissa had made for him together. They'd giggled over it for two hours, huddled on the couch with Tallulah's laptop, and he'd been listening to it on repeat ever since. It reminded him of them. It reminded him of home.

Textbooks on the table. Three people bumping into one another in the kitchen while making ice cream sundaes. The crinkle of a paper bag full of bagels on Sunday morning. A jumble of winter boots by the front door. Mint, sumac, and cumin scenting the air.

Lying on their backs outside on the roof garden and looking up at the night sky, talking about everything and nothing.

Laughter. Music. Dancing.

That was his home now.

And the person who'd come along and created his bright, colorful new world was currently in the brick building to his right, taking her final exam before earning her master's in marine biology, after which they were going to meet Lissa for brunch at a restaurant adjacent to her high school. Having nearly completed her freshman year, his daughter was now fiercely independent and flourishing. She still preferred reading to socializing, but a couple of times this season, he'd returned from practice to find Tallulah kneeling in front of their coffee table, giving manicures to a handful of high school students.

Yeah, his kid had friends now, but more importantly, she had good judgment. A backbone. A way of looking at the bigger picture, instead of sweating the small setbacks. A lot of that came from her mother, of course—who now came over regularly for dinner with her new husband—but a huge helping of Tallulah's influence was there, too. And who knew . . . maybe he'd helped Lissa come into herself by transforming at the same time. Becoming someone who embraced change and new experiences, instead of turning his back on them.

A growling rap song drifted into his ears—one Tallulah swore would get him hyped for games—and he sighed into a smile, looking at the entrance to the building. His girlfriend was definitely a hockey fan now. Through and through. Burgess was almost tempted to tack on one more year to his career, just so he could watch her cheering in the family section a little longer, dressed in his jersey. But . . . no. This one would be his last. He'd come back from his back injury and proven himself resilient, a vital member of the Bearcats, but it was time to pass the captain's torch to Sig.

There were adventures waiting for him, after all. Him and his family.

Someone tapped on Burgess's shoulder and he turned, finding a man in his twenties looking back at him. The dude seemed caught off guard by Burgess's smile, obviously wondering if he had the right person, so Burgess replaced it with a scowl.

The guy relaxed.

"What's up?" Burgess asked, removing one of his earbuds.

"Sir Savage. I'm Irving Randell from the *Globe*. Funny enough, I'm actually on campus to report on the lacrosse team winning state, but I happened to see you sitting here. I'd love to ask you a few questions, if you have time. Would earn me some points with the sports editor."

Burgess glanced back toward the building, then down at his watch.

"Okay. You've got me until my girlfriend walks through that door. Once I see her, I probably won't hear a word out of your mouth."

"You're waiting for the au pair?"

"*Former* au pair. Current . . . everything."

There was no other way to describe Tallulah. She was everything. The love of his life and reason for opening his eyes every morning. His best friend and co-parent. His cheerleader. His inspiration. His heart. Life hadn't been the same since they'd returned from Costa Rica nearly seventeen months earlier, reuniting with a sobbing Lissa on the sidewalk in front of the Beacon. Yet somehow, it felt like Tallulah had always been there. As though a gap had existed in their lives that only she could see or fit into. Thank God she'd saved his life by filling that hole. Thank God she'd been created, period—a thought Burgess had periodically while watching her wake up in the glow of morning sun, beside him in bed.

The reporter cleared his throat, subtly letting Burgess know he'd drifted.

Burgess deepened his frown.

"Are your questions about her?"

Irving hedged. "Well . . . it's the subject that would earn me the most points with my editor. You've refused to talk about the relationship with your daughter's nanny in the past."

"That's because it's nobody's business."

"Sure isn't."

Irving raised an eyebrow, nonetheless, waiting to see if he'd talk about Tallulah, regardless . . . and maybe it was the king-sized balls on the reporter that made him want to share. Or maybe Burgess just couldn't help himself, because the happiness inside of him was a great, big thing and overflowed like a dam after seventeen months of rain.

"As you know, I'm retiring after this season . . ." he started, before clearing his throat. "First thing I'm going to do is take my girls to Istanbul. Tallulah misses her family, and Lissa and I want to get to know them." He cocked a brow. "After that, I'm getting certified in scuba."

"Okay. I . . . didn't see that coming."

He nodded at the building. "Tallulah is a marine biologist. I want her to take me down there and show me everything she loves. I want to know the name of every single thing she loves in this world and that includes the ocean." He paused, imagining his woman surrounded by sunsets, marketplaces, winding through skyscrapers, skinny dipping across the globe—but this time, he'd do it with her. He'd say yes to all of it. "Something tells me this next chapter is going to be better than the first one."

Irving blinked at him. "You're nothing like I expected you to be."

"A couple of years ago, I might have been."

"But . . ."

"She happened."

"I see." The reporter shifted, a bemused expression creeping onto his face. "I hope you don't mind me saying this, but based on the way you talk about her, I'm surprised you haven't popped the question yet."

Burgess acknowledged that with a rumble. "She wanted to wait until she finished grad school. Otherwise, she'd have been Mrs. Abraham seventeen months ago."

"Right." Irving rubbed at his chest. "I have the sudden urge to call my girlfriend."

"Do it."

"I'm not reckless enough to say no to you." The other man

opened his mouth, hesitated. "Since we're talking romance and personal relationships, I don't suppose you're willing to comment on the whole Sig Gauthier situation. You know, with his step—"

"That's their story to tell," Burgess interrupted with a head-shake. "Not mine."

"Fair enough."

Burgess saw movement in the building and narrowed his eyes, trying to make out Tallulah's silhouette behind the glass. There. Books pressed to her chest, that soft strut, like she was walking a personal runway, hair in a side braid that draped over her left shoulder. There was his Tallulah. He'd know her shape blindfolded. It fit against him perfectly. Those inner thighs never failed to lock into the grooves of his sides, allowing him entrance to her body with a sharp scoop of his hips, their mouths stifling breathless moans first thing in the morning, the friction of their skin, harsh breathing, and low creak of the mattress springs his favorite sounds, easily replacing the slap of a puck.

Christ, this morning had been hot as hell.

Intense.

She'd ended up on top, tits raking up and down his sweaty chest, finishing with a muffled scream into his neck.

Great, now his pulse was out of whack.

And when she fully emerged from the building and spotted him, her face lighting up with a grin, his heart only beat faster.

Damn, he loved this woman.

Damn.

"Turn off the recorder and open your camera," Burgess advised Irving in a rasp.

The reporter fumbled his phone slightly. "Why?"

"Trust me."

And that's how Burgess ended up on the front page of the *Globe* the following morning, down on one knee in front of Tallulah with an open ring box in his hand, under the headline "Sir Taken."

Keep an eye out for

WINDOW SHOPPING

Tessa's next standalone novel, a feel-good
opposites-attract holiday romance!
AVAILABLE OCTOBER 2024!

ABOUT THE AUTHOR

#1 *New York Times* bestselling author Tessa Bailey can solve all problems except for her own, so she focuses those efforts on stubborn, fictional blue-collar men and loyal, lovable heroines. She lives on Long Island, avoiding the sun and social interactions, then wonders why no one has called. Dubbed the "Michelangelo of dirty talk" by *Entertainment Weekly*, Tessa writes with spice, spirit, swoon, and a guaranteed happily ever after. Catch her on TikTok @authortessabailey or check out tessabailey.com for a complete list of her books.

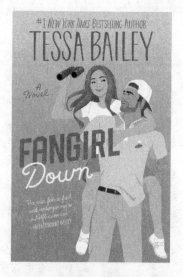